'_____ me about?"_

She stood and wiped her hands down the sides of her trousers. "I think you should come and take a seat and—"

"Stop fudging! Don't delay any longer, Sarah. Out with it."

"Fine!" She folded her arms, stuck out a hip. She swallowed, but lifted her chin. "I'm pregnant."

For a moment her words made no sense. He even momentarily reveled in the relief that she wasn't planning to leave Melbourne. "You're—" he rubbed his nape "—pregnant?"

She nodded. "That's right."

"And…?"

She flopped down to her stool. She lifted her arms and then let them drop back into her lap. Her mouth trembled and her eyes were full of fear and sadness and tears and, strangely, some laughter. Her eyes contained the entire world. "And the baby is yours, Majed."

SARAH AND THE
SECRET SHEIKH

BY
MICHELLE DOUGLAS

MILLS
BOON®

First Published in Great Britain 2017
By Mills & Boon, an imprint of HarperCollins*Publishers*
1 London Bridge Street, London, SE1 9GF

© 2017 Michelle Douglas

ISBN: 978-0-263-92327-8

23-0917

Our policy is to use papers that are natural, renewable and recyclable products and made from wood grown in sustainable forests. The logging and manufacturing processes conform to the legal environmental regulations of the country of origin.

Printed and bound in Spain
by CPI, Barcelona

Michelle Douglas has been writing for Mills & Boon since 2007 and believes she has the best job in the world. She lives in a leafy suburb of Newcastle, on Australia's east coast, with her own romantic hero, a house full of dust and books, and an eclectic collection of sixties and seventies vinyl. She loves to hear from readers and can be contacted via her website: www.michelle-douglas.com.

To my Auntie Ellen and Uncle Reg for letting me
run wild on their Mount Vincent property when
I was a wee, small thing…and for trusting
I'd neither inadvertently drown myself in
the dam or be eaten alive by the wildlife.

CHAPTER ONE

SARAH SLID ONTO a stool and held her hand up for a high five as Majed passed on the other side of the bar. The palm-on-palm contact from the sexy barman sent heat ricocheting up her arm.

His raised eyebrow told her he was intrigued and she had to tamp down a laugh of pure, ridiculous exhilaration. His briefly raised finger told her to give him a moment while he served someone down the other end of the bar.

She settled onto the stool. She'd happily wait a hundred moments to share her news with him.

A hundred moments?

She rolled her shoulders and shook out her arms and legs. Maybe not a *hundred* moments. It wasn't as though she thought of Majed in *that* way. Even if he was sexy as all-get-out, with his dark hair, tawny skin, and eyes as dark as a desert at midnight. She bit back a dreamy sigh. Eyes that were edged with long, dark lashes that should be wasted on a man but weren't in this case as they only made him look more exotic.

But no. It wasn't because Majed was hot with a capital H that she'd quite happily wait until closing time to tell him her news but because she knew he'd *understand*. An easy-going friendship had sprung up between them over the past year when she'd barely been paying attention and she gave thanks for it now.

He prepared the order for the three women at the far end of the bar—mojitos—with a casual elegance Sarah envied. The women all flirted with him—flashing smiles and cleavage with a good-natured abandon that had Sarah biting back a grin. He said something that made them laugh, looking for all intents and purposes completely at ease, yet she sensed he held some part of himself back.

Majed: man of mystery, man of contrasts. He managed this bar but he didn't drink. He attracted women in droves—and some men—and was equally pleasant and courteous to all. He could have his pick from the beautiful people who frequented this inner-city Melbourne bar but she'd never seen him go home with anyone.

Mike, her best friend's older brother and the owner of the bar, had asked her to keep an eye on Majed, to give him a hand if need be. As he was letting her crash at his swanky inner-city apartment for the six months of his current overseas sabbatical, it had seemed little enough to promise in return. Mike called her his house-sitter but, as he had no cat to feed or houseplants to water, Sarah had secretly dubbed herself his charity case. Mike had simply taken pity on her.

Pity or not, she'd jumped at the chance to cut forty-five minutes each way from her daily commute.

And keeping an eye on Majed had proved no hardship at all.

Mike had mentioned that he and Majed had gone to university together. She knew where Mike had gone to university. Majed should be a banker or a businessman or some hotshot lawyer. Like Mike, he should have a whole chain of bars, restaurants and resorts across the world—or at least be working towards it. What he shouldn't be doing was twiddling his thumbs behind some bar in Melbourne.

Oh, right, and you think you're qualified to be dispensing vocational advice, right?

She winced.

Good point.

She knew all about treading water in a job that was going nowhere. She knew all about not living up to her potential. She ought to. Her mother reminded her of it every single time they spoke.

Majed moved back down the bar towards her and she resolutely shoved her mother's voice out of her head.

'Your usual?'

Her usual was a glass of house white. She straightened and rubbed her hands together. 'I'll have bubbles, please.'

That eyebrow rose higher. 'Celebrating something?'

She laughed because she couldn't help it. 'I can't drink alone tonight. Let me buy you a drink.' He opened his mouth but she cut him off. 'Be a devil and have a lemon squash on me.'

Shaking his head, he did as she bid, and she noticed that at her end of the bar his smile was more relaxed and his shoulders swung a little freer. The fact he relaxed around her loosened the hard knots that the working day had wound up tight inside her.

He slid a glass of bubbles in front of her and she promptly clinked it to his glass of squash. 'To the fact that I am now officially a single woman again.'

Stunned midnight eyes met hers and his smile, when it came, was low and long and sent a spiral of heat circling through her belly.

He leaned towards her. 'You did it? You broke up with Superior Sebastian?'

Ah...not exactly. Sebastian had been the one to dump her. But it came to the same thing—she was single and rid of the awful boyfriend. And Majed looked so happy for her...he looked *proud* of her. It had been an age since anyone had looked at her like that, so she didn't have it in her to correct him.

She pointed to herself. 'Free woman.' That, after all, was

the material point. She then waved her hand through the air, assuming supreme indifference. 'I've kicked his sorry ass to the kerb. Never again, I tell you.' And she meant it. She was having no more of Sebastian's on-again, off-again mind games. She couldn't even remember why she'd put up with it all in the first place.

Majed took a long pull on his drink and she couldn't help but notice the lean, tanned column of his throat and the implicit strength in the broad expanse of his shoulders. He set his glass down. 'Never again?'

She shook her head. 'Never.'

'Cross your heart?'

She crossed her heart. In one smooth movement Majed leaned across the bar, cupped her face in big, warm hands and then his lips slammed down on hers in a brief but blistering kiss.

When he eased back all she could do was stare.

He frowned. 'I shouldn't have done that.'

She tried to marshal her scattered wits, tried to corral her racing pulse. 'Oh, yes, you should.' She found herself nodding vigorously. 'You *really* should've done that.'

Whatever he saw in her face chased his shadows away. He shrugged, and she swore it was the sexiest thing she'd ever seen. 'I couldn't kiss you when you were going out with another man.'

Majed had wanted to kiss her? If she'd known that, she might've broken up with Sebastian sooner.

Her heart pounded. 'I was an idiot to put up with Sebastian and his so-called *"this is for your own good"* sermons for so long. It's just…' It was just that sometimes she was *hopeless*.

Majed folded himself down on the bar until he was eye-level with her. 'You will get his voice out of your head right now and you won't let it back in. You hear me? You do *not* need to lose weight. You do *not* need to wear more makeup. You do *not* need to do your hair differently. And there is absolutely nothing wrong with ordering a fluffy duck rather than a martini, because you *don't* have to be too cool for school, Sarah Collins. You're perfect just the way you are.'

She stared at that mouth uttering those delicious words—words she sorely wanted to believe—and her chest coiled up tight and her mouth dried. She glanced up and moistened her lips. He watched the action and midnight eyes glittered and sparked. Her blood pounded so hard it made her thighs soften. 'Now I want to kiss you,' she whispered.

'That wouldn't be wise.'

But he was staring at her lips with unadorned hunger and he didn't move away.

'Perhaps not, but it'd be fun.'

He gave the tiniest of nods in acknowledgement.

She lifted her chin. Mike *had* asked her to keep an eye on him. 'When was the last time you had fun, Majed?'

His pupils momentarily dilated. 'A long time.'

In those eyes she saw unexplained pain before heavy lids lowered to block it from her sight.

She sat back and surveyed him. He'd been counselling her for months now, telling her she deserved something better than a constantly critical boyfriend. And he'd been right—she did deserve better. And so did he. The way he was going, he'd work himself into an early grave.

She pursed her lips. That might be an exaggeration. She was rubbish at the work side of things but she could make up for it on the play side of the equation. 'Do you ever drink?' she asked.

He straightened. 'I'll be back.'

He moved away to serve a customer. When he returned he folded himself down into the same eye-level position. Did he know how sexy that was? Did he know she'd only have to close the space with a small forward movement to kiss him? If she did…

'You have very speaking eyes.'

His grin was full of temptation. It was all she could do not to swoon—or kiss him. She settled for grinning back at him instead. 'I'm feeling happy, free…and in the mood for some fun.'

She'd never been this bold before, but she couldn't find it in herself to regret it. She'd made a fool of herself over far less worthy things.

She shrugged but she doubted it was one of those confident, nonchalant gestures all the cool girls managed. Something in the gesture, though, made Majed's face soften. 'What can I say, Majed? I like you.'

He was quiet for a long moment and just when she'd started readying herself for a hot squirm of embarrassment, and the shame of a kindly worded rejection, he said, 'Brandy. Sometimes, late at night when I'm home alone, I'll indulge in a small glass of brandy.'

Her heart grew so big it blocked her throat, leaving her temporarily unable to speak. Finally she swallowed. Air flooded her lungs and her blood danced. 'Maybe you'd like to have a brandy with me tonight? When you're done here?'

He reached out to wind his finger around a lock of her hair. 'There's no maybe about it. I'd like it very much.'

Ooh! Ooh! She found it impossible to form a coherent thought.

He gestured towards the far end of the bar to the waiting customers. 'Don't go anywhere.'

'I'm not going anywhere.' She couldn't believe how strongly her voice emerged when the rest of her felt as weak and shapeless as smoke. Well…it felt weak until his smile sent her floating up towards the ceiling.

Sarah stretched and encountered a warm male body.

She opened one eye to find Majed sending her a low, sexy smile that warmed her blood. Her other eye flew open as the events of the previous night flooded her. Their love-making had… Wow! She gulped She hadn't known it could be like that.

'Good morning.'

She couldn't contain a grin. 'From where I'm lying, it's a *very* good morning.'

She lifted a hand to trace the firm contours of his bare chest. Majed sucked in a breath. And then three loud knocks pounded on her front door. Her hand stilled. Majed raised an eyebrow.

She lifted a finger to her lips. 'If we're quiet they might go away.'

The knocking started up again.

And again.

Majed's lips twitched. 'They don't seem to want to give up.'

She bit back a sigh before pointing a finger at him. 'Don't go anywhere.'

He brought her finger to his lips and kissed it. 'I'm not going anywhere.'

She slipped on a robe and belted it at her waist. 'I'll be back. *Very* soon.' She'd get rid of whoever it was in double-quick time.

And then maybe they could resume last night's…delights.

Majed shucked up the bed, resting his hands behind his head. The sheet threatened to slip beyond his waist. All she had to do was grab the sheet in one hand, tug, and…

If it were possible, Majed's smile grew wider and sexier. 'Answer the door, Sarah.'

Oh, yes! The sooner she got rid of her unwelcome visitor the sooner she could get back to bed…and Majed.

It was all she could do to contain a shimmy when she flung open the door.

'What the hell took you so long?' Sebastian barrelled into the room.

Her jaw dropped and then she pointed back the way he'd come. 'Leave, Sebastian. Right this moment. We've nothing to say. We're done, so just please go.'

'Hey, baby, don't be so hasty.'

He tried to take her in his arms, but she side-stepped him. Majed had been *so* right about Sebastian. Why hadn't she realised that sooner?

Because you wanted to annoy your mother.

'Aw, Cuddles…'

'Don't call me baby and do *not* call me Cuddles!' God, how she loathed that nickname. It made her sound like an over-fed cat. A neutered over-fed cat. 'We have nothing—'

'I'm sorry, baby. I know I was awful yesterday. I'd had a terrible day at work. I didn't mean what I said, and I don't want to break up with you.'

Had she honestly fallen for this tripe in the past? 'I don't want you to want me back, Sebastian. What I want is for you to leave. *Now.*'

He frowned evidently baffled. Shame, hot and queasy, made her stomach churn. When had she let herself become such a pushover? When had she decided to settle for so little?

He straightened and moved towards her, determination glinting in the hard twist of his mouth. Good God, did he mean to kiss her into submission? If he tried it he'd find himself on the floor clutching his groin. Her mother had taught her about men like him.

'If you touch the lady, I'll be forced to take action.'

Majed leaned against the doorway to the bedroom, wearing nothing but a pair of snug cotton trunks—royal blue—that did nothing to hide his…impressiveness. Her mouth dried at the sheer magnificence of six feet of honed muscle lounging in the doorway, waiting for *her* to come back to bed. A sigh of pure appreciation rose through her.

Sebastian stared from Majed to Sarah and back again. It would've been almost comical if his surprise hadn't been so darned offensive. Finally he swung around and called her a one-word name that made her flinch.

With the casual elegance she envied, Majed strode across and landed a right hook to Sebastian's jaw. Hauling him off the floor, he dragged him to the door and flung him out into the hallway before closing the door on him.

He did it efficiently. Like a trained warrior. And Sarah had no hope of getting her pulse back under control. 'Um… thank you.'

'You're welcome.'

Her heart thundered in her ears. Would it be really poor form to push Majed back into the bedroom and have her wicked way with him? Or should she offer him coffee first? Actually, she had no intention of doing anything without his signal consent because…

She swallowed. Because at the moment he looked seriously forbidding.

She gripped her hands in front of her and prayed for her fantasy lover—the Majed of last night—to come back.

'You lied to me.'

She blinked. 'When?'

'You told me you'd dumped him.'

She swallowed, her hands twisting together. 'I told you I was a free woman.'

'But you deliberately let me believe the break-up was at your instigation, yes?'

Her heart sank. She had. He'd been so proud of her… and she'd wanted to revel in the sensation. She refused to compound the lie with another one. She couldn't speak, so she nodded instead. She wished he'd smile. She tried for levity. 'Are you going to punch me on the nose now?'

He did smile, but it was the kind of smile that made her heart ache. 'I would never do anything to hurt you, Sarah.' He strode over and lifted her wrist to his lips. 'I've had a wonderful night.'

She did what she could to swallow the lump that tried to lodge in her throat. 'So did I,' she whispered. 'But from the look on your face, I'm guessing this is goodbye.'

'Yes.'

He let go of her hand and it felt as if she'd been cast adrift on an endless grey sea. 'Goodbye...for good?'

He nodded.

'Even though I didn't instigate the break-up, I wanted it just as much as Sebastian did. I was relieved that it was over.'

'So why do I now feel as if you were searching for a distraction last night to take your mind off your hurt?'

That wasn't true! But she could see he wouldn't believe her. She'd ruined it—ruined the chance at something amazing—with one careless lie. She tamped down on the sob that rose in her chest. 'I messed up.' *Again.* 'I'm sorry.'

'Ah, Sarah.' For a moment regret stretched through his eyes. 'You're on the rebound, and I'm in an impossible situation. There really wasn't anything to mess up.'

He kissed her cheek and then strode back into the bedroom to dress. Sarah stumbled into the kitchen to make coffee and try to formulate a plan to salvage something from the situation. The click of the front door told her not to bother.

She walked back into the living room and stared at the closed door. With an effort, she straightened and pushed her shoulders back. Majed was right. Great sex didn't automatically make for a great relationship.

For heaven's sake, she didn't need a boyfriend. What she needed was some time alone to get her head straight—work out what she really wanted. It might be for the best if she didn't drop into the bar quite so regularly this week. Maybe not drop in at all for a couple of weeks.

But the thought of not seeing Majed at all caught at her in a way that made her ache. Not to have the chance to chat with him or share a joke…

She dragged both hands back through her hair. 'No, Majed, you're wrong. I did mess up. I messed up bad.'

Majed sensed the exact moment Sarah walked into the bar.

Even though he had his back to the door.

Even though it was a Wednesday night and she hardly ever came into the bar on a Wednesday night.

Not that she'd shown her face in here all that often in the last six weeks.

He set a Scotch and soda in front of the customer he was serving, took their money and gave change, all the while readying himself for the jolt of seeing her. He glanced towards the door. She'd stopped to chat to a table of her friends—other regulars—and he did what he could to ignore the clutch low down in his gut. She'd had this effect on him from the very first moment he'd met her. In all likelihood she'd have it on him till the day he died. Some things were just like that—desert sunsets, palm fronds moving in a breeze, the scent of spices on the air…and the sight of Sarah.

It didn't excuse the fact he'd been an idiot to go home with her. He should've resisted the temptation. After all, he'd managed to avoid desert sunsets, date palms and spice markets with remarkable ease.

He pushed the memories away—memories of home. They might haunt his sleeping hours, but he refused to dwell on them when he was awake.

He pinched the bridge of his nose. He still couldn't believe he'd relaxed his guard so much.

It was just…

He grabbed a cloth and vigorously wiped down the bar. She'd made him feel like he could be someone different—that he *was* someone different. When she spotlighted him with those pretty blue eyes of hers, she made him feel worthy. And, God forgive him, but he'd been too weak not to revel in it.

The man at the far end of the bar tapped his empty beer glass. Majed got him another. He bent down to check the stock in the fridge. But, rather than rows of wine bottles and mixers, all he could see was fragments from the night he'd spent with Sarah. They replayed through his mind on an endless loop—the curvaceous length of her leg, the way her body had arched to meet his, the taste of her. They drew him so tight, his muscles started to ache. That night had been spectacular—unforgettable.

But the morning after…

He straightened in time to see her laugh at something one of her friends said. Her stupid lie—it hadn't even been a big lie—had reminded him of the mistakes that lay in his past. His hands clenched. Mistakes he had no intention of repeating.

And it had reminded him of all that he owed his family. He forced his hands to unclench. Where on earth did he think a romance with an Australian woman could go? He grabbed a tray of dirty glasses and stacked them in readiness for the dishwasher. If he wanted to redeem himself in the eyes of his family he'd have to submit to a traditional marriage—a marriage made for political purposes that would cement democracy in his beloved Keddah Jaleel and ensure peace for future generations.

Love for his homeland welled inside him. He missed the desert night sky. He missed walking beneath the date palms on the banks of the Bay'al River. He missed the bustle of the undercover markets, the air heavy with the scent of clove and nutmeg. He missed…

His throat started to ache. When he returned—*if* he returned, *if* his father ever countenanced it—Ahmed wouldn't be there to greet him, and he didn't know how he could bear to live there without his brother. He didn't know how he could meet his father's bitter disappointment every single day, or how to assuage his mother's heartbreak. He missed his homeland but he didn't know how he could ever return.

And yet for one night Sarah had made him forget all of that. He hungered now for the respite she represented— the respite she would probably still offer to him freely if he asked for it—but he had no right to such respite. And the thought of making love to a woman who was in love with another man was anathema to him. Pride forbade it.

He lifted his chin and didn't pretend not to see her as she made her way towards the bar…and him. 'Good evening.' The words growled out of him and she stopped a pace short of the bar. He could've bitten his tongue off for sounding so damned forbidding. He tried to inject a note of friendliness as he flipped a coaster onto the bar in front of the nearest stool and said, 'Your usual?'

She eyed him warily as she slid onto the stool. 'Just a lemonade, please.'

It might be a work night but that had never stopped her drinking before. Not that she ever got rollicking drunk. She'd once told him she drank in an effort to anaesthetise herself to the mind-numbing mundanity of her life. It had made all the sore places inside him ache.

Fellow feeling—that was what he and Sarah had shared from the first.

And attraction. At least on his part. It had been instant. And insistent. And it had had nothing to do with his covert—and not so covert—scheme to rid her of Superior Sebastian.

He set her lemonade in front of her. 'Has Sebastian been giving you any trouble?' Was she seeing him again?

She paused in the act of reaching for her drink. 'Good God, no. Not since…'

Not since Majed had thrown him out of her apartment?

'And good riddance to him.' She drank deeply and then shot him a mischievous, if half-hearted, grin. 'Sebastian who?'

He wished he could believe her. She deserved better than the likes of the Sebastians of this world. He took in her pallor, the dark circles under her eyes, and wondered how long it would take her to get over him. 'You're better off without him.' Sebastian had never been worthy of her, had never appreciated her the way she ought to be appreciated.

'I know.'

He could almost believe her…

'Look, Majed, I didn't come here to talk about Sebastian. I—'

She broke off to bite her lip. Something in Majed's gut coiled at the way her gaze slid away, at the way she compulsively jiggled her straw in her drink. 'What have you come here to talk about?'

She glanced around the room. It was a quiet night but there were still a dozen people in the bar. 'It's not the time or place. I was hoping to talk to you once you'd closed. Or…some other time when you're free.'

He didn't want to be alone with her. He folded his arms. His right foot started to tap. 'Can't you just tell me now?'

She stopped jiggling her straw to fix him with a glare. 'No. You deserve more respect than that. And so do I.'

Her gaze slid away. Again. She had a lock of hair that always fell forward onto her face. She'd push it back behind her ear, but it would always work its way free again. Majed held his breath and waited… He didn't release it until it had fallen forward to brush across her cheek. That silly, defiant, joyful lock of hair could always make him smile.

Stop it!

He continued to gaze at her. She didn't look like other women. At least, not to him. Which made no sense at all because, of course, she looked like a woman. And while she wasn't stunningly beautiful, she drew his gaze again and again. He found her...lovely.

Her hair was neither gold nor brown, her skin was neither fair nor olive, and it had taken him a while before he'd realised her eyes were a clear brilliant blue, but once he had he couldn't forget them. Her features were regular, though some might claim her mouth was too wide, but nothing about Sarah immediately stood out. Not physically. Except... She exuded warmth, as if she housed her own internal sun, and everything about her made his fingers ache to reach out and touch her. He had to fight the urge now, and the effort made his muscles burn.

But... There was something in the set of her shoulders.

It hit him then, why she was here, and his hands slammed to his hips. Her eyes caught the movement...followed it... The pink of her tongue snaked out to moisten her full bottom lip and he went hot all over. He cleared his throat. 'You've lost another job.'

His rasped accusation had her gaze spearing back to his but the heat continued to circle in his blood. Her cheeks went pink but, whether at the accuracy of his accusation or the fact he'd caught her staring, he didn't know.

'Well, yes.' One shoulder lifted. 'But that's not what I came to talk about either.'

No?

She stared down her nose at him. 'Mike told you to keep an eye on me, didn't he? He told you to give me a job if I needed one.'

He had, but Majed had no intention of admitting as much.

'Don't worry, Majed, I haven't come to beg you for a job.'

He gave thanks for that mercy. If he had to work with

her day in and day out, he didn't know how he'd manage to keep from touching her.

'Mike asked me to look out for you too, you know?'

He jerked upright. 'I don't need looking out for.'

A smile hovered at the corners of her lips. 'Oh, that's right. I forgot. You're an island unto yourself.'

That was *exactly* what he had to become if he was to ever return to Keddah Jaleel, and the fact she found the idea so nonsensical irked him. Sarah was more than happy to tell anyone who'd listen that she was a complete flake, but she had a perspicacity that was remarkable in its accuracy.

'I don't need looking after either, despite appearances to the contrary. I might be a flake…'

There she went, putting herself down.

'But I'm an independent flake.'

'I don't consider you a flake at all.'

She gave a short laugh. 'I'm going to ask you to hold that thought in the forefront of your mind when we have our conversation.'

What on earth had she come here to discuss?

He stiffened. Was she leaving Melbourne? Had he some-how left her feeling that she had to leave?

Damn it all to hell!

He strode into the middle of the room and clapped his hands together. 'Excuse me, everyone, but something has come up and I need to close early. Can I ask you all to fin-ish your drinks and leave?'

When he'd locked the door behind the last customer he spun to face Sarah. 'What did you want to talk to me about?'

She stood and wiped her hands down the sides of her trousers. 'I think you should come and take a seat and—'

'Stop fudging! Don't delay any longer, Sarah. Out with it.'

'Fine!' She folded her arms and stuck out a hip. She swallowed but lifted her chin. 'I'm pregnant.'

For a moment her words made no sense. He even momentarily revelled in the relief that she wasn't planning to leave Melbourne. 'You're—' he rubbed his nape '—pregnant?'

She nodded. 'That's right.'

'And...?'

She flopped down to her stool. She lifted her arms and then let them drop back into her lap. Her mouth trembled and her eyes were full of fear, sadness, tears and, strangely, some laughter. Her eyes contained the entire world. 'And the baby is yours, Majed.'

CHAPTER TWO

THE SHOCK OF brandy hitting the back of his throat had Majed jolting back to himself. It was only then he realised Sarah had pushed him into a chair, had poured him a snifter of brandy and was urging him to drink it.

He did what she demanded because he was at a loss to know what else to do. *She was having his child!*

'I know it's a shock.' Sarah moved to the chair opposite. 'And I didn't mean to blurt it out quite so baldly.'

But he'd ordered her to.

Heat scored through him, followed by a wave of ice. He stared at her. Was she okay? It didn't matter what kind of shock he might be experiencing, it had to be far worse for her. Physically he was exactly the same as he'd been before she'd told him the news. But, regardless of what decision she made, Sarah would never be the same again. He had to focus on what she needed from him—and do his best to provide it.

She was pregnant with his child!

He opened his mouth but before he could speak she said, 'I understand your reservations concerning the baby's paternity.'

She thought his silence indicated that he didn't believe her?

She'd lied about instigating the break-up with Superior Sebastian.

She wouldn't lie about something as big as this.

'Sarah—'

'Please, just let me explain. It's taken me this long to screw up my courage and now that I've started I'd…I'd rather just keep going.'

He gave a terse nod, hating the thought that she'd been afraid to tell him her news.

'So, the thing is…' She drew a loop of circles in the condensation of her glass. 'Sebastian had mumps when he was fifteen, which means the likelihood of him being able to father children is pretty slim. But, besides that—'

She broke off to stare at her hands. He reached out and wrapped one of his hands around both of hers. She had such small hands, and every protective instinct he had surged to the fore. 'Don't be frightened of me, Sarah. I'm not angry. Just stunned.' He made his voice as gentle as he could. 'I want to help in any way I can.'

Her lips trembled. 'That's lovely of you.'

'You've had a lot to bear on your own. I want you to know you're not alone now.' *She was having his child!* He forced himself to swallow. 'What were you saying about Sebastian?'

'Oh.' Her lips twisted. 'Before we broke up…for the two months before we broke up… Sebastian and I…'

'Yes?'

She disengaged her hand from his to rub her nape. 'We hadn't been intimate.'

He'd always known the man had rocks in his head. This simply confirmed it.

'I don't doubt your word.'

The little moue she made informed him she didn't entirely believe him. 'We'll have a paternity test done to put your mind at rest. If I decide to keep the baby.'

If. His heart clenched at the word, though he wasn't sure

why. A child was the last thing he'd expected at this point in his life. It should be the last thing he wanted.

But the ultimate decision rested with Sarah. It was her body and he'd support her whatever she decided to do.

'Are you and the baby healthy?'

'The doctor says so.'

'You've been to see a doctor? That's good.'

She frowned. 'You're taking this very calmly.'

Inside he was a mass of conflicting emotions but he refused to reveal them. 'We're in this together. I want you to know you're not alone. Between us we'll sort it out.'

Her mouth opened but no words emerged.

'Have you eaten this evening?'

She wrinkled her nose. 'I haven't had much of an appetite.'

He rose and took her hand. 'Come, I'll make you an omelette.'

He switched off the lights to the bar and led her upstairs to the flat above.

'You can cook?' she asked when he'd seated her at the breakfast bar of his open-plan kitchen-dining-living room.

'I make omelettes that are out of this world.'

She glanced around and he wondered what she made of his bachelor pad. 'An omelette sounds kinda nice.'

It wasn't until Majed pulled the eggs from the fridge that he remembered pregnant women were supposed to avoid certain foods. What about eggs? He swung back. 'Will you excuse me for a moment?'

He sped into the bathroom and pulled his phone from his pocket to open his web browser. He typed in his query and then read down the list of foods that pregnant women shouldn't eat. Right—the eggs shouldn't be runny. Okay, he'd cook the omelette a little longer than usual... Actually, he might cook it a lot longer than usual, just to be on the safe side. Hard cheeses like cheddar were fine too.

Right. He snapped his phone shut. He'd keep it simple with a plain cheese omelette. Well cooked.

Sarah tried to find some trace of Majed in his flat—in his furniture and in the décor—but… Well, it was all very comfortable and commendably tidy, but something was missing, though she couldn't put her finger on what it was.

'What do you think of the place?'

She glanced around from the window that overlooked the busy inner-city Melbourne street to find Majed surveying her from the doorway. And just like that her heart started to jackhammer. 'It's nice.' She ignored his raised eyebrow to add, 'I've always been curious to see up here.'

He stared at her for a bit longer. 'The bathroom is just down the hall on the left.' He pointed back behind him. 'And the bedroom is at the end of the hall. Feel free to take a look.'

'Oh, no, I'm all good.' She couldn't invade his privacy that much.

She slid onto her stool again when he started clattering pots and pans and whisking eggs. She knew they were skirting around the main topic of conversation but…dear Lord…the shock on his face when he'd finally realised what she'd been trying to tell him. It made her stomach churn just remembering it. She wanted to give him a chance to get a little more used to the idea before they launched into a discussion about what they would do.

Frankly, she had no idea what that might be.

He moved with easy grace in his compact kitchen and it was no hardship to watch him rather than make small talk…or think. He started to slide her omelette onto a plate, and then jerked, as if he'd burned himself. His gaze speared hers before he seemed to recall himself and finished serving her food.

She stared at the plate he pushed in front of her and

had to fight a frown. This did *not* look like an out-of-this-world omelette—it looked flat and rubbery. And brown. Her stomach gave a sick little squeeze but she gamely forked in a mouthful. He *had* gone to all the trouble of making it for her.

His hands went to his hips as he watched her eat. It only made her stomach churn harder. She set her fork down. 'What?'

'Did you lose your job because you're pregnant? They *cannot* fire you for being pregnant.'

She picked up her fork again. 'True. But apparently they can fire me for calling the manager a weasel of a bully who's nothing more than a boil on the backside of the universe that's in dire need of lancing.'

He choked. 'You didn't?'

'I did. And I can't begin to tell you how utterly satisfying it was.' But now she had no job. And she had a baby on the way. Could her timing have been any worse? Talk about irresponsible!

She blew out a breath. She was such a screw-up.

Just ask Sebastian.

Just ask her mother!

'Eat your omelette,' Majed ordered.

She didn't know if it was her self-recriminations, or if the eggs hadn't agreed with her, but she only just made it to the bathroom before losing the contents of her stomach. Majed held her hair back from her face while she was sick. He pressed a cool, damp cloth to her forehead, and through it all she wished she felt well enough to feel even a modicum of embarrassment.

Eventually she closed the lid of the toilet and sat on top of it. The concern in Majed's face caught at her. She tried to find a smile. 'Did you know that *morning* sickness is a misnomer? Apparently it can happen at any time of the day.'

'It's...*wrong*!'

'It's certainly unpleasant.' But her legs finally felt steady enough to hold her so she rose and rinsed out her mouth. 'Majed, I know we have a lot to talk about, but I'm feeling beat and—'

The rest of her words stuttered to a halt when he lifted her off her feet and into his arms. 'You need to rest, *habibi*. It's been a difficult day for you. Sharing with me your news has been nerve-racking, yes? We have time yet to talk and make decisions.' As he spoke, he carried her down the short hallway to his bedroom. Very gently, he lowered her to the bed. She had an impression of vast luxury and comfort and had to bite her lip to prevent a sigh of pure bliss escaping as softness enveloped her.

'I shouldn't—'

'Of course you should.' He pulled off her shoes.

'Maybe just a little rest,' she murmured as he pulled the covers over her.

'Rest for as long as you like,' he murmured back.

'Majed?'

'Yes.'

'What did that word mean—*"habibi"*?'

'It's a term of endearment…like "sweetheart".'

A sigh fluttered out of her. She suspected it would be rather lovely to be his sweetheart for real.

Sarah woke as the first fingers of dawn filtered through the curtains of Majed's bedroom windows. She lay still and listened intently but couldn't sense any signs of movement throughout the rest of the flat. Very quietly, she pushed back the bedclothes and tiptoed into the living room to find Majed sprawled across the sofa that barely contained his bulk, fast asleep.

Most people when they slept looked unguarded, younger… vulnerable. Not Majed. If anything he looked slightly forbidding and stern. It suddenly struck her that the easy-going façade he assumed every day at the bar might be exactly that—a front.

Or maybe your news has given him unpleasant dreams.

She scratched her hands through her hair. How long had he sat up last night, churning over her news? She'd had a few extra days to get used to the idea. Yesterday evening her sleepless nights had finally caught up with her. She felt rested and well now, though, and she didn't have the heart to wake him.

A shiver shook through her. When she got right down to it, how well did she *know* Majed? Barely at all. She had no idea if he wanted a child. She gripped her hands together. For all she knew, he might welcome a child with unbridled enthusiasm. Or the idea of fatherhood might be a total anathema to him. Surely one should know these things about a man before becoming pregnant by him?

Your mother didn't.

Perhaps not, but she didn't intend to take her parents as role models. They'd spent her entire childhood using her as a pawn in their war to score points off each other. That was the only thing she was certain of—that she wouldn't do that to any child of hers. If she had this baby she'd do her best to ensure its childhood was happy and carefree—not a battleground.

If.

Slipping onto a chair at the dining table, she lifted her feet to the seat and hugged her knees. She and Majed had to decide what to do about this baby and she had no idea where to start.

A pen and notepad rested in the middle of the table. She pulled them towards her with the thought of writing a list of pros and cons. She'd start with the cons, because there were so many: the pregnancy was unplanned, she was unemployed, so how would she support not just herself but a baby as well? Her mother would have a fit and there'd be no end to the recriminations. Her father would take the opposite stance and think an unplanned pregnancy was an inspired idea. She was only twenty-six—there was plenty of time yet before she needed to start thinking about having children. She was a total screw-up and surely a child deserved better than that for a parent?

There'd be more cons—lots more—but the length of the list had started to dishearten her. She needed something in the pros column to balance it out…just a little bit.

She stared at the page and bit her lip. There had to be one reason to keep this baby. A solid logical reason that made perfect sense. Her throat ached. The page in front of her blurred. She reached out and wrote a single sentence:

I love this baby already.

She stared at the words she'd just written and blinked hard. She did love this baby, but was it enough? A child deserved a better home than Sarah could give it. But, no matter how much she might wish to, she couldn't draw a line through that single entry on her 'pros' list.

Perhaps she should try a different tack and list all of the options available to her instead. Biting back a sigh, she turned the page…only to find that Majed had made a list of his own. Her heart started to pound. Would it be an invasion of privacy to read his list?

Invasion or not, she had no hope of stopping herself.

At the top of the page in bald, ugly print he'd written a single word: *abortion.*

She couldn't stop herself from flinching, even though it had been the first option that had occurred to her too. Even though it was an option she was still considering.

Beneath that he'd written: *adoption.* She swallowed. Did she have the strength for that? If she loved this baby then wouldn't she want the very best for it? Wouldn't she fight to give it the very best, regardless of the cost to her personally?

She froze when she realised that was *exactly* what she'd do. She loved this baby. All she had to work out now was what would be in the baby's best interests.

She pulled Majed's list back towards her. Two hard, dark lines separated those first two items from the rest of his list. Pulling in a breath, she read on…

Majed watched Sarah's eyes widen as she read down the list he'd made. He knew when she'd reached the end of the list because it wasn't possible for her eyes to go any wider.

She glanced across at him and saw him watching her. Something arced in the air between them before she gave him a brave little smile that cracked open something in his chest and started up an ache that he feared would never go away.

He couldn't afford to fall in love with this woman. He couldn't afford to fall in love with anyone. Love clouded one's judgement. And when one's judgement was clouded it put the people one cared about at risk.

He couldn't fall in love with Sarah, but he could look after her.

'Good morning,' she whispered.

Her voice emerged on a rasp, as if her throat was dry, and he threw off his blanket, rose and strode to the kitchen. 'Let me get you something hot to drink. You should've helped yourself.'

'I didn't want to disturb you.'

He came back with glasses of apple juice and steaming mugs of herbal tea. His body cried out for strong black coffee but, if Sarah was avoiding caffeine the way most pregnant women he knew did, then it would be cruel to drink it in front of her.

He nodded at his list. 'I tried to cover every possible option I could think of. Are there any you've thought of that I've missed?'

She shook her head and sipped her tea. He watched carefully for any signs of nausea but she merely closed her eyes and inhaled the steam as if welcoming the warmth into her body. Her clothes looked rumpled from having been slept in, and she had bed hair, but beneath all of that a vitality and vibrancy that had been lacking yesterday had started to emerge.

'You've thought of things that hadn't occurred to me.' She pointed to the very last item on the list. 'That's a bit over the top, don't you think?'

He shrugged but his gut tightened. 'My purpose was to list every option I could think of, without making value judgements.'

He'd spent a lot of time in the West. Four years in the UK at Oxford University with trips to the USA in the summer breaks. For the last four years, he'd worked in Australia. But he'd grown up in Keddah Jaleel—a world of ancient tradition, arranged marriages and duty. He knew exactly what his family would expect of him in this situation.

He had no intention of forcing those expectations onto Sarah but...

'I want you to know that whichever one of those options you settle on, whichever you deem is in your and the baby's best interests, I'll support you one-hundred percent.' He didn't want her to doubt that for a moment.

She set her mug down, a deep furrow marring her brow. 'What?'

'Your happiness is just as important as mine.'

He didn't deserve happiness. He didn't say that out loud, though. It was a sentiment that would horrify her. He nodded at the list. 'None of those options make me unhappy.'

Her raised eyebrow told him she didn't believe him. She pointed towards the top of the list. 'This line here is rather dark. It looks angry. Does that mean you hate the idea of abortion and adoption?'

He tried to keep his face unreadable. 'I've no ethical objection to either. It's just…' He reached out and wrapped her hand in his. 'It's just, I don't dare care for the life growing inside you if those are the routes you're considering.'

She stared at him with such intensity his mouth went dry. The pulse at the base of her throat pounded and he could feel an answering throb start up at the centre of him.

'You care about this baby?'

The question was raw, Sarah's voice full of heartbreak and hope, and he didn't know which one would win out.

He nodded. There wasn't a single doubt in his mind that if Sarah had this child—*if*—he would love it with everything that was inside him.

Then tell her that. You need to give her more.

But he didn't want to pressure her one way or the other. She winced. 'Majed?'

He realised he was all but crushing her hand. He loosened his grip immediately and massaged her hand gently before releasing it. 'Last night I found myself getting excited about the prospect of a baby.' *A grandchild for his parents—what a gift!* 'I know this is completely unexpected. Not in a million years would I have thought… I mean, we were careful.'

'We were. This is so…*unplanned.*'

'But it doesn't follow that it's not a blessing.'

She went still and he chose his next words with care. 'I had to rein in my excitement last night because you deciding not to go ahead with the pregnancy is a valid choice, and an understandable one.'

She sat back and massaged her temples. The conflict he saw mirrored in her face tore at him. Without a word, she reached out and turned over the first page of the notepad. She'd written a list of pros and cons. Only one item was listed under the 'pros' heading. He read it and something fierce gripped his gut. He didn't bother reading her long list of cons. He seized her hand again. 'If you love this baby, Sarah, then you must keep it.'

Her gaze dropped from his. Her hand trembled. She pulled it free and reached for her tea. 'This baby deserves more than I can give it.'

'We're in this together. I'll help you financially. Between us—' He broke off, his heart thundering in his chest. 'You won't deny me access to the child…will you?'

Her mug clattered back to the table. 'Of course not. I wouldn't dream of it—not if you want to be a part of the baby's life.'

'I want that *very* much.' He wanted them to be very clear on that point.

'But, Majed, I'm not talking about the financial arrangements here. I have—' she rolled her eyes '—marketable skills. I don't doubt my ability to get another job.'

It would be so much harder with a baby, though. And they both knew it.

It took a beat longer for what she wasn't saying to hit him. He wanted to take her hand again, to offer her silent support, but she had both hands wrapped tightly around her mug. His heart continued to pound. 'Then tell me what you're really afraid of.'

She lifted her gaze and the shadows in her eyes made his stomach clench. 'I think we need to be completely honest with each other from this point forward, if we're going to have a baby together. Don't you?'

There was so much she didn't know about him. And she'd need to know. He resisted the urge to lower his forehead to the table. 'I agree.'

'I need to be honest with you, even if it means you come to despise me.'

For good or ill, his opinion mattered to her. It was why she'd let him think she'd broken up with Superior Sebastian rather than the other way round. He couldn't let her down now. Gently, he reached out to brush the backs of his fingers across her cheek. 'I could never despise you. The idea is unthinkable.'

She took his hand and squeezed it before releasing it with a smile. 'That was the right thing to say.'

Everything inside him sharpened. He sat back with folded arms, his hand still warm from where he'd touched her. 'Now, if I can only get you to believe it. Come, tell me what you're afraid of.'

She swallowed and her throat bobbed. 'Majed, there's a hole inside me—as if there's something essential that I'm missing. And I try to fill it up with things—like my relationship with Sebastian, a relationship I knew wasn't good for me—in an effort to distract myself from that sense of lacking something. It's why I bounce from job to job. Once I start to feel settled in a job, the emptiness starts gnawing away at me. And…and I have to create upheaval to keep it at bay.'

He stared at her. 'Is that why you invited me back to your apartment that night?'

'No, *that* was something I *wanted* to do. I was feeling jubilant and happy and it felt right.' She met his gaze. 'The night I spent with you, I wasn't thinking about filling up any kind of shortfall or lack inside me. I wasn't trying to distract myself. I'm not sure I was thinking at all. I acted on impulse, yes, but on instinct too.' Her frown deepened. 'I felt as if I was living—as if I were properly alive. It was… exhilarating.'

It merely meant she hadn't had time to become bored with him yet. 'And you're afraid that a baby won't be a big enough distraction? You think you'll find yourself becoming bored with the baby, the way you do with your jobs?'

Shocked eyes met his. 'That's *not* what I mean at all. No. I'm afraid that I'll make the baby the very centre of my life—that I'll use it to fill all those empty places inside me. That'd be wrong. It wouldn't be fair to put that kind of pressure on a child. I have a feeling it would be *shockingly* unfair.'

Her honesty stunned him.

The care she was already taking for her child humbled him.

He had empty places inside him too, but he knew exactly what had caused them—the guilt and responsibility he bore over his brother's death. How did he mean to protect a child from those?

'You sense it in me too, don't you?'

'No.' He shook his head. 'You don't appear to me as if some essential part of you is missing. You don't strike me as lonely, or even as if you're afraid of loneliness.' She had a wide network of friends. He'd seen her with them in the bar. From the outside, Sarah's life seemed full. 'Before Sebastian, you were nearly a year without a boyfriend, yes? You don't strike me as a person who needs to constantly be in a romantic relationship to feel whole.'

'The emptiness has nothing to do with romance or loneliness. If it did, I'd be able to fill it.'

'What does it have to do with, then?'

She shrugged but her gaze slid away. Instinct told him not to push. 'Sarah, you don't strike me as someone who is lacking. You strike me as someone who is searching.'

She swung back to gaze at him. 'Searching for what?'

'I expect you're the only person who can answer that.' Though he'd do anything he could to help her find the answer.

She scrubbed her hands down her face. 'I don't want my...*lack*...to hurt the baby.'

'If we're both aware of it as a potential problem then we can remain on our guards against it—cut it off at the pass, so to speak.'

She bit her lip but it didn't hide the hope that flared briefly in her eyes. 'You make it sound easy.'

'I don't think it'll be easy. I think raising a child must be the most challenging thing a person can ever do in this life. I think it must also be one of the most rewarding.'

She sagged back in her chair. 'You make me believe that I could do it.'

She could do it! And how much he wanted to do it too—with her—should scare him. Instead, it elated him.

She pointed at his list. 'Which of these options is the most attractive to you?'

His heart thundered so loud it was all he could do to hear his thoughts over it.

She tapped a finger to the notepad. 'Do you have a…for the lack of a better term…*favourite* here?'

'Yes.' She'd just been completely honest with him. She deserved the same in return.

'Okay,' she whispered. 'Hit me with it.'

'You want the truth? Right now?'

She moistened her lips. 'What are *you* afraid of?'

'Terrifying you.'

After a beat, she started to laugh. 'Being pregnant terrifies me. Wondering whether I'll be a good mother or not terrifies me. But, Majed, *you* don't terrify me.'

Without another word, he pointed to the last item on the list. 'This is my preference.'

Her quick intake of breath told him she hadn't expected that.

'You want us to marry?' she whispered. 'You want to marry me and take me and the baby to live in Keddah Jaleel with you?'

'Yes.' The word croaked out of him. 'Have I terrified you?'

'Umm…no.'

He didn't believe her. But nevertheless it was time to

tell her the truth. 'Sarah, there's something you need to know about me. My father is the ruling Sheikh of Keddah Jaleel…and I'm his heir.'

Her face remained blank for a disconcertingly long time before she straightened. 'You…you mean that you're…like a king?'

'My father is the king.'

'But you'll be king one day?'

Acid burned the back of his throat. 'Yes.' *Maybe.*

'And if we marry, and our child is a boy, he'll one day be king too?'

He had to force his answer out. 'Yes.'

She folded her arms tightly in front of her. 'Okay, you can now colour me terrified.'

CHAPTER THREE

SARAH WASN'T SURE at what point she stopped listening. Majed's rich tones continued to wash over her but her mind whirled in a million different directions. He was the son of a king. *He was a prince!* And then one of his statements cut through all her confusion, crystallising into an overarching and urgent question.

'Whoa, wait!' She held up a hand. 'You were sent away from Keddah Jaleel *for your own safety*? Because of border infractions and rebel activity?'

He dragged a hand down his face and she hated how grey he'd gone. 'Majed?'

'Yes.'

'And yet this is a place you want to take me? You're prepared to put your unborn child in danger?'

'No!' His head shot up and his eyes flashed. 'I would never knowingly place you or our child in danger. The skirmishes were minor and quickly smothered, the perpetrators dealt with. It wasn't necessary that I leave, but it put my parents' minds at rest.'

Her heart thumped so hard she swore it would leave bruises. 'Then why have you stayed away from your homeland for the last four years?'

He shot out of his seat to stalk across the room. 'That is not something which I wish to discuss. You have my word of honour, though, that is has nothing to do with fearing for my safety.'

He wanted her to take his word for it? Maybe, if it were only her life at stake here, she would. But it wasn't. She had a baby to consider. She could no longer afford to be reckless or irresponsible.

Rising, she ran her hands over her blouse in a vain effort to smooth out the wrinkles. 'I think it's time I went home.'

Her apartment—Mike's apartment—was only a couple of blocks away. A walk in the early-morning air might help.

Or not. Probably not. But it wouldn't hurt.

His nostrils flared. 'You'll consider my proposal?'

'No.'

Not a single muscle moved and yet he seemed to sag. 'You think the idea too outrageous?'

It was utterly preposterous, yet it wasn't outrage that gripped her. 'I'm not going anywhere near Keddah Jaleel when I've no idea why you've stayed away so long. I know no one there. You'd be my only friend and support, and if I can't trust you…'

Her stomach churned. 'I am not putting myself in that position, Majed. My mother taught me better than that.'

He swung away to pace the length of the room before swinging back to face her. Agitation—anger, perhaps?—crackled from him like a force field. 'An Internet search will provide you with everything you need to know.'

She located her purse and slung it over her shoulder as she made for the door. 'Goodbye, Majed.'

'That is not enough for you?'

She swung back. 'I'm surprised you even need to ask that question. We're going to have a baby and yet you can't be honest with me.' Her hands clenched. 'If you can't see the problem with that, then I'm not going to try and explain it to you.'

His nostrils flared. His chest rose and fell. And for a

moment he looked so forbidding, her mouth went dry. He'd never hurt her, she knew that, but she could suddenly see the legacy of his heritage—the fierce and fearless warriors who'd fought and won innumerable wars on the ancient sands of Keddah Jaleel. Their blood flowed in his veins and, beneath his veneer of polish, that same fierceness resided in Majed's DNA.

'You're going to do it. You're going to keep the baby.'

His words were more statement than question. He smiled and she felt as if she were falling. She opened her mouth and then closed it again, realising that she'd come to a decision in spite of herself. Her heart beat hard. She and Majed would be tied to each other always through this child. And, regardless of what happened between them, the thought of the baby could still make him smile. And that mattered.

She rubbed a hand across her chest, trying to dislodge the ache attempting to settle beneath her breastbone. 'I…' She pulled herself up to her full height. 'Yes, I am. I'm going to have this baby.' If nothing else, this morning had made that crystal clear to her.

And that was something to be grateful for.

He strode towards her, and for a moment she thought he meant to hug her, but he stopped short and she saw shadows gathering in his eyes, ousting the excitement and tenderness that had momentarily lit them.

He dragged both hands through his hair. 'Four years ago my brother was killed by the rebels.'

The floor bucked beneath her feet. Sarah braced herself against the door, pressing her spine back until the hard wood bit into her.

'He'd organised a secret assignation with a woman who couldn't be trusted. It was a reckless and foolish thing to do and he paid heavily for it. Too heavily.'

The anguish in his eyes tore at her. 'Oh, Majed.' She reached a hand towards him but he flinched.

'I loved my brother, Sarah. I've not returned to Keddah Jaleel because I cannot imagine living in my homeland without him.'

She wanted to hug him but everything in his posture forbade it. 'I'm sorry,' she whispered.

He nodded, but all she could see in his face was pain and anger. Her stomach churned in a sickening slow roll. *Oh, no you don't.* This was *not* the time to throw up. Closing her eyes, she rested her head back and concentrated on her breathing.

'Come, Sarah.'

Her eyes sprang open at the touch of warm fingers against her arm.

'Come take a seat on the sofa.'

She couldn't fight the nausea and talk at the same time so she let him lead her across to the plump comfort of the sofa. Once seated, she shoved her head between her knees, murmuring, 'I'll be right as rain in a moment.'

When she was finally sure she'd mastered the nausea, she lifted her head. 'I'm sorry about that. I—'

'I shouldn't have told you in such a way!'

'I'm glad you did tell me.'

'Has it made you more afraid to journey to Keddah Jaleel?'

'Not more afraid, just sadder.' And to her surprise she realised she spoke the truth. 'Your brother...'

'Ahmed.'

She swallowed. 'Did Ahmed not follow proper security protocols? I assume you have security measures in place?'

He nodded. 'It's necessary for any ruling family. But that night Ahmed gave his bodyguard the slip.'

Nobody deserved to pay such a high price for wanting a single night of freedom.

'Why did they kill him?' she whispered. 'What did they hope to achieve?'

'My father is a progressive monarch. At some future point, he'd dearly love to introduce democracy to Keddah Jaleel. There are still those in my country, however, who cling to the old ways.'

'Progressive? Is he working towards gender equality? Will, for example, the daughters of the ruling sheikh ever be allowed to rule?'

For the first time that morning, he smiled—really smiled. 'Ah, Sarah, we're progressive…and we'll continue to work towards a fair and just world for all of our citizens…but change cannot always be introduced as quickly we would like.'

'Meaning?'

'Progress takes time. And we must be seen to respect the traditions of our people, even as we move beyond them. If they believe us to view our heritage as worthless, then we would lose their trust and loyalty. If our child is a daughter, and if she shows an interest in politics, then she'll have some kind of leadership role.'

'But she won't be ruler?'

'I cannot see that happening for the next generation, no. But, if we have a granddaughter, things may be different for her.'

She stared at him and her heart thumped. What a difficult task it must be to lead a country. This man was a prince—one day a ruler by birthright. She had no right telling him what he should and shouldn't do politically, not when she had no notion of what his people held dear, what they valued and what they hoped for.

She swallowed. 'Your family have paid a heavy price for their service to your country, Majed. I'm more sorry than I can say about the loss of your brother.'

This time when she reached out to touch his hand he didn't flinch. Instead, he turned his palm upwards and laced his fingers though hers. The scent of amber and spices—

cloves and cardamom—teased her senses as a thick, pregnant silence wrapped about them. It was all she could do not to chafe the gooseflesh that rose on her arms.

'There is one other thing you need to know.'

His tone lifted the tiny hairs at her nape.

'Ahmed was my *older* brother.'

'Do you have any other siblings?'

He shook his head and that was when she realised what he was trying to tell her. 'Oh!' Her heart started to thump. 'You… Ahmed was supposed to ascend to the throne, not you?'

'Not me,' he agreed.

Wow! Okay. 'And…and that's another reason you haven't wanted to return?'

'Yes.'

And yet he was prepared to face his demons because he had a baby on the way—because he wanted to be a good father. 'I think you'll make a fine ruler, Majed. I know you must miss Ahmed, but you haven't usurped him.'

'I know that in my head. But it's not the way it feels in my heart.'

'What would Ahmed tell you to do?'

He spoke a phrase in Arabic that she didn't understand. But then he laughed and he suddenly looked younger. 'He'd tell me to stop over-thinking things. He'd tell me I need to curb my impatience for change and to tread with respect in relation to the traditional ways.' A sigh shuddered from him. 'He'd tell me to take my place at my father's side. He'd want me to fight for it.'

Fight for it…?

She wasn't sure what that last bit meant but, as she stared into his face, she couldn't agree more with Ahmed's advice. Majed was destined for great things. It was time for him to embrace his destiny.

'Will you come to Keddah Jaleel with me, Sarah? Will

you at least come and see the life you could have there, the life I can give you and our child?'

'What will your parents think about a baby?'

'It will…' The lines about his mouth deepened. 'It will bring them joy.'

She had a feeling that there were family issues at play here that she had no hope of understanding.

'Our unmarried status will not thrill them. It will… disappoint them. But if you find you like Keddah Jaleel then maybe you will stay.'

'And marry you?'

'That is my wish.'

'And what kind of marriage do you think we can have?'

'One based on respect and honesty. One based on friendship.'

She pulled in a breath. 'What about love?'

He dragged his hand from hers. She immediately missed the warmth and connection. He pushed that hand back through his hair once…twice. 'We said we would be honest, yes?'

She couldn't speak. She could only nod. He was going to tell her that he could never love her…and she didn't know why, but she wasn't sure she could bear to hear him say it.

'I do not believe in love.'

She blinked.

'And if I did, I'd not want it in my life.'

What on earth…? So it wasn't that he *couldn't* love her *in particular*. It was that he *wouldn't* love any woman at all.

'Love—romantic love—leads people to do wild and foolish things. It clouds their judgement. I want no part of that.'

Her mouth went dry. He was talking about Ahmed and the woman who had entranced him so completely that he'd thrown caution to the wind.

Oh, Majed.

'I can sincerely assure you, however, that I believe my happiness in marriage with you has a better chance than with anyone else I know. I *like* you, Sarah, and that has to count for something.'

He said that now. But what would happen when he met a woman who stirred his blood? How much would he resent the ties that bound him then—and the woman and child responsible for those ties? Would he become like her father? Would she become like her mother?

She couldn't let that happen.

She moistened parched lips. 'Do you believe in fidelity?'

His eyes flashed. 'I do.' He took her chin in a firm grip and forced her gaze to his. 'I can assure you that, if you marry me, you will not think of other men.'

And then his lips slammed to hers with a force that was far from polite and more demanding than any kiss she'd ever experienced. One hand slid to her nape to prevent her from drawing away, while the other remained at her jaw, holding her still while he plundered her lips with a ruthless and seductive intent that had her melting even as she wanted to resist. The relentless, primal possession continued, sending the blood stampeding through her veins while the strength leached from her muscles until it finally tore his name from her throat.

He lifted his head, his eyes glittering. 'Are we clear on this point?'

She lifted fingers that trembled to swollen lips. That kiss had been an outrageous attempt at domination, yet she wanted him to kiss her like that again…and not stop.

'I'm clear on the fact that you expect fidelity from me. Do you demand it of yourself?'

'Naturally.' His chin tilted at an arrogant angle. 'But then, I expect my future wife to make sure my mind does not stray to other women.'

She tossed her head, dislodging his grip, thrilled and

appalled in equal measure. But before she could give him the put down she was sure he deserved, his lips were on hers again—warm, gentle…playful. They teased and tantalised until her anger had dissolved and she threaded her fingers through his hair to pull him closer.

He obliged until she lay half-sprawled beneath him, their only barrier the thin material of their clothes, his kisses sending something inside her spiralling free. She wanted all barriers between them gone. She wanted to move to the dance he'd taught her six weeks ago. She craved the spiralling pleasure, the adventure of it all, and the peace that followed. She ached…

A whimper broke from her when he lifted his head. He muttered words she didn't understand but could translate all too easily.

There'd be no more kisses today.

He lifted himself away from her and then helped her back into a sitting position with a gentleness that had the backs of her eyes burning.

'I'm sorry.'

He physically removed himself from the sofa, his words emerging clipped and short. If she hadn't heard the regret threading through them, she might've fled in mortification.

'I'm only sorry you stopped.' She'd aimed for levity but fell far short of the desired mark. It was the truth of her words that rang in the space between them rather than humour. What the heck, she'd made a fool of herself over lesser things. 'Why did you stop?'

He moved to sit in an armchair. She'd love to flatter herself that it was because he couldn't trust his control when he was near her, but she wasn't that kind of woman. She didn't inspire that kind of passion in men.

'I don't want to do anything to make you resent me.'

'And…sex can be complicated?'

'That is my experience, yes.'

Hers too, but she and Majed had already been lovers, they were having a baby—he wanted to marry her, for heaven's sake! Surely…?

'From here on, Sarah, it has to be all or nothing. I won't settle for anything less.'

She gulped.

'As the mother of my future child, you're entitled to my respect and consideration.'

Uh huh.

'I don't want… I should hate to come to resent you. We may marry or not—whatever you decide—but I think it important that we do our very best to maintain our friendship.'

'Absolutely.' Desire continued to shift through her in an insistent ache, an itch and prickle in her blood, but she forced herself to focus on his words. Friendship was important. She remembered what it had been like growing up with warring parents. She'd do anything to protect her child from that. But… 'If you don't believe in love, Majed, why should you come to resent me if we became lovers? I don't understand.'

'I have my pride, *habibi*. Just like any man.'

She was starting to suspect he might have more than his fair share. 'Meaning that, if we became lovers and I then chose not to marry you, that would hurt your pride?'

'Deeply.'

Wow. Okay. He really did mean all or nothing. And she had no intention of rousing his resentment. He could think what he liked of her but she had to make sure he never resented their child.

'I'd resent being the tool with which you recovered from a broken heart.'

Her jaw dropped. 'Broken heart? You mean… Sebastian? Oh, *please*! He didn't break—'

'We promised to be honest with each other.' His lips twisted. 'Do not lie to me now.'

Her hands clenched. 'Sebastian did not break my heart!'

She glared at him but Majed's face had gone opaque. 'Perhaps that is what you want to believe. Perhaps that's what you wish were true.'

She shot to her feet. 'That's the kind of privileged-male superiority that seriously ticks me off! Oh, the poor little woman can't possibly know her own mind—she's just a hysterical female! I'll tell her what she really thinks because she's not clever enough to think for herself.'

The lines bracketing his mouth turned white. He shot to his feet too. 'That's not what I meant.'

'It's what you said.'

He raised his arms. 'You want me to believe Sebastian didn't break your heart?'

'Your belief is your own affair. Just…just don't presume to know my thoughts and feelings better than I do myself.'

They were both breathing heavily. Eventually he nodded. 'You are right. That was wrong of me…and stupid. I resent Sebastian—I resent the way he treated you. The only possible explanation I could come up with for why you accepted that treatment was because you were in love with him.'

'There are other reasons.'

'Such as?'

She fell back into the sofa. 'Do we need to talk about this now? There're a whole lifetime of reasons and it makes me tired and ashamed to think of them.'

He sat again too, his eyes dark and intense as they scanned her face. It suddenly occurred to her that maybe he found her just as baffling as she found him. It comforted her a little, but his continuing seriousness made her fidgety. She shot him a smile. 'Perhaps you'll understand if you ever meet my mother.'

'I want to meet your mother.'

That made her laugh, though not in a particularly humorous way.

'Why do you laugh?'

'My mother will try and eat you for breakfast.'

'Meaning?'

'She subscribes to a particularly militant brand of feminism.'

'And you don't?'

'I'm a feminist—don't doubt that for a moment. I believe in equal rights for women, in equal pay and in equal opportunities. I also believe men can be feminists.'

'But your mother doesn't?'

She shook her head. 'She thinks I'm deluded.'

He rubbed his nape. 'I'm the son of the ruling sheikh in a patriarchal society. She's going to hate me.'

She grimaced. 'Pretty much.'

'I see. It won't be a comfortable meeting, then.' He lifted his chin and met her gaze squarely. 'I still want to meet her.'

Brave man.

'And then I want to meet your father.'

'I suspect that'll be impossible. At least, in the short-term. He's in America at the moment. But we can call him if you like.'

'Yes. It's necessary.' For a moment a silence stretched and then he said, 'After that…will you come to Keddah Jaleel and meet *my* family? Will you come and see the life you could have there?'

Her heart started to thump so hard, it was all she could do to breathe. Did she dare?

How can you not? This will be your child's heritage. Whether you stay or not, you owe it to this child at least to experience Keddah Jaleel for yourself.

'Majed…'

He leaned towards her, his face intense and so intent on her that it made her pulse pound in her ears. 'Yes?'

'Do I have your word that, if I want to leave Keddah Jaleel, you and your family won't prevent me?'

He smiled, but it was the saddest smile in the world, and Sarah hated herself for putting it there. 'You've heard horror stories of kidnappings in the Middle East?'

She'd promised him honesty, so she nodded.

He came back to the sofa but he didn't take a seat. Instead, he knelt before her and took her hand in both his own. 'You have my word of honour that you'll be free to leave Keddah Jaleel at any time you choose.' He hauled in a breath that left him pale. 'If you have the baby in Keddah Jaleel and then want to leave, you have my word of honour that you can leave with the child if you wish.'

She saw how much it cost him and she believed him utterly.

'Thank you,' she whispered. 'I…I have something else I want you to promise me.'

'Yes?'

She swallowed. 'If you and I end up hurting each other— I know that's not what either one of us wishes, but this is a situation that has the potential to…matter a lot. And it's unfamiliar territory for us both.'

Midnight eyes bored into hers. 'It doesn't have the *potential* to matter. It already matters a great deal.' He frowned when she remained silent. 'What are you trying to ask of me?'

'I grew up with warring parents, Majed.' She rested a hand on her stomach. 'I don't want that for this child. It would be my worst nightmare.'

His face grew grim. 'I see.'

Her chest clenched. 'I've offended you.'

He shook his head. 'I'm just sorry you had such a difficult childhood.' His gaze met hers, confident, steady and full of belief. 'You and I will never descend to such pettiness.'

How could he be so sure?

'But, if it will set your mind at rest, then you have my word. I will never use this child as a weapon against you. I will always speak of you to this child with respect, whether we are together or not, whether we are friends or not. I promise you this.'

'And I promise it too.'

'No. You need make no such promise. I already know you wouldn't do such a thing.'

She wished she had an iota of his confidence.

'So, Sarah, will you come to Keddah Jaleel with me?'

It was her turn to pull a steadying breath into her lungs. 'Okay, here's what I think we should do.' He allowed her to pull him up to sit beside her, but he refused to relinquish her hand, and she was glad of it. 'We wait until the twelve-week mark in my pregnancy to make sure…' She didn't want to jinx them by saying the words out loud.

Majed nodded. 'Yes, I understand this. You're healthy and young, and I don't envisage that anything will go wrong, but perhaps it would be best to wait.'

She nodded, grateful he'd phrased it so tactfully. 'Then you and I will announce the news to my parents.'

He nodded again.

'And then…and then we go to Keddah Jaleel. Initially for a month.'

'A month?' His eyes flared. 'You'll give me a month?' He lifted her hand to press a kiss to her palm. 'Thank you.'

CHAPTER FOUR

THE ENVELOPE IN Majed's top pocket felt as if it were burning a hole to brand his chest through the thin cotton of his shirt. He glanced at Sarah. Was she ready to go to Keddah Jaleel with him yet?

Three days ago she'd had her twelve-week scan. When she'd asked him if he'd wanted to go with her, he'd said yes with such force it had laid him bare. He dragged a hand down his face. It should've appalled him to reveal such vulnerability but it hadn't. Sarah understood his feelings for this baby. She shared them. She wouldn't toy with his emotions when it came to their child. He knew that in his heart. He knew it in his bone marrow. He held tightly to the knowledge.

Her relief at his affirmative answer had laid her bare too, though. She didn't want to do this parenting thing alone. She wanted her baby to know its father. She wanted her baby to know *him*, and the realisation had set something inside him alight.

And then there'd been the moment they'd seen their baby…

The breath jammed in his throat and his heart started to hammer. *His baby!*

He'd been completely unprepared for the rush of love that had gripped him as he'd stared at the image on the monitor. If asked, he'd have said he already loved this child, and had from the moment Sarah had told him about it, but actually to see the baby…hear its heartbeat…

His hands clenched and unclenched. He'd been ridiculously nervous beforehand. He had no idea why. He wasn't prone to histrionics. He didn't have a predilection for envisioning gloomy outcomes. Sarah was young and the picture of health. There was absolutely no reason why she and the baby should be anything but hale and hearty.

But those moments before the monitor had been turned towards them had felt like an eternity. His heart had lodged in his throat, making his lungs ache with the effort to keep breathing. They ached again now at the memory.

Sarah had felt it too. She'd reached for his hand and had squeezed it with all of her might. He'd understood her fear and he hadn't let go of her hand again until the scan was complete. She'd needed his strength and he meant to give her whatever she needed.

And then the technician had turned the monitor towards them and Sarah's grip had changed—strong, still, but charged with relief…and with awe and excitement. In that instant he hadn't known what was more beautiful—the child on the screen or the love that unfurled across Sarah's face in a warm, golden glow as elemental and awe-inspiring as a sunrise. It had stolen his breath. It had made him ache.

And then she'd met his gaze and her smile had been so big and so *real* that all the breath had flowed back into his body. Her smile had included him so completely and utterly that he hadn't been able to resist it. It had said, *this is our child. Look what we've made. Isn't it beautiful?*

Suddenly they weren't two people thrown together in difficult circumstances trying to work out the best way forward, but two people looking at the life they'd created. In that moment the shadowy, insubstantial bond they shared had crystallised, cementing them together. No matter what happened in the future, they were parents of this child. And they were determined to do whatever was best for it, regardless of the expense to themselves.

He glanced across at her again. They'd taken to spending Monday nights together—dinner out at one of the many local restaurants followed by coffee and conversation, or sometimes a movie back at Sarah's apartment. They always sat—or sprawled—on adjacent sofas, careful not to touch. Sarah dropped into the bar several times a week—just like she used to—but somehow they'd not managed to recapture their old camaraderie.

Because you slept with her. And you want to sleep with her again.

He didn't just *want* it—he *ached* with it. It plagued his dreams at night. It teased and tormented him. But…

He lifted his chin. He refused to allow passion to cloud his judgement or sway his decisions. He'd been blindsided by desire and lust before and it had cost his brother his life. He would *not* let that happen again.

He stared at his hand. The memory of the way she'd gripped it during the scan rose again in his mind. Sarah wanted what was best for this child. With a deep breath, he pulled the envelope from his pocket and slid it across to her.

'What's this?' With a glance at him, she took it…and then stilled. He watched the bob of her throat as she swallowed and a familiar thirst rose through him. The friendship they'd been trying to establish for the last seven weeks did nothing to cool the stampede of heat in his blood, or dispel the ache that gripped him when he gazed at the plump promise of her bottom lip. He craved to suck that lip into his mouth, bite down gently on it, before laving it with his tongue. He…

'These are tickets to Keddah Jaleel.'

He pulled his mind back from X-rated visions of Sarah naked, to find her staring at him with wide eyes. Perspiration prickled his top lip. 'Are you really surprised?'

'I… Well, I guess I shouldn't be.'

But she was. Maybe he should've led up to this more gently. 'The date is open-ended. You, of course, get to decide when we fly out.'

'Have…have you organised a replacement manager for the bar?'

He nodded. His second-in-command was ready to step up to the job whenever Majed asked it of him. He'd spoken to Mike, and Mike had no objections.

Sarah bit her lip as she stared at their tickets. He understood her anxiety, but her vulnerability caught at him. Although they were constantly careful not to touch—other than that isolated incident during the scan—he was tempted to move across to her sofa and take her in his arms. His pulse quickened. *Don't be an idiot.* 'What are you worried about?'

'That your family will hate me.'

'They won't hate you. That'd be impossible.'

'But they might disapprove of me. They might be disappointed in us both.'

'If they are, they'll be too polite to say so in front of you.'

She managed a short laugh. 'I wish I could promise you the same good manners from my mother.'

This child would go a long way to healing his parents' hearts. He longed to alleviate their pain. Nothing and no one could ever replace Ahmed in their lives, and his father might never be able to look at Majed in the same way again—not since the details surrounding Ahmed's death had emerged—but he'd dote on a grandchild. It seemed the least Majed could do. In time, his father might even find a way to forgive him.

But what if Sarah didn't want to stay?

The thought burned a path of acid through him. His hands clenched. He'd have to return to Australia with her, turn his back on Keddah Jaleel and any hope of becoming his father's heir…and on any hope there might be a way he and his father could repair their relationship. Darkness—thick and black—tried to settle over him. He did what he could to beat it back. He'd do what he needed to do. His child's wellbeing and happiness came before all else.

He lifted his head, recalling the way Sarah had gripped his hand during the scan and the deep love that had transformed her as she'd stared at the image of their baby. A deep-seated recognition coursed through him. Like him, Sarah would do what was right for this baby, regardless of the personal cost to herself. She wanted her baby surrounded by love. She'd never deny it a father who loved it, a father who wanted to be an integral part of its life.

He pushed his shoulders back and found he had to fight a fierce smile. He could offer this baby and her a life of unparalleled luxury and opportunity. For their child's sake she wouldn't be able to turn her back on all that Majed could provide—the privileged life he could offer their child—even if she cared nothing for such things for herself.

She'd come to the same conclusion once she'd been to Keddah Jaleel and had fallen in love with his family, his country and his people. Her loyalty to her child would win out. But with Sarah a gently-gently, softly-softly approach would be best. He had no desire to force her hand. She needed to feel that she'd made the decision herself, that she hadn't been led…that she was free from pressure and expectation. She needed to come to the conclusion in her own time, not his. And he'd do everything in his power to facilitate that.

He loved this child. He wanted to be a part of its life. She knew that and it meant something to her. She'd do the right thing.

Sarah scrolled through the calendar on her tablet. 'I only need to give the temp agency a week's notice. So…' She shuffled to the end of her sofa nearest to him and he moved to the end nearest to her. 'What if we have dinner with my mother this coming Saturday night…? And we can talk to my father that evening too. And then…and then we could fly out to Keddah Jaleel on the following Saturday? It should give us ample time to get ourselves organised.'

'Perfect. I'll let my parents know to expect us then.'

'Are you going to tell them about the baby?'

'We'll do that together once we arrive—face to face.'

Her smile trembled and he broke their unspoken no-touching rule to reach out and grip her hand. 'It'll be okay, I promise. Just give it a chance.'

'And I thought that you choosing dress-making as a career choice was your greatest mistake!'

Beside Majed, Sarah flinched.

Irene Collins fixed first her daughter and then Majed with a martinet's stare that managed to make him feel he was ten years old again and on the receiving end of a serious scolding from his paternal great-grandmother, who hadn't held with Majed's father's form of parenting. She hadn't been a 'spare the rod' woman. She'd terrified both him and Ahmed.

Irene Collins terrified him in a similar fashion now.

Don't be a coward.

He'd been tutored in the art of diplomacy. He should find this interview—confrontation—relatively easy. Relative, say, to mediating between warring nations, or introducing a new system of government into his homeland, this *should* be a doddle.

But it wasn't.

'Let me see if I have this right,' Irene repeated—she even insisted that Sarah call her Irene. 'Not only are you pregnant, but you're going to *voluntarily* allow this man to escort you to his country *in the Middle East*?'

'His name is Majed, Mother, and I'd appreciate it if you'd maintain some semblance of civility and use it.'

It hadn't taken him long to figure out that, whenever Sarah wanted to annoy Irene, she called her 'Mother'.

'Majed isn't some stranger I picked up in a bar on the spur of the moment and had a random one-night stand with. We've been friends for quite some time. And, whatever else happens, we mean to maintain that friendship. I…' Sarah lifted her chin. 'I insist you treat him with respect.'

Go, Sarah! Something akin to admiration warmed his chest. In her own way she was just as strong as her mother. He wondered if she realised that.

Irene folded her arms. 'At least you got rid of that ridiculous specimen you were dating previously. What was his name?'

Majed's lip curled. 'Sebastian.'

Irene—her spine ramrod-straight—eyed him from her armchair opposite the sofa where he and Sarah sat. Although she evidently shared Majed's opinion of Superior Sebastian, he couldn't detect an ounce of softening in her gaze. Sarah had told him that Irene was the area manager for a building society. He was simply grateful she wasn't his boss.

He yearned to reach out and take Sarah's hand—offer her support, provide a united front—but she looked as untouchable as her mother. It occurred to him then that she might've kept Sebastian around so long simply to annoy her mother. Childish, undoubtedly, but understandable.

Irene flicked a piece of lint from her trousers. 'Have you spoken to that patriarchal, profiting pillock of a father of yours?'

Majed choked.

'Not yet.'

That seemed to unbend Irene a fraction.

Sarah didn't elaborate further and Majed didn't blame

her. They were planning to speak to Sarah's father tonight. He started to see why she'd made him promise never to let their child become caught in a tug-of-war battle between them. His heart ached for the young Sarah who'd had to suffer through all of that.

'I take it you're well?'

'Very. I've had a little morning sickness, but that seems to have passed. The baby is due in October.'

Irene stuck out her chin. 'You know my feelings on men.'

Sarah glanced at Majed. 'Irene doesn't believe a man is necessary to a woman's happiness.'

He met Irene's gaze. 'You don't believe in love?'

'Romantic love? No.' Her raised eyebrow challenged him. 'Do you?'

He believed in it. He just didn't want it. 'My parents have a very successful marriage, but their union was arranged by their families. It has made me see that love is not a necessary component for a successful marriage. I believe mutual respect, shared values and friendship are far more important—and will bring more long-term happiness to one's life. My parents value and respect each other deeply.'

Love could be such a fleeting emotion—an emotion that in his experience was worth neither the heartache nor the upheaval. 'They have been wonderful role models. My childhood was very happy.'

'And are *they* happy?'

His gut clenched. He could feel his face turn wooden. 'Several years ago my brother died. They have had a difficult time since then.' How did one learn to accept the unacceptable, adjust to the un-adjustable?

Irene sat back a fraction, an almost imperceptible sigh infinitesimally loosening her shoulders. Sarah leaned forward, as if sensing that Majed needed a moment's respite—a moment to re-gather his resources. For the last four years he'd managed to avoid any mention of Ahmed, but in the last few weeks he'd been forced to acknowledge his brother's death. And each time it felt as if a sword were slashing his vitals.

'There's more you should know.'

'Dear God, don't tell me you're considering marrying this man, Sarah? Don't be such a little fool! It's completely unnecessary. I'll make sure you're looked after, that you have everything you need—you and the baby.'

Irene's unswerving show of support comforted a part of him that he hadn't known needed comforting. Irene might be tough and uncompromising but she loved her daughter.

'You cannot be serious!' Irene shot to the edge of her chair when Sarah remained silent. 'I raised you with more street smarts than that!'

'That's my own concern.' Sarah stuck out her chin. 'I haven't made a decision yet. The *more* you need to know is that Majed's father is the ruling Sheikh of Keddah Jaleel and that…'

She gripped her hands together, her white knuckles betraying her nervousness.

'Majed is his heir.'

Majed *should* be his heir, Majed corrected silently. If his father disowned him completely then that would change. It was too difficult to try and explain. They'd travel to Keddah Jaleel and he'd discover if he still had a place there.

'I see.' Irene took several agitated turns about the room before resuming her seat. 'What do you know about Keddah Jaleel?'

'I know where it is on the map. I know its climate, its primary industries and the name of its major river.'

She did?

'But I won't pretend that's what you want to know. You mean, what do I know about the politics of the place.' She pressed her hands together. 'Majed's father and uncles are transitioning the country to a democracy with a view to their family becoming a constitutional monarchy—much like Great Britain. At the moment Sheikh Rasheed—Majed's father—is something midway between an absolute ruler and a prime minister.'

'And from where have you had this? From Majed himself?'

Sarah actually laughed. 'For heaven's sake, Mum, you taught me better than that.'

Her 'Mum' sounded far more natural—and affectionate—than her previous 'Irene's or 'Mother's.

Irene's gaze speared to him. 'I assume there's an under-representation of women in both civic and industry leadership roles in your country?'

'Yes, but—'

'No buts! It's appalling.'

'No more appalling than it is in this country.' It took an effort to keep his voice level. 'It's an issue my father is working hard to address, but this kind of change doesn't happen overnight. Currently we're making more university places available to women.' He straightened. 'We intend to have the best educated female population in the world.'

'Which will do them no good if they're not allowed to use their education to better their own situations.'

'That will come.' He found himself on his feet, his fierce love for his country and his people rising through him. 'Tell me what it is that you really fear. Why are you worried about Sarah's visit to Keddah Jaleel?'

Irene stood too. She stabbed a finger at his chest. 'I'm *worried* that once you get her there she'll be a virtual prisoner. I'm *worried* that you and your family will compromise her reproductive autonomy. I'm worried that you'll take the child and that if Sarah proves troublesome—and, believe me, my daughter knows how to be troublesome—you'll imprison her...or worse.'

He swore softly in his native tongue. 'Madam, I am not a barbarian. Nor are my family or my fellow countrymen.

Sarah—and her child—will be free to come and go as and when they choose. It's true that I hope Sarah will marry me but I would never force her.'

'A marriage that will be more to your benefit than hers.'

'A marriage that will be *mutually* beneficial.'

'Mum!' Sarah hissed. Grabbing Majed's arm, she tugged him back down to the sofa beside her. 'I'm going to visit Keddah Jaleel for a month but I've made no decision beyond that.'

Irene smoothed a hand down her trousers and sat. 'It occurs to me that the wife of the ruling sheikh could do a lot of good in Keddah Jaleel.'

No doubt she meant in relation to women's rights. It occurred to him that he hadn't really considered the political implications of marrying Sarah. All he'd thought about was how a grandchild would help to heal his parents' hearts. Marrying Sarah could be the final nail in the coffin of Majed's hope to work alongside his father for his country's betterment.

Would his countrymen accept Sarah?

He pushed his shoulders back. If Sarah accepted his proposal of marriage then they'd have to. Somehow he'd make it work.

They hung up from the call they'd just had with Sarah's father, and for a moment Majed didn't know what to say.

'I did warn you,' Sarah said.

Dear God, she'd had to grow up with these people? His heart ached at the thought of the young girl she must've been, and all she must've suffered being at the centre of the tug-of-war between two such embittered people—people who'd once claimed to love each other.

'He liked you,' she offered.

'Only after discovering your mother didn't approve of me.' He'd actually called Irene a 'ball-busting old witch'.

'He didn't even congratulate you on the baby.' He'd just gone off into ugly torrents of laughter when he'd imagined the look on Irene's face as she'd heard their news.

'He offered me money instead.'

He knew people showed their love in different ways, but…

He shoved his shoulders back. Nobody in Keddah Jaleel would treat Sarah with unkindness or disrespect; he wouldn't let anyone turn her into a pawn in a game. He'd make sure of it.

He made his smile gentle, calm…encouraging. 'Are you ready to come to Keddah Jaleel now?'

She gave a half-laugh that tightened his chest. 'Yes, it's time for me to face the dragons on your side of the fence.'

'No dragons,' he promised. At least, not for her. He'd draw all their fire on himself if need be. It was the least that he could do.

CHAPTER FIVE

'No! You're joking!'

Sarah stopped dead on the tarmac to stare at him, and he had to swallow back a laugh. 'No joke,' he assured her.

Her eyes widened even further. 'You have your own private jet?'

'It belongs to my country, not to me or my father personally.' But his father *had* very thoughtfully provided it for them. That had to be a good sign.

'So, what you're telling me is that we're travelling in that?'

She pointed at the sleek jet gleaming in the mid-morning sun and he nodded. 'Lovely, isn't it?' With a laugh, he took her arm. 'Wait until you see inside. It's amazing. Mind your step. The stairs are steep.'

He waved the flight attendant away and buckled Sarah into an armchair-sized seat himself, taking delight in her simple astonishment and growing awe. *It's for the plane, remember, not for you.*

He buckled himself into the seat beside her. 'What do you think?'

She ran her hand over the cream leather of the seats and pulled her feet from her sandals to dig her toes into the plush carpet. 'I understand textiles are a big industry in Keddah Jaleel.'

'We're proud of our textile industry—justifiably so.

We have some of the finest artisans in the Middle East. We make exquisite carpets, beautiful silks and the finest cottons. Only the best materials and most skilled workers were employed for the kitting out of the jet.' He glanced at the stewardess standing nearby. 'Even the flight attendants' uniforms have been made locally. Would you like a pre-flight drink?'

Sarah ordered a lemonade and then pointed with a shy smile at the stewardess's scarf. 'That is truly lovely.'

The stewardess returned with glasses of lemonade and sparkling mineral water, as well as a complimentary scarf for Sarah, who went into immediate raptures over it. Her cheeks grew pink when she became aware of Majed's scrutiny. 'I'm sorry.'

'Don't apologise. I'm pleased it finds favour with you.'

'I dreamed of being a designer…once upon a time.'

He recalled Irene's scathing, *'And I thought you choosing dress-making as a career was your greatest mistake!'* He remembered the way Sarah had flinched.

'I soon wised up on that front, but I still have a passion for fabric and cloth.'

He fought back a frown. 'What do you mean, wised up? Why did you not pursue this passion?'

She rolled her eyes. 'Because passion doesn't always translate to talent. One needs more than enthusiasm.' She shuffled upright in her seat and touched her glass to his. 'To a good flight.' She sipped and then let out an exaggerated sigh. 'Real crystal?'

He nodded. 'Real crystal.'

'This is how you live in Keddah Jaleel?'

He tried to see the luxury through her eyes. He hadn't missed it, but maybe he'd taken it for granted. 'The economy of Keddah Jaleel is flourishing. It allows the Sheikh a great deal of…'

'Opulence? Luxury? Splendour?'

'Comfort,' he countered. 'You have to understand that a display of this kind of statesmanship is designed to impress, to give a sense of largesse, to showcase the country's prosperity.'

'Is that another way of saying "to show off"?'

He chuckled. There was something about Sarah that made him feel young. That made it easy to laugh. 'I see I'm going to have to teach you the art of diplomacy.'

Despite her teasing, though, he could see that the jet, the luxury and the respect afforded him from the flight crew impressed her. And he meant to push every advantage he had at his disposal. 'We're very fortunate to be able to enjoy such a lifestyle. If you choose to, Sarah, you can enjoy all of this too.'

Rather than wriggling with excitement, or staring at him with wide eyes, her gaze slid away and she sipped her drink, rubbing her free hand across her chest as if to ease an ache. He'd read that pregnant women often suffered from heartburn. 'Do you feel unwell?'

'I'm fine.' She turned back with a smile that didn't quite reach her eyes. 'What did my mother say to you before we left last night?'

He allowed the abrupt change of subject. He didn't doubt that it had been preying on her mind. 'She told me that she had a lot of resources at her disposal—that she knows important people—and if I thought I could hold you against your will then I had another thing coming.'

She winced. 'I'm sorry.'

'Don't apologise. I don't blame her for her fears, or for doing what she can to ensure your safety.' He sipped his drink before sending her a sidelong look. 'She said that the two of you have a code word…and so I'd better watch myself.'

That got a laugh from her. 'We do.'

He turned to her more fully. 'Really? What is it?'

'My mother taught me better than that, Majed,' she chided, piquing his curiosity further. 'It's a secret—just between her and me. That's the point of it.'

She surveyed him for a moment, head cocked to one side. 'You know, it wouldn't hurt us to have a code word too. Just in case.'

'Just in case of what?' He laughed. 'So I can rescue you if one of my relatives starts to bore you half to death or…?'

'Oh, no! A code word isn't to be used for trivial things, but only in the direst of circumstances. If one of us utters it, or writes it down, or somehow or other telegraphs it to the other, then it means they're in terrible trouble and to get help. We're talking big help here, Majed—like the police.'

He stiffened. 'I'll let no harm come to you in Keddah Jaleel, Sarah. I swear. Are you frightened?'

'I'm nervous about meeting your parents. I'm not frightened for my life or my freedom. But it's a fact of life that people—women—are murdered every day. Random events happen. It never hurts to have a code word.'

He supposed not. But the thought of Sarah needing one disturbed him. He didn't want his perturbation to worry her, so he forced himself to smile. 'You're right. It won't hurt.' *And if it'll put her mind at rest…*

He turned back to find her staring at his mouth, as if totally mesmerised. On cue, a roaring hunger surged through him. She could take him from laughing, to perplexed, to arousal in less than three beats of his heart. She shook herself, her cheeks turning pink. 'You and your father are important men. Don't you have code words with each other… with your bodyguards?'

He couldn't answer for his father but as for him… 'No.'

'Then you should.'

If the future panned out the way he wanted it to, he'd consider it. Until then… 'Let's create one now. It can't be something we'd use in normal conversation?'

'No.'

He stared at her face, at the colour of her lips. 'Coral... Will that suffice, do you think?'

'Coral?' She nodded. 'Perfect.'

If Sarah had been impressed by the deference Majed had been treated to from the moment they'd arrived at the airport in Melbourne, it was nothing to how impressed she was at the pomp and ceremony he received once they'd landed in Keddah Jaleel.

She'd had a brief impression of blazing sands, a glittering ocean and an unexpectedly green belt of land before the plane had descended. She'd turned to Majed and had said stupidly, 'You have beaches!'

The closer they'd got to Keddah Jaleel, the more morose Majed had become. She knew his thoughts must be with Ahmed but she didn't know how to comfort him. She sensed he wouldn't welcome any attempts on her part to intrude into his solitude. He'd been so solicitous towards her, so supportive, that she'd remained quiet and left him to the privacy of his thoughts.

But her words now made him laugh. 'You're surprised, *habibi*?'

Heat curled in her abdomen. She liked it when he called her that. She liked it a little too much. She fought back a frown. 'I shouldn't be, I suppose. I mean, I looked Keddah Jaleel up on the map. I knew it wasn't land-locked.' But beaches hadn't occurred to her.

'My family has a villa on the coast which we sometimes use for vacations. We could spend a few days there, if you would like.'

'That sounds...wonderful.' Australia was renowned for its beaches. It was one of the things she thought she'd miss if she moved to Keddah Jaleel.

If.

Nerves immediately made her stomach churn. Then the plane was on the ground and her entire body turned to jelly. *Please let his family like me.*

Upon landing, Majed's conviviality fled. He became almost grim. She knew he must be going through a hundred different kinds of hell, and she refused to trouble him with her own anxieties—they seemed so paltry in comparison—but...

She slid her hand into his. 'Majed, I know you're thinking about Ahmed and missing him, but this is your home. You have happy memories and associations here too. You're *allowed* to be happy that you're back.' He shouldn't feel guilty about that.

Dark eyes turned to meet her gaze. 'This country is in my blood, and it's leaping to be back here, fired with something more elemental than joy—a recognition that this is where I belong.' His brows drew together, his eyes dark with confusion. 'I didn't expect that.'

Wow. Sarah had never felt that about any place.

'I've stayed away too long.'

He glanced at their linked hands, and a sigh shuddered out of him, and before her eyes he transformed into another man—the same, yet different. He became taller, broader, more serious...and, if it were possible, more tempting. His spine straightened, his jaw lifted and hardened, and determination filled his eyes. She suddenly saw a man who was destined to be king.

It should make her want to flee.

Her heart started to pound as all her mother's dire warnings bombarded her, even as something traitorous softened in her stomach. If she married Majed, she'd have him in her bed every night. She moistened parched lips.

You can't make such an important, life-altering decision based on hormones.

There was no denying, however, that the thought was an alluring one.

Seductive.

Tempting.

'Sarah!'

Majed's sharp tones snapped her back, and she realised she hadn't been attending to a single word he'd said. She swallowed, and prayed he hadn't deciphered the directions of her thoughts. 'I'm sorry.'

His eyes flashed. 'Never mind—the journey has been a long one.'

She couldn't help thinking that it took all his patience to keep his tone level and gentle. She swallowed again. All her life she'd tried people's patience. Now, it appeared, she'd try Majed's. 'What were you saying?'

His eyes scanned her face before he spoke. 'My parents will receive us at the palace, but there'll be a small reception on the ground here at the airport to welcome me home.'

He undid her seatbelt and helped her to her feet. She had to lock her knees to keep them from shaking.

'There are protocols it'd be best for you to follow.'

'Such as?'

'Remain a few paces behind me. Don't address me unless I speak to you first.'

She took a step away from him, her stomach rebelling. What had she let herself in for?

His chin shot up. 'Don't look at me like that. I hate this as much as you do, but this is only until we get to the palace. If I take you out there on my arm, like I wish to, we'll have an entire country thinking we're engaged.'

The flight attendant stood waiting patiently in the doorway. Majed turned and snapped a few rapid-fire words at her, and she immediately withdrew, quietly closing the door behind her.

She'd done his bidding, just like that. Without asking questions or demurring or…anything!

It hit her then that Majed would one day be a king. He might not hold the title at the moment, but he'd been bred to rule.

And she…? She was a nobody!

And here he was, advancing on her with a determined light in his eye, and she found herself giving way before him.

'Have you come to a decision yet, *habibi*? Would you perhaps like to be married to the ruling sheikh and live a life of privilege and luxury?'

'Don't be ridiculous.' But her words emerged breathily… huskily….as if she were inviting him to…

The backs of her legs hit the long bench-seat, and she'd have sprawled along its length if Majed hadn't reached out and pulled her against the hard, masculine length of his body.

'You look at me with such hungry eyes that…that I'm tempted to undress you right now—to make love to you until you beg me not to stop.' His hands drifted down to her hips with seductive slowness. 'Until you cry out my name at the pleasure I can give you.'

His fingers curled into the flesh of her hips, sending coursing flames of desire licking through her veins, and she swayed into him. He held her so close, she could feel the hard length of him pressing against her belly. Both their chests rose and fell too quickly.

She tossed her hair and met his gaze. 'If we make love now, Majed, I can promise you that I won't be the only one crying out my pleasure.'

His nostrils flared, his gaze narrowing in on her lips. 'And afterwards I'd take you out there on my arm.'

She pulled air into lungs that felt as if they were going to burst. 'Then you'd risk looking a fool in the eyes of your countrymen if I decide to not stay in Keddah Jaleel. I'm sorry, Majed, but you can't seduce me into submission.'

'Are you sure about that?' One side of his mouth hooked up in a deliciously wicked grin. 'You bring out the barbarian in me. I find myself tempted to take up your challenge.'

One of his hands travelled from her hip to her armpit, brushing the side of her breast with delicious intent that had her biting her lip as her nipples pebbled into hard nubs that pressed against the thin cotton of her blouse. He stared at them in hunger…and triumph.

Suddenly, she *wasn't* sure, and it frightened her like nothing else had. She wrenched herself out of his arms. 'Positive!'

He stared at her for a moment and then gave a curt nod. 'That's better. You have colour in your face again.'

Her jaw dropped. *He'd…he'd done that on purpose?*

Before she could tell him what she thought of his tactics, he'd turned on his heel and strode out of the plane, leaving her to scrabble her composure into place and scramble after him.

'That was a dirty, rotten trick.' She started the moment the limousine pulled away, the tinted glass shielding them from the crowd's curious gaze, the soundproof barrier between them and the driver securely in place.

'It was, but we were running out of time.' He sent her a sidelong glance. 'But none of it was lies. I'd very much like to…'

'Don't!' She pointed a finger at him. 'Enough of that.'

He took her hand and laced his fingers through hers. 'The fact is, there's a lot at stake here, and appearances are important. I want to shield you as much as I can from unwanted attention and curiosity. For that to happen, you need to be almost invisible—in the same way a brisk, efficient aide would be invisible.'

What he'd done hit her then, and she couldn't help but be grateful for it. If she'd appeared on that welcome committee's red carpet looking nervous…as if she wanted to run…she'd have drawn attention to herself and questions would've been asked. The sense of outrage he'd evoked in her, along with his assured, autocratic arrogance, had protected her from that. Still…

'Couldn't you have just explained all of that to me?' She wasn't stupid. She'd have understood.

'I tried to, but you weren't listening.'

Heat burned her cheeks. She'd been too busy fantasising about Majed to pay attention to anything he'd been trying to tell her. And if she hadn't been such a complete and utter twit she'd have realised there would be protocols it would be best for her to follow.

She was such a flake—a screw-up. What on earth made her think she could successfully move in the same circles as Majed? If he married, he needed an assured diplomat at his side…not someone like her.

'Are you going to be sick?'

His concern tugged at her. 'I'm fine. Just appalled at my own naivety. You better tell me how to address your father and mother, and any other protocols I should be aware of.' Majed had shown her nothing but wholehearted support. The least she could do in return was not embarrass him.

She listened intently as he gave her a quick rundown on palace protocol.

She moistened her lips. 'And what kind of…welcome can I expect from your parents?'

'In public, they'll be very formal, and I expect they'll rarely address you.'

'In private?'

Majed's cheekbones, high and angular, suddenly seemed to stand out in stark relief to the rest of his face. His eyes went pitch-black. Generous lips pressed into a hard line.

'My father is a reserved man. He keeps his true feelings under lock and key.'

Right. She shouldn't expect a warm welcome from him, then. She glanced at Majed out of the corner of her eye. His relationship with his father sounded complicated.

'My mother is the opposite—effervescent and warm. She'll take you under her wing and treat you like a baby chick.'

Her lips twisted. 'Nothing like the welcome you received from my mother, then.'

He laughed, and the hard lines of his face momentarily softened, but he stared out of the window and not at her. 'Look.'

He pointed and she followed the line of his finger. Her jaw dropped.

'The royal palace of Keddah Jaleel.'

On a hill to their right, overlooking the city of Demal— the capital of Keddah Jaleel—stood an enormous palace of white stone and gleaming blue enamel. It had a huge central dome made of silver that gleamed in the sun. There was a cascade of descending half-domes, vaults and ascending buttresses. Numerous slender minarets rose into the sky with a grandeur and grace that left Sarah breathless.

She'd researched Keddah Jaleel's history and geography, its climate and economy. She'd read about Demal's religious diversity and knew that it boasted several mosques, a Catholic cathedral and several Buddhist temples, but she hadn't thought to research its royal palace.

'It's…amazing.'

'We're rather proud of it.'

'It looks like a cross between a fortress and something from the *Arabian Nights*.'

His eyes glowed. 'It has seen a lot of history.'

And then they were gliding through the towering gates and being ushered into the inner sanctum of the palace grounds. An enormous fountain stood in the middle of a generous square that was lined with date palms and drenched with the scent of jasmine and cloves. The water sent a rainbow arcing through the air, fragile and yet beautiful against the fierce blue of the sky. She wasn't sure she'd ever seen anything more beautiful in her life.

She stood to one side and did her best to look deferential, trying to keep her eyes on the ground, rather than darting from side to side to take in all the splendour. Majed held an arm out towards her. 'Come.'

He led her through one of the nearby arches and along a corridor that afforded her glimpses of exotic courtyards and grand rooms.

'We've been lucky to be spared a formal reception.'

She couldn't tell from his tone or his expression whether he considered that a good thing or not.

'Instead we've been summoned to my parents' private apartments.'

Sarah's heart immediately hammered up into her throat. She'd thought she'd have a chance to freshen up before meeting Majed's parents.

He smiled down at her. 'You don't need to be afraid. They're rulers, but they're also people like you and me. Just be yourself.'

Oh, right. She could just imagine them being impressed by a complete and utter flake.

They were halfway across a courtyard—shadier and more beautiful than any other she'd so far seen—when a woman came flying across from the building opposite. 'Majed! Majed, my son!'

The woman flung her arms around Majed and held him tight. Sarah watched them embrace and a lump unexpectedly lodged in her throat. This woman hadn't seen her son in the flesh for four years. Sarah felt like an intruder.

'You must be Sarah?'

She glanced around to find a pair of dark eyes, identical to Majed's, surveying her. 'Your Highness, I...'

She went to curtsey, but he held up his hand. 'You must call me Rasheed.' And to her utter amazement he embraced her, kissing her on both cheeks before holding her close. 'Thank you for bringing my son back home to us, my dear,' he whispered in her ear.

Sarah found herself hugging him back.

CHAPTER SIX

WHEN HIS MOTHER finally loosened her arms from about his neck, Majed turned to greet his father, his insides coiling up tight.

To his surprise, one of his father's hands rested on Sarah's shoulder, and it was evident from the relief in her eyes and the pink in her cheeks that he'd greeted her warmly.

Majed let out a pent-up breath before bowing formally, as was the custom, and when he straightened he found his father's warmth had retreated behind an impenetrable wall of reserve. Even though it was what he expected, it made Majed's gut clench. 'Hello, Father—it's good to see you.'

'Hello, Majed.' He nodded towards Majed's mother. 'It is good to see your mother so happy.'

He felt the sting of the reprimand like a whip against bare flesh. *How could you be so heartless as to make your mother suffer?* He understood immediately what his father hadn't said—that Majed's presence did not make *him* happy. He'd tolerate his son's presence for his wife's sake and that was all.

Sarah glanced at Majed and his father and back again, her brow crinkling. He didn't blame her for her confusion. Should he have given her a clearer picture of how things stood between him and his father?

In all honesty, he hadn't known if things had changed dur-

ing his absence, whether his father's attitude had softened…
or whether he'd still feel the same way.

His hands clenched. Evidently it was the latter.

Evidently he still held Majed responsible for his brother's
death.

And why shouldn't he? Majed still blamed himself. He
didn't deserve forgiveness, but there was still the possibility that he could bring some measure of light into his
parents' lives.

He gestured Sarah forward. 'Mâmâ, this is my friend,
Sarah Collins.'

'Your Highness.'

Sarah curtsied in the fashion of his people and he stared
at her in surprise—when had she learned to do that?

'It's a great honour to meet you.' And then she held her
tongue. One did not speak to the Sheikh or Sheikha unless addressed first.

To his further surprise, his mother didn't embrace
Sarah. She didn't even offer her hand. She merely said,
'I hope you'll be comfortable during your stay.' And then
she turned back to him. 'Majed, you owe your mother a
little of your time, surely? Come now to my sitting room.
We have so much to catch up on. You must give me time
to feast my eyes upon you.'

What on earth…? He glanced back at Sarah.

'The servants will see to your friend.'

Sarah smiled at him and nodded, encouraging him to go,
but he sensed the nerves behind that brave little smile—
saw the way she pressed her hand to her stomach, as if to
protect her child from an unseen force. *His child.* Sarah deserved his consideration. He wouldn't abandon her at the
first available opportunity.

'I'm sorry, Omme.' He used the formal term for mother.
'I'd prefer to attend to Sarah myself. Please give us half an

hour to freshen up after the flight and we'll meet with you and Abii in his private sitting room.'

'As you wish.'

It was all he could do not to wince at the coldness that threaded his mother's voice or the way she swept from the courtyard. Very few people denied the Sheikha her wishes…except on occasion her sons. She did deserve better from him, but she'd understand once she learned that Sarah was pregnant.

His father's eyes flashed a reprimand in Majed's direction but he touched Sarah's arm in a courtly gesture of leave taking and told her he looked forward to speaking with her more, before he too set off in the same direction as his wife.

When they disappeared from view, Sarah spun to him. 'You should've gone with her, Majed. She's not seen you in four years.'

He glanced meaningfully towards a shady corner where a servant waited patiently. Sarah swallowed and bit her lip, but nodded her understanding—they weren't alone and anything she'd prefer not to be overheard needed to wait. She didn't speak again until the servant had led them to the guest quarters. As Majed had requested, Sarah had been given the best suite of rooms.

The servant melted away at a signal from Majed and Sarah glanced at him with a raised eyebrow. 'Is it okay to speak now?'

'I know you wish to berate me for not going with my mother but, Sarah, my first duty is to you.'

Her face turned wooden. 'Duty?'

He bit back a sigh. 'I didn't mean it that way. I don't see you as a duty. But I promised you every care and consideration while you were here, and I meant it. I've no intention of failing you—abandoning you—the moment we arrive.'

'I'd have understood.'

'I know, but…' He raked a hand through his hair, want-

ing desperately to change the subject. 'What do you think
of your quarters?' She had a sitting room, a bedroom and a
lavish bathroom, all decorated in mother-of-pearl and lapis
lazuli. 'Do you approve of them?'

She glanced around, her hands twisting together.
'They're very beautiful—rooms fit for a princess.'

If she married him, she would be a princess.

As if realising that, some of the colour leached from her
face. Was it the thought of marrying him that caused it, or
the thought of becoming a princess?

And, if it were the latter, why would that frighten her?
He'd had women tell him that becoming a princess was a
dream, a fantasy akin to winning the lottery.

'There are things here I don't understand...undercurrents
with your parents.'

'I... Yes. I thought that in four years things might've
changed, but...' But it was as if no time at all had passed.
And he felt damned to hell because even now, at any moment, he expected Ahmed to sweep into the room and pull
him into a bear hug.

Sarah strode across to an arched window. Her room had
a view onto a beautiful courtyard, but when she turned
back to face Majed he realised she'd not even seen it. He
could see her wishing herself a million miles from him
and Keddah Jaleel.

In three strides he was in front of her and gripping her
shoulders. 'Trust me, Sarah, please. I don't have time to
explain it all to you now. We're expected soon in my father's private sitting room. What I can say is that I didn't
go with my mother because I wished to present a united
front with you first. I don't want them to doubt where my
loyalty lies. I want to tell them our news and then I'll humour my mother with as many private interviews as she
wants. I promise.'

She pulled in a breath and finally smiled, but he saw

what it cost her. 'Please tell me I have time to shower and change?'

'Only just. I'll be back to collect you in twenty minutes.'

She nodded. 'You're right. We should get this over with as soon as possible.'

He reached out to trace a finger down her cheek. The memory of their almost-kiss on the plane flared back to life between them. He dragged his hand back from temptation. 'You're not facing a judge, jury and executioner, *habibi*.'

She rolled her eyes, but he suspected it was more an effort to ignore—and deny—the heat flaring between them than anything else. 'No, it's just your parents. And they're *way* scarier.'

And yet, somehow, she could still make him laugh.

'So you are pregnant, then? It's as we feared, Rasheed.'

Majed's heart pounded when his mother strode to the window, her back ramrod-straight. He'd expected his father to be the one to pace, the one whose voice would be strained with disapproval.

Before Majed could speak, Sarah said, 'Your Highness—'

'We do not stand on ceremony in here, Sarah,' Rasheed said. 'In private you must call me Rasheed and my wife Aisha.'

Sarah blinked. 'That's very kind of you. I—'

'And you must allow me to offer you my felicitations.'

To Majed's surprise his father rose, took Sarah's hand to bring her to her feet and embraced her. If he hadn't seen it with his own eyes, he wouldn't have believed it.

'Congratulations, Majed.'

Majed shook the hand his father offered him, feeling as if he'd stepped into a dream.

'Do the two of you plan to marry?'

Sarah glanced at him and it was only the steadiness reflected in her eyes that unglued his tongue from the roof of his mouth. He read her intent to step into the breach if needed, but he had no intention of appearing weak or feeble in front of either her or his father. 'We've not decided yet.'

His father sat with a heavy sigh. 'It will be a great scandal if you do not.' His glance towards Sarah, however, was not unkind.

'Nonsense.' Aisha spun around. 'These things can be hushed up.'

Rasheed continued as if Aisha hadn't spoken. 'I know things are done differently in your country, Sarah, but it will be a scandal whichever path you choose.'

His mother's eyes flashed and Majed readied himself to intervene as she came storming back towards them, her eyes fixed on Sarah. 'You will steal my son from me!'

'Mother!'

'No, Majed, don't.' Sarah swallowed and nodded, but not in agreement with his mother. 'That's what my mother accused Majed of too, though she phrased it differently. And it's not my intention to steal your son from you, Aisha. I've come to your country to see…to see if there's a place for me here. To see if I could live here.'

His mother stilled for a moment. With a smooth, graceful motion she sat and folded her hands in her lap, although her chest rose and fell furiously. 'You would consider moving to Keddah Jaleel rather than forcing my son to turn his back on his birthright?'

Rasheed shot to his feet and started to pace. And, though he cast a dark glare at her, Aisha stoically ignored him.

Sarah nodded. 'It's why I'm here.' She turned to Rasheed, who still paced, a frown darkening his face. 'I want you to know that your son has acted honourably. He's asked me to marry him. It's I who have yet to come to a decision.'

Majed moved to stand beside Sarah. 'I'll not have Sarah

pressured. She'll have the freedom to make up her own mind without interference.'

Sarah stared at him with those big blue eyes as if he were a super-hero. It made him stand taller.

His mother waved an imperious hand. 'Oh, do please sit down, Majed. You're looming and it makes my neck ache.'

He saw Sarah seated first and then sat beside her. All the while he was aware of his father's dark gaze.

Aisha cleared her throat. 'Sarah will be free to make up her mind. As free as the rest of us are.'

He stiffened. 'She's not bound by our laws.'

'No, but you are, my son. And Sarah needs to be aware of the repercussions to you of her decision. It's only fair that she knows all the facts before she makes a decision.'

Sarah stared at Majed and then Aisha. 'What repercussions?'

Majed took her hand—a show of solidarity—but his heart pounded and his nerves stretched tight. 'I'm interested to hear those myself.'

She squeezed his hand and it helped to steady the nerves jangling through him.

His mother shot him a sharp look. 'You know them as well as I do. If you do not marry the woman who bears your child, our people will see it as a sign of weakness and moral degradation. Your father has fought for reform in this country and he needs an heir who is strong—who is seen by the people to be strong. There are those still wedded to the old ways who would use any perceived sign of weakness as a reason to incite civil unrest.'

His heart pounded. At least his mother saw a role for him in the governance of his country. *If he married Sarah.*

Sarah's white-knuckled grip on his hand tore at him and, while he appreciated the truth of his mother's words, he wished she'd held her tongue. 'You need to decide what will be best for you, Sarah—for you and the baby—not for me. And there is time yet before that decision needs to be made. Don't forget that.'

Her grip eased and she nodded. Her low, 'Thank you,' pierced him. He admired her courage in the face of his parents' stateliness, and her veneer of steadiness in the face of her own panic.

'But it *will* need to be made. And *soon*.'

'Mâmâ!'

'And…and if I do decide to marry Majed…?'

His heart clenched with a fierceness that took him off guard—part possessive triumph and part primal, masculine desire that she would be in his bed, that he would have the right to make love with her every single night.

He rubbed his nape and tried to get his rampaging hormones back under control. He was no better than his marauding forebears!

'If I marry Majed will your people see him as a strong ruler—will they see him as someone who can take their country into the future? Will they follow him?'

'It's impossible, my dear.' Rasheed moved back to his seat. 'Our people will never accept a Western woman as their Sheikha.'

Each of his words pounded into Majed like blows. The fact they weren't true made no difference.

'They would come round if *you* showed your support!' his mother all but shouted in Arabic. 'She could show our women a new way, a way forward.'

In Arabic, his father told her to hold her tongue. Majed had never heard him speak to her in such a hard tone before.

Majed squared his shoulders. 'So you still do not see a place for me here? You refuse to countenance me as your heir?'

'I—'

'Stop!' Sarah surged forward to stare into the older man's face. 'What are you doing?' she whispered, and this time it was Majed who felt he didn't understand the undercurrents in the room.'

'You are welcome here, Sarah, but you are an outsider.'

'She's not an outsider.' Majed shot to his feet. 'She's bearing your grandchild.'

His father's chin lifted and his eyes flashed. 'And as such she is entitled to my care, my consideration and my assistance. She also has my gratitude. But it is the same now as it was four years ago, Majed. I plan to make your cousin, Samir, my heir. You are free to return to the West.'

Sarah stared at Rasheed in growing horror. What was he doing?

And why was he doing it?

From the stricken expressions on Aisha and Majed's faces, not only had he hurt them—'gutted' would be a more precise description for them—but he was going against some kind of traditional royal protocol.

'You cannot!' Aisha had gone deathly pale. 'The ruling sheikh hasn't done that in over two hundred years, Rasheed!'

'Hush, Aisha, it's for the best.'

How could this possibly be for the best?

Thank you for bringing my son home.

No!

Sarah clapped her hands, turning all eyes to her. She made herself smile—not over-brightly, because she couldn't manage that, but enough to cover her confusion. 'Majed, your mother has long desired a private interview with you. She hasn't had the opportunity for four long years. Surely it's time to grant her wish now that we've announced our news?'

Majed opened his mouth but she cut him off. 'I'll be perfectly fine. I'm not a child that needs looking after. Besides, I'm very much looking forward to getting to know your father better.'

Rasheed's head came up. 'As much as I echo that sentiment, I'm afraid it will not be possible this afternoon. I have state business that demands my attention.'

A likely excuse if she'd ever heard one! 'You don't have ten minutes to spare for the mother of your future grandchild, sir?'

She hoped he'd correctly interpret the almost-glare she sent him. If he didn't give her ten minutes of his time now, she'd speak her mind in front of everyone…and she had a feeling he'd hate that.

But she refused to hold her tongue. She and Majed might not love each other—and they might not marry—but he was her friend and she was on his side.

'How delightful,' Rasheed murmured. 'I'm sure I could spare you ten minutes, my dear.'

They were said pleasantly enough, but Sarah had a feeling his words were forced out through gritted teeth.

Majed and Aisha left, and Rasheed led her into an even more splendid room than the one they'd just left. But if he thought the pomp and splendour would intimidate her then he was sadly mistaken. 'What on earth are you doing?' She rounded on him. 'You've lost one son. Why on earth would you want to banish another?'

He paled at her words but drew himself up to his full height and stature. 'You know nothing of the politics of my country or my family.'

'Oh, no you don't, Rasheed.' She was too het up to stand still. She paced up and down in front of him and stopped to point a finger at him. 'You might be supreme ruler of Keddah Jaleel, but at the moment you're simply Majed's father. I care about Majed and I care what happens to our baby.'

His gaze lowered to where her hand curved about her abdomen and before her eyes he seemed to age. Her heart thumped. Biting back something rude, she took his arm and led him to a sofa embroidered in such rich cloth it almost distracted her from her aim of talking sense into Rasheed.

'I know you love your son, so why would you banish him from the homeland he loves?'

The older man stiffened. 'I do not banish him.'

'That's exactly what you're doing if you deny his right to ascend to the throne when the time comes.'

Rasheed stare back at her stonily.

Had nothing she'd said made any impact on him? She gripped her hands together. 'Would it really be so problematic if the heir took a Western bride?'

His gaze slid away.

'If the answer to that question is yes…' She swallowed. 'Then the solution is simple. I'll leave Keddah Jaleel and never return. I'll deny Majed all access to his child.'

Rasheed surged to his feet. 'You cannot do that. It would kill my son.'

The way he'd said 'my son' gave her hope.

'And, as Aisha said, it can all be hushed up. No one need ever know that Majed has a child. If we take that course of action, it should surely remove what you see as a major stumbling block to Majed succeeding you.'

The Sheikh's chest rose and fell. 'You cannot deny him his child!'

She didn't know what she was searching for… 'Though, I suppose, Majed and I could continue to live here in Keddah Jaleel. I'm certain Majed could find a role here, even if it wasn't as the supreme ruler.'

Rasheed's face tightened and he slashed a hand through the air. 'That is out of the question!'

Behind the anger she sensed something else but she wasn't sure what. Fear? Resentment? Regret? Her mouth dried. 'Do you really think Majed would make such a poor ruler?' Did he not know his son at all?

Rasheed's chin shot up and for a moment she swore she

saw affront in his face, before it became opaque and calm once again—his statesman's face, she suspected. He lifted his arms. 'What do you want of me, Sarah Collins?'

What did she want? She pushed her shoulders back and refused to dwell on the fact that she was berating a supreme ruler and interfering in the politics of a country she didn't understand. 'I want you to give Majed a chance.'

'A chance to do what?'

She moistened parched lips. 'A chance to prove that he should be your heir.'

'And if I do not do this?'

'Then I'll leave. And I'll make sure I never see Majed again.'

Her heart thumped. What on earth was she doing? What if the Sheikh told her to go now and pack her bags?

She pressed a hand to her stomach and glanced about the stately room. 'I refuse to be responsible for denying Majed his birthright.'

'Instead you will deprive him of his child!'

'It is you, sir, who tells us this situation is impossible.'

He rose to stalk about the room. Something in the slant and set of his shoulders reminded her of Majed so much that an ache pressed against the backs of her eyes.

Rasheed swung around but his stately reserve crumbled when he stared at her. 'My dear, do not cry.'

She lifted her hands to her cheeks, surprised to find them wet. A lump stretched her throat as she tried to mop them up. 'I'm sorry.' To her mortification the words emerged on a sob. 'Pregnancy hormones—they're making me all…all emotional.'

He sat down beside her and patted her hand. 'Do not distress yourself. It cannot be good for you or the baby.'

'Oh, Rasheed, don't you want to know your grandchild?'

'Of course I—'

He broke off and folded his arms, his brow lowering. 'You are either very clever or very ingenuous.'

She dried her eyes. 'I suspect I can be both at different times, but I'm not trying to trick you into admitting anything you don't want to. I'm just wanting to do what is best for my baby. And the best for Majed. And myself too.'

'In that order?'

She smiled. 'Now I think it's you who's trying to be clever. The baby comes first. As for the rest...' She lifted her shoulders and let them fall.

For a moment, silence stretched between them. Sarah's heart thumped and her temples ached. On impulse she reached out and touched Rasheed's arm. 'I'm sorry Ahmed is no longer with you. I wish he were. I know how much Majed wishes it too.'

Rasheed went grey but he didn't pull his arm away. She must be breaking a hundred royal protocols but she didn't care. 'I can't imagine the pain of losing a child.'

'I pray you never will.'

She met his gaze. 'Please don't punish Majed because he isn't Ahmed.'

A wall came down in those eyes and Sarah couldn't help feeling she was missing something significant, some piece of the puzzle that would give her the clue she needed to understand. Before she could try and work it out, Rasheed had risen and was offering her his arm. She took it and followed him as he led them back the way they'd come.

Aisha and Majed broke off when she and Rasheed entered what Sarah guessed must be Aisha's private sitting room. One glance at Rasheed's face and they rose. If possible, their faces grew even more serious.

'Zawj?'

Husband. It was one of the few Arabic words Sarah knew.

Beside her she could feel the tension radiating from Rasheed. 'Majed, Sarah has convinced me to reconsider my position.'

Aisha clapped her hands beneath her chin, her eyes glowing.

'She has convinced me to give you a chance.'

'A chance, sir?'

'You have the next month to prove that you're willing and able to step into my shoes, to prove you should be the heir to the throne of Keddah Jaleel—to prove that you can rule with courage and love.'

Relief ripped through Sarah. Majed's expression, though, turned opaque.

He gave his father a short bow. 'I will not let you down, Bábá.'

Had Majed and Aisha heard the Sheikh's sigh? Something in it tugged at Sarah's heart.

'Sarah.' The Sheikh turned to her. 'If my son does prove himself worthy, you need to know this…'

'Yes, sir?'

Her heart started to thump. Would he banish her and the baby?

'To ascend the throne, Majed must marry you.'

Her heart leapt into her throat to pound there, making it impossible to speak.

'This is not blackmail. It is the tradition of our people. It is the only way Majed will be able to maintain the respect and loyalty of his subjects. Do you understand?'

She couldn't speak but she managed to nod.

'If you'll excuse me now…'

The Sheikh left and Majed immediately moved to her side, his eyes scanning her face. 'You're pale. And you're shaking. Come, sit down.'

He pressed a glass of cold water into her hand and she sipped it gratefully.

'Are you feeling better?'

Dark eyes peered into hers but she could read nothing in them. It was as if Majed had closed himself off from her. Why didn't he look happy or relieved, or something positive?

'Would you like to see a doctor?'

'Don't fuss, Majed. I'm fine. It's just… I've never… Well, your father…'

'The situation has been nerve-racking, yes?' Aisha supplied.

The warmth in her smile settled Sarah's nerves more than anything else could have done. 'Exactly. But I think perhaps the worst is over now.'

Aisha reached out and patted Sarah's hand. 'I think so too. Majed, you should take Sarah back to her room to rest for a bit. I'm looking forward to getting to know you better, Sarah.'

Majed didn't speak on the long walk back to Sarah's quarters. Not once. He didn't speak until he'd seen her seated in her sitting room. 'What did you say to my father?'

She lifted a shoulder and let it drop, trying to smile. 'Probably things that in the olden days would've had me beheaded.'

His lips lifted, as if by rote, but the smile didn't reach his eyes. Her stomach started to shrink.

'We've not had capital punishment in Keddah Jaleel for more than a century.'

'That's a…um…comfort.'

He didn't even attempt to smile this time. His eyes blazed into hers. 'Sarah?'

His tone was even but relentless. It told her he meant to get an answer to his earlier question, and he meant to get it soon.

She bit back a sigh. 'I told him that if he didn't give you a chance to prove yourself that I'd…um…'

He folded his arms. 'That you'd…?'

She swallowed, her throat suddenly dry. 'That I'd leave Keddah Jaleel and…and deny you all access to the baby.'

The lines about his mouth turned an ominous shade of white. 'I see.'

She suppressed a shiver as his eyes froze over.

'Did you mean that?'

'I don't know.'

'So you *lied* to him?' The light in his eyes was utterly relentless. 'Either that or you've lied to me.'

'I was just trying to make things…better.'

'*Better?*' He stared at her as if she spoke a language he didn't understand.

She lifted her chin. *In for a penny…* 'And I told him it wasn't fair to punish you for not being Ahmed.'

His mouth dropped open. 'You. Did. *What?*'

He flung his arms outwards, each word shooting from him with bullet-like precision, piercing her with his incredulity and censure. He paced the room, letting forth a torrent of Arabic that she didn't understand but which sounded far from complimentary, and her shoulders started edging up.

He swung back. 'You've no idea what you've done, do you?'

Evidently not.

'You've all but promised to marry me if he makes me his heir. You've all but promised him and my mother that you'll raise our child here in Keddah Jaleel. And if you don't keep your word now you'll break their hearts all over again. Not only have they lost a son, but now they must lose a grandchild?'

'No, I—'

'You told him I want to be his heir and you've promised him I'll fulfil the role!'

He paced the room, muttering imprecations under his breath. She tried to claw her panic back under control. All she'd done was defend him, stick up for him. What was so bad about that?

He turned, his eyes black. 'You've made all of these promises on our behalf and neither one of us yet knows if we can keep them, let alone live up to them!'

Her mouth dried. 'You don't want to be the ruling sheikh?'

His hands slammed to his hips. 'Do you know yet if you want to marry me?'

No.

'Precisely,' he shot back at her, as if he'd read that thought on her face.

She'd thought she was making things better. Instead she'd made them worse. *Flake. Disappointment. Failure.* The words pounded at her, making her feel small and stupid.

He slashed a hand through the air. 'You've no idea in what you're meddling. You shouldn't have interfered!'

That put steel back into her spine. 'Then why don't you tell me? Why don't you fill in the blanks I'm so obviously missing? In Australia you told me you were your father's heir, and then I get here and find out there's a whole big question mark over the issue. If you don't give me all the information, Majed, how on earth do you expect me to negotiate the situation here?'

He didn't want her negotiating the situation! He'd negotiate it for both of them.

Even as he thought it, though, he knew he wasn't being fair.

Sarah hadn't meant to put him in a difficult position. All she'd done was fight for the chance she thought he wanted. She'd stuck up for him, had shown loyalty…and he was railing at her like a martinet.

'It's all well and good for you to reprimand and slam me, but I at least told you what to expect from my mother.'

Her eyes flashed. 'I didn't throw you in at the deep end without any warning!'

Yes...but she'd told Rasheed to stop punishing him for not being Ahmed. He wanted to drop his head to his hands and howl.

Her chin shot up. 'You don't trust me, do you? Despite all your promises of friendship and whatnot, you don't trust me enough to tell me what's going on here.'

She moved in closer, her eyes continuing to flash. Her scent bombarded him and he had to grit his teeth against it.

'How on earth do you think we're going to successfully co-parent if you keep important information from me?'

His heart pounded so hard his chest started to hurt.

She folded her arms, her glare increasing. 'Why does your father have such an issue with you becoming the next sheikh? And don't even think of putting me off, Majed. Whether you like it or not, this is going to affect our baby. You *will* tell me the truth.'

Or what? She'd leave?

He bent at the waist, hands braced against his knees to draw deep, ragged breaths into his lungs.

When he glanced up, he found she'd pressed a hand to her brow as if to keep a headache at bay. She was pregnant. She needed to rest—for her own sake and for the baby's too.

She won't rest until you tell her every loathsome, repugnant detail.

He straightened. 'I hate talking about this.' The words left him on a growl but that didn't seem to perturb her in the least.

'That much is evident.'

He motioned for her to take her seat again. 'To understand my father's attitude, you need to become better acquainted with the circumstances surrounding Ahmed's death.'

CHAPTER SEVEN

SARAH'S KNUCKLES TURNED WHITE. 'I know this can't be easy to talk about.'

Yet she still meant to make him utter the words out loud. Majed swung away. 'I told you it was a woman who was responsible for leading Ahmed to the rebels.'

'Yes.'

He stared at a spot on the wall and forced himself to continue. 'I was the one who introduced Fatima to the palace... and to Ahmed.'

Her gasp—loud in the silence of the room—speared into him.

'My father blames me for that. As he should.'

'No, Majed, you're wrong. Even a stranger can see—'

'Let me finish!' The words left him on a bellow, but he couldn't help it. 'There's more to this sordid story yet.' *So much more.* 'I was the one dating Fatima.' His lips twisted and he finally turned to face her, steeling himself for the condemnation and pity he expected to see. 'I was the one who fancied himself in love with her.'

Her jaw slackened. 'She betrayed you with Ahmed?'

Yes. Which meant Ahmed had betrayed him too.

His skin felt as if it were on fire. He tried to bury the pain coursing through his chest, pounding at his temples, threatening the strength of his knees. 'Obviously the rebels' sights were initially set on me, but when Fatima found she had access to a greater prize—the Sheikh's actual heir—she took her chance.'

She stared at him and it was almost impossible not to shift under that gaze. It made him tense...and the tension made him cruel. 'Have I satisfied your curiosity?'

Her head reared back. 'Curiosity? Is that what you think this is?' She shot to her feet. 'I can't believe you let me go in front of your parents without telling me this. I'd never have said the things I said to your father if I'd known.' She dragged her hands through her hair. 'How insensitive and... and *cruel* he must think me.'

She broke off to pace. His heart thumped. She was right—it hadn't been fair. But talking about Ahmed and Fatima tore the very heart out of his chest and...he couldn't bear it.

His heart pounded. Sarah had stood up for him. She'd had the courage to defend him. A strange warmth filtered into his veins, warming him from the inside out. Majed loved his father but he knew how intimidating Rasheed could be. Sarah had promised him friendship and she'd delivered. While he...he dragged a hand through his hair... he'd put her in an impossible situation.

He pinched the bridge of his nose. 'I'm sorry.'

She swung back. 'Because you're afraid I'm going to leave?'

His hands fell back to his sides. 'Because I promised you friendship and I fell at the first hurdle.'

She stilled.

He moved across and took her hands. 'You deserved better from me. You deserved my full disclosure. I've been weak. Talking about Ahmed is...it's very painful for me. I've avoided talking about this for the last four years. I can see now how wrong that was. I'm sorry my weakness put you in such a difficult position.'

Her hands trembled. 'Wow, you can do a really good line in guilt when you want to.'

She said it to make him smile and he did his best to oblige her. 'I'm an expert.'

He said that to make her smile, and something in his chest started to ache when she managed a weak one.

'I want you to know I'm grateful for the opportunity to work with my father.' He squeezed her hands lightly and then released her, stepping away before he pulled her into his arms and tried to erase the events of the day in the mind-boggling pleasure of making love with her. It might work in the short term, but in the long term it would probably prove a disaster. He had no intention of doing anything that might make her leave. He did his best to banish the images from his mind. 'You'll stay?'

She stared at him for a long moment, before nodding. 'For the moment.'

His knees almost gave out in relief and gratitude. 'Thank you.' *Do not kiss her!* 'I should leave you now. You should get some rest.'

'Sarah?'

Majed tapped on the open door to Sarah's sitting room. She glanced up from her seat on the sofa where she was flicking through a magazine. She closed the magazine and sent him a guarded smile that had his chest cramping. She gestured him into the room. 'Good morning.'

'Did you sleep well?'

She started to nod and then slumped back. 'About as well as you did, I expect.'

'Things will get easier. I promise.'

She nodded.

'Which makes what I'm about to say all the harder.'

She tossed the magazine to the coffee table. 'You better give it to me straight. I've been banished or—'

'Nothing of the sort. My mother can't wait to show you about the palace and introduce you to the women of the family.'

'But your father?'

'I haven't spoken to him since our interview yesterday.' He grimaced. 'However, ten minutes ago one of his aides informed me that I'm to take up the mantle of my royal duties today.'

She straightened. 'Oh, wow. But…that's good, isn't it?'

He didn't know. He hoped so.

'But you're feeling bad because you believe you're abandoning me?'

Bingo.

'Don't worry about me, Majed. I'll be fine.' She suddenly smiled. 'I expect your mother will make sure of that.'

So did he. It was just… *He'd* wanted to be the one to introduce her to his country.

'I can tell them it's impossible for me to take up my duties until next week.'

'You'll do nothing of the sort!' She shot to her feet. 'It's obvious this is a test.'

'Of my—?'

'Of *our* determination and…and steadfastness.'

She made it sound as if his father was trying to scare them away. She could have a point.

'Do you have time to talk?'

He'd make time. 'Yes.' He sat.

She sat too. 'I've been going over things.'

He didn't want her going over things. He didn't want her worrying and stressing. He wanted her… He bit back a sigh. He wanted her to fall in love with Aisha and his country, and to leave all the hard stuff to him.

But Sarah wasn't built like that. So he'd simply have to find a way to ease her mind about whatever was worrying her.

'I want to have a *difficult* talk.'

He lifted his chin. He had no intention of shying away from a difficult discussion again. He set his shoulders. 'Shoot.'

She pulled in a deep breath. 'You think your father holds you responsible for Ahmed's death.' She moistened her lips. 'You think…you think he can't forgive you.'

She was spot on, but his throat had closed over and he couldn't speak. He nodded.

'I think you're wrong.'

The certainty in her voice had him glancing up. He fought the urge to yell and fling wild words at her. She didn't deserve his anger. She deserved his gratitude. If it weren't for her, they'd be back on a plane bound for Australia, and who knew when he might've stepped foot on home soil again?

She moved to stand in front of him and he realised he'd shot to his feet. He stood there with hands clenched at his sides, breathing heavily. His feeling of vulnerability appalled him but he could not do anything about it. Talking about the events of four years ago had ripped the scab off a wound that would never heal and it made him want to tear at rock with his bare hands.

She reached up and touched his cheek, laid her hand flat against it, and her warmth seeped into him, helping to ease the storm raging in his soul.

'You've suffered so much. You all have. My family is fractured but that's because my parents have allowed their bitterness to consume them. It means I can recognise that kind of vitriol. There's something different happening with your family, Majed. I'm not sure what it is, but between us maybe we can work it out.'

And then she removed her hand and retreated back to the sofa, staring at him expectantly. Swallowing, he nodded and took the seat beside her. 'I'm listening.'

Her gaze never wavered. 'This is going to take courage from you.'

He stiffened. 'I am no coward.'

'*Emotional* courage.'

His jaw clenched. Was that her opinion of him? 'As I said, I'm not a coward.'

'But your feelings have been hurt. You believe your father blames you for Ahmed's death because you blame yourself. That's colouring your judgement.' She lifted a hand skyward. 'You think I've just called you a coward when I don't believe that for a moment.'

His head rocked back. His mouth dried. 'I wasn't aware I took offence so easily. My apologies.'

'I don't want your apologies, Majed. I want you self-aware and concentrating. Something is happening here and we need to get to the bottom of it.' She dragged in a breath. 'My child's happiness depends on it.'

'*Our* child,' he corrected.

She stilled and then nodded. 'Our child.'

'Go on.'

Those steady eyes of hers speared him again. 'You need to put your sense of guilt and blame to one side for the moment—discount them if at all possible. Can you do that?'

He couldn't explain why, but her calm logic helped to ease the storm raging within him even further until it was nothing more than a distant rumble on the horizon. 'I can try.'

Her smile anchored him.

She turned to him more fully. 'The first words your father spoke to me were, "thank you for bringing my son home".'

His jaw dropped. His heart started to thud.

'And then, to you, he acted all cool and regal and distant.'

He recalled her bafflement at the meeting and it started to make sense.

'Why would he hide his joy, his happiness, at seeing you *from* you? It makes no sense.'

If what she said was true...

'Of course, you were just as cool and regal and distant in return.'

His mouth dried. Should he have given his father more? He suddenly saw what she meant by emotional courage. Did he have the courage to allow himself to be completely vulnerable to his father...and risk rejection? Again.

'I told your father that if it were truly impossible for you to rule with a Western wife I'd return to Australia without you, deny you access to the baby, and we could all keep the baby's paternity secret.'

His hands clenched so hard his entire frame shook. 'Did you mean that?' *She'd deny him his child?*

'Keep your mind focussed on your father for a moment.' Her voice had gone sharp. 'He was utterly horrified that I would even consider doing such a thing.'

His breath got caught midway between his chest and throat.

'He told me I couldn't do it. He said denying you your child would kill you.'

He had?

'If you had to choose between your kingdom or your child, Majed, which would you choose?'

'My child.' He said it without hesitation.

'And your father knows that.'

Hence the reason for his reprieve.

'Because I'm pregnant, my mind is filled with thoughts of our child. My love for it...all I'd endure and suffer for it if I had to. So when I look at your father and find his words and actions in relation to you in such conflict, I ask myself, what's causing it? I ask myself, what does he fear?'

Majed's first thought was that his father feared his second son wasn't up to the task of leading his country. But that was the old guilt—the doubts Sarah had asked him to put to one side.

'What kind of father was he when you were growing up?'

'Loving.' He half-smiled at the memory. 'He was strict too, but he was also loving. He made time for his family, despite the many demands of his position. He said his family was his strength.' Ahmed's death had struck him and revealed his most vulnerable site—it had devastated him.

Majed tried to breathe through the pain raking his chest. 'It's possible he's still grieving. Perhaps he's not yet ready to move on. Nobody can replace Ahmed. The idea is ludicrous but…'

'But someone will need to step up and be ruler when your father's reign comes to an end,' she finished for him.

Was it possible that Rasheed didn't blame Majed for Ahmed's death? Could it simply be that his younger son's presence reminded him so forcefully of his older son's absence? It was a possibility Majed hadn't considered. His heart pounded so hard he found it difficult to breathe. 'I have to make this right. I'm not sure how, but my father deserves peace.'

She nodded and it hit him then that if it weren't for her he'd have never had this insight into his father. He'd have continued to wallow in a sea of self-pity. Sarah had forced him to look beyond his own hurt and instead of despair he'd discovered hope. He gripped her shoulders. 'I cannot thank you enough. I hadn't thought of looking at it in a different way.'

'You don't need to thank me. I'm simply trying to make things as good as they can be for our baby.'

His mind was no longer on the baby but on her. It occurred to him now that he wanted to marry her for *her*, not just because of the baby. He wanted her in his bed every night. She might not be a native of Keddah Jaleel but she'd make him a fine wife.

As if aware of the direction of his thoughts, she scrambled out of his grip and across to the sideboard to pour herself a glass of water. He followed. He didn't mean to, but something stronger than rational thought made him move across to her. Without giving himself time to think, he swept the swathe of hair from her neck to press a kiss there.

Her gasp arrowed straight to his groin.

The glass clattered to the counter and both her hands clutched the sideboard, as if for support.

He grazed his teeth lightly across her earlobe, breathing her in deeply.

'What…what are you doing?'

Her chest rose and fell. She wanted him just as much as he wanted her. He couldn't explain the craving in his blood where she was concerned but it helped that she felt it too. 'I am kissing you, *habibi*.'

'But…why?'

She stiffened, so he ran his hands from her shoulders down to her hips, pulling her back against him so she could feel the hard length of him against her back, glorying when she arched into the kisses he pressed to her neck. 'I want you, Sarah. I want you like I've never wanted any woman before.'

A moan broke from her lips. 'You said you wanted all or nothing.'

And she couldn't promise him that yet…

They both stilled. For a moment the next move hung in the balance. He could make love to her now, as his aching flesh longed to, with no promises made. Or…

With a groan, he stepped away from her and the action felt like a physical pain. 'I'm sorry. Forgive me. I forgot myself.' Regardless of what his barbarian forebears might've done, he couldn't seduce Sarah into marriage. She needed to make that decision with her head, not her hormones.

She was going to be the mother of his child.

She'd won him a major concession from his father.

She didn't deserve pressure or coercion. She deserved his support.

He glanced at his watch. 'It's time for me to go. An aide will be along in half an hour to take you to my mother. I wish you an enjoyable day.'

With that, he turned on his heel and strode from the room.

One week later Majed strode along the corridor leading to the women's quarters. He had aunts and cousins who lived here and others who often came to visit. He hoped they'd taken Sarah to their bosoms, praising their life in Keddah Jaleel and making her want to live here too.

He'd not spent anywhere near enough time with her this week. He'd wanted to introduce her to the delights of his country but instead he'd found himself swamped with royal duties—meeting overseas delegates, taking part in trade negotiations, overseeing the introduction of a science, technology, engineering and maths syllabus at a new women's university in the capital.

He'd relished every moment of it. But it didn't change the fact he hadn't spent enough time with Sarah.

Maybe she was relieved with the current state of affairs. Maybe she was as afraid as he was that they'd give into the overpowering temptation of their desire for each other... afraid of the consequences that might bring.

His mother had kept him abreast of Sarah's activities—most of which she'd taken upon herself to arrange. Earlier in the week they'd visited a master artisan at his textile shop. Majed's lips lifted. Sarah had waxed lyrical about all she'd seen. The artisan had sent her back to the palace with bolt upon bolt of material. She'd been overwhelmed at the generosity. Little did she realise the prestige that came with the title Royal Supplier.

His mother and several of her aides had taken Sarah on a tour of the undercover markets. She'd returned smelling of incense and he couldn't help wishing he'd been able to share the experience with her—to witness her delight and curiosity. Rather than talk about her own experiences, though, she wanted to hear about his.

Did she recognise his new sense of purpose? Did she sense that he'd found the place where he belonged? For the last four years he'd felt cut adrift from all that mattered. Now he felt as if he were finally fulfilling his destiny. And that was all down to her.

Without a single doubt in his mind, he knew now he wanted to be his father's heir. He wanted to lead his country into the future and see his father's—and Ahmed's—vision for Keddah Jaleel become a reality.

He'd stayed away for so long in an attempt to bury the pain of his father's perceived rejection and in the process he'd buried his true desire—that he wanted to take over the throne from his father when the time came. This was his destiny.

Did she sense all that? Did it frighten her?

If so, she gave nothing away. What she wanted to know was if he and his father had *talked* yet.

So far, Majed had to answer in the negative. He'd spent a great deal of his time in his father's company, but never alone. Twice he'd requested a private interview but both times he'd been stonewalled. He'd ask again soon. Eventually Rasheed would grow used to his presence. And then, maybe, they could work on rebuilding their personal relationship.

Music drifted from the large common room at the end of the corridor. It wasn't traditional Keddah Jaleely music. It wasn't even Arabic music. It was... He frowned. And then he laughed. It was kitsch Western pop music.

He moved to the doorway and his grin widened at what he saw. Half a dozen women—his mother included—were following Sarah's lead in a series of dance moves that had them all laughing and breathless.

The pop music was completely out of place in this room with its richly coloured decorative tiles, arched windows and carved columns, yet the women had such large smiles and the music was so much fun that he had no words for the sense of wellbeing that flooded him. Sarah was...

Dear God! He gulped. She was wearing a traditional Bedouin dancing girl's costume in pale blue with a silver-and-lapis-lazuli medallion belt riding low on her hips. The costume left her belly bare and drew the eye to her generous curves.

Desire fireballed in his abdomen. He backed up a step. He shouldn't intrude...

'Majed!'

His mother's greeting prevented his retreat.

The other women in the room all spun to him with smiles of welcome. Sarah sent him a half-grin—as if to share the joke of a disco in an Arabic palace with him—but a moment later her cheeks flamed pink and she attempted to cover her bust, and all that delicious cleavage, with her folded arms... Then she seemed to realise that her stomach was bare and her hands flew down to cover it.

She stood there staring at him with eyes too big for her face, one foot rubbing the top of her other in delicious awkwardness, and a wave of tenderness washed over him. Her pregnancy hadn't started to show yet, but he'd done research on the Internet and he knew that she'd develop a baby bump within the next couple of weeks.

He couldn't wait to feel the baby kick. He hoped she'd let him share that with her.

'Majed,' his mother murmured in an undertone. 'It's impolite to stare.'

He started to find that Sarah's cheeks had gone even redder. The other women didn't know why Sarah was here, but there'd be speculation. They knew Sarah was his friend.

And now he'd added fuel to the fire.

Sarah cleared her throat. 'We've been having a cultural exchange. Your cousins have been teaching me how to belly dance.'

He noticed then that Sarah wasn't the only one wearing a traditional dancing girl's costume.

'While I've…' Her grin peeped out again.

'While you've been polluting their ears and minds with *pop music*.'

She shook her hair back, feigning superiority. 'I'll have you know that this isn't just any pop group, thank you very much. They're *the* pop group.'

As she spoke, she strode over to a nearby chair and pulled on a shirt that buttoned down the front, hiding all her delicious curves from sight. Majed wanted to go down on his knees and beg her not to.

Sarah's pulse fluttered in her throat like a crazy, wild thing. The hungry twist to Majed's lips, the way he surveyed her as she buttoned her shirt—the gleam in his eyes—made her want to incite him to action—make him haul her into his arms and kiss her. And not stop.

Dangerous.

The word whispered through her.

But delicious.

Very.

But she had her baby's welfare to consider and muddying the few rational thought processes she could muster with hormones… Well, it would be irresponsible. And she was trying so very hard to leave that part of herself behind.

She pulled in a breath. She needed to create a better family for her baby than she'd had. She would not give her child a legacy of warring parents and bitterness—a sense of always being pulled in two different directions. They all deserved better than that.

Friendship first.

She pasted on a smile. 'We've been having a lot of fun today. Your family's hospitality is boundless. An offhand comment about needing to buy a pair of wireless speakers, or a wistful remark that my sewing machine is in Austra-lia, and—*voilà!*—these items seem to magically appear!'

He blinked and a sigh welled through her. He had such beautiful eyes.

'Sewing machine? You've taken up your old hobby again?'

'Oh!' She shook herself. 'Just a…whim.' She waved what she desperately hoped was a nonchalant hand through the air. His eyes narrowed and she rushed on. 'After coming home with all that gorgeous cloth the other day, I…'

'Come and see what this remarkable girl can seemingly whip up out of thin air.'

Aisha took Majed's arm and led him towards the other end of the room where two sewing machines and an over-locker had been set up for Sarah's benefit. Her pulse went into hyper-drive. 'Oh, I'm sure Majed isn't the least inter-ested in my silly little bits and bobs.'

He glanced at her, one devastating eyebrow cocked. 'Then you'd be wrong.'

'Bits and bobs!' Aisha scoffed. 'Majed, the girl is an ab-solute marvel. She could be an artisan herself.'

Ha! Sarah's heart crunched up tight. She gave what she hoped was a light laugh. 'A flattering exaggeration.' But it was still an exaggeration.

Aisha's brow furrowed. She said something low to

Majed that Sarah didn't catch but it had his gaze turning thoughtful.

'Look at this.' Aisha held up the piece Sarah had spent the morning working on. 'Is it not stunning?'

Majed took the creation, his hand travelling thoughtfully over the material, and Sarah had to force her attention away from his hands…and the thought of how they'd feel if they moved over her naked flesh with the same appreciation. A shiver shook through her.

'Granted, it's pretty.' She shifted her weight from one foot to the other. 'But that's really down to the material. It's flawless. And a delight to work with.'

He turned to her. 'This is…it's remarkable! Why must you put it down?'

She snapped her mouth shut, her heart pounding.

'I'd no idea you could do such fine work. What inspired this piece?'

It was a riff on a kaftan. Many of the women in the palace wore gaily coloured kaftans. But this one had a Western influence. 'I was just playing with the idea of East meets West.'

She had to swallow. She did all she could to tamp down the old enthusiasm that rose through her. Nothing could come of it. It would only lead to disappointment. She had a baby on the way, for heaven's sake! She'd given up such folly long ago.

'And?'

She shrugged. 'I love the style of dress here—the long kaftan shirts and the loose, flowing trousers, the long, sheer scarves. They look so comfortable, but I love Western styles as well. I wanted to create something I could wear that was…' She searched for the word.

'A compromise?'

'A complement—the best of both worlds.'

'We want her to make us all one.'

She gestured to the piles of fabric nearby. 'I'd be delighted to. All you need to do is choose the material you'd like.'

Sarah reached out and took the tunic from Majed. 'It's not really finished yet. I've not finished off the seams properly and…and other things.' She showed him a seam to prove her point. 'But we've just been playing and experimenting and having some fun in the process.'

He opened his mouth but she hurried on. 'How has your morning been? I'll warrant ours has been more enjoyable.'

'The kaftan is not the only thing Sarah has made this morning.'

To Sarah's discomfit, Aisha handed Majed a tiny baby's nightie made from the softest cotton threaded with a yellow silk ribbon at the bodice. 'The detail is breath-taking,' Aisha continued. 'Just look at these pintucks.'

She doubted Majed knew what a pintuck was. In fact she doubted Majed even heard his mother. She couldn't speak as she stared up into his stunned and suddenly vulnerable face. She knew he was imagining their child in that nightie. He was imagining holding their baby, seeing it for the first time…and the hunger in his eyes hollowed out her heart.

He loved this child as much as she did.

How could she deny him the chance to co-parent, to be a part of his child's everyday life?

Could a marriage based on friendship be enough?

And desire. Friendship *and* desire.

But desire didn't last…

She snapped back when Aisha said her name, to find everyone surveying her. 'I'm…I'm sorry. I was a million miles away.'

Aisha smiled but Sarah wasn't sure why. 'Would a cruise down the River Bay'al be to your liking this evening? The worst of the day's heat will be gone and it's cool on the river. And very pretty. We're rather proud of it.'

How could she say no to that? 'I'd love to. It sounds wonderful.'

A gleam briefly lit Majed's eyes. 'I'll collect you at six,' he said, before turning on his heel and disappearing.

'It sounds delightful.' She turned back to Aisha with a determined smile. 'What shall we wear?'

'Not we, my dear—*you*.'

It would be just her and Majed? A traitorous pulse leapt at the thought. Wouldn't it be dangerous, the two of them alone together…?

She folded her arms. Majed, her *and* all his staff. They wouldn't be alone. She did her best to quash her disappointment.

'I think you should wear this.' Aisha took the tunic from Sarah's limp fingers. 'And I think you should make those trousers you were describing to us.'

Another riff on the ones the women here wore—except a little more fitted and cropped just above the ankle.

'We're eager to see them. We're eager to see what they'll look like on. Please, my dear, put us out of our suspense.'

'By all means.' Everyone had been so kind that it was the least she could do. And she had a feeling that keeping busy for the rest of the day would be a very good idea. When she sewed the rest of the world fell away, and she found she needed the comfort of that today.

She turned to the piles of fabric. 'We have so much to choose from and—'

'But only this will do.'

Aisha pulled forth a black silk, so finely made it was almost sheer. Sarah could imagine how decadent it would feel against her skin—like a lover's caress. She could imagine Majed's eyes darkening in appreciation when he saw her in them. It would set off the myriad blues in the tunic perfectly. Without a word, she took the fabric, spread it out and set to work.

* * *

'I need to pinch myself.' Sarah kept her voice low, not wanting to disturb the twilight hush of the river. To the west the sky was a burst of orange, slowly shading to breath-taking pinks and paler mauves. All the colours were reflected in a river that was millpond-smooth. Something about it eased the burning in Sarah's soul.

'You like it?'

Majed's caramel voice bathed her skin in a warmth that lifted all the fine hairs on her arms. 'Like it?' She started to laugh. What wasn't there to like? They were drifting down the river on a slow-moving barge reclining on a bed of silken cushions beneath a canopy of blue-and-silver satin. The luxury was unimaginable and the scenery stunning. '*Like* is far too weak a word. I…' She swallowed. 'I can't believe how beautiful it is.'

Date palms, tall, majestic and seemingly ancient, lined the riverbanks. Beyond them stretched a fertile flood plain green with crops. Majed had told her the river was a hub of activity during the day, with trading boats that travelled from the south, but at the moment it was quiet with only an occasional pleasure craft or tradesman's boat to share its great breadth with them. The palace security patrol ensured that nobody could approach the barge.

'It is beautiful.' Majed turned to her, surveyed her from beneath lazy brows. 'You're beautiful too, *habibi*. I'm honoured to share this with you.'

Majed wore traditional robes and a headdress, and her heart had nearly stopped when she'd first clapped eyes on him. He looked like a stranger—a beautiful, exotic stranger. His robes highlighted the masculine breadth of his shoulders and the lean, hawk-like angles of his face.

A great thirst welled up inside her. 'Um…thank you.'

He rested back against the cushions on one elbow and turned more fully to her. A pulse started up in her abdomen. With a deliberate finger, he reached out and traced a path from her knee to her mid-thigh. She sucked in a breath. 'What are you doing?'

The smile he sent her could only be described as wolfish. 'I like to touch you…and the clothes you wear invite me to touch them. Was that not your intention?'

'Of course not.' Her pulse hammered. *Liar.* 'Don't be ridiculous.'

'That's a shame.'

He held out a dish of delicacies to her—locally made Turkish delight that melted on the tongue, dates that were fatter and more luscious than any she'd ever had and a pastry, whose name she couldn't pronounce, which was filled with nuts and honey and tasted of the gods. Normally she'd have eaten her fill, but not this evening. Majed unsettled her too much. 'No, thank you.'

He selected a pastry and bit into it slowly, his tongue snaking out to collect a stray flake from his lips, his gaze on hers the entire time. He made a murmur of appreciation that was so lover-like, heat flooded her cheeks. She swallowed convulsively. 'What are you doing?' she whispered. She wanted to look away, but she couldn't.

He finished the pastry slowly, deliberately…and with obvious relish. 'I promised myself that I wouldn't pressure you one way or the other into marriage with me, Sarah, but I think that was a mistake.'

'Oh, I don't! I think—'

His finger against her lips halted her words. 'I think you ought to know how invested I am in you marrying me. I think you ought to know how much I want you in my bed.'

She jerked away from him, her heart thumping hard. 'Stop it.'

'Why? Because when I talk to you like this you find it hard to hold onto your own restraint? Find it impossible to ignore your body's demands?' He smiled, as if he'd read the affirmative answer in her face. 'Good. I burn for you, *habibi*, and I want you burning for me too.'

He leaned towards her, dredging her with the scent of amber and spice. 'If I were an old-time sheikh I'd order the sides of this canopy lowered until we were cocooned in our own private world and I'd have my wicked way with you until you were replete with pleasure.'

The picture he created was so vivid in her mind, her lips parted to draw in more air.

He leaned back. 'You're lucky I'm a more civilised man than my forebears.'

Was she?

Of course she was!

Her heart thumped. It took a moment for her to master her voice. 'You forget we have a baby to consider.'

His nostrils flared. 'I do not forget that for a moment. Our child is always on my mind.'

Of course it was. He wanted the baby, not her. She couldn't forget that.

Oh, no, he wants you too.

In his bed but not in his heart. Could she settle for that? She cleared her throat. 'Be that as it may, we need to decide what will be best for this baby.'

'And why do you doubt that marrying me won't be in our baby's best interests? If you marry me our baby will have a privileged life. He or she will want for nothing. Every opportunity will be open to him or her. What could be better than that?'

His eyes flashed and an answering frustration pierced her. 'Parents who love each other,' she shot back.

He rolled into a sitting position. 'That is impossible. Besides, your parents must've loved each other once and looked what happened to them. We can give our child a more solid foundation. We can give it parents who respect each other.'

Respect? She bit back a sigh. Respect was *important* in a relationship. So why did it sound so…dreary?

'We can give this child a family, Sarah. Brothers and sisters.'

She'd wanted a tribe of siblings when she was growing up. She could have all the things she'd wanted from a family *now*…if she put aside girlish daydreams and fantasies.

It didn't seem too much to ask, did it?

CHAPTER EIGHT

'I WILL DO everything in my power to make you happy, Sarah. I mean that.'

The expression in his eyes told her he meant his words. He was no longer trying to convince her through the force of their desire for each another. He was no longer trying to cloud her judgement by leaning in too close and making her blood leap and her pulse pound.

It should've made her happy! Majed was vowing to do everything in his power to ensure that she and their child would have not just a good life but a wonderful life.

Except give you his love.

She swallowed. Why did that have to matter so much? Love would come. It would evolve naturally from mutual respect and friendship.

Oh, but it would be a pale imitation of what she'd expected whenever she'd thought about love and marriage in the past.

But...

Maybe Majed was right. Their relationship would never descend into the bitter acrimony that her parents' marriage had. Hadn't she vowed to do anything to spare her child that?

'Tell me more about this old design ambition of yours.'

She glanced across at him. He half-reclined against the cushions and stared out at the river as the barge slid across the water. He looked lazy, at ease…almost slumberous. It occurred to her that she'd not seen him the slightest bit relaxed since they'd arrived in Keddah Jaleel. It soothed something inside her.

She crossed her legs and reached for a piece of Turkish delight. 'Oh, it was just a phase—like wanting to be a fire-fighter when I was ten or a mermaid when I was seven.'

'You wanted to be a mermaid?'

His slow grin warmed her blood…and her heart. Press-ing both hands to her chest in exaggerated longing, she said, 'Desperately,' making him laugh. And then she popped the Turkish delight into her mouth before it melted in her fingers.

He leaned forward to pour her a glass of exquisite home-made lemonade. 'How old were you when you decided you wanted to be a designer?'

'Fourteen, I think.' It was hard to feign nonchalance but she did her best. 'I always loved making things—as a kid I loved anything crafty.' The desire to make pretty things had always lived inside her, but it wasn't until she'd discovered sewing that it had really flared into life, filling her with a sense of purpose. 'I intended to study design at university.'

'You didn't?'

'I started.' She sipped her lemonade, hoping its sweet-ness would help counter the bitterness of the disappoint-ment that could still rise up inside her all these years later, reminding her what a flake she was…what a failure.

Her heart thumped and she risked a quick glance at Majed's profile. He deserved a better wife than she'd ever make—a more polished and accomplished wife.

'You started?'

His gaze speared hers, belying the laziness of his pos-ture, and for a moment it felt as if he were plumbing the depths of her soul and laying bare all her secrets. She dragged her gaze from his, feigning interest in a passing cargo boat.

She forced herself to continue. 'I completed a year of study.' And, according to her marks and her teachers, she'd been doing well... 'But in the summer break my mother organised for me to be an intern with Inguri Ishinato.'

He refilled her glass. 'The famous designer?'

She nodded and made herself smile. 'She's wonderful, isn't she?'

'I don't know. Some of her creations seem outrageous for outrageousness' sake. But I understand that she has an enviable reputation.'

'Oh, she was a name all right. Working at her studio opened my eyes.'

'You didn't enjoy your experience there?'

Quite the contrary. She'd loved it but...

'You decided it wasn't the right career for you?'

She rolled her eyes in an attempt to mock herself, doing her very best to smile with wry self-awareness. 'If we hadn't sworn to be honest with each other, I'd be tempted to lie now and save my battered ego, but the truth is I don't have the talent to be a designer. At the end of the internship Inguri took me aside and told me I was a very competent seamstress, but that my design talent was mediocre at best.'

Majed shot into a sitting position. 'She what?'

'She suggested I'd find it more rewarding to make dress-making a hobby rather than a career, and more profitable to find work in a different field.'

He stared at her. 'So you quit design school?'

His disbelief made her fidget. 'It seemed the wisest course of action.'

'Wise?'

He stared at her with such unmitigated astonishment her shoulders started to hunch.

'One setback! You let one person's opinion dissuade you from pursuing your dream?'

She'd bet once Majed set his sights on something he wouldn't let anything or anyone dissuade him. But she wasn't like him. 'It wasn't just any person, Majed. It was a world-class designer whose opinion I valued.' Inguri Ishinato had been her hero.

He folded his arms, his nostrils flaring in the twilight. Her heart lurched. The man was magnificent, truly magnificent. But she wished he wouldn't stare at her like that.

'My mother had been warning me for years that the industry was cutthroat and fickle…and how difficult it would be to earn a decent living. So I decided to be sensible.'

'And learn office administration instead?'

His lip curled and he spat out the words as if they tasted bad on his tongue. She shoved her shoulders back. 'It's a skill that's always in demand. The qualification I got ensures I'll always be able to find work. You can scoff at that all you like, Majed, but it's something I refuse to take for granted.'

'But does it fill your soul? Does it chase the emptiness away?'

She flinched and threw up an arm as if to ward off his words. How could he use her confession against her like this? It was…cruel!

He reached out, his fingers shackling her wrist. 'Is it really that easy to deter you from striving towards what you want? Do you really lack the confidence—the courage—to try?'

He stared at her…almost in fury…and her mouth dried.

'If I started a campaign to undermine your confidence in your ability to be a good mother, would you give way so easily?'

'Don't be ridiculous!' She shook off his hand. 'That's completely different.' She *loved* this baby.

You loved designing too.

His face turned cold and pitiless. 'Your mother didn't appear to approve of your career choice. Did you never question her hand in helping you to acquire this internship with Inguri Ishinato?'

His meaning was clear and her stomach clenched. 'My mother would never sabotage me like that.'

'She didn't need to sabotage you. She simply put a single roadblock in your path. And you crumbled with barely a whimper.'

He was wrong about that. It was just that she'd kept her whimpers to herself.

'I haven't seen a sewing machine in your apartment. I've never even heard you speak about designing or sewing until recently.'

'My equipment was packed away in my move. I haven't got round to unpacking it.'

The fact of the matter was that she hadn't had the heart to look at her sewing machine after Inguri's pronouncement. She'd put her things away and had let the emptiness grow. She'd resisted the temptation to dabble—how could she just dabble when it meant so much more to her than that? She'd not been able to face it until here, now, in Keddah Jaleel, where her old world had dropped away. With all of that delicious fabric tempting her…calling to her. Today when she'd sewn, she'd felt at peace—and whole—for the first time in years.

There had been one other time.

The pulse fluttered in her throat. When she'd made love with Majed, the empty places inside her had filled then too.

But that had to have been an illusion.

'You have a fear of failure.'

The disgust in his voice snapped her spine straight. 'Everyone is afraid of failure, Majed, even you.'

'It won't stop me from trying, from striving, from doing my very best and giving my all.'

Her heart started to thump. Did he think her incapable of those things?

Well...aren't you?

She didn't give her all in her work—it was so darn boring and unchallenging that she found it hard to remain engaged—but her employers deserved better than that. The realisation made her reach out a hand to steady herself against the cushions.

She didn't give her all in her relationships either. She was always waiting for someone to find fault with her. If they didn't, she saved them the time by pointing out her myriad flaws first—all under an umbrella of humour and self-deprecation, of course. But it created a distance inside her that was impossible to breach.

She swallowed. Was that what she wanted to teach her child?

At nineteen she'd let someone deter her from following her dream and she hadn't felt whole since. And yet, not once had she dared to resurrect her dream.

Because she lacked courage.

When had she settled for being a flake and nothing more than a flake?

'I want to be the best father I can be to our child. I want to be the very best role model I can be.'

The iron in his voice pounded at her.

'I also want to be happy. I want to show my children that they can be happy too. You, Sarah—I think you're afraid of being happy.'

Pain radiated out from her chest to all her extremities—even the tips of her fingers and the soles of her feet ached. 'I'd like to return to the palace now.'

Her words emerged clipped and short...distant. Without even looking at her, Majed gave the order to return to the palace. They didn't speak a single word to each other again until they reached the palace and Majed gave her a clipped, 'Goodnight.'

Her throat had closed over so she couldn't return the pleasantry. Not that it mattered. He strode off so fast, he'd not have heard it anyway.

Sarah returned to her rooms to find one of Rasheed's aides waiting for her. 'Sheikh Rasheed understands from the Sheikha that you have a desire to become acquainted with the palace protocols and duties surrounding the role of the Sheikha?'

'Um…' She stared at the file the man held out to her. It was so thick!

'He had this compiled for your benefit.'

She took it, her heart sinking. 'Please thank His Highness for me. It was very considerate of him.'

The aide bowed and left.

Sarah carried the file to the desk and stared at it. Majed's reproof rang in her ears before she'd even lifted the cover.

As she read, her heart sank further and further.

Sarah didn't clap eyes on Majed for the next two days. Her lips twisted as she sewed the seam for a sleeve. No doubt he was trying to find a way tactfully to retract his offer of marriage. The thought made her heart burn though she didn't know why. It would make things simpler all round if he did.

The plan had been for her to shadow Aisha these past two days but, for reasons she wasn't privy to, those plans had been cancelled. At Majed's command, perhaps? But nor had Aisha gone about her duties, leaving Sarah to the mercy either of her solitude or the other women's ministrations. Instead, she declared herself on holiday and spent her time in the women's quarters with Sarah and whoever else felt like joining them. They all urged Sarah to work at her sewing machine, to show them the things that she could make, to teach them some of the techniques they admired.

She complied gladly, though Majed's reproof about being afraid to be happy constantly rang in her ears. Sewing—making clothes, handbags, cushion covers and other soft furnishings—*did* make her happy. Why had she denied herself this pleasure so completely? Why had she turned her back on it?

'May I have a word, Sarah?'

Majed's voice sounded next to her and she jumped, nearly sewing her finger to the tunic she was making for Aisha.

'Forgive me, I didn't mean to startle you.'

He didn't look angry, for which she gave thanks. Instead he looked… Actually, she couldn't decipher his expression. But she could guess the contents of the conversation they were about to have and she couldn't prevent her heart from sinking.

This is for the best.

Of course it was, but…

She stood. 'Of course.'

She expected him to lead her to a quiet corner of the room but he led her out to a private courtyard instead. A fountain tinkled in the quiet air and the cool shade beckoned a welcome invitation. She gave a low laugh. 'You've chosen a pleasant spot for your unpalatable news, Majed.' She appreciated that, appreciated his thoughtfulness in providing her with this shield of privacy.

'I don't know what you mean. What *news* do you think I have come to give you?'

He'd accused her of a lot of things—being afraid of failure, of not fighting hard enough for what she wanted—all true. But she refused to be a coward now. She turned to face him. 'After our discussion on the river the other evening, I expect you've come to retract your marriage proposal.'

He paused in the act of motioning her to a bench padded with brightly coloured cushions. 'You are most wrong, *habibi*.'

The whispered promise of the endearment softened her stomach. She wanted to sit, to move away from his overpowering masculinity and the need it sent rocketing through her, but he took her hand and she found she couldn't move a muscle.

'Would that news have been unpalatable to you?'

Oh, um... Before she could concoct a reply, he lifted her hand and pressed a kiss to her wrist at the point where her pulse jumped and jerked. He grazed it with his teeth and she could barely contain a gasp.

'I'm fully committed to marrying you, Sarah Collins. The final decision rests with you. If you choose to not marry me, it will hurt me very much.'

She reclaimed her hand. It would hurt his pride, not his heart.

Though, that wasn't completely true. It would hurt him if she denied him his child. Not that she'd ever do that, but... It would hurt him as much as it would hurt her, and that knowledge plagued her.

'No, *habibi*, I came to apologise.'

Apologise!

'For the things I said two evenings ago. It was wrong of me. It shames me to remember them. I've no right to judge you. I've had privileges you could only have ever dreamed about. I've had parents who encouraged me to strive for whatever it was I wanted. The disparity in our backgrounds...' He shook his head. 'I had no right to call you a coward.'

He sat and, resting his elbows on his knees, he dropped his head to his hands and muttered what she suspected was some kind of curse in his native tongue.

She sat too and touched his arm. Warmth immediately

sparked through her fingers and she reefed her hand back. 'There was truth in your accusations, Majed. I didn't want to admit it then, but—'

'No!'

He spun to look at her and slowly he straightened. Something in his eyes made her mouth dry.

'You're no coward. You lack confidence, that's all. And it's *that* which made me so angry. Not at you,' he rushed to reassure her, 'but at the circumstances in your life that have robbed you of believing you've the right to chase your dreams, that have prevented you from recognising and taking pride in your own talents.'

The regret in his face touched her.

'I'm sorry I railed at you like I did. I—'

'Stop, Majed. Stop feeling so bad about this. I accept your apology. I also accept that there was truth in some of your words—even if I didn't like hearing them.'

He took her hand. 'But the failings aren't your fault. You've not had anyone to believe in you and encourage you…until now.'

Something in his tone… She straightened. 'What do you mean *until now*?'

'I've invited the master artisan you visited the other day to view the things you've been making for my mother and the other women. He's with them now.'

Sarah shot to her feet, her heart pounding. 'You've done what?'

She'd only just rediscovered her love for all of this. She wasn't sure she could bear anyone putting a dampener on her joy just yet and telling her she had only a mediocre talent. Which made no sense at all, because she hadn't had any delusions of grandeur while she'd been playing with all of that gorgeous fabric. And that was what it had felt like—playing. There'd been joy, freedom and fun, nothing more.

'You're angry with me?'

You promised honesty.

She swallowed. 'Hiding behind anger would be easier than facing the truth.'

She went to stride away—to pace up and down the court-yard—but he caught hold of her hand and, before she knew what he meant to do, she found herself tumbled onto his lap. Warm arms encircled her. Warm lips hovered just cen-timetres from hers…so tantalising and tempting. The scent of amber and spice surrounded her.

'I enjoy having you in my arms, *habibi*, and I could very easily lose myself in you this very minute.' The words growled out of him. 'But that would be unforgivable.'

She'd forgive him!

He stroked the length of her jaw with one lazy finger. Beneath it her blood heated. 'You're afraid the artisan will damn your work with faint praise.'

She nodded, not trusting herself to speak.

He stared down at her solemnly. 'I don't know what he'll say. He's promised to provide an honest assessment, that's all.'

Her heart jerked in her chest.

'But I want you to know that, whatever he says, my opin-ion of you won't change.'

She stilled.

'I'll still admire you, regardless of his assessment of your skill. I'll still enjoy your company and the way you make me laugh. I'll still think you intelligent, warm and generous.'

Very carefully—as she was sitting in his lap and they needed to be careful when they were this close to each other—she shuffled into a more upright position. It brought their mouths closer together. His gaze rested on her lips for a moment. He swallowed and she saw the effort it cost him to control himself. A ripple of triumph quivered through her.

His lips curved. He said something she didn't understand then. 'If you agree to marry me, I'll look forward with much pleasure to our wedding night.'

'You'd make me wait that long?'

'It is the custom of our people. I must honour you with every token of reverence and esteem. But there can be pleasure to be found in delayed gratification.'

He leaned forward and grazed his teeth across her ear. Heat shot straight to her core and need pounded through her with a prickling awareness that made her want to press against him to assuage the ache, to inflame him, to incite him to lose control. If she did that... The fat file Rasheed had sent to her rose in her mind. Biting back a sigh, she pressed a hand to Majed's chest and pushed him back. Beneath her palm his heart raced just as hard as hers.

He glanced into her face and murmured something under his breath. 'This is a dangerous game we are playing. Come.' He gently lifted her to her feet. 'Let us go and see what our artisan has to say.'

Us. Our. The sense that they were somehow in this together lent strength to her knees. She pushed her shoulders back and ignored the craven urge to flee. She'd face this with the same courage that Majed faced the future.

The moment they entered the common room, an elderly man raced over to them, his face alight. 'Your Highness Sheikh Majed, who is this talent you have found? What is his name? I would take him for my apprentice in a heartbeat if he is free to engage in such study.'

'Arras, that is a great honour.' Aisha moved to stand beside him, sending Sarah a speaking glance. 'You have to understand that Arras has not taken on an apprentice in more than five years.'

The older man shook his head. 'I am getting old and I'm not as patient as I once was. I give my time now only to the extraordinary. And, while some of this work is raw and undeveloped, it has a great energy and sophistication that mark it as an exciting talent.'

Sarah couldn't believe her ears. She'd forgotten to pull her hand from Majed's upon entering the room, and she gripped it now as if her life depended on it. She didn't care what rumours it would excite among the women.

Arras glanced at their linked hands and he broke out into a radiant smile. 'It is this lovely young lady who possesses this talent, yes?'

'It is.'

The pride in Majed's voice as he introduced them made everything inside her feel bright, as if she had her own internal sun. 'You…you really like my pieces, Arras? You think they have promise?'

'I do, yes! Come, come.' He hustled her over to the table that held the pieces Aisha had evidently assembled for him. 'I'm impressed with the East-West fusion of this tunic…'

They spoke for nearly two hours, the rest of the world receding as they discussed design principles and techniques. Before he left, Arras pressed his card into her hand. She promised they'd talk again soon.

When he was gone, it was only she and Majed left in the common room. He sat on a deeply cushioned sofa but he rose when her gaze founds his.

She pressed a hand to her chest. 'You did this for me?'

She didn't know what to say. She was absurdly close to tears. How could she thank him for all he'd done? He'd helped her to overcome her worst fear. And in facing it she'd discovered that her most cherished wish could come true. That it was true—she had a unique and remarkable gift—and she no longer intended to deny it. In that moment the emptiness that had been a constant part of her since she'd given up on her dream vanished. She'd found what she was destined to do.

Could she do that *and* be Majed's Sheikha?

'I told you I'd do whatever I could to make you happy. I meant that.'

'Wouldn't your people have a problem with the Sheikh's wife doing…that?' She waved a hand towards her sewing machine. 'With her having a career beyond her royal duties?'

'I see no reason why they should.'

She stared at him and her heart started to pound, thumping relentlessly against the walls of her chest. Wind roared in her ears, blocking out everything but the truth. She loved Majed. She loved him heart and soul. She loved *his* heart and soul. She loved his kindness, his sense of honour and his unselfishness. She loved his confidence and his ability to solve problems, his ability to meet obstacles with his head held high. She loved his…big-heartedness.

A vice tightened about her chest. But he didn't love her. *Does it matter?*

She swallowed. Of course it mattered. But it didn't mean she couldn't marry him.

Rasheed's fat file rose in her mind, and a sigh pressed against her throat, but she refused to let it escape.

'Sarah?'

She shook herself. What on earth was she doing just standing here like a dummy? She made herself smile and then she strode across to him. Placing her hands on his shoulders, she reached up to press a kiss to his cheek. His eyes glittered, his lips parted and for a moment she thought he'd sweep her into his arms and kiss her senseless. She stepped back quickly, the blood thundering in her ears. 'I…' She had to swallow. 'Nobody has ever done such a thing for me before. I can't tell you how much it means to me.' She shrugged, unable to find the words. 'You're an amazing man. I feel lucky and blessed to know you.'

'I feel exactly the same way about you.'

Not *exactly*. And that stung in ways she hadn't known

possible. But she did have his friendship and his respect. And there was little doubt that he desired her.

He reached out, as if to touch her cheek, but his hand fell short and dropped back to his side. She knew why. The spark between them was too strong. A single touch could unleash a raging inferno. But there was too much at stake. She couldn't get this wrong. This wasn't something she could screw up.

Her hand curved about her abdomen, unconsciously protective. For once in her life she had to be as unlike a flake as possible. Majed's eyes lowered to where her hand rested. When he lifted them they glowed with a possessive pride.

'You make me believe impossible things are possible,' she blurted out.

He nodded. 'Good.'

'I…I need to go somewhere quiet and process all of this.' She turned and made for the door.

'Sarah.'

She pulled in a breath before turning to face him again.

'There is time. You have time. I don't want you feeling pressured. I don't want you feeling stressed.'

Even now, when he must sense how close her capitulation was, he thought first of her welfare.

He didn't love her, but maybe she had enough love for both of them.

She had to work out what she wanted. And then, somehow, she had to find the courage to fight for it. With a nod, she left.

Majed stood in front of his father. For the last three weeks he'd worked tirelessly at his father's side. The older man hadn't given him a single word of praise, but he had sought Majed's opinion on several tricky issues. Majed didn't flatter himself that it was because his father valued his opinion. It was all part of a larger test. He just didn't know yet if he'd passed or not.

He squared his shoulders. He'd given it his all. He'd made no secret of the fact he wanted a role in taking Keddah Jaleel into the future. He'd held nothing back.

'Greetings, Samir.'

Majed's gut clenched as his cousin—older than Majed by two years—entered the stateroom. Everyone else had been ordered to leave, even the Sheikh's most trusted aides.

The cousins clapped each other on the shoulder in greeting. Majed loved and trusted his cousin.

'As you both know,' Rasheed started, 'I intend to choose one of you to be my heir.'

'Sir—' Samir started, but Rasheed held his hand up for silence.

'As you must be aware, I have long favoured you, Samir. You're smart and steady, and loyal to the people of this country. You'd lead our people well.'

'Thank you, but—'

Again that hand rose, demanding silence.

Majed glanced at his cousin's profile. Samir didn't want the title—not at what he considered to be Majed's expense. Last week the two of them had engaged in a long and serious discussion on the topic.

'Majed, in these past weeks you've proven yourself adept and surprisingly canny in foreign affairs.' Rasheed's lips momentarily pressed into a thin line. 'Additionally, Samir has informed me that if he does become ruler of Keddah Jaleel he envisages a role for you among his trusted advisors.'

It was the role he'd have played if Ahmed had lived. It was what he'd been trained and groomed for. There was no hiding the displeasure in his father's eyes, however, at that prospect.

Majed wanted to throw his head back and howl. Did his

father still hold him so comprehensively responsible for Ahmed's death? Would he never forgive him? Did the sight of his younger son still cause him so much pain?

To spare his father, maybe he should leave Keddah Jaleel for good. *Which would kill your mother.*

It was all he could do to stop his shoulders from sagging.

In the next moment he pushed them back. What of his child's destiny? Did his child not have the right to know and love this land as much as Majed did? He'd fight any battle for his child's welfare and honour.

Rasheed blew out a breath, his dark eyes troubled. 'Majed, if Sarah agrees to marry you, then the throne will one day be yours.'

A fierce gladness gripped him. His father had seen his worth! Majed would work tirelessly to prove to his father that his faith had not been misplaced. 'Thank you, Bábá.'

'I believe you're as committed to bringing democracy to this country as both I and Ahmed.'

Pain raked his heart at the mention of his brother but he forced his chin up. 'I am. I'd infinitely prefer that Ahmed were here, but he's not.' He broke off, fighting the burning in his throat. 'Thank you for giving me the opportunity to prove myself.'

At Majed's mention of Ahmed, Rasheed lowered himself to the seat behind his desk, his hand covering his eyes. When he lifted it away, Majed was shocked to see how old his father looked. He wasn't old! He was only sixty-three!

'Majed, if Sarah decides not to marry you, I'd ask that you leave Keddah Jaleel.'

Ice tripped down Majed's spine, vertebra by vertebra.

'I'll not make it an order, but there will be a scandal that our enemies will do their best to use against us. I cannot let that happen. I'll not allow your brother's death to be in vain.'

CHAPTER NINE

'This is amazing!'

Majed glanced across at Sarah as she peered out of the helicopter's windows, straining against her seatbelt in her efforts to take in the view, and was glad he'd taken the time away from his duties to show her more of the land he loved.

They'd been in Keddah Jaleel for three weeks and two days now. He needed to know if Sarah had come to a decision. He needed to know if she was going to marry him.

Don't pressure her. You've no right to pressure her.

His grip tightened about the helicopter's control stick. It was one of the most difficult things he'd ever done—maintaining this façade of patience and calm, of not doing all he could to sway her decision...or to not sway it more than he already had.

But if she left Keddah Jaleel with his child...

His stomach lurched. He couldn't bear the thought.

He knew she wouldn't keep their child from him. There'd be visits and holidays, but he wanted to be a part of their child's everyday life—an integral part, not a figure on the edges.

He swallowed. He'd shown her the beauty and luxury of life at the palace—the lifestyle she could enjoy as his wife. He'd tried to show her the kind of consideration and respect she would receive from him as her husband. He'd demonstrated that she could pursue her dreams and carve out a career for herself here too.

He hadn't pointed out how much more difficult it would be for her if she decided not to marry him, if she returned to Australia instead. His heart clenched at the thought. She already knew those difficulties—had lived through them with her own mother. Even if they shared custody, life would still be far more difficult.

For them both.

He'd avoided mentioning how much her decision would affect his own destiny.

That'd be emotional blackmail.

He hadn't mentioned the scandal that'd break once it was known that the Sheikh's only son had a child out of wedlock. He hadn't told her of the press storm that would explode, the fact it would follow her to Australia…or that an intense media interest—and presence—would follow their child throughout his or her life.

He refused to terrorise her with such horror stories. At the moment her health had to be his primary concern. She should be entitled to make her decision in peace.

'This is such a contrast to Demal.' She breathed.

Her awe reached him through the headsets they wore. He manoeuvred the helicopter lower so she could observe the landscape at closer quarters.

'This is what I imagined Keddah Jaleel would look like.'

They'd left behind the capital with its fertile coastal plain, green fields and glinting river to pass over the high hills to the west. Here the topography changed dramatically to an arid rocky landscape that eventually merged with seemingly endless dunes of shifting, golden sand. A heat haze shimmered in the distance.

He glanced at her again. 'What do you think of it?'

'It's utterly terrifying. Like Australia's Great Sandy Desert. I can't imagine how awful it would be to find yourself stranded alone in it.'

He opened his mouth to tell her she need never fear such a thing when she swung to him.

'It's utterly magnificent. It's so…*beautiful*.'

She saw the same beauty in this landscape as he did and something inside him shifted. He feigned preoccupation with the myriad dials on the helicopter's control panel, but his heart started to pound. This woman had an uncanny ability to get beneath his skin.

He'd dismissed it as desire. Well…he hadn't exactly *dismissed* it.

He wanted her. His desire for her burned through him, hot and fierce. It kept him awake at night. He hadn't *dismissed* that desire but he'd used it to explain away his other reactions to her—other more disturbing reactions.

He clenched his jaw. She was carrying his child. It was only natural he should feel possessive and protective but he couldn't allow that to compromise his common sense, his caution or his ability to reason—the way those things had been compromised with Fatima. The way Ahmed's ability to make good decisions had been overset by his brother's girlfriend.

That Ahmed had betrayed Majed demonstrated the evil that accompanied such a passion. It showed the selfishness and the potential for self-destruction that resided at the heart of such passion. He ground his back molars together. He wanted no part of that kind of love again. He'd dig out every grain he found forming within and he'd destroy it.

If Sarah married him, he'd become Keddah Jaleel's ruling Sheikh. Sarah's welfare, their children's welfare and his people's welfare would rest with him. It would be his duty to protect them and keep them safe. They deserved the very best he could give them. They deserved his very best efforts. He would not fail them.

'Majed?'

Sarah stared at him with pursed lips, a question in her eyes. She'd been speaking but he hadn't been attending to her words. He swallowed. He wouldn't allow himself to fall in love with her, but nor would he neglect her.

Visions of exactly how he wouldn't neglect her rose in his mind. Heat and perspiration prickled his nape. He needed a long, cold drink. 'I'm sorry, *habibi*. It's been a long time since I flew a helicopter. It's requiring more concentration than I remembered.'

The purse of her lips became more pronounced—*those luscious lips!*—and an ache stretched through him, pulling his nerves taut. A teasing light deepened the blue of her eyes. The fact she was oblivious to his preoccupation should've comforted him but it only strained his muscles further.

'Exactly how long has it been since you flew a light aircraft? Should I be worried?'

He laughed—how could she make him do that? 'I think we can risk it. There's the oasis now. See how it emerges from the desert like a jewel?'

An hour later they were sitting beneath a fringed canopy that protected them from the fierce heat of the sun. A small breeze made the fringe dance and cooled their hot flesh as it made its way across the deep pool of water in front of them. They sat on silken cushions scattered across a brightly coloured carpet that Sarah had spent an inordinate amount of time studying. That was, until she'd suddenly spun to him and started pelting him with questions. How many people lived at this oasis? How many people did it service? How did the people here make a living? How many oases like this one were scattered across the Keddah Jaleely desert?

He'd answered each of her questions as best as he could

until he found the opportunity to ask one of his own. 'From where does all of this interest spring?'

She glanced out at the water before taking her time to select a date, but something in her face had become shuttered. He leaned towards her. 'Sarah?'

Her shoulders suddenly drooped. 'I feel so utterly ignorant about everything, Majed—Keddah Jaleel's people, your country's history, its geography…and everything! There's so much to learn.'

He started to laugh. 'You don't need to learn it all at once. You don't need to learn it at all if you don't want to.'

She rose and he found himself staring at a very rigid back. Glancing around, he dismissed the attendants. They melted away without a sound. Rising, he moved behind her. Placing his hands on her shoulders, he pulled her back against him.

For a moment he thought she might resist, but then she softened and nestled back, and he had to grit his teeth at the desire that fired through him. 'Would you like to tell me what's troubling you?'

He felt rather than heard her sigh. 'Not really.'

Instead of pressing her, he simply pulled her more firmly against him, one of his arms encircling her just below her collarbone, and he just held her, running his other hand from her shoulder to her elbow and back again in an attempt to give her comfort…and a safe haven in which to relax. They stood like that for a long time, staring out at the sparkling sheet of water. Very slowly, the tension drained from her. A fierce gladness gripped him. He always wanted her to find comfort in his arms.

Eventually he said, 'In another five days we'll have been in Keddah Jaleel a month.'

She nodded and her hair tickled his face. 'The time has whizzed by so quickly. More quickly than I thought it would.'

Did she mean she wasn't yet ready to make a decision?

'But I know in five days' time you'll ask me again if I'll marry you.'

There was something in her voice. He turned her to face him. 'Do you doubt my desire to marry you?'

She searched his eyes and then shook her head. 'No.'

He couldn't help it. He traced his right hand from her shoulder and up the clean length of her throat to cup her jaw. Her pulse quickened beneath his fingers and his own leapt in response. 'Do you doubt our ability to deal well with each other?'

She shook her head again and the warm slide of her skin against his fingers pulled something tight inside him.

'No, I don't doubt that. The fact is…'

The sudden vulnerability in her eyes caught at him, though he sensed she tried to shield it from his sight. 'The fact is?'

Her lips lifted as if they couldn't help it. 'The fact is I…I like you.'

Both of his hands cupped her face as he wrestled with the sudden fierce joy that gripped him. 'You like me?'

'I know it doesn't sound like much, but—'

'It is everything!' And then he couldn't help himself. He kissed her. He'd meant it to be nothing more than a swift press of his lips to hers, but her surprised gasp sent warmth washing across his lips and he found he couldn't pull away. He dipped his head again, his tongue plundering her softness and warmth, and then she was pressed against him, her fingers entwined in his hair, and Majed found himself lost to sensation.

From somewhere he eventually found the strength to pull back.

Her chest rose and fell as deeply and quickly as his. She touched trembling fingers to her lips and then shot him a shaky smile. 'And I know how much you also like me.'

A laugh burbled in his chest. It would be fun being married to this woman. 'I desire you greatly, *habibi*. I've made no secret of it. But I want you to know that I *like* you too. You've honesty and integrity, and those things are diamonds to me. I think you'll be a wonderful mother—I see the care you already take of our child and it humbles me. A man could ask no more than that. And yet you know how to laugh too, how to make me laugh. I do not think you know how much I value you.'

'Oh!' She pressed a hand to her heart and swallowed. He could see how furiously the pulse in her throat worked. He reached out and brushed his thumb across it. 'Your heart is racing.'

'Isn't yours?'

In answer, he took her hand and pressed it to his chest. 'It races like a wild thing.'

'No man has ever treated me the way you do, Majed. Even when you're angry with me, you still show me kindness and…respect.'

'It's my intention to always do so.' She'd not been shown enough kindness in her life. If she let him, he'd do his best to make that up to her.

'I've a very big question to ask you, Majed. I beg that you'll answer me truthfully.'

His mouth dried but he nodded. They'd promised each other honesty. He wouldn't fail her now.

'Could the people of Keddah Jaleel eventually accept a Western woman as their Sheikha? Would your rule survive that?'

Her earlier unspoken worries made sudden and perfect sense. He nodded, not in assent but in recognition of her concern. 'This is a question I've had to consider carefully. I know it is not *romantic* to admit as much.'

'We're something other than a romance, Majed.'

Her tone was crisp, yet…did she mind? Did she miss

romance so very badly? It was true that women loved romance and he'd tried to give her the façade of it—the sunset cruise on the river, this picnic at the oasis…he'd shower her with such treats for the rest of her life. She deserved them. But the two of them weren't a love match. And he couldn't pretend otherwise.

But she *liked* him, and even now that knowledge thrilled him.

'We're something better than a romance,' he told her.

Her gaze dropped from his but when she spoke her voice was steady. 'Yes, we're going to be parents.'

He pulled in a breath. She understood. 'I've thought hard on this issue, Sarah. I'll not do anything that will hurt you or our child, or that'll hurt my country.'

Her gaze met his again. 'It's a big ask.'

'But not an impossible one. I won't lie—there'll be some among the more conservative sections of Keddah Jaleely society who'll try and make an outcry if I marry you— who'll attempt to create outrage in the general population, accuse my father and me of not holding to or valuing the old ways—but we can weather that.'

'How?'

He admired her need to understand. He respected it. If she married him, his people would become her people. And they'd be lucky to have her as their Sheikha. 'My father is popular with our people and his rule is strong. He's only sixty-three. Our line has, thus far, been blessed with good health and long life.'

Realisation dawned in her eyes. 'His rule could last for another twenty years.'

'Or more. Our people will have a chance to get to know you.'

'To grow used to me.'

'While I work side by side with my father, taking on more and more of his duties as he gets older.' In the same way Sarah would take over more and more of his mother's duties. None of them would throw Sarah in at the deep end. Everyone would have ample time to grow used to the idea.

She nodded. 'I see.'

'So what do you say, Sarah? Will you marry me?'

Will you marry me?

The words pounded at her. He needed an answer. Maybe not right at this moment but in a few days' time. And she'd have to give him one.

Her mouth dried. She'd spent several days shadowing Aisha as the other woman had gone about her duties. Sarah's hands clenched and unclenched, that fat file of Rasheed's rising in her mind to plague her. How could she hope to live up to Aisha's grace and confidence? How could she live up to Aisha's inspiring speeches, wise words and innate dignity as she'd visited countless schools, libraries business centres and hospitals?

Majed has told you there'll be time. She didn't need to step into the Sheikha's role immediately...or even in the near future. There'd be time and opportunity to learn all she needed to know.

She'd moved away from Majed to stride around the perimeter of the awning. She turned back to him now. Leaning against one of the tent poles, she curled her fingers around it for support. If she married him, their baby would grow up living with two parents who loved it. *You'll both still love it, even if you don't marry.* But Majed's family were in a privileged position and if she didn't marry Majed she'd be denying her child that position. Could she do that?

And, if she didn't marry him, Majed would be passed over for the throne.

It's not a woman's role constantly to martyr herself in the service of others.

That was her mother's voice, and she agreed with the

sentiment, but one could hardly call living in the lap of luxury and getting a chance to study design under a master artisan an act of martyrdom.

What do you *want?*

She loved Majed.

Would marrying a man who didn't return her love become an exercise in self-destruction?

Only if you let it.

What *did* she want?

She stared at Majed. He hadn't moved. He watched her closely but he didn't say a word. He didn't try to pressure her, just gave her the time she needed. He…waited. In that moment she knew exactly what she wanted. And for perhaps the first time in her life she meant to fight for it.

She lifted her chin. 'Yes, Majed, I will marry you.'

He moved towards her so swiftly she barely had time to draw a breath. He reached out, as if to grip her shoulders or take her hands, but stopped short. She didn't know whether to be disappointed or relieved.

His eyes throbbed into hers. 'Do you mean that?'

Behind the hope she sensed his vulnerability. 'Yes.'

He stared at her, as if he could barely believe it. 'Do you want to consider it for a few more days before we make the announcement?'

'I see no reason for that. You've given me plenty of time to think about it and I'm grateful for that.' She swallowed. 'But now that I've made up my mind I've no intention of changing it.'

'I want to kiss you.' His chest rose and fell. 'But I'm afraid that if I do I won't be able to stop. And we will be seen.' He swallowed, his hands opening and closing convulsively. 'I want the people of Keddah Jaleel to hold you in the highest regard—the way I do. So…'

She blew out a breath, doing what she could to hide her

disappointment. 'Well, you better not kiss me, then. But how long do we have to wait for the wedding night?'

She wasn't ashamed of her desire for him, and when his eyes flashed an ache burst to life inside her.

'We'll make it a short engagement.' He took her hand and pressed a kiss to her palm. 'You'll not regret this, *habibi*, I promise you that. Is there any other promise you'd like to extract from me?'

Her palm tingled from the heat of his lips. He didn't release it either and she found it hard to concentrate. 'I...' She swallowed. 'I'd like us to mean our wedding vows.'

'I wish that too.'

A frown suddenly built through her.

'Sarah, why are you strangling my hand?'

Oh! She loosened her grip but he refused to allow her to pull away. 'Are your wedding vows here in Keddah Jaleel the same as the ones we have in Australia? I'll promise to love, honour and cherish you but I refuse to have "obey" in there. This is the twenty-first century and my mother taught me better than that.'

She broke off when he started to laugh. 'We can have whatever you want. I promise.'

She pulled in a breath. 'I just want us to promise to do our best to look after each other.'

He stilled. And then he lifted her hand to his lips again. 'That is not a promise for which you need to wait until our wedding day. I can promise that to you now.'

If she hadn't already fallen in love with him, she would have in that moment. And, when his lips touched her smouldering flesh, she swore that this time they left a mark.

'We must have a betrothal ball!'

Aisha clapped her hands, her delight at Sarah and Majed's announcement a balm to Sarah's nerves, even as the thought of being the focus of a formal event stretched them tight again.

She turned to her prospective father-in-law. Rasheed had paled, the lines bracketing his mouth deepening. His evident lack of pleasure at their news cut at her. She glanced at Majed. How much more deeply must it cut at him?

Rasheed rallied, though. Lifting his chin, he said in formal tones, 'I felicitate you both.'

Her heart gave a sickening thud in her chest. 'Thank you,' she managed to murmur.

Majed stared at his father for a long moment and then bent at the waist to rest his hands on his knees, as if someone had punched him in the stomach. 'Bábá, if it causes you so much pain to see me in Ahmed's place then I will step aside.'

The older man's nostrils flared. 'You'd leave Keddah Jaleel?'

'He'll do no such thing!' Aisha cried.

Majed straightened, meeting his father's stare. 'I'll take up the role I'd have had if Ahmed were still alive. I'll become Samir's advisor instead.'

Nobody said a word.

'Maybe,' Majed started, 'when you see me in my rightful role, you won't be reminded so strongly of the son you lost. Maybe then you'll find peace.'

Sarah shot forward. 'Your rightful place is as your father's heir!' She hadn't known she believed those words until she'd uttered them.

Rasheed lowered himself to an armchair as if his legs would no longer hold him. Sarah dropped to her knees in front of him and gripped his hand. 'I know you love Majed.'

He met her gaze but she didn't understand the heartbreak reflected in his face.

'Your son has taught me a lot this past month about finding my courage.'

He sent her a half-smile. 'You think I lack courage, my dear?'

'I think your heart has been broken and it hasn't mended yet.' Her eyes filled. 'Majed would mend it for you if he could,' she whispered.

Rasheed nodded as if he knew that.

Sarah had no idea how to help mend it either. Her knees hurt. Her back hurt. Her heart hurt. 'What would Ahmed say to you at this moment?'

She rose and took a step back. 'What words of comfort or wisdom would he offer you? What advice would he give?' She gripped her hands together. 'Who would *he* choose to take his place?'

The silence became so deep, Sarah thought she might drown in it. 'I'm sorry,' she finally managed, their white faces spearing into her. 'I had no right to say anything. Please forgive me.'

Majed drew her to his side. 'You're a part of this family now. You have every right to speak up. The decisions we make now will affect you and our child's life and destiny.'

Rasheed's head came up at the word 'destiny'. 'Ahmed would have chosen you to take his place, Majed.'

She could feel the tension crackle from Majed. 'Are you sure about that, sir? Because I'm not.'

Her jaw dropped.

And then Majed turned on his heel and strode from the room.

After three panicked beats of her heart, Sarah swung back to Aisha and Rasheed. 'Will you please excuse me?' she said, before scurrying after Majed.

She caught up with him in the long corridor that led towards the private apartments.

'Not now, Sarah.'

Yes, now, but she didn't say the words out loud. Instead,

she faked a cough and pressed a hand to her stomach. 'Will you be a gentleman and see me back to my room?'

He pulled to a halt and glared at her, so she faked another cough for good measure.

'That is not convincing. You're aware of that, no?'

She didn't say anything and eventually he shook his head, but the lines that tightened his mouth eased a fraction. 'You won't be able to make me laugh today, Sarah. So, pray, don't even try.'

She slipped an arm through his and turned him right at the end of the corridor towards her rooms, instead of letting him go in the other direction. 'We're in this together, remember, Majed.'

'That doesn't mean either one of us will not desire solitude from time to time.'

'You can have your solitude in due course, just not right at this moment.'

They'd entered her sitting room but she didn't release him. He glanced at their linked arms and then raised an eyebrow.

'Are you going to run away the moment I let you go?'

His nostrils flared. 'Of course not.'

She let him go and he strode across the room to pour her a glass of water. 'For the tickle in your throat,' he said with a wry twist of his lips.

She sipped it and tried to think of a way to ask him nonconfrontationally what he'd meant back there with Rasheed.

'You want to know why I said I'm far from convinced that Ahmed would choose me to take his place.'

She coughed for real this time. She hastily set her glass down and nodded.

'And I'll get no rest until I tell you want I meant, is this right?'

She shrugged. 'Pretty much.'

His chest rose and fell. 'You'll make me say the words out loud?'

Dear God! The expression in his eyes—the pain in them—raked through her. She went to him and pressed her hand to his heart. 'Majed?'

'He betrayed me, Sarah. He knew how I felt about Fatima and yet he still…'

She ached for him.

'I've tried to forgive him. The price he paid far exceeded the crime but…but it doesn't change the fact that he betrayed me—*his own brother*!'

His hand covered hers, his eyes dark and full of confusion. 'He didn't choose me then, and I cannot see that he'd choose me now.'

He peeled her hand away. 'And why should it matter so much still anyway?'

With those words he strode towards the door. His figure blurred as she stared after him. 'Because you still love him.'

He halted and she could almost physically see him count to three before he spun back round. He strode back to her and gripped her shoulders. 'I sent him to his doom! I'm responsible for the misfortune that has befallen my family. How can I possibly take his place with that knowledge weighing on my heart?'

He'd have whirled away again except she captured his face in her hands. 'That's not true. Ahmed made his own choices the day he died. They were poor choices on more than one level. You're entitled to your anger and disappointment, but the fact you still love him—that his opinion still matters to you—tells me he must've been a good man.'

Tears fell down Majed's cheeks unchecked. Her throat thickened and her eyes filled.

'Majed, that makes me think he'd have been truly sorry to have hurt you. It makes me think he'd have sought your forgiveness if he'd lived.'

Anger, pain and despair all warred in his face.

'The two of you were deceived by a clever but wicked woman. Isn't it time you forgave him for that? Isn't it time you forgave yourself?' She pulled in a breath. 'If your positions were reversed, wouldn't Ahmed forgive you?'

CHAPTER TEN

IF THEIR POSITIONS were reversed…?

Majed stared at Sarah. His chest rose and fell, a band tightening about it. He'd have never betrayed Ahmed with a woman. *Never!*

What if Ahmed had met Sarah first?

His hands clenched and unclenched and a shout of pure, possessive outrage boiled up inside him.

'What if Ahmed had brought home a girl who tempted you beyond all reason? What if she let slip that, while she respected your brother, she wasn't really happy…that she didn't love him? What if all her words and actions made you think she had an overwhelming desire for you? Would you have done nothing?'

He stared at Sarah and a chasm opened up before his feet. He couldn't recall the power of his passion for Fatima. Not any more. It had been swallowed by pain—the pain of Ahmed's betrayal, and the utter devastation of Ahmed's death. But the desire he had for Sarah burned like an all-consuming flame through him now. An irrational part of his brain told him he'd kill anyone who touched her.

It's because she carries your child.

Was it?

He took a step away from her, finding it hard to breathe.

'Majed?'

'What you say is true.' He had to force himself to speak,

but as he did the resentment that had festered in his chest for the last four years started to drain away. And he let it. He gave thanks for it. He didn't want to hold onto it. He wanted to remember the Ahmed he'd laughed and schemed with…the brother he'd loved with all his heart.

'I can see now how Fatima manipulated us both. Such passion is dangerous.' He took another step away from her. 'It's why I'll never again allow such a passion in my life.'

She took a step towards him but he held up a hand to tell her to keep her distance. Her frown deepened. 'Love doesn't have to be destructive.'

He wasn't taking that risk.

'It's high time I forgave Ahmed. You're right about that. It's been weak and foolish of me to hold onto my sense of injury for so long.'

'You've been neither weak nor foolish!'

Her voice was sharp but he was too busy building a wall about himself—a wall to contain the uncomfortable feelings she roused in him—to heed it.

'What about yourself?'

'What do you mean?'

Her eyes flashed. 'You've forgiven Ahmed. Will you now forgive yourself?'

For introducing a viper into his family's nest? Never!

She folded her arms and glared. She could glare all she liked but she couldn't change the past or undo the mistakes he'd made.

'So…' Her hands slammed to her hips. 'If your father felt responsible for this incident with Fatima, you'd want him wracked with guilt, to lash himself with blame for the rest of his life?'

He'd started to turn away, wanting to escape from her and her too-difficult questions and demands, to escape the far too simple demands of his body, but he swung back now. 'You talk nonsense! My father is in no way responsible.'

She thrust out her chin, her eyes flashing. 'He's the se-nior member of your family, isn't he? He sees it as his duty to protect you all.'

His mouth dried. *No!*

'It was *his* palace security that failed.'

Majed's heart thumped.

'How old were you, Majed—twenty-five? Your father was a vigorous fifty-nine-year-old who had more experi-ence of politics, rebels and women than either you or your brother. What if he feels he should've protected you better?'

'That is not true! He has always been the best of men and the best of fathers!' The words bellowed from him. 'He has nothing to reproach himself for. Do you hear me? *Nothing!*'

'I know.'

Her soft voice filtered through the tempest roaring through him. He stilled and met those clear blue eyes. 'You do?'

'He has nothing to blame himself for, Majed, and nei-ther do you.'

His heart thumped and pain radiated from his chest. 'I don't wish to speak about this any more today.'

She stared at him for a long moment. That damned lock of hair did that beguiling almost-falling-into-her-eyes thing and he had to bite back a groan. 'Okay,' she finally whis-pered.

He pulled in another breath. He couldn't leave her with such fraught words simmering between them. 'I'm glad beyond words that you've agreed to marry me.'

The smallest of smiles touched her lips. 'You're such a big, fat liar. At the moment you're wishing me to the blazes. I expect *glad beyond words* is far too strong for this par-ticular moment. But, I know you were glad. And I know you'll be glad about it again.' She lifted a shoulder and let it drop. 'I can live with that.'

Miraculously, some of the knots inside him loosened.

How did she do that? Without giving himself time to think, he seized her shoulders and pressed a kiss to her forehead. 'Thank you.'

Her quick intake of breath speared straight to his groin. And he released her—fast.

She moistened her lips. 'We're going to fight sometimes. You know that, right?'

He took a careful step away from her and considered her words. 'When we feel we're in the right, neither one of us wants to give way.'

She blew out a breath. 'Just as long as you haven't deluded yourself into thinking you're gaining yourself a restful wife.'

He found himself laughing. 'No, *habibi*, I haven't. A restful wife wouldn't suit me. Besides, it'll be fun to make up after our spats.'

'I'm counting on it.'

She waggled deliberately provocative eyebrows at him and that made him laugh anew. He took another step away from her. 'I must go now.'

She nodded but he felt her eyes follow him as he left the room. He left with a lighter heart than he could've thought possible. And with much to ponder.

Still, it was all he could do not to sweep back into her room and kiss her soundly.

A week later they held the betrothal ball. Majed wore traditional robes that bore the royal insignia in blue and silver. A scimitar in a gilded scabbard set with precious gems hung at his side.

His breath snagged when he caught his first sight of Sarah for the evening.

His. His. His. The word drummed through him in a possessive tattoo.

The traditional tunic that Arras, the master artisan, had

made especially for the occasion flowed over Sarah's body in a fall of silken temptation that had him curling his hands into fists. A headdress of precious gems and gold rested against her hair and a ruby the size of a walnut dangled low on her forehead, making her look exotic, unfamiliar… and utterly desirable.

Her eyes went satisfyingly round when she saw him, making his breath jam in his chest. It was her smile, though, that speared him. It was more beautiful than the ruby on her brow.

He lifted her hands to his lips, kissing both of them, letting his lips linger against her soft flesh. She smelled of honey and lavender. 'All the men of my country will envy me when they see you.'

'You…' Her breath hitched as she surveyed him. 'You look amazing, Majed. The single women of Keddah Jaleel will be in mourning that you're no longer eligible.'

She stood in the reception line beside him and welcomed the invited dignitaries and guests who came to congratulate them, charming them all with her warmth and her attempts to speak in Arabic. He hadn't even known she'd been having language lessons! She kept up a *sotto voce* commentary that had him biting back inappropriate laughter, but her grip on his arm betrayed her nervousness.

'You're doing brilliantly,' he assured her. 'Everyone is enchanted.'

'You great big fibber. It's obvious that the jury is still out in some quarters.'

He followed her gaze to the three older gentlemen standing on the other side of the room, all heads of important Keddah Jaleely families. 'We'll win over Omar and Youssef eventually but nothing we do will win Hamza's acceptance.'

She turned that clear blue gaze to him, one eyebrow raised, and he shrugged. 'Back before I was born, Hamza had great hopes that his sister would marry my father. Their family is an old one and the match would have been politically savvy.'

'But your father married Aisha instead. And they've been very happy.'

He squeezed her hand. 'We will be happy too.'

'Of course.'

But her voice wobbled and he gazed at her sharply. 'Come, you should rest for a bit.'

'Oh, but surely that'd be rude and—'

'Nonsense.'

After a quick word with his mother, he bore Sarah off to an empty antechamber and made her sit and drink a glass of the pomegranate juice she'd grown so fond of. 'Not having second thoughts, are you, *habibi*?' He'd do whatever was necessary to reassure her, to quieten her fears and doubts.

'Of course not!'

Her shock calmed the burning in his chest.

'I find being in the spotlight nerve-racking, that's all. Public engagements intimidate me.'

'They'll get easier,' he promised, taking the seat beside her.

She sent him a shaky smile. 'I hope very much you're right about that. Aisha has said the same.'

She'd spoken to his mother about this? He leaned towards her. 'You're truly worried about appearing in public?'

'Doh!' She rolled her eyes but she smiled as she did so. 'You've been born to all of this. I know I'm going to make mistakes and…'

'And?'

'And I don't want them to reflect badly on you. I'm… I'm not used to this level of attention.'

And she didn't like it. The revelation disturbed him. He'd been focussing on all the good things he could give her, the life of luxury she could live if she married him, without considering the sacrifices she'd also have to make.

She shrugged. 'There's a price to be paid for having such a privileged life, and I'll do my best not to let you down.' She drained her glass and started to rise. 'Come, we should get back out there and—'

He pulled her back down beside him. 'You'll have lots of help, Sarah, and you won't have to take on the Sheikha role for many years yet. You'll have the opportunity to grow comfortable in the role.'

She sat back, evidently recognising the worry in his face. 'I know that too. It's why I'm still here. The thought of being Sheikha filled me with fear at first—especially when I realised all that the role entailed.' She glanced down at her hands. 'I don't have a great track record when it comes to holding down a job, so even considering taking on the role seems a cheek.'

'But?'

She glanced up. 'But if I get the chance to follow my design dream…'

'Which you will.'

'Well, that gives me strength.' She frowned. 'And a measure of confidence. If I can be good at that, then maybe I can be good at…at other things. The fact is I'd sacrifice a lot to follow my dream.'

His heart thumped. She was sacrificing a lot.

'You've made that possible for me. It only seems fair that I do what I can to help make your dream come true too. You've the right to follow in your father's footsteps.'

'And you've made that possible for me.'

Taking his hand, she held it against the gentle swell of her stomach. 'This baby has made it possible—for the both of us.'

His hand curved protectively about her. And then he froze, his gaze spearing to hers. She laughed. 'Did you feel that? It was the baby kicking. I believe he or she agrees with me.'

He couldn't speak and she rested her hand over his. 'Majed, instead of running away, I've decided to face my fears and fight for the life I want. It won't always be easy, but I'm aware of that…and you should be too. Please stop worrying that I'm going to change my mind. I'm not having second thoughts. I promise.'

He wondered if he'd ever wanted any woman more than he wanted her in that moment.

She started to laugh then pressed a hand to the centre of his chest and pushed him gently back. 'Oh, no, you don't! You're *not* going to ruin my lipstick. Not tonight.'

So he told her in a rush of Arabic exactly what he wished to do with her. And what he'd do once they were married.

Her eyes widened and her breath quickened. 'You're… I only understood about a fifth of what you just said but… you're a wicked man, Majed.'

He laughed and took her hand to lead her back out into the grand reception room, pleased with the renewed colour in her cheeks and the sparkle in her eyes.

Majed glanced up from his desk when a knock sounded on the door. He always kept the door to his office partially ajar when not in a private conference. His father's aide stood there, his face grim. Majed motioned him in.

'Your father would like to see you.'

'When?'

'Immediately.'

Majed did his best to hide his surprise. His father rarely requested to see him—their meetings, summits and conferences were all arranged well in advance and entered into Majed's diary by efficient secretaries.

He logged out of his computer and rose, his senses sharpening when the grim expression on the aide's face didn't abate. What on earth…? Was something wrong? He knew better than to question the man—his loyalty to Rasheed was absolute and his adherence to palace protocols unshakeable.

He entered his father's library, the aide close at his heels. A sense of dread settled in his chest when he saw his father was alone. 'What's the matter?' Fear clenched his gut tight. 'Sarah…?'

'Sarah is well. This has nothing to do with her. Please sit.'

The sense of relief didn't last. The expression on his father's face chilled Majed's heart. 'Abii?' *Father?*

'There's no easy way to convey this news to you, Majed. There has been a sighting.'

Rasheed broke off to drag a hand down his face. Majed leaned towards him. 'Of…?'

'Fatima.'

He couldn't move. He couldn't speak. His heart pounded so hard he thought it might burst.

'We thought she was dead, yes,' Rasheed continued, as if he could read the questions burning in Majed's mind. 'But her body was never discovered.'

They'd thought she'd died, caught in the crossfire between the rebels and the Keddah Jaleel special force that had put down the insurrection. The military had searched the rubble and caves for her body but it had never been found.

'What does she want?' His voice didn't sound as though it belonged to him.

Rasheed's mouth whitened. On his desk his hands clenched to fists. 'Intelligence believes she wants revenge on you.'

On him? He shot to his feet. 'She's the one who led my brother to his death! If anyone wants revenge it should be me.'

Rasheed stared at him stonily, as if frozen. 'When our

forces crushed the uprising, her husband and brother both lost their lives.'

Majed fell back into his chair. Against his father's wishes, he'd led those forces. He swallowed. 'She was married?'

His father gave a heavy nod.

Dear God. He and her, they'd... He swallowed. 'This woman is unstable.'

Rasheed met Majed's eyes. 'And very, *very* dangerous.'

The blood pounded in his ears. If she wanted revenge on him, then there was every chance that she'd target Sarah. Fear almost immobilised him, cramping his chest and gut. 'Sarah must leave.' The words croaked from him. 'We have to get her out of Keddah Jaleel.'

'You must try and think clearly! Sarah will be safest here in the palace. So will you.'

No! He had no intention of hiding in the palace. He meant to find the woman and wring her neck with his bare hands! 'The palace is *not* safe. Fatima infiltrated it once before. I don't doubt that she could do so again.'

'Majed, I—'

He slammed to his feet, his heart burning and his throat constricting. 'She won't go after Sarah if she believes our engagement to be broken.' She'd go after him instead.

Rasheed's gasp sounded loud in the deathly quiet of the room. 'You cannot do that! You'll shame both her and yourself in the eyes of our people.'

He didn't care. He'd suffer any indignity to keep Sarah safe. He'd suffer any fate. The thought of losing her, of Sarah no longer being in the world... He couldn't stand it!

His father surged to his feet. 'This is madness! She will not go. She is committed to you. She is committed to Keddah Jaleel.'

'She won't go if she knows the truth.' He knew that in the very marrow of his bones. Sarah had her flaws but she was brave—she'd stare danger in the eye and would do what she could to defeat it. He cared for her and their child passionately, and he feared he'd allow his compulsive need for her to cloud his judgement.

He muttered a curse and started to pace. Such need was too dangerous for a man in his position. It put people at risk—people such as Sarah and the baby.

He swung back to glare at the other two men in the room. 'But we will not tell her the truth. Do you understand me?' He met the men's gazes individually. 'Not a single whisper of this is to reach her ears. Do you hear me?'

He trembled with the force of his emotions but could do nothing to contain them. Rasheed finally gave a heavy nod and his advisor followed suit.

Majed let out a breath, some of the tension easing out of him. He'd ensure that Sarah and the baby were safe. 'Leave it to me. I know exactly how to make Sarah leave.'

It wouldn't be pretty, but it would be better than Sarah dying at a crazed woman's hand.

And the sooner he did it, the better. Without another word he strode from his father's library, his heart growing heavier with every step.

'Sarah!'

Sarah swung round from where she and the women of the female quarters were enjoying a gossipy morning tea. They were bringing her up to date on the political leanings of many of the people she'd met on the night of the betrothal ball. Along with their bad habits, the skeletons in their closets and their secret ambitions.

From what she could tell, no one in Keddah Jaleel had a secret they could call their own.

The smile of welcome that sprang to her lips wavered when she saw the expression on Majed's face. Good Lord!

What on earth could be wrong? One of the women beside her murmured what sounded like a prayer.

Sarah stood.

'May I have a word?'

The words snapped from him, short and clipped. Without a word, she followed him from the room, automatically searching her mind for some palace protocol she might've breached in the last few days. She'd been so careful!

She glanced at him and something cold touched her heart. In Arabic, she said, 'Majed, you look so grim.'

Startled eyes met hers. 'Your Arabic is improving.' He spoke in his native tongue too.

'Shukraan.' Thank you. 'My pronunciation is getting better. I need others to speak slowly to catch what they're saying, but I'm finally starting to believe it'll come and that one day I might be fluent.'

His lips pressed together into a thin line. She didn't understand. Normally he'd be pleased, would congratulate her on her progress. Something weighed heavily on his mind. She'd love to make him laugh—just for a moment—to help lighten his load.

She glanced at him again from the corner of her eye. 'Mind you, we won't mention my written Arabic. Still, I love looking at the script. It's very beautiful, but my tutor keeps telling me it's not aesthetic appreciation he wants from me.' She gave an exaggerated shrug of self-deprecation. 'What on earth could he mean, I wonder?'

Nothing. *Nada. Diddly-squat.*

'If I could find a way to communicate the written word via my sewing machine, I expect it'd make everyone's lives easier.'

He led her to her suite of rooms and then swung to her with a frown. 'I'm sorry?'

He hadn't heard a word she'd been saying! She swallowed. 'It was nothing important.' She sat because she had a feeling she'd need to sit for this conversation.

Majed poured her a glass of iced water and set it on the coffee table…and then paced.

Sarah ignored the water. 'Will you tell me what's on your mind?'

'I'm trying to find the words.' He swung back briefly, his eyes hooded. 'I don't wish to hurt your feelings. I want to give you as little pain as possible.'

'Oh, this sounds promising.' She folded her arms but it did nothing to allay the dread that settled in her stomach.

He sat and went to take her hand but she tugged it free and moved further down the sofa away from him, until she was wedged tight against its corner. 'I don't want you to touch me, not when you look at me like that.' *As if he pitied her.*

'As you wish.'

She could barely believe it when he moved away from her to the sofa opposite. This had the classic hallmarks of a break-up scene. But…that couldn't be possible, surely? They were going to be married in two weeks!

'There's been more political backlash than we expected at my choice of bride. Certain parties are bringing more pressure to bear on my father than we expected.'

'But you both foresaw this would happen.'

'Not to this extent.'

She tried to beat back the panic that wanted to seize hold of her. 'You said Rasheed's rule was strong, that it could withstand a certain amount of disapproval.'

He swung out of his seat to pace again, his face twisting in…fury. Her heart cramped so suddenly it was all she could do to keep breathing. Was he furious with her because…she was questioning him?

'My father is unwell. I don't want him taxed with having to fight this particular fight. It now appears I'll have to take on the role of ruling sheikh sooner than expected.'

She shot to her feet. 'Oh, Majed, I'm so sorry! Is there anything I can do?'

Agonised eyes met hers. 'Go quietly.'

It took a moment for the import of his words to sink in. She sank back to the sofa, her legs shaking too hard to support her. 'Are you…? You're breaking off our engagement?' It took all her courage to ask the question.

He couldn't meet her eyes and maybe that hurt worst of all.

'Yes.'

Acid burned her throat. 'So in the end you choose your kingdom over your child?'

He loved this child. She knew he did.

'My father needs me.' His hands clenched. 'And a man in my position must be prepared to make sacrifices.'

'And what about when this child needs you?' She pressed a hand to her stomach. His eyes followed the movement. 'You promised me friendship and…and respect.' She'd believed him… 'That was all lies?'

He slashed a hand through the air. 'You'll want for nothing. The child will want for nothing. You have my word.'

The child. No longer *our* child.

'Your word means nothing!' She surged to her feet. 'That's neither respect nor friendship. It's simply you doing your paternal duty and nothing more. It's what any man should do.'

She strode around the coffee table until she stood toe to toe with him. 'You love this child, I know you do, but now you mean to deny it?' If he wanted to be ruler he couldn't admit to having an illegitimate child. It would outrage his people.

Rasheed's words came back to her. *You cannot deny him his child. It will kill him.*

She swallowed and tried to rein in her pain and fear. 'If your father needs to step down then couldn't you…couldn't Samir step into the role? I know it means you wouldn't be ruler, but you'd be a trusted advisor. You'd still have a privileged role leading Keddah Jaleel into the future…and you'd get to keep your child!'

He didn't have to marry her but he could still have a relationship with their child. Surely that was better than the alternative?

'Samir doesn't want to be ruler.' He stared at her with pitiless eyes. 'And why should his life be ruined as well?'

He meant marrying her would ruin his life. Colour leached from the edges of her vision. She retreated to the window and concentrated on pulling in one deep breath after another.

'Your instinct about your unsuitability as Sheikha was, as ever, unerring. I should've heeded it. I'm sorry.'

Flake. Disappointment. Failure. The accusations speared into her. It was obvious she'd been living in Cloud Cuckoo Land. Had she seriously thought she could measure up to the demands that would come with being the wife of such an important man?

'I know I've disappointed you.'

How she hated that voice—so smooth, calm and rational.

'All I can do is tell you I'm sincerely sorry. But, Sarah, this was never a love match. Your pride has been hurt, perhaps, but your heart remains intact.'

She turned at that and lifted her chin. 'Is that what you think, Majed?' She made her voice as pitying as she could. 'Then you'd be wrong. You might have your heart under lock and key, but I'm much freer and more generous with mine.'

He paled. His hands clenched and unclenched.

'The only reason I agreed to marry you—the *only* reason—is because I love you.' She gave a short laugh that nearly choked her. 'You once accused me of cowardice but what an act of courage that was—you'll have to agree—to consent to marry a man who I knew didn't love me back. I never realised I could be so...*optimistic*.'

If possible the lines about his mouth went even whiter, stark in his tanned face.

'I won't let you off the hook that easily. My baby and I will be perfectly fine without you in our lives, but I refuse to allow you to operate under the misapprehension that you haven't hurt us, because you have—deeply.'

He stood there frozen, his nostrils flaring and his hands clenched at his sides. 'There are no words to convey the depths of my sorrow at having caused you such pain.'

At least none that he was prepared to utter out loud. She simply raised an eyebrow—a show of bravado. 'Evidently.'

'I'll make your travel arrangements.'

She turned away to stare down into the serene courtyard below. If he thought she'd thank him for saving her the trouble of making the arrangements, he was very much mistaken. When she finally turned back, he was gone.

She pressed one hand to her heart, the other curved about her stomach. She couldn't think. All she could do was feel. And she didn't want to! Pain scored through her as if a thousand whips flayed her heart. The taste of blood filled her mouth, as her teeth clamped down on her lips to bite back the cries that rose through her. How was it possible to feel so much? How could she bear it?

'Sarah!'

Sarah came back to herself to find Aisha gently shaking her arm. She still stood at the window. The shadows of the courtyard had shifted and lengthened. How long had she been standing here—an hour...maybe more?

'Come.' Aisha led her to a seat and pressed a glass of

water into her hand. 'Drink, please. You must think of the baby.'

Oh, yes! She couldn't fall ill. She wouldn't allow her heartbreak to harm her baby's health. She drank the entire glass of water in three gulps. 'I'm sorry, I…'

What could she say—*your son has broken my heart and I'm in shock*? Aisha was his *mother*.

Aisha's eyes narrowed. 'What did Majed say to you? What has he done? I've not been able to get near either Rasheed or Majed all afternoon. They've locked themselves away in meetings.'

She pulled in a breath and told herself to not cry—it would only upset Aisha. 'Majed has broken off our engagement. I'm to return home to Australia.' Except Australia didn't feel like home any more. Nowhere felt like home.

Aisha rattled off an angry spate of exhortation in her native tongue. 'My son…he is a fool! He loves you and yet he tries to send you away. Why does he do this?'

'He doesn't love me, Aisha. He never did. But I know he loves this baby.'

'Pah, this is nonsense of which you speak. Tell me everything my son said to you.'

She stared into her now empty glass, tapping her index fingers against it. *Fight for the life you want.*

She lifted her gaze to Aisha's. 'You really think Majed loves me?'

'Of course he loves you. It's in his eyes when he looks at you. It's in his every action—though I do not know if he is aware of it himself. He has been frightened of love since that wicked Fatima.'

Sarah's fingers curved into claws. If she were ever to come face to face with the other woman, she'd quite cheerfully scratch her eyes out.

'But you are unsure of his love for you and this is why you let him send you away.'

She'd started to think that, given time, Majed might start to feel something deeper for her. But, that aside, she knew how much he wanted to be a part of his child's life and…

That could *not* have changed so comprehensively.

Aisha shook her head. 'And this is why you do not put up a fight.'

Sarah shifted on the sofa to face Aisha squarely. 'You just said he *tries* to send me away.' She moistened her lips. 'Are you saying that, if I don't want to go, he can't make me?'

Aisha's shoulders went back and her chin came up. 'He is not supreme ruler yet. And I can assure you, my dear Sarah, that the current supreme ruler will *not* dare countermand me on this.'

Her confidence and outrage almost made Sarah laugh.

'Now come, tell me all that Majed said.'

So she told her, finishing with, 'I'm sorry that Rasheed is not well.'

'Pah! It is nonsense. Rasheed has been living too much of the high life, but he is as fit as a fiddle. His gall bladder was removed earlier in the year, but he has recovered beautifully. He is a very vigorous man still, I assure you.'

Sarah's cheeks warmed when she realised exactly what Aisha meant. Aisha patted Sarah's hand with a laugh. 'Just as his son is vigorous…and virile.'

Dear Lord! Where to look?

'But there is something else at work here.'

Like what? If Majed and Rasheed weren't frightened for their country or their rule, what had them so spooked?

'And these men—' Aisha waved her hand through the air '—they think that they can organise the world according to their whim, expect it to run according to their demands and design. Well, they cannot rule us.' She fixed Sarah with her dark eyes. 'Do you have the courage to fight, Sarah?'

Her mouth went dry. Majed didn't want her. And she

had no intention of begging him for his love. That would be… It would be too humiliating!

But he did love the life growing inside her. Only a very strong fear would have him sending his child away.

She pressed her fingertips to her temples. Was she just trying to find excuses to make his rejection hurt less? 'Your son doesn't think I can make a suitable Sheikha.'

'What do *you* think?'

Her fears pounded at her. *Failure. Hopeless. Flake.*

But she lifted her head. Majed had deliberately played on her deepest fears. He'd said things deliberately to distance her. Why would he do that?

There was a mystery here and she needed to solve it. *Did she dare…?*

Her heart pounded and her mouth went dry. She loved Majed. If he truly wanted to turn his back on her and their child, then she'd leave. But first she had to make sure.

She lifted her chin. 'I think I could make a fine Sheikha.'

'Bravo.'

Sarah reached out and clasped the other woman's hand. 'Aisha, I have a plan—but I'm going to need your help.'

CHAPTER ELEVEN

'WHAT THE HELL do you think you're doing?'

Majed stormed into Sarah's bedroom. It was all he could do not to step forward, throw her over his shoulder and toss her onto a plane himself. Slamming his hands to his hips, he glared at her. She glanced round from the suitcase open on her bed, not looking the least perturbed at his martial tone. That damned lock of hair fell forward, brushing her cheek, making him want to reach out and touch it…touch her.

She gestured to the suitcase as if what she was doing was self-evident. 'Packing.'

His entire body started to shake. 'To go home to Australia?' The words growled out of him in a voice he didn't recognise. They'd been supposed to emerge as a command. Instead they sounded more like a question.

She sent him a look of such pity it made him want to shake and hug her at the same time. 'Don't play the fool, Majed. It doesn't suit you.'

The fool? He started to shake even harder.

'Your mother rang not two minutes ago.'

No doubt to warn her he was on the warpath.

'So I know you're aware of our plan.'

'She's a treacherous—'

He broke off at the glare she sent him. Anger would evidently get him nowhere. He drew himself up to his full imposing height. Thrusting out his jaw, he forced a coldness into his eyes and voice that he was far from feeling. 'I forbid it.'

She stared at him…and then she started to laugh. *To laugh!*

'You've met my mother. Do you honestly think she raised me to put up with nonsense like that? Oh, if only she were here now. She'd have a field day with you.'

She straightened and stuck out one hip. It drew his attention to the shape of her…to her lush curves and the delights her body held. The need to sweep her up in his arms, to kiss her and make love to her, nearly overcame him. But if he did that she'd know—she'd know how he felt about her—and then she'd never leave. *It would put her in danger.*

That was why this kind of passion was so dangerous. It flouted all reason and common sense. Sarah *had* to leave. There was no other way to keep her safe. He would not allow his passion for her to endanger her further than it already had.

'I'm sorry, Majed, but the moment you broke off our engagement you lost any right to make demands of me—reasonable or otherwise.'

She flipped the lid of her suitcase closed and zipped it up before glancing at her watch. 'You don't have to marry me—that's your right. But you've no right to tell me where I can live or what I can do. You've shown me that I can have a wonderful life in Keddah Jaleel.'

She shrugged. And smiled. *Smiled!*

'I don't have to be married to you to study design and textiles under Arras. I can live here in Keddah Jaleel and give my child a thorough grounding in his or her Keddah Jaleely heritage. We can holiday in Australia. It appears, Majed, that I can have it all.'

But what if Fatima got to her? They couldn't risk it!

He straightened, stiffening every muscle. She'd said she loved him. It would be a dastardly card to play… But her safety was paramount—it was his only priority—and he'd stoop as low as he had to. 'And what about me? You said you cared for me.'

She went to lift her suitcase to the ground but he stepped forward, brushed her aside and did it for her. 'You shouldn't be lifting anything heavy. It's not good for the baby.'

She sent him an odd look—an assessing look—and then nodded, as if satisfied about something. 'Then I'd be grateful if you placed it by the door.' And then she swept past him, out of her bedroom and into the sitting room. 'As for what about you, Majed, I expect you can have it all too. You can marry some Arabian princess that your people will endorse.'

He didn't want to marry an Arabian princess. He wanted to marry Sarah!

Sweep her into your arms. Tell her you love her. You can find another way to keep her safe.

What other way? Marrying him would place her in danger and he wouldn't allow that.

'And you can be supreme ruler of Keddah Jaleel, be king of all you survey and live a blessed life.'

He didn't want a blessed life. He wanted…

If he turned his back on Keddah Jaleel, would Fatima still want her revenge? He squared his shoulders. It wasn't a chance he was prepared to take. Sarah's life was too precious to risk as a stake in such a dangerous game.

'That won't happen once word gets around that my mistress has borne a child out of wedlock.'

'Aisha is confident we can hush that up.'

'You're a fool if you believe that. You want to revenge yourself on me! You want to dash my hopes. I don't know why it should surprise me. After all, it was the way you were raised.'

Her head reared back and he knew he'd scored a point, but it gave him no pleasure.

'I don't see it'll make any difference where I live. You still mean to deny your child. I'll lie for you publicly. So you don't need to fear—your reputation will remain intact.'

'I don't care about my reputation!' He roared the words, fear making his extremities throb.

She came to stand in front of him, her blue gaze unwavering. 'Then what is this about? Would you care to tell me the truth?'

If he told her the truth, she'd stay.

He made his voice ice-cold. 'It's about not being constantly reminded of a mistake that I'd prefer to forget.'

Her quick intake of breath speared into his heart. *I'm sorry,* habibi. *I'm sorry, my love.*

'Cruelty isn't your style, Majed. It doesn't suit you any better than stupidity.' She turned away and wound a scarf— a scrap of sheer chiffon—about her neck. 'Demal is a large city. I doubt our paths need ever cross.' She glanced again at her watch. 'If you'll excuse me, my driver is here.'

What on earth…? She couldn't go to his mother's villa! It was on the other side of the city. He shoved his shoulders back. 'I may not be able to force you to leave Keddah Jaleel, but my father can.'

Her answering laugh infuriated him.

'Good luck with that. He'll have to get through Aisha first, and I don't like his chances. Goodbye, Majed.'

She didn't even offer him her hand.

And then she was gone.

It took two hours before Majed could see his father. His father's aides had to physically restrain him from breaking in on the delicate negotiations Rasheed had been involved in with the delegates from a neighbouring nation. But, when Rasheed was finally back in his office, Majed stormed in and, ignoring everyone else in the room, slammed a fist to the desk. 'You must banish Sarah from Keddah Jaleel! You must have her deported to Australia! She must leave!'

Rasheed stared into Majed's face and then with a few quiet words dismissed everyone else from the room. He motioned to a chair. 'Sit!'

Majed didn't want to sit, but the expression on his father's face had him biting back his anger and planting himself on the chair. 'Has there been news of Fatima?'

'Not yet. I've ordered a dozen men from the special forces unit to be placed around the perimeter of your mother's villa.'

'Have you told her about Fatima?'

The older man hesitated. 'I didn't want to stir up bad memories. She's suffered enough on account of that woman.'

Majed dragged in a breath. 'You could stop this all now if you sent Sarah home.'

Rasheed rested his head in his hands. When he lifted it again, the fine lines fanning from his eyes had deepened. Majed's heart started to pound. His father looked so...tired.

Rasheed lifted his chin but his sigh sounded about the room. 'Do either of us have the right to make that decision for her?'

'It'll keep her safe!'

'But it will make her unhappy.'

He couldn't deny it...

'How would you feel, Majed, if someone made that decision for you? Would you not be outraged? Would you be able to forgive it?'

Something in his father's voice had a cold hand tightening about his heart. 'What are you talking about?'

'Did you not wonder why I sent you away when Ahmed was killed?'

Acid burned the back of his throat. 'You said it was for my own safety. You said I had to leave to save my mother from more fear and worry. When you didn't ask me to re-turn, when you didn't *speak* to me, I believed it was because you held me responsible for Ahmed's death.'

The older man shook his head heavily. 'I never held you responsible, Majed. It was my fault that palace secu-rity was breached.'

'That's not true!'

'Before Ahmed's death, I'd never really understood how dangerous it was to be the son of the ruling sheikh. Oh, I understood it academically, but it had never felt real until that moment. And I knew then that the danger and fear would be present forever. I understood that you were also in danger.'

Majed's heart gave a sickening kick in his chest. 'You... you sent me away and encouraged me to stay away be-cause...'

No. His father would not be cruel enough to let him think he blamed him for Ahmed's murder.

'Because I was afraid of what would happen to you oth-erwise? Yes. I couldn't face the thought of losing you the same way I had lost Ahmed.'

Majed surged out of his chair. The world no longer felt solid beneath his feet. He lurched from one side of the room to the other. 'But Keddah Jaleel is my home. It's where I belong.'

Rasheed's shoulders drooped, as if a heavy weight pressed down on them.

'I...I thought you blamed me for everything!'

Those shoulders sunk further. 'I know.'

He fell back into his seat, not believing what he was hearing. 'How could you let me go on believing that?'

'I considered it a small price to pay in return for your safety.'

'*Small?* I—' Blood thundered in his ears.

'Your Sarah, although she's not aware of it, made me see

how wrong I was. She made me realise I was placing *my* need to keep you safe above *your* happiness. I told myself that you would suffer in the short term but would become reconciled to it all eventually and live a full and long life. And, son...' he met Majed's gaze '...I want that life for you more than anything. But... I placed the demands of my own heart above yours. I'm only starting to see now how wrong that was. I am truly sorry, Majed. I do not know if you will ever be able to forgive me.'

There could be no denying his father's sincerity. He leapt up again, the agitation coursing through him demanding an outlet. 'I... A year ago I'd have stormed out of here and... and I don't know when I'd have spoken to you again.' *If ever.* 'But now that I have a child of my own on the way—' now that he had Sarah '—I'm starting to understand the power of fears I'd not considered before.'

He went to his father and embraced him. 'I forgive you, Bábá. But if you ever do anything like that again...'

Rasheed hugged him back. 'I am glad to have you at my side once again, Majed. You may rest assured that I will never again interfere in your destiny in such a way.'

A weight lifted from Majed—a weight he'd been carrying for four years—making him feel both freer and stronger.

'But...' Rasheed pulled back and met Majed's eyes. 'Can you find the courage to do the same for Sarah?'

He froze. He wanted her safe!

Like your father wanted you safe.

He had no right to take away her autonomy, no right to make decisions on her behalf without her knowledge. His hands clenched. But how would he bear it if he lost her?

He shook his head and spun away. He had to keep her safe, whatever the cost.

But...

He raked both hands through his hair. If his father had

held to that course of action, Majed would be back in Australia by now with a wound that would never heal burning in his soul.

He spun back. 'I want to keep her safe!'

'Then work with her to do that,' Rasheed said. 'Not against her. I've had to learn to do that with your mother. And I have to learn to do it with you.'

Majed let his father's words sink in. His heart pounded when he recognised the expression in Rasheed's eyes. Adrenalin flooded every atom. 'You love Mâmâ?'

'Yes.'

'I don't mean simply feel affection for—?'

'I love your mother with every atom of my being!'

It took an effort of will to prevent his jaw from sagging. 'But…your marriage was arranged.'

Rasheed's eyes flashed. 'I fell in love with her the moment I saw her. My father knew that.' His lips lifted in a sudden and sweet smile. 'I made sure he knew it. It's why he selected her from among the other possible choices.'

'You married her because you *loved* her?' Not out of duty, as he'd always thought. The world moved on its axis a fraction. It was love that had made his parents' marriage so strong, not duty, respect or friendship.

'Yes, my son.'

Majed's heart hammered. It suddenly hit him. The real reason he'd wanted to marry Sarah—the reason he'd hidden from himself—was because he loved her, heart and soul. Like his father loved his mother. It was the same reason he'd tried to send her away.

Dear God, had he ruined everything? He spun on his heels. 'I have to go to her. I have to tell her the truth.'

He prayed to God she'd forgive him for what he'd almost done.

He prayed to God that he could keep her safe.

* * *

Sarah swam a lazy lap in the sumptuous pool before turning on her back to float. The pool house was attached to Aisha's villa and, the moment she'd seen it, she hadn't been able to resist a dip. She stared up at the tiled ceiling and allowed the cool water to soothe her. The combination of colours—sage-green, cream and dusky pink—helped to ease the burning that gripped her soul.

Majed had been so angry!

She blew out a breath and tried a relaxation breathing exercise, but she couldn't concentrate. She frowned up at those lovely tiles. Something had lain beneath Majed's anger. Had it been fear? She'd thought so…until he'd turned icier than the Arctic. She shuddered now, remembering it. If she let them, her insecurities would get the better of her, but she couldn't heed them. They'd misdirect her.

What do you know for certain?

One: Majed wasn't a cruel man—it wasn't in his nature—yet he'd been deliberately cruel to her.

Two: he might not love her, but his friendship had been sincere. She'd stake everything on that.

Three: he loved this child. She touched a hand to her stomach. *He loves you, little one.*

So…what could he be afraid of if, indeed, it was fear prompting this out-of-character behaviour?

She made a face. It was possible he did fear for his reputation, but she didn't think so. It didn't ring true somehow. In the same way his cruelty hadn't rung true.

So, if he didn't fear for himself, it had to be that he feared for his father's safety…or his mother's.

She frowned. Or hers and their child's. But, if that were the case, why hadn't he told her?

Her heart started to hammer. She straightened and brought her hand down hard, the slap sending water high into the air. *Of all the…!* Because he knew it wouldn't work!

He knew it wouldn't make her leave. Her nicely cooled skin heated up again in temper and she slapped her other hand down on the water. Did he think her a child?

A movement in the far corner of the pool house snagged her attention. She turned to find herself staring at a slim and stunningly beautiful woman. All of the hairs on her nape lifted. It suddenly occurred to her exactly the kind of danger Majed might have been trying to protect her from.

Oh, Majed, why didn't you tell me?

Her pulse raced and her heart thundered. She wanted to sink beneath the surface of the water and pretend that nothing bad could happen but…

She had a baby to protect.

She bit back all physical signs of panic that might alert this intruder to her fear. A thread of steel shot through her. She wouldn't let anyone harm her baby. 'Hello,' she said in Arabic. 'May I help you?'

'You are Sarah?'

The woman's English was good, though thickly accented. Sarah considered lying but since the betrothal ball her picture had featured in all of Keddah Jaleel's newspapers. 'Yes.'

'My name is Fatima.'

Then she held up a gun and pointed it directly at Sarah.

Sarah's heart hammered in her throat but she merely resumed floating. *Show no fear. Don't freeze up. Keep thinking.* '*The* Fatima, I presume? I've been curious to meet you.' She cocked her head to one side and considered the other woman. 'You're as beautiful as I thought you must be.'

The woman smirked her satisfaction. 'You have heard of me, then?'

'Oh, yes. You have them all in a flap at the palace at the moment.'

She stiffened and glanced behind her. 'They know I'm in Demal?'

Sarah assumed so. It would explain Majed's ridiculous behaviour. 'They have nothing concrete—at least, not that they've told me. Just rumours.'

Fatima tossed her mane of glorious black hair. 'The security of Aisha's villa is appalling. I could not believe how easy it was to break in.'

Keep her talking.

'Ah, there's a perfectly good explanation for that.'

'Which is?'

Very slowly, Sarah shook her head. 'You first, Fatima. I'll satisfy your curiosity if you satisfy mine. Why are you pointing that gun at me? What threat do you think I pose?'

'Threat?' She gave a scornful laugh. 'None! You are just a pampered Western girl.'

She was neither pampered nor a girl. But she let it pass. She wasn't the one holding a gun. 'So why do you want to shoot me?'

'Revenge,' she purred. 'Majed killed my husband and my brother. He will know the agonies I suffered when I kill his bride.'

Her stomach gave a slow, sickening turn. 'Well, as he broke off our betrothal yesterday, it appears I will no longer be his bride.'

The gun waved wildly in the air. 'You lie!'

'I wish.' She gestured around the pool house—*slowly*. 'It's why the security around here is so lax. You see, Majed was very much hoping I'd be on a plane to Australia by now. He's livid that I'm not. He thinks I'm going to cause him trouble. It's all been rather unpleasant. I couldn't remain at the palace any longer. That's why I'm here.'

Fatima stared at her as if she didn't know whether to believe her or not. She hitched up her chin. 'What kind of trouble could you cause?'

An avid look, almost of madness, had come into Fatima's

eyes. Sarah had to repress a shudder. 'Look, do you mind if I get out? It's getting a little chilly in here.'

She might have very little chance of getting the gun away from Fatima on dry ground, but she had no chance at all in the pool.

Fatima motioned with the gun towards the steps at the far end of the pool. 'Any sudden movements...'

'I get the picture.'

Sarah moved up the steps—slowly—until she was no longer in the water and was clearly visible. She turned side-on and stood there dripping, touching a hand to her stomach. 'I think you can see the kind of trouble I could cause.'

Fatima's eyes went wide.

Sarah pointed to her towel—slowly—and then reached for it and started drying her hair—slowly. 'I'm afraid that if you kill me you'll be doing Majed a service rather than an injury. With one bullet you could make this nightmare go away for him.'

Please let her swallow this nonsense.

The gun wavered. 'Why should I believe you?'

'Why risk it when you can verify the truth in the next day or two? I expect the broken engagement will make the headlines. And I'm probably being a little hard on Majed. If you kill me, he will feel guilt and regret, but he won't be heartbroken...and he will be relieved.'

Maria, Sarah's bodyguard who was posing as a maid, entered the pool house. Sarah had thought her own private bodyguard an over-the-top measure, but Aisha had insisted, and she gave thanks for it now. Maria pulled up short when she saw that Sarah wasn't alone. Fatima had pulled the gun down by her side where it was hidden by the material of her tunic. Sarah wanted it to remain there.

Show no fear. 'Ah, Maria, this is...Sinna, an acquaintance of mine. Would you be kind enough to bring us some tea? Or would you prefer coffee?' She turned to Fatima. 'Strong Turkish coffee?'

Fatima gave a short sharp nod.

'Right, Turkish coffee for Sinna, and I'll have some of that lovely chicory coffee.'

Chicory was the code word she and Maria had set up and, to her credit, Maria didn't so much as bat an eyelid. 'Very good, miss. Also, His Highness Majed is on the phone.'

Sarah blew out an exaggerated breath. She had to maintain this charade. 'Can you tell him I'm not available? You can repeat that, as long as he meets my demands, I won't go to the press. Oh, and can you tell him he'll find his mother's coral necklace in the top drawer of the dresser in the guestroom I was using?' She glanced at Fatima. 'The last thing I need is for the palace to accuse me of being a thief.'

'Yes, miss.'

Maria disappeared and Sarah pulled on a blouse. 'She's German. I think they're afraid I'll corrupt a nice Keddah Jaleely girl.'

'She's probably spying on you.'

Sarah shrugged. 'Suits me. If she tells Majed I'm not alone, he'll leap to the conclusion that I'm talking to the press. That suits me nicely.'

'Why didn't you give me away?'

She nodded at the gun. 'Call me sentimental, but I'd prefer not to be shot. I'd prefer that Maria wasn't shot either, even if she is spying on me. She's just a servant girl.'

To her relief, some of Fatima's agitation—the fanatical light in her eyes—receded. 'What are these demands you're making of Majed?'

She gestured across to the patio furniture. 'Shall we sit?' She led the way and hoped that Fatima would follow, her heart pounding. 'Just money.'

Fatima sat. 'A lot?'

Sarah sat too. 'I think it's a lot. I've asked for a million dollars. I don't care that Majed wants to deny his paternity, but he can jolly well ensure that the child is financially secure.'

'You should've asked for more.'

She still held that damn gun in too secure a grip for Sarah to risk trying to take it from her. 'You think? How much would you have asked for?'

'Two million. In American dollars.'

She feigned dismay. 'I said Australian dollars.'

Fatima snorted her disgust. 'You have no idea what you're doing!'

Sarah slumped back. 'I'm a rank amateur.' *Wasn't that the truth!* 'I've never tried to blackmail anyone before. I—'

She broke off when Maria entered with a clattering tea tray but, before she reached the table, footsteps sounded on the far side of the pool house. Majed strode in, all tall and powerful-looking with those broad shoulders and strong thighs, and Sarah's heart leapt into her mouth. He was such a big target!

'Oh, look, my two favourite women.'

Her gaze snagged with his. Had he heard the nonsense she'd been feeding Fatima? How long had he stood out there listening? She hoped he had the entire villa surrounded with police and bodyguards.

'Plotting my demise, no doubt.'

Don't lose it now! 'Checking up on me, Majed?' She made her words a taunt.

He raised an eyebrow, but she could practically feel his eyes scanning her for signs of hurt or injury. 'Do you blame me, *habibi*? I like to keep my enemies close.'

Fatima rose and pointed her gun at him. 'I'm going to enjoy killing you, Majed.'

He moved towards them slowly with panther-like grace

and Sarah's heart pounded. She wanted to shout, *'Turn and run!'*

'Will you kill me quick or will you make it slow, I wonder?'

A scream pressed at the back of her throat. She could see he was playing for time as Maria manoeuvred herself into position behind Fatima, but he was putting himself in such danger!

With a superhuman effort Sarah pulled herself together. She would not let this crazed woman kill the man she loved!

'Do you want to know how Tabor died? Shall I tell you the gory details? Do you want to know whose name he shouted in his death throes?'

Dear God, he was deliberately taunting Fatima to keep her attention on him.

Fatima paled and her face tightened. She cocked the revolver.

No! Nobody was going to kill Majed. She wouldn't allow it.

At that precise moment, Maria flung steaming hot coffee and it hit Fatima in the centre of her back. Fatima screamed, rearing back automatically in reaction, giving Sarah the split-second chance to bring her hand down hard on Fatima's arm in a karate-chop move her self-defence teacher had taught her when she was eleven…and thirteen…and fourteen… and again at seventeen.

The gun slid across the floor and she kicked it away, before catching Fatima in an arm lock that left the furious woman immobilised and screaming in frustration.

'You lied to me!'

She didn't bother responding. She couldn't.

In the next moment, Maria had taken over and a dozen men surged into the pool house. Fatima was handcuffed, hauled to her feet and dragged from the room.

Sarah found herself swept up into strong arms and Majed's lips were pressed to her ear, murmuring words that sounded like a prayer. Arms and lips that made her feel safe, cherished…and loved.

Tears pricked the backs of her eyes. He didn't love her, but he had risked his life for her, and she clung to him now. *He was safe. He was safe.*

'Shh, *habibi*, the danger is now past.'

It was only then that Sarah realised she was crying. 'I—I thought she was going to kill you,' she hiccupped.

He lifted her into his arms, carried her into the house and took her into the sitting room, where he settled on the sofa with her ensconced securely on his lap. He held her close, his hands making soothing circles on her back. She finally pushed herself up a little to stare into his face. 'You were so brave. My heart nearly stopped when you walked in. I wanted to yell at you to run.'

'You were the one who was brave.' He smoothed her hair back from her face, cupping the back of her head and staring at her with such admiration she almost believed he cared for her.

Of course he cares for you. Just don't mistake it for more.

'The way you played for time…played on her prejudices and need for revenge… It was so clever! And you appeared so calm. I was in awe of you.'

'I was shaking inside.'

'I knew you were brave but I've never been more afraid than in that split second when you brought your hand down on Fatima's arm.' His hands gripped her shoulders, his fingers digging into her flesh as his face twisted. 'All I could think was that Fatima would injure you badly—she's expert in martial arts. But you disabled her so quickly and then had her in an arm lock before I was even halfway to you. I—' his hands gentled '—I was never more proud of anyone in my life. Where did you learn to do that?'

Sarah suddenly found that she could laugh. 'My mother, of course. Every year from the age of eleven through to eighteen she bought me a course of self-defence lessons for my birthday. I guess some of it stuck.'

'She is a wise woman. I will tell her so next time I see her.'

Sarah moistened suddenly dry lips. 'Fatima is the reason you tried to send me away?'

His eyes darkened and the lines about his mouth momentarily deepened. 'Yes.'

She tried to shift away but he wouldn't let her. She turned her face towards the door. 'Don't you want to go after them—the guards—to make sure that the woman who killed your brother is—?'

'I don't care about her! I don't care about my revenge! I care about you. I…I care about you, *habibi*.'

She stilled. Her heart thudded. She finally found the courage to turn back and face him. He looked so ragged and vulnerable that she wanted to pull his head down to her shoulder and comfort him the way he'd just comforted her.

'I'm sorry I lied to you, Sarah. It was my father who made me realise how wrong I was.'

She blinked. 'Rasheed? What did he say? I…I thought he wanted me gone too.'

'No, *habibi*, he wanted *me* gone. For the same reasons I tried to make you leave Keddah Jaleel.'

Her heart gave a sudden kick of recognition. 'He'd lost one son. So…he wanted to keep the other one safe. And that's why he sent you away?'

He nodded. 'But you made him see how wrong he was.'

'Me?' she squeaked.

'You forced him to recognise that my home and destiny— my happiness—would always be linked to Keddah Jaleel. He saw that I'd never be happy anywhere else, although I might be safer elsewhere. He realised that he had no right to interfere in my destiny in such a way.'

She leaned back into him. 'Wow.'

'He made me realise I couldn't rob you of your choices and your freedoms either.'

She pulled in a breath. 'You realised that if I knew the truth—that Fatima was on the warpath—that I wouldn't agree to leave.'

'My fear put you in danger. I'll never forgive myself. I should've confided in you and we should've come up with a plan to keep you safe.'

She nodded.

His eyes bored into hers. 'I learned also another valuable lesson.'

Her heart started to race with a different kind of tempo. 'Oh?'

'I can see now how love can make you strong, if you let it.'

Two beats passed before his words sank in. He continued talking but she didn't hear his words. 'Whoa, wait!' She sat bolt-upright in his lap. 'Did you just say...*love*?'

Midnight eyes stared into hers. His lips curved in a way that made her pulse pound. 'But of course, Sarah. Surely you must know now that I love you?'

She could only stare. And then she could only shake her head.

Very gently he took her face in his hands. 'Little one, you are the light of my life. I love you with all my heart and soul—and very soon I will love you with my body... if you'll let me. If you'll still marry me.'

Of course she was going to marry him...

'I've been fighting it for a long time.' His face darkened. 'I was stupid. I thought love made men weak and easy to manipulate. Not being true to love is what makes a man weak. I allowed my fear of love, and my fear of being betrayed, to rule me. It is those things that made me weak. And it could've ended in disaster. If you had come to harm…'

His regret and self-recriminations tugged at her. She touched his cheek. 'I'm safe, Majed. We're both safe and the threat has been dealt with.'

His hands caressed her from shoulder to wrist, making her shiver. 'Because of your code words.'

'Because we worked as a team.'

He stilled, his gaze burning into hers. 'I want us to always work as a team. I will not make the same mistakes again. I swear that to you. Can you forgive me, *habibi*?'

Her breath jammed in her lungs. 'Say it again.'

He pulled in a breath, his expression intense, his eyes not leaving hers. 'I am sorry. I will never—'

'No, not that.'

He stared into her eyes and then he smiled. 'I love you, Sarah Collins. I love you with all that I am. I will love you forever.'

Warmth radiated through her chest, his words leaving her feeling weightless and grounded at the same time.

'If I promise to honour our vow of love, will you marry me?'

'Yes,' she breathed. 'A million times yes. I love you, Majed.'

She lifted her face to meet his kiss, her arms winding about his neck. She was no longer afraid of having to hide her love from him, no longer overwhelmed at all she felt for this amazing man.

Firm lips captured hers and he kissed her so thoroughly, with such tenderness and intensity, that it made the blood pound in her ears. It left her in little doubt of the depth of his feelings for her.

The baby suddenly kicked, as if to share in her joy, and with a laugh she took his hand and laid it on her abdomen.

'Who'd have thought we would all end up here like this? Who'd have thought an…accident would end so happily?'

'No, *habibi*, not an accident. This baby might not have been planned but it was no accident. It was destiny. It brought you to me, and you brought me home.'

She touched her hand to his cheek, placing her other hand over his on her stomach. 'This baby has helped me find a home—a place where I belong. It has helped me find my courage. While you showed me that I should never give up on my dreams.'

'This baby is a blessing.'

She couldn't argue with that. Reaching up, she pressed a kiss to his cheek. 'Please tell me we can marry soon.'

His eyes gleamed. 'We will be married very soon, *habibi*. I can promise you that.'

And then his lips claimed hers in a kiss that left her breathless, and looking forward to the future with more anticipation than she'd ever dreamed possible.

* * * * *

If you've enjoyed this book, then you won't want to miss
THE SPANISH TYCOON'S TAKEOVER
by Michelle Douglas.
Available now!

If you're looking forward to another secret baby romance, then make sure to indulge in
CLAIMING HIS SECRET ROYAL HEIR
by Nina Milne.

"I wanted to check on Rhett."

He moved closer, crowding her a little. But she didn't step back. She stood her ground. "That's not all you want," he whispered.

There weren't enough words in the English language to cover all the things she wanted from David. From life. From this moment.

"Ask me again," he told her, threading his fingers through her hair. The desire she saw in his blue eyes mesmerized her. A longing that matched her own, making her need grow that much more intense. "Ask me to have an affair with you."

"Kiss me," she said instead. Those two words were the only ones she could force her mouth to form at the moment.

He lowered his mouth to hers, claiming her lips with a force she felt all the way to her toes. How could the way he touched her feel both infinitely gentle and demanding at the same time? She wound her arms around his neck and gave herself over to the sensation. It was too much and not enough, and she whispered the one word that pounded through her whole body, "More."

* * *

Crimson, Colorado:
Finding home—and forever—in the West

ROMANCING THE WALLFLOWER

BY
MICHELLE MAJOR

First Published in Great Britain 2017
By Mills & Boon, an imprint of HarperCollins*Publishers*
1 London Bridge Street, London, SE1 9GF

© 2017 Michelle Major

ISBN: 978-0-263-92327-8

23-0917

Our policy is to use papers that are natural, renewable and recyclable products and made from wood grown in sustainable forests. The logging and manufacturing processes conform to the legal environmental regulations of the country of origin.

Printed and bound in Spain
by CPI, Barcelona

Michelle Major grew up in Ohio but dreamed of living in the mountains. Soon after graduating with a degree in journalism, she pointed her car west and settled in Colorado. Her life and house are filled with one great husband, two beautiful kids, a few furry pets and several well-behaved reptiles. She's grateful to have found her passion writing stories with happy endings. Michelle loves to hear from her readers at www.michellemajor.com.

To all my favorite Broadmoor Elementary teachers.
Thanks for everything you do for our kids.

Chapter One

"Stop staring at the hottie brewmaster's butt."

Erin MacDonald choked on the gulp of strawberry daiquiri she'd just swallowed. "I'm not staring at anyone's butt," she said as she grabbed a wad of napkins and dabbed at her chin and shirtfront. "And don't talk so loud."

Melody Cross, one of the second-grade teachers at Crimson Elementary, snorted. "It's a crowded bar on a busy Thursday night. No one can hear me."

But Melody had the kind of booming voice that could quiet a room full of squirming eight-year-olds the afternoon before summer break. The tall table they stood at was a good five feet from the bar, but Erin swore she saw the man's broad shoulders stiffen.

"Want me to take a picture of him?" Suzie Vitale, her fellow kindergarten teacher, offered with a tipsy smile. "It lasts longer."

Before Erin could stop her, the curvy blonde aimed her

phone at the backside of the gorgeous guy who not only worked the bar but also owned Elevation Brewery. The brewpub had opened a little over a year ago and had become a popular hangout for both locals and tourists in the quaint mountain town of Crimson, Colorado.

Erin had noticed David McCay, the brewery's owner, the first time she'd stepped into the nouveau rustic—and very on-trend for Colorado—space. He was tall and lean, with dark blond hair that curled around the collars of the flannel shirts he favored. David McCay was as handsome as a movie star and built like he spent endless hours tossing huge sacks of barley—or whatever it was beer brewers did.

Erin, who was built like she spent her days sitting cross-legged on a reading rug, had surreptitiously watched him each time she came into the bar with friends or coworkers for a random happy hour or birthday celebration. He was often tending bar or sometimes she'd spot him coming out from the back, wearing the heavy rubber boots and backward ball cap that she'd quickly learned were his uniform when actually brewing beer.

Colorado was known for its craft brews, and the fact that Elevation had made a name for itself so quickly was a testament to his hard work and talent at running a business.

At least that's what Erin wanted to believe. Her mother liked to remind Erin that she too often assumed the best about people, which allowed them to regularly take advantage of her.

But David McCay hadn't taken advantage of her, even though it was the stuff of her fantasies. Even though his nephew, Rhett, was now in her kindergarten class and David had been with the boy and his mother for back-to-school night. Erin had barely been able to put a sentence together with David towering over the other adults in the back of her classroom, but he hadn't bothered to acknowledge her. Heck, it was doubtful he even knew she existed.

Except when she blinked and looked up, he was staring straight at her. Sparks of awareness flamed through her body, setting every inch of her skin on fire. He lifted one thick brow as if he could read her thoughts. Which might be impossible since it felt like all of her brain cells had spontaneously combusted under the weight of his stare.

She heard Melody giggle behind her, and Suzie gave her a little shove forward. David now stood at the edge of the bar, only a short distance from her, with movement all around him. Customers in groups laughed and talked. A waitress set her tray on the rich wood bar top. A group of women near the edge of the bar vied for his attention. But his focus remained on Erin.

Then something—someone—suddenly blocked her vision. Cole Bennett, Crimson's recently elected sheriff, was talking to David. Cole was also tall and broad, and to use one of her mom's favorite expressions, made a better door than a window.

Erin shifted to the right as she overheard Cole mention Rhett, David's nephew. David's gaze hardened and his jaw clenched. Unable to stop herself, she moved forward, sidestepping a couple heading toward the back of the bar and a group of twentysomething guys who looked like they'd just come off a hiking trail, until she stood directly behind the sheriff.

She was five feet four inches tall in the clogs she favored for work, so both men towered over her and were completely unaware she was listening to their conversation. Invisibility was Erin's unintentional superpower. She knew much more than she should about her coworkers and neighbors, simply because people didn't notice she was there.

"Rhett is safe," Cole told David. "But they can't get him to come out."

"What the hell was Jenna thinking?" David asked, then scrubbed a hand over his jaw. "No, don't answer that."

"She's in trouble, David. The crowd she's running with—"

"I'll handle it." He pulled a set of keys out of one of the pockets in his tan cargo pants. "I just need to tell Tracie I'm leaving for the night. I'll be over for Rhett."

"I have to call Social Services," Cole said softly, and Erin felt the tension ratchet up a notch.

"Give me some time with him first, okay?"

"Can you—"

"I'll handle it," David repeated. He moved behind the bar and spoke to the woman filling two pint glasses from the tap.

The sheriff walked out of the bar, patrons instinctively clearing a path for him although he wasn't in uniform tonight.

When she looked up, David McCay stood toe-to-toe with her. She realized she'd moved forward to block his path from behind the bar.

In her daydreams, she'd compared his eyes to the brilliant summer sky above the ragged peak of Crimson Mountain or the iridescent cobalt of a tropical lagoon. But now his frosty stare was more like the ice blue of a glacier, so cold a shiver passed through her.

"I don't have time for this, sweetheart. You and your friends are going to have to play your liquid courage bar games with someone else."

"It's not a game," Erin said.

"Darlin', you ordered a froofy drink in my bar. It's either a game or a joke."

This close to David, the heat and frustration radiating off him made her feel different from the woman she knew herself to be. She was aware of her body in a way that was new and exhilarating. She wanted more. She wanted... something she couldn't name. Still, the promise of it made her weak with longing.

Also braver than she'd ever been. Or maybe *crazy* was a better word, because when he moved to step around her, she placed a hand on his arm.

"I can help with your nephew."

His sleeves were rolled up to the elbow. His skin burned hers, and the rough hair on his forearm tickled her fingers. A current passed through him, the force jolting Erin like she'd been struck by lightning. He stilled and the power it took to rein in all the things she imagined he was feeling right now made an answering strength bubble up inside her.

"Let me help, David." It was the first time she'd spoken his name out loud. To her friends, he was simply "the hottie brewmaster."

"You're drunk," he said, his gaze focused on where her fingers wrapped around his arm.

"No. I only had one drink. I'm fine now. Promise." She lifted her hand. "Rhett is in my class," she said, in case this enormous, angry man truly had no idea who she was.

"I know." One side of his mouth almost quirked. "I came to back-to-school night."

So she wasn't quite invisible to David McCay. A little thrill tickled down her spine. "I've connected with him. He responds to me."

David's cool blue gaze met hers again, and he gave a brief nod. "Let's go then."

Erin swallowed. This was really happening. "I just need to tell my friends I'm leaving."

"My truck is out front," he said, his voice a low rumble. Then he turned and walked away. Erin had the distinct impression if she didn't get her butt in gear, he'd readily leave her behind.

No chance she was letting that happen.

"I've got to go," she said as she rushed to where Melody and Suzie stood gawking. She grabbed her purse from the tabletop.

"With the hottie brewmaster?" Melody asked, her voice a high squeak.

Suzie pumped a fist. "No beating around the bush tonight."

"It's not like that." Erin glanced over her shoulder but David was already out the door. "I can't explain now. I'll see you at school tomorrow."

Before her friends could respond, she hurried toward the brewpub's entrance. The young, flawlessly mountain-chic brunette at the hostess stand gave her the once-over and arched a brow, wordlessly communicating that a woman like Erin had no business following David McCay out into the night.

Normally Erin would agree, but this was more than her hidden crush on the man. It was about helping a troubled five-year-old boy. Erin's students were family to her, and she took her responsibility to heart. She had a Spidey sense for the ones who needed a little extra; whether it was the child or their family circumstances, Erin made it her mission to connect with every student in her care.

From the moment Rhett McCay had slunk into her classroom clutching his beautiful mother's arm, Erin's radar had been on high alert. Jenna McCay clearly loved her son, yet the woman seemed high-strung and flighty.

Erin had the impression Rhett's home life was anything but stable.

She might not have the guts to talk to David on her own, but she was fearless when it came to one of her kids.

A huge black Chevy truck idled near the curb, and she knew David was behind the wheel. Not that she was a stalker or anything, but Crimson was a small town and she'd seen him drop off and pick up Rhett at school several times.

"I'm fearless," she whispered to herself when her legs wanted to stop on the sidewalk. It was late September and the evening air was crisp, the changing season scenting the breeze.

If Erin were an ice cream flavor, she would be straight-up vanilla. Everything about her life was ordinary, ordered and infinitely normal. Somehow she knew getting into David's truck was going to add a whole slew of strange toppings to the mix. She might long for adventure, but this wasn't what she had in mind.

She conjured up Rhett's sweet face, with his shaggy blond bowl cut and mischievous blue eyes. With a calming breath she moved forward, opened the passenger-side door and climbed in.

"You ready?" David asked in that deep, hot-caramel-syrup voice of his.

Absolutely not, Erin thought.

"I'm ready," she answered.

David was going to kill his little sister, if she didn't manage the task on her own first.

He concentrated on navigating the route from the bar to Jenna's small apartment complex on the outskirts of Crimson as fast as he could without breaking any laws. He took slow breaths in and out to calm himself. Of course any thoughts of doing her harm were a joke, although she seemed hell-bent on getting into as much trouble as she could find.

Which had been one thing when they were teenagers, but Jenna had Rhett now. The constant stream of dead-end jobs, loser boyfriends and wild partying wasn't only hurting her. The thought that Rhett would end up some-how irreparably scarred kept David up more nights than he cared to admit.

He'd moved to Crimson from Pittsburgh almost two years ago to watch out for them. But between the hours he'd put in opening the brewery and Jenna's resentment over what she saw as his attempts to control her life, he hadn't spent nearly as much time with them as he wanted.

His greatest fear was that he would fail his nephew the same way he'd failed Jenna.

"I'm guessing you and your sister are pretty close?"

David blinked and glanced at the woman sitting next to him in the truck's cab. Lost in his own thoughts, he'd almost forgotten about his uninvited passenger. What the hell had possessed him to allow Rhett's kindergarten teacher to come along on this mission anyway?

David was a master at keeping everyone in his life at arm's length, even Jenna and Rhett. How had this tiny woman with the thick ponytail the color of maple syrup and big eyes to match managed to slip through his defenses?

"We're Irish twins," he offered as an answer. "Ten months apart."

"That must have been fun growing up," she said, her voice gentle. The exact kind of voice that could lull a class-room of restless kids into sitting in a quiet circle to learn. Most kids anyway. He still had trouble believing Rhett could calm his squirmy body enough to sit still.

"Not for our mom."

She gave a small laugh. "If Rhett takes after the two of you, your mother had her hands full."

"Yeah," he agreed, and felt the knot in his chest loosen slightly at the affection in her voice. David had no problem with his nephew's rambunctious personality, but he was normally in the minority.

He didn't say anything more, and Erin didn't speak for a few minutes. David liked quiet, but other than Tracie at the bar, most women he knew couldn't tolerate it. The silence that filled his truck now was strangely comforting, like an extra blanket thrown over the bed on a cold winter night. Like all good things, it didn't last.

"What happened tonight? Is your sister in trouble? Is Rhett okay?"

David sighed. He knew the questions were coming, and he owed the soft-spoken teacher an explanation before they reached the apartment. "How much did you overhear from Cole?"

"No details. Just that there was a problem and Rhett wasn't cooperating."

"He's hiding," he said, trying in vain to stop the anger and frustration from trickling into his voice. He could feel it seeping through his pores, making his blood run hot and raging. "Apparently he's wedged under the kitchen sink. Jenna had a party, and things got out of hand. The cops busted it up and found drugs."

Erin gave a sharp intake of breath, rousing his temper even further, like a backdraft making a fire blaze out of control. "Jenna loves that boy with all her heart, but she's in a bad way. It's why I moved to Crimson in the first place."

"To help your sister?"

To save her, he wanted to answer, but he only nodded.

David knew his limitations better than anyone, and he was nobody's hero.

"She's been clean for almost two years," he said without emotion. "It's been tough, but I thought she had her demons under control. Cole took everyone to the station. They didn't realize Rhett was there until the place was empty and he made a noise. The deputies tried to get him out, but he freaked and scratched one of the officers. I know Cole so he called me before the social worker."

He bit the inside of his cheek and waited for the recrimination he deserved. He should have seen the signs that Jenna was teetering on the edge. He knew her better than anyone. Why the hell couldn't he keep her safe?

He pulled into the parking lot of the shabby apartment complex. There were two buildings, both with faded siding and balconies that looked like they wouldn't hold the weight of a litter of kittens. He'd begged Jenna to let him help her move to a better place, but his sister was stubborn and resented any time he tried to "take control" of her life.

"We'll make sure he's safe," Erin said as he turned off the truck's engine.

Safe. The word had haunted him—and tainted every relationship in his life—for over a decade. Now this too-sweet-for-her-own-good woman offered it to his nephew like she had that kind of power. Damn if David didn't want to believe it was true.

He shifted to face her, the dim light of the parking lot illuminating her face so that her creamy skin looked like something out of a dream. Unable to resist, he ran the pad of his thumb over the ridge of her cheekbone, marveling at how soft her skin felt.

The inherent goodness radiating from her drew him in at the same time he knew he should push her away. Someone like Erin MacDonald had no business knowing the ugly details of his sister's struggles. She was Rhett's teacher and nothing more. But he couldn't let her go quite yet. Tonight she was his talisman. He had to believe having her close would keep the darkness always skirting the edges of his life at bay.

He dropped his hand and they got out of the truck and started toward Jenna's apartment. Toward the little boy David was determined to keep safe, by any means necessary.

Chapter Two

"Come on, buddy. You've got to come out."

The muscles bunched in David's broad shoulders as he shifted his weight to one arm and leaned closer, reaching into the open cabinet under the kitchen sink.

A high-pitched scream split the air and several bottles of household cleaners tumbled out onto the scuffed linoleum floor.

David sat back on his knees with a muttered curse. "He bit me," he said, examining the back of his hand where a semicircle of angry red teeth marks was clearly visible.

"Same thing happened to me," Cole Bennett whispered. Cole had been waiting at Jenna McCay's cramped apartment, clearing out the other officers when David and Erin arrived. "I didn't want to force him out because I was worried he'd get hurt banging his head on the pipes if he struggled."

The two men, both so strong, looked absolutely baffled

at how to lure the young boy from his hiding spot. Erin glanced around the apartment and suppressed a shudder. On every surface, abandoned beer bottles and red plastic cups competed for space with fast-food wrappers and empty chip bags. It looked like a college fraternity house the morning after a huge party. The colorful drawings stuck to the front of the refrigerator were the only hint that a kindergartner lived here.

One of the crayoned pieces of art gave Erin an idea. She moved toward the narrow hallway, stepping over trash until she got to a half-open bedroom door. The space was neat and clean, untouched by the mess in the rest of the apartment. Toys lined one wall and the small bed was covered with a football-themed comforter. She grabbed the stuffed blue dog sitting on top of the pillow and hurried back to the kitchen.

David was once again on all fours in front of the cabinet, speaking so softly she couldn't make out his words, only the rough yet surprisingly gentle timbre of his voice.

She crouched low next to him and tilted her head until she could see Rhett's eyes, wide and still terrified. "Rhett," she said, "It's Ms. MacDonald. I found your stuffed dog and wanted to let you know he's okay."

A faint whimper came from the cabinet. "Ruffie," the boy whispered.

"Ruffie is safe," Erin said, using the same tone she would when soothing a child scared of letting go of his mother's leg on the first day of school. "You're safe, too. Your uncle David is going to take care of you. But we need you to come out now."

The boy wedged himself farther into the corner, as if he could make himself invisible. God, Erin did *not* want this child to feel like he needed to be invisible. David's large hand settled on the small of her back, and the steady pressure and warmth of his skin were more of a comfort than she would have guessed.

"Ruffie needs you." She placed the small dog in front of her, just on the edge of the cabinet. "He's scared and needs a hug. Can you do that for him?"

She held her breath for what felt like an eternity, then released it as the boy slowly unfolded his body and climbed out. Her fingers remained wrapped around the stuffed animal's back leg to make sure Rhett wouldn't try to grab it and retreat again.

Once he was in the light, she could see the smudge of dirt on his chin and the tearstains on his ruddy cheeks. Her heart broke for what this young boy had already seen in his life. David made a sound low in his throat and scooped up his nephew and the raggedy blue dog. It was as if a dam broke in Rhett and his whole body began to shake as he burrowed into David's embrace.

She straightened and stepped away, closer to the sheriff. Somehow it felt wrong to bear witness to the moment between David and Rhett, both tender and raw. It was obvious David was trying to keep his emotions hidden, but pain and guilt were bright on his handsome features, like a stoplight in the dark.

"Nice work," Cole Bennett said and put a hand on her elbow to lead her to the apartment door. "You're like a kindergartner whisperer." She started to turn but stopped at the sound of David's voice.

"Stay."

One word, but the intensity of it rocked her to her core. She glanced up at Cole, who arched a brow.

"I'll stay," she told him.

He nodded. "Someone from Social Services will be here soon. I can let them in. They'll want to talk to David and the boy."

"We'll be ready," she said with more confidence than she felt.

She turned back and followed David to the couch, quickly cleaning off the coffee table and dumping everything into the trash before lowering herself next to him.

Rhett still clung to him, chubby fingers holding fistfuls of flannel shirt in a death grip. "Where's Mommy?" he asked in a tiny voice.

"She's…" David paused and his gaze slammed into hers. The pain in his eyes made her want to wrap her arms around both him and Rhett and make this whole night go away. "She's safe. Sheriff Bennett is taking care of her."

Erin wondered exactly how Jenna McCay was being cared for, and she hoped that whatever was happening Jenna was coherent enough to feel horrible about the situation she'd created for her son.

"It was loud," Rhett said. "Mommy's friends woke me up. I came out to tell her, but there were so many grown-ups and I couldn't find her. Then everyone started yelling and I got scared and hid under the sink."

"That was real smart of you," David told the boy, his hand smoothing Rhett's sleep-tousled hair.

After a moment Rhett tipped up his head to look at David. "When is Mommy coming home?"

"I'm not sure, buddy. But I'll stay with you until she does, okay?"

Rhett chewed on his bottom lip for a few seconds, then nodded. After a knock at the door, Cole let in a gray-haired woman who appeared to be in her midfifties. She wore a plain white button-down shirt and dark pants and looked about as no-nonsense as they came.

The woman spoke to Cole in hushed tones for a few minutes, then they both approached.

"This is Becky Cramer from the county Human Services department," Cole said.

Becky gave David a small nod, then bent to look at Rhett. "You've had quite a night," she said gently.

"It was loud," Rhett said, turning in David's lap but not releasing his shirtfront.

"I'm David McCay." David offered the woman his hand. "Rhett's uncle. He'll stay with me while we sort out things with Jenna."

Becky shook his hand, then glanced at Erin.

"I'm Rhett's kindergarten teacher, Erin MacDonald." She saw a flash of surprise pass over Becky's sharp features.

Right. How was she supposed to explain why she'd ended up on the couch with David and Rhett, caught up in the middle of family drama that had started long past regular school hours?

"Erin is a friend of mine," David answered. Becky seemed to have no issue with that response, whereas Erin had trouble keeping her jaw from hitting the floor. Friends with David McCay? In what lifetime?

Men like David didn't have boring kindergarten teachers as friends. Before he came to Crimson, he'd been a major-league baseball pitcher. He must be used to drop-dead gorgeous women who were exciting and sexy.

Erin knew she was boring. And ordinary. Not at all David's type. She'd had a boyfriend last year—an accountant at a firm in town. He was quiet, average and exactly her type. Greg had broken up with her to date someone who was better than average, but that didn't mean Erin could change the person she was on the inside. No matter how much she wanted to try.

David had been her unrequited crush since the moment she'd first seen him. It was a harmless fantasy with no chance of rejection. Never had she expected to get to know him, let alone be part of his life in this kind of personal way.

Her mind drifted to that moment in the car when he'd traced his thumb over her cheekbone. The simple touch had sent shock waves rippling through her and ignited a kind of flash-point desire Erin hadn't realized she was capable of feeling.

"It's important the school and the family work together," Becky said, bringing Erin back to the current conversation with a jolt, "to keep the boy's life as stable as possible during this time."

She looked at Rhett, who had fallen asleep in David's arms. "Let me put him to bed," she whispered, "while you two finish talking."

David relaxed his grip, allowing her to lift the boy into her arms. She made sure to take the stuffed dog, too. Rhett remained asleep as she tucked him back into bed, sighing when his head hit the pillow. Erin sat on the mattress for several minutes, rubbing the boy's back to make sure he didn't wake again. She couldn't imagine how scared he must have been earlier, unable to find his mother and with the wild party in full swing.

She made a silent vow. She *would* keep him safe, no matter how far out of her comfort zone—and tangled up with David McCay—that led her.

It was almost two in the morning before David let himself into the apartment, exhausted and emotionally drained. Erin had agreed to stay while he went to see Jenna. Cole was keeping her overnight on possession charges but had agreed to drop them if she entered a rehab program.

David had helped his sister get clean once before, and it

was a rough road. She swore that tonight's tumble off the wagon was a onetime occurrence. David wanted to believe her, yet he'd heard so many excuses over the years. All he knew was he had to protect his nephew. There could be no repeats of what Rhett had gone through tonight.

It never should have happened in the first place, and he couldn't stop blaming himself.

The apartment was quiet when he entered, and he found Erin asleep on the couch, curled on her side as if she didn't want to take up too much space. It blew his mind that the buttoned-up schoolteacher had so willingly pitched in to help with his hot mess of a life. He understood that Rhett was her student. But David had never encountered a teacher like her.

Hell, he would have paid a lot more attention in school if he'd had someone like Erin MacDonald in his corner.

If possible, she looked more luminously beautiful asleep than she did awake. She was like a damn fairy-tale princess with her creamy skin, straight nose, rosy cheeks and the long, dark hair that fell over her face. It was easier to study her now than when those too-knowing bourbon-colored eyes were staring back at him.

He covered her with a blanket and went to check on Rhett. Unlike Erin, the boy was sprawled across the bed, arms and legs reaching out like a starfish. Jenna claimed she'd meant to have only her new boyfriend and a few of his buddies to the house to watch the Broncos play, but things had gotten out of hand. According to Cole, the boy-friend was serious bad news, having had more than a few run-ins with law enforcement over the years.

How the hell did Jenna manage to attract the biggest scumbags on the planet every time she found a new man? He would have asked her, wanted to rail and shout, but she'd looked so defeated sitting alone in the holding cell.

She understood she'd messed up and he knew from experience that heaping on more condemnation would only put her on the defensive.

Fear and guilt had warred in his sister's pale blue eyes, along with the remnants of a long-ago pain that she could hide from most of the world, but not from him. She'd agreed to check into a treatment program, so finding a place for her would be the first thing on his to-do list after getting Rhett to school in a few hours.

He lowered himself into the recliner next to the couch. Erin had cleaned the messy apartment, another debt of thanks he owed her. David hated owing people anything, had learned the hard way to only depend on himself. Yet he couldn't help but be grateful for the chance to simply sit and rest for a few minutes.

His eyes drifted shut, although he didn't intend to fall asleep. The next thing he knew, someone was shaking him awake. He blinked and found himself staring into Erin's huge brown eyes.

"I have to go," she whispered. "I need to shower and change before school."

David blinked and tried to look more with-it than he felt. "What time is it?"

"Almost six in the morning." She moved away and he had the ridiculous urge to pull her down against him. These past few hours had been the soundest he'd slept in years. Something about having this woman close soothed the demons that waited for him in the dark.

"I'll give you a ride," he told her, rising from the chair. His lower back ached, and as he looked around the small apartment, reality came crashing over him like a tidal wave. Today was going to be awful. "I'll need to wake Rhett and—"

"One of my girlfriends is on her way." Erin shoved a

thick lock of hair behind one ear. "Rhett needs all the sleep he can get. He's coming to school today, right?"

"Yes," David answered, mentally listing all the things he had to get done. "He needs a routine now more than ever."

"How's your sister?"

"She feels terrible and says she's committed to straightening out her life once and for all. I need to pick her up this morning and then make arrangements to get her to a treatment facility."

"So Rhett will be staying with you while she's in rehab?"

"Yes. Not here. I live in a loft above the brewery."

"How long is the program?"

He sighed. "A month. Rhett doesn't know she'll be gone. I'll tell him when he wakes up, but she won't leave until tomorrow afternoon. I want him to spend time with her—to know that she's okay."

"It could be traumatic," Erin said with a nod. "But we'll get him through."

He didn't want to admit how much her words resonated with him. When had he suddenly become afraid of dealing with things on his own? David prided himself on never being dependent on anyone, let alone a woman who'd been a stranger only twelve hours ago.

She worried her bottom lip between her teeth, a nervous habit he'd seen her do several times since they'd left the bar. That moment when he'd caught her staring at his ass felt like a lifetime ago.

He ran a finger across the seam of her lips. "You need to give that lip a break. It's too pretty to take so much abuse."

"Oh," she breathed, pink rushing into her cheeks. He wasn't sure what had surprised her more—his touch or the fact that he thought her mouth was pretty. Pretty and far too kissable to be good for either of them.

"I appreciate your help," he said, the words rusty and unfamiliar on his tongue. "I'm going to make sure Rhett has a stable home life, but having a teacher who understands what he's going through will be important."

She inclined her head to study him. After everything she'd witnessed and what she'd clearly inferred about the dysfunctional McCay family, it must seem odd for him to suddenly be speaking so formally.

"Of course." Her brows knit together, causing a small crease to appear on her forehead. He resisted the urge to smooth it away...barely. "I should go. Melody doesn't live far from here. She'll be waiting."

She moved across the small space, and he didn't say anything until the door to the apartment had almost closed.

"Erin."

She turned, one hand on the doorknob. "Yes?"

"I'd like to repay you for last night." The thought of remaining in debt to her—to anyone—chafed his skin like an itch he couldn't quite reach.

"There's no need—"

"There *is* a need." The need pounding through him to claim her. He tried to convince himself the longing would be quenched if he could do a favor to repay her for—in large part—rescuing him last night. "I could make a donation to your class or host the school's Christmas party at the bar, free of charge. What do you want?"

She stared at him for several long moments, the air between them growing thick and hot. She cleared her throat and said clearly, "I'd like to have an affair with you."

Then she was gone, the door clicking shut behind her.

And David was left staring after her, wondering if the whole thing had been some kind of bizarre dream.

Chapter Three

"You asked him to hit the sheets?" Melody let out a hoot of laughter. "Who are you and what have you done with my friend Erin?"

Erin kept her palms pressed tight against her cheeks, willing her face to stop burning. "Oh my gosh," she repeated for the tenth time since she'd climbed in Melody's minivan and told her friend how she'd left things with David. "I'm nobody. I'm delusional. He's going to think I'm crazy. Maybe I *am* crazy."

"You're not crazy." Melody reached out and gently pulled Erin's hands away from her face. "But did you ever think of asking him out on a date?"

"Clearly I wasn't thinking at all." Erin shook her head. "And of course I didn't ask him for a date. David McCay would never go out with someone like me."

"Bargaining for sex seemed like a better idea?"

Erin groaned. "Oh my gosh."

"Why wouldn't he go out with you? You're cute. You're nice. You have decent teeth."

"Decent teeth? My best friend thinks one of my top three selling points is decent teeth? This is even worse than I thought."

Melody laughed softly. "Suzie and I saw the way he looked at you at the bar last night. It was kind of hot."

"The way he looks at a parking meter is hot. That's David. He's not for me. We both know he's not for me."

Her friend didn't deny it, and Erin wasn't sure whether to feel justified or hurt by the silent validation.

"Then why make your little request?"

Erin thought about how she'd felt with David watching her across the small apartment. The way she'd seemed to come alive when he'd placed his hand on the small of her back. The longing for something more in her life.

"He asked me what I wanted and my mouth formed the words before my brain could catch up. He *is* what I want. Not forever. Not for real. But the chance to be with him…"

Melody sighed. "Can you imagine?"

For Erin, fantasizing about David was akin to fan-girling over a comic book superhero played by some hot Australian actor on the big screen—larger than life. He was so handsome he took her breath away, but was a whole galaxy out of her league.

He'd probably even look darn good in tights. Erin giggled at the thought, and the fact that she *had* asked him for an affair. What had she been thinking?

"I want to be seen," she said softly. "I'm tired of being invisible."

"We see you," Melody answered. "The kids see you."

"They see Ms. MacDonald. For a school year. Then we have kindergarten graduation and they move on. They grow up. They aren't *mine*." She took another breath. "It's the same reason I'm working with Olivia Travers at the community center on the Crimson Kidzone project."

"You're comparing starting an after-school program for at-risk kids to sleeping with the town hottie?"

"Yes." Erin shook her head. "No. I mean, not when you put it like that. But Kidzone will belong to me. I can make a lasting difference in this community."

"You do that already. That's what being a good teacher is all about. Elaina loves you."

"She's a great kid, but you know that already." Melody's daughter, Elaina, was in Erin's class this year and was the same mix of sweet and spunky as her mother.

"Takes after her dad," Melody said with a wink. Melody had two young kids and a husband who worked long hours as one of Cole Bennett's deputies to provide for his family.

She pulled to a stop at the curb in front of Erin's apartment building. Erin had lived in her apartment in the converted redbrick Victorian since she'd moved back to Crimson after college. All of her furniture was hand-me-downs from her mother. She had white walls and a shower that never got hot enough and it was all…adequate.

"I want to do more, Mel. I want to *be* more. Average has always been enough for me, but sometimes I want more than an ordinary life."

"David McCay sure isn't average."

Erin smiled. "It was a stupid request, and I'll have to apologize. Or maybe he'll pretend it never happened and save us both a lot of embarrassment."

"Is that what you want?"

"It's what I *should* want. I didn't help him last night because I expected anything in return. Rhett's a special kid, but it's clear his life hasn't been easy. He definitely has some behavioral issues, but we were making progress in class. He was responding to me. I don't want him to slip through the cracks."

"Don't take it back, Erin. How many women like us get a chance with someone who looks like that?"

"Says the woman with a ridiculously handsome husband."

"I love Grant to distraction, but we're already a boring married couple. Let me live vicariously through you and your little adventure. I vaguely remember what it was like to be single and playing the field."

"You and Grant started dating when we were juniors in high school."

Melody rolled her eyes. "I said vaguely."

"I need to shower and get ready." Erin opened the car door, the morning breeze tickling the hair that had come loose from the ponytail she wore almost every day. "It's going to be a long one. I'm meeting Olivia at the community center after school to finalize the details on the outreach program."

Melody leaned over the console as Erin hopped out of the car. "At least reassure me that this business with your hottie brewer has nothing to do with the jerk ex-boyfriend."

"Nothing at all," Erin confirmed, and shut the door behind her, never revealing that the fingers of her other hand were tightly crossed behind her back.

Erin parked around the corner from the Crimson Community Center later that afternoon and kept her head down as she moved along the bustling sidewalk. Growing up, Crimson had been nothing more than a sleepy mountain town, always in the shadow of nearby Aspen, which felt to Erin like the more glamorous and showy older sister. But in recent years, Crimson had come into its own, attracting new residents and an influx of visitors who appreciated the town's laid-back vibe and the myriad outdoor fun available in the mountains surrounding it.

Now the town was busy most weekends, even though the summer crowds had dispersed and they had a good two months before ski season kicked off.

She'd managed to avoid David at both drop-off and pickup today, although she'd pulled Rhett aside during reading groups after she'd watched the boy purposely knock a bin of markers to the floor, then blame the mess on Elaina Cross, who sat next to him. At first he'd refused to speak or even make eye contact when she'd brought him into the hallway. Eventually he blinked away tears and told her his mommy was going away to a place that would make her better and he had to stay with his uncle David.

Wrapping Rhett in a tight hug, Erin had reassured him that both his mother and his uncle loved him. She'd cautiously brought up the previous night and they'd talked a little about his fears and how important it was for him to feel safe.

While she couldn't avoid David forever, a little distance might work to Erin's advantage. A fierce war was raging between her brain, which wanted the whole embarrassing situation to disappear, and the rest of her body, which was singing the "Hallelujah" chorus at the mere thought that David might agree to her outrageous request.

Erin had been with one and a half men in her lifetime. Well, two men to be exact, but she only counted the first as a half because he'd gotten so drunk during their date that he'd fallen asleep kissing her. Talk about a blow to the ego, and her ego hadn't been much of a force in the first place. But the jerk ex-boyfriend Melody had referred to was the final nail in Erin's confidence coffin.

She and Greg Dellinger had dated for six months, and

their relationship was fine. *Fine.* That should have been her clue to run away as fast as she could. She'd watched enough rom-coms to know that falling in love was supposed to be better than *fine.*

It had been Greg who'd broken up with her, blissfully explaining that he'd fallen in love with a woman who was beautiful, sexy and exciting. Tacitly implying that Erin was none of those things. Not a big shock, but it stung.

Maybe she owed Greg a thank-you, though, because it had been while reevaluating her life—halfway through a carton of Chunky Monkey—that Erin decided she wanted more.

Deserved more.

Changing up her love life was a daunting project, so she'd started her be-more-than-ordinary makeover by contacting Olivia Travers. Ever since she was a girl, Erin had wanted to be a teacher—to help kids learn but also give them a chance to discover all their potential and coax it out.

The same way she'd wished for someone in her life to notice her. With Crimson's ever-expanding population and changing demographics, she was afraid that the neediest kids in the community were getting overlooked. Lost in the shuffle or with families that didn't want the stigma of coming forward for assistance.

Olivia, who'd founded the community center two years ago, had the best of intentions but funding was often difficult to come by for free programming. Erin had outlined her plan for Crimson Kidzone, scheduled a meeting and pitched her idea, offering to volunteer her time to start the program and also work on grant writing to gain additional support.

Her friends at school had encouraged her, while her mom wondered why she'd want to spend more time with

children than she already had to for her job. Maureen Mac-
Donald was a quiet, keep-to-herself type of woman. She
loved Erin and had done her best after Erin's father died
of a sudden heart attack when she was in kindergarten.
But Maureen dedicated more of her time to her psychol-
ogy practice than she did to motherhood, and she and Erin
had little other than genetics in common. Her mother was
content to remain in her introverted bubble and that's how
she'd raised her only daughter.

Erin was stepping out of that bubble, even if the encounter with David made her want to jump right back
into it.

Her nerves disappeared as soon as she walked into the
community center. Her personal life might be a hot mess,
but she knew in her heart that the after-school project
would be a success. She wouldn't settle for anything less.

Olivia was waiting at the reception desk for her, a
chubby-cheeked baby cradled in her arms.

"I hope you don't mind an audience for our meeting,"
she said apologetically. "The babysitter called in sick."

"Any opportunity to get my dose of snuggles." Erin
shifted her backpack so she could reach for baby Molly,
who was the most scrumptious five-month-old she'd ever
seen.

The little girl was a perfect mix of her mom and dad.
She had eyes the same striking green as her mother's. But
instead of Olivia's dark hair, she was a towheaded baby
with wispy blond hair the same color as Logan Travers's,
Molly's doting daddy. Erin wasn't part of the Traverses'
wide social circle, but she'd seen the group of friends
around town enough to know that Logan, while big and
brawny on the outside, was absolute putty in his daughter's hands.

"You're a natural with kindergartners *and* babies," Olivia said as she transferred her daughter to Erin. Coming from Olivia, who was naturally beautiful and had the gentle spirit to match, Erin was grateful to receive the compliment. "Did you grow up in a big family?"

A little pang of disappointment passed through Erin as she shook her head and pressed a kiss to the baby's soft forehead. "I'm an only child, but I always thought it would be fun to have a big family. I love babies."

"You were meant to be a mother."

The other woman's words made something go soft and melty in Erin's heart. She wanted to be a mother, to have someone—or even better, multiple someones—to call her own. The thought of a baby with David McCay's big blue eyes made her chest flutter.

"I have a gut feeling," Olivia continued, "just like I did when you contacted me about the after-school program." She leaned in closer. "Any potential suitors or shall I put the word out? I've learned to trust my instincts."

"Praise the Lord for your instincts," a deep voice said, "or you never would have taken a chance on me." Erin glanced over her shoulder to see Olivia's husband, Logan, standing right behind her. And next to him...David McCay.

Molly let out a little squeak as Erin squeezed a bit too tightly. She rocked the baby and Molly immediately grinned and tugged on the ends of Erin's hair.

"That's right," Olivia said, leaning into her husband when he moved around Erin and draped an arm across her shoulders. "Can you blame me for wanting everyone to be as happy?"

"I'm happy," Erin whispered, even though it wasn't quite the truth. She could feel David's eyes on her, and although she didn't meet his gaze, the intensity of his stare made the hair stand up on the back of her neck.

"How about you, David?" Olivia lifted a brow. "You're single, right?"

"Yep," came the rumbly answer.

Olivia smiled. "Crimson is the perfect place to find true love."

"David is here to talk about the beer for Oktoberfest," Logan said, dropping a kiss on the top of Olivia's head. "Although I'm sure he appreciates your matchmaking efforts."

Erin risked a glance at David, who shrugged. Suddenly she was terrified he might reveal what she'd asked him. It was crazy, but she couldn't stop the fear coursing through her. He opened his mouth but before he could answer, she blurted out the first thing that came to mind, even though it was an obvious lie. "I've got a boyfriend."

Olivia looked disappointed. "Well, I guess I wasn't meant to be a matchmaker after all."

"We'll have to find other ways to keep you busy," Logan said.

"Right now, Erin and I need to go over the last-minute details for her after-school outreach project. The program starts Monday." She scooped the baby out of Erin's arms and handed her to Logan. Molly gurgled happily, curling a fist in the soft denim of her daddy's shirt.

Olivia moved toward the hallway that led to the community center's classrooms. "You coming, Erin?"

Erin realized she was staring at the baby, her arms strangely empty without the lotion-scented bundle. "Right." She darted a glance at David, who arched a brow in response.

One small brow arch she felt all the way to her toes.

An imaginary boyfriend. That should end things before they even got started.

Forcing a smile, she looked from David to Logan. "See you both later," she called, and hurried after Olivia, ignoring the regret that surged through her as she walked away.

Chapter Four

David waited outside the community center's front door, watching groups of people take to the streets of Crimson on this beautiful fall Friday night. The temperature was quickly cooling, typical at altitude once the sun dipped behind the majestic peak of Crimson Mountain to the town's west.

He imagined the crowds heading toward Elevation for a drink with friends, a reminder that he should be tending bar tonight. He'd been lucky with the brewery, opening just as the picturesque mountain town was hitting a resurgence and having a knack with brewing the ever-popular craft beers.

But he didn't take his success for granted. After destroying his baseball career thanks to one night of reckless stupidity, he'd learned to work hard for what he wanted. He should be working now. Or checking in with Jenna, who was spending the night with Rhett in his loft before they drove to Denver tomorrow to put her on the plane headed for the rehab center in Arizona.

He should be a dozen places that didn't involve standing in the shadows waiting for Erin. David was long past the days of making stupid choices when it came to women, and he'd never had any interest in the type who looked as wholesome as a tall glass of milk.

The door opened and Erin walked out, and all the reasons David shouldn't be waiting for her disappeared under the relentless drumming of need pulsing through his body. He might not understand his reaction to the beautiful schoolteacher, but neither could he ignore it.

"Tell me about the boyfriend," he said, stepping out to block her path.

She stumbled back a step, pressing her hand to her cheek. "Holy cow! You scared the pants off me."

David felt his mouth curve at that. If only.

"No one says *holy cow* in real life," he muttered, reaching out a hand to steady her.

She shrugged off his touch. "Clearly people do say *holy cow*," she countered. "Because I just did." She crossed her arms over a chest that could benefit from a low-cut blouse. Oh, yes. David would definitely like to see this woman in something far more revealing than the conservative pastel-colored shirts she seemed to favor.

The thought of undoing a few of her buttons made his blood run alarmingly hot.

"Why are you skulking around out here?"

"I'm not skulking," he told her. "I'm waiting for you. You were just about to explain why you asked me for sex when you have a boyfriend."

Her delicate brows winged up. "No, I wasn't." She glanced over her shoulder. "Keep your voice down. I don't want anyone to hear…" Even in the waning light he could see color flood her cheeks. When was the last time he'd been around a woman who actually blushed?

"That you propositioned me?" he supplied.

"Stop," she said on a hiss of breath. "It wasn't like that."

"It sure sounded like that to me. But I guess you need to keep me your dirty little secret since there's a *boyfriend* in the picture." He tapped a finger on his chin, as if pondering the concept. "I've never been a kept man before. I'll admit it has a certain appeal."

Her eyes narrowed. "You're teasing me."

He didn't bother to hide his grin. "You seem unfamiliar with the concept."

She stared at him a moment longer, then gave a small sigh. He could almost feel on his skin the puff of breath that left her lips. Damn, but he wanted to feel it. He wanted to taste her to gauge for himself whether she was as sweet as she looked. He eased closer to her, slowly, as if she might spook if he moved too fast.

He'd meant to confront her, demand what the hell she'd been thinking when she'd made that shocking request. But he liked the easy banter they fell into far too much. His life had never been easy, and a bit of innocent flirting with Erin gave him a few minutes' reprieve from all the things he couldn't control.

She bit down on her lip but didn't shy away. He liked that, too. "I don't have a boyfriend," she mumbled.

"Really?" he asked, even though he'd guessed as much.

"Olivia was intent on playing matchmaker, and I didn't want you to be forced into asking me out or anything. That's a horrible feeling and I'm not…"

"Interested?" He chuckled. "We both know that's not true."

A shadow clouded her gaze, and he wasn't sure what he'd said wrong, but he wanted to kick himself for it.

"I'm not your type," she said through clenched teeth, coming up on her toes and tipping back her head so that he got his wish and felt her breath tickle his chin. Her scent was a mix of cinnamon and sugar, like he imagined a kitchen might smell with a batch of cookies baking in the oven. Warm, inviting and the exact opposite of the cramped galley kitchen in the apartment where he'd grown up.

He was so caught up in his reaction that he almost missed the words she spoke. As it was, by the time he opened his mouth to correct her, she'd brushed past him and was around the corner of the building.

"Erin, wait," he called, but instead of slowing she moved faster. It only took a few strides to catch up to her.

"I need to go," she said, keeping her gaze on the ground in front of her when he blocked her path.

"Why do you think you're not my type?" He was curious to know whether her reasons matched his.

She gave a little shake of her head.

"Erin."

"Am I your type?" she asked suddenly, her honey-colored gaze slamming into his.

He opened his mouth, shut it again. How was he supposed to answer that? When she made to move around him again, he settled for the truth.

"You're way too good for me."

The comment earned him an eye roll. "If you say the words *it's me, not you*, I'm going to punch you."

"I'm guessing you don't go around punching people."

"You make me want to start."

He laughed again. "How is it that I'm the bad guy right now?"

"You're not," she whispered. "I should never have made

the request. I was tired, and it was stupid and embarrassing. Can we just forget about it?"

He wished he could. Getting involved with this woman—in any capacity other than as his nephew's teacher—was sure to be trouble for both of them. Why couldn't he make himself walk away?

"No one," he said softly, unable to resist stepping into her space again, "would have to force a man to ask you out."

It was her turn to laugh, but there was no humor in it. All the light was gone from her golden eyes, and he wanted nothing more in life at that moment than to reignite it. "I know who I am, David."

He lifted his hands to cup her cheeks and felt a slight shiver pass through her. It drove him crazy with need. "Take another look," he said, and touched his lips to hers.

Erin's eyes drifted closed even as her body opened like the petals of a flower unfurling in the warm sunshine. Take another look? She'd planned to hold on to this moment like a priceless piece of art. If she could she'd frame it and hang it on her wall so she could always remember.

David McCay was kissing her, and quite thoroughly at that. His lips were soft but firm as they glided over hers and she couldn't resist darting her tongue into his mouth. He rewarded that bit of bravery with a small groan, which made sparks dance across her skin. She leaned into him, her breath hitching when his fingers laced through her hair and tugged gently.

A whistle from a passing car made her wrest away from his embrace. She squeezed her hands into fists and pressed them to her sides when all she wanted was to wrap herself around him and hang on for dear life.

"Women like you don't do PDAs on the sidewalk," he said, his voice rougher than normal.

She bit down on the inside of her cheek and looked up at him through her lashes. "I don't make it a habit," she admitted. The truth was she'd never before had the opportunity. But it was Friday night and it wouldn't be good for one of her students or another teacher to catch her in a full-blown make-out session on a public sidewalk.

"Too good for me," David repeated, and Erin realized he'd actually meant the words when he'd said them earlier.

Her ex had said something similar when he'd broken up with her, but the insinuation behind the comment had been quite different. *Good* had been another way of saying *boring*. But if the heat in David's gaze was any indication, he didn't find her the least bit boring.

Erin's long-suffering ego broke out into a little happy dance, but she quickly pulled the plug on the music. "That isn't true," she said, pressing a hand to lips still tingling from his kiss.

"You asked me for an affair, sweetheart." He smoothed a loose strand of hair away from her face. "Not a date. We both know what that means."

"Would you have gone out on a date if I'd asked?"

He shook his head, and she tried to ignore the pang of disappointment that snaked through her.

"You're a white-picket-fence girl. America and apple pie. What you saw at my sister's apartment pretty much sums up how I was raised. I come from that world. It's what I know."

Right now that didn't matter. This man had flirted with her, then kissed her senseless. Twenty minutes with David had been more exciting than the sum total of the rest of her life. Heck no, she couldn't have an affair with him, even if he was willing. She was liable to spontaneously combust. It was time to get the subject back to safer ground.

"How's Rhett doing?" she asked, reaching into her purse for her keys. She moved to the edge of the sidewalk where her Subaru hatchback was parked at the curb.

"He's with his mom tonight. They're staying at my loft."

"Is your sister okay with going into treatment?"

He nodded. "Deep in her heart she doesn't want to repeat the mistakes our mother made. I have to believe last night was a wake-up call for her."

"Then maybe it was a blessing in disguise. I hope she gets the help she needs." She hit the remote start on her key fob.

"I hope Rhett and I survive the next month together." He ran a hand over his jaw and the scratching sound made her want to whimper. She was truly pathetic.

"He's welcome at Crimson Kidzone in the afternoon. It starts Monday at four. Sign him up if you need a break."

When he stared at her, she held out a hand. "No strings attached or indecent proposals from me. Promise."

He took her hand but instead of shaking it, pressed a lingering kiss on her knuckles. "That would be a huge disappointment."

Erin sighed. Cue the weak knees. "You don't mean that," she whispered.

"I might have enough willpower to leave you alone, but that doesn't mean I won't be thinking about how good we could be together."

He released her hand and she clutched it against her stomach, feeling ridiculously like a teenage girl who wanted to hold on to the imprint of that kiss. "Good to know," she told him.

He winked at her. "Night, Erin. Sweet dreams."

* * *

"Seriously, McCay? Your nephew's kindergarten teacher?"

David blew out a breath at the annoyance in the feminine voice behind him.

He hoisted a bushel of hops over his shoulder and turned. "I don't know what you're talking about, Tracie, but I promised Rhett I'd take him fishing after thirty minutes of screen time so I need to make the most of my electronic babysitter."

It was early Sunday morning—too early considering David hadn't gotten to sleep until after 3:00 a.m. He'd paid one of the waitresses to babysit his nephew last night, which had left him short-staffed since his best—if mouthiest—bartender Tracie Sheldon had taken the evening off for a date with the local orthopedic surgeon who'd been asking her out for months.

Tracie stood behind him now, wearing running shorts and a long-sleeved athletic shirt. Her short blond hair stuck out from under a bright pink headband and he guessed she'd stopped into the bar in the middle of her daily five-mile run.

"Besides, shouldn't you be busy basking in post-date glow or doing the walk of shame or something?"

"I'm not that kind of girl," she shot back, then added softly, "anymore. Besides, it wasn't a good match."

With a quiet sigh, David dropped the heavy bag to the floor. "Why not? Your doctor has bellied up to the bar several nights a week for the past month, even when he's on call and drinking root beer. We might serve up a helluva plate of chicken wings and some crazy good nachos, but there's only so much bar food a man can take."

He leaned in closer. "Unless he has another compelling reason for becoming a regular."

"Compelling." Tracie snorted. "Right. He's a surgeon, Davey, my boy. I'm a high-school dropout bartender. We have nothing in common."

"I've spent some time talking to Luke Baylor. He's a decent guy, Tracie. Worked his way through med school. You work hard, and you're not a high-school dropout anymore. It won't be long until you graduate nursing school. You should hold your head high."

"So tell me about the schoolteacher," she countered, placing her hands on her hips.

"I don't know what you've heard, but there's nothing to tell."

"Do you like her?"

"Do you like Doc Luke?"

She arched a brow. "We had dinner at Carlo's Bistro last night. Remember Lance who washed dishes here for a while?"

"Yeah." David nodded. "Punk kid."

"That's the one. He's a busboy at Carlo's and was all too happy to stop me on the way to the restroom and report he saw you and a dark-haired librarian type sucking face on the street."

David felt a headache begin to pulse behind one temple. "No one was sucking face."

"I figured it was the teacher after seeing the way she looked at you Thursday night. Like she was a kid in a candy store and you were her favorite flavor."

He didn't want to admit how much he liked the idea of that. "You're changing the subject."

"You started it."

"We're quite a pair." He wrapped an arm around the tiny blonde's shoulders—she barely came to his chest—and pulled her in for a hug. "I'm not going to stop trying to make you believe you deserve some happiness."

"Goes both ways," she said, and gently elbowed him in the ribs.

He grunted and squeezed her shoulders. "Rhett's happiness is what matters to me now."

At that moment, Rhett gave a small shout. "Ms. Mac-Donald," he yelled, and scrambled out of the booth, his iPad forgotten on the table.

Tracie took a step away from him as David turned to see Erin, backlit in the doorway of the bar by the morning sunlight. Her dark jeans hugged her curves and a cranberry-colored sweater with a scooped neckline made her skin look even more luminous. It was difficult to read her expression, but her gaze was bouncing between him and Tracie in a way David didn't like one bit.

"Don't just stand there staring," Tracie muttered. "Go to her. I'm going to slip out through the kitchen."

"Tracie, you don't need to…" David started, but he was talking to her back.

"Ms. MacDonald, I live in a bar now." David cringed as Rhett's voice carried across the empty space.

"We don't live in the bar," David corrected as he moved forward. *Go to her*, Tracie had said. What he wanted to do was swing her into his arms and bury his nose against the crook of her neck. Her thick hair was pulled back into another ponytail.

Did she ever wear it down? Right now he would give just about anything to see it falling in waves over her shoulders. He'd been too long without a woman if he was now obsessing over Erin's hair.

"I know," she answered. "You have a loft upstairs. I didn't mean to interrupt." Her gaze traveled past him to where Tracie had disappeared. "I was heading to the bakery and your door was open…"

"You're not interrupting," he said quickly, coming to

stand behind his nephew. "Tracie works here, and she stopped by after her run. She had a date last night." She bit down on her lip and he quickly added, "With some-one else. Not me. We're not..." He raked a hand through his hair. "She's a friend. The guy she went out with is a doctor. A surgeon. He—"

"Uncle David, why are you talking so fast?" He glanced down to find Rhett staring up at him, then raised his gaze to Erin's. He was babbling. He'd never babbled in his en-tire life.

She flashed a shy smile. "I'm going to grab breakfast at Life Is Sweet, then head over to the community center to set up a few things for tomorrow. I thought Rhett might like to help me if it's okay with you."

He felt Rhett fidget against his legs. "What do you think, buddy? We can head to the river a little later if you want to help Ms. MacDonald."

"I might mess things up," Rhett said, kicking the toe of one ratty sneaker against the scuffed wood floor. "I have to stay out of the way around here."

David sighed. He'd said those words this morning—pre-coffee—when he'd set up Rhett with the iPad.

"You won't mess up anything." Erin crouched down in front of the boy. "In fact, some of the supplies I'm using are way back in a closet and I need someone small enough to crawl in and push them out to me."

Rhett nodded. "I can do that."

"Then we've got a deal." She straightened, and David expected to see censure in her big eyes, but instead they were gentle in a way that made his heart hammer in his chest.

"Can I go in my pj's?" Rhett asked.

Erin smiled. "This might be a good time to get dressed for the day. Can you do that?"

"Me and Ruffie have a bedroom upstairs." He pointed to the raggedy blue dog sitting on the booth where he'd been playing a video game. "He gets nervous when we're not together."

"He's welcome to come with us," Erin offered.

"Yeah," Rhett agreed. "He'd like that."

He ran to the table, grabbed the dog and then headed for the hallway leading to the staircase that accessed the upper floor. There was also an entrance off the street, but David used the one that led directly into his office in the back of the bar when things weren't busy.

"I suck at this," he mumbled when Rhett was out of sight. "Jenna hasn't even been gone twenty-four hours and Rhett feels like he's in the way."

"It's a big change for both of you. How did it go yesterday?"

"Jenna cried. Rhett cried. He was sullen all day yesterday, and the first thing he asked this morning is when she's coming home. I felt like a total ass for arranging her stay in rehab. Maybe she could get clean and still be here, you know?"

"It's not long in the grand scheme of things and could make a real difference. That would make everything worth it. A kid deserves to grow up feeling safe. Your sister is lucky to have you to step in and help her. You're giving both of them another chance."

He blew out a breath. "How did you know exactly what I needed to hear this morning?"

Color rose to her cheeks. "It's the truth."

It wasn't just the words she spoke that made him feel better. It was the fact that she'd come to check on him. Okay, maybe she'd come to check on Rhett, but David still reaped the benefit. *She* was exactly what he needed. "Thank you."

They stared at each other for several long moments, and the spark of awareness that connected them seemed to shimmer and thrum in the air. It made him want to pull her in and kiss her again, but then he thought of Tracie and the kid who'd reported him Friday night. Normally, David didn't care who saw him doing what, but Erin was different. She was too good to be dragged through any sort of gossip mill, especially when she was starting her new program at the community center.

He crossed his arms over his chest to resist the urge to touch her. "Rhett won't be long." He made his tone purposefully chilly.

Disappointment flashed in her brown eyes before she cocked her head and studied him, as if she was trying to riddle out secrets. "This place is different during the day," she said, moving away from him and trailing her long fingers over the polished mahogany of the bar. He could imagine a lot of other places those fingers should be traveling. Namely all over his damn body.

"The architecture is beautiful." She pointed to the vaulted ceiling, where rough-hewn beams stretched across the open space.

"Logan helped me design it," David said, following her as she moved through the high tables. Following her like a puppy on a leash. Never had he felt so under a woman's spell as he did with Erin. The crazy part was she had no idea the power she had over him.

"Did he do the renovations, too? When I was growing up, this place was a grocery store, then it stood vacant for a number of years."

He'd forgotten that she was a Crimson native. The town was a tight-knit community and everyone seemed to know their neighbors and their neighbors' business. But before Rhett started school, David had never heard of Erin Mac-

Donald. "The building was bank-owned when I bought it. I got a great deal."

She smiled at him over her shoulder. "You must have had a clear vision."

"I went to college on a baseball scholarship, but only lasted a couple of years. It sounds crazy now, but I took a brewing lab sciences class freshman year and got hooked on the process. I was good at it, but baseball came first. When I got drafted, the beer brewing moved to the back burner for a few years. I stopped playing ball, but then Jenna needed me out here. I needed a job and had enough money to make the business work."

"Why did you give up baseball?"

He gave a harsh laugh. "Not exactly my choice. I screwed things up pretty good. Not worth rehashing the details, but suffice it to say it was totally my fault."

"You do that too much," she said, moving toward him until she was directly in front of him. "You take the blame for anything that goes bad."

David felt his eyes narrow. "Only when I deserve it."

She poked him in the chest. "It seems like you're of the opinion that you always deserve it."

He clamped his mouth shut and stared down at her. There was no right way to respond to that. He didn't always do the wrong thing, but the times he'd messed up in his life had resulted in grim consequences for the people around him.

"You can't control everything. Sometimes bad stuff happens no matter what you do to prevent it."

He wrapped his hand around her finger and lowered it. "Other times it can be prevented, and I've often failed at that."

He expected her to wrench out of his grasp, but she

surprised him by gently squeezing his hand. "I wish you saw yourself the way I see you."

David felt her words like a vise clamping around his heart. The ways this woman could wreck him boggled his mind. Pulling away from her, he took several long steps toward the back hallway. "Rhett, you almost ready?" he called up the stairs.

"Coming," the boy shouted as his small feet pounded down the steps. He bounded into the hallway, the ever-present blue dog tucked against his side.

"Shoes, buddy," David said softly. His nephew had a habit of putting his shoes on the wrong feet.

With a sigh, Rhett dropped to the floor and undid the Velcro straps of his superhero sneakers and switched them to the correct feet. David's heart squeezed even harder as Rhett's tongue darted out the corner of his mouth. It meant he was concentrating hard and was the same quirk Jenna'd had as a girl.

David ruffled Rhett's hair as he stood. "Listen to Ms. MacDonald and do what she says," he told the boy. "No trouble."

"Okay."

He turned and looked at Erin, but her attention was focused on Rhett. "I'm glad you're coming with me this morning," she said.

Rhett gave a sharp nod and inched forward.

"I need another hour or so to get things settled here," David told her. "I'll pick him up after that."

"No rush," she answered, but still didn't look at him. "We'll stay busy."

He'd been the one to pull away a few minutes ago, but now the distance separating them seemed wider than simply physical space. It felt like he was losing something that had never belonged to him in the first place. The sensation made him want to throw a tantrum, like a baby whose favorite toy was taken away.

Erin held out her hand to Rhett, and the boy placed his smaller one in it. They walked out the open door and disappeared into the cool autumn morning.

David stood in his empty bar, staring at the dust motes that floated through the rays of sun shining in from the bar's front windows. He'd never minded being alone before. Why did it feel so damn uncomfortable now?

Chapter Five

"I owe you for this morning."

Erin almost stumbled off the end of the fishing dock at the sound of David's voice directly behind her.

He reached out a hand to steady her, but as much as she wanted to lean into his touch, she shrugged it off. Not going there, she reminded herself.

"You don't owe me. I told you I wanted to help with Rhett."

One side of his mouth quirked as he stared at her from behind dark sunglasses. "You also told me—"

"Don't say it." She held up a hand. "We've agreed that request was a moment of sleep-deprived stupidity on my part."

"I haven't agreed to anything." His deep voice once again set off tremors inside her.

"I thought you and Rhett were going to look for rocks to skip."

David gestured to where the boy was busily digging in the sand and gravel that made up the shoreline of Crimson Reservoir. "He got distracted."

She smiled as she watched Rhett, crouched low and with his too-long hair hanging over one eye, his attention completely focused on his task. "This is good for him, David. He needs some time to just be a kid in nature."

"This place can make anyone feel better."

She lifted her gaze to take in the awe-inspiring scenery around them. They were standing on the east side of the seven-mile-wide reservoir situated about thirty minutes outside of town. Rhett had insisted she accompany them on their planned fishing trip when David came to pick him up at the community center.

She should have said no. It had been a spontaneous decision to make the boy part of her morning on her way to the bakery earlier. A good decision, she thought, because both Rhett and David had looked grateful and relieved at her offer. But spending too much time with David was dangerous for her emotional health.

She'd spent far too much time since Friday replaying their kiss in her head. Instead of satisfying her, it had made her want more, even though she knew she shouldn't.

This afternoon only heightened her need. Having a crush on David was one thing, but watching his patience with Rhett and how hard he was trying to connect with the boy made Erin like him on an entirely different level. Once Rhett got tired of fishing, he'd gone to play on the shore, leaving David and Erin together on the dock.

Sunlight sparkled on the water, and a breeze made the changing aspen leaves flutter and sing around them. The breathtaking view of Crimson Mountain on the far side of the water made the reservoir one of the most beautiful places she'd ever seen. It seemed funny now that she'd never come out here before.

Her mom hadn't been much for outdoor activities. Erin knew kids came to the lake to hang out in high school, big groups or on dates. She was pretty sure the scenic overlook they'd passed on the way to the parking lot was still a popular make-out spot for teens in town. But she'd never been part of that crowd.

Now she wished she had been.

"I'd give way more than a penny to read your thoughts right now." David bent and picked up the fishing pole that he'd left next to her on the dock.

"I was thinking about what I still need to do to be ready for tomorrow," she lied.

"That makes you blush?"

She pressed her hands to her cheeks. "I'm not blushing."

He chuckled. "Want to throw in a line yourself? All you've gotten to do so far is watch me teach Rhett to fish."

"He likes it out here. Outside. Sitting in a classroom all day is tough for boys, and a lot of them go home and spend the rest of the day playing video games or watching TV."

"Like my nephew?"

She shrugged. "I'm sorry. I'm not trying to criticize your sister."

"It's fine," David answered, his voice tight. "Just because I moved to Crimson to help doesn't mean I knew how to or that Jenna wanted me involved. I should have been paying more attention. She was hiding things from me. Turns out Rhett was alone a lot more than I realized. He's pretty addicted to his screen time."

"Then today is even more of a treat for him."

David stepped closer, and she could see the shadow across his jaw that meant he hadn't shaved that morning.

He wore faded jeans and an olive-colored T-shirt with the Elevation Brewery logo across the front. Everything about him fascinated her.

"So you gonna do some fishing?"

"I don't know how," she answered, but took the thin pole he held out to her. "I mean, I was listening when you showed Rhett but..."

"I'll give you a lesson, too." He grasped her shoulders and turned her so she was facing the water. Then he moved to stand behind her, his body touching hers from chest to thigh. A crazy buzzing started in her head, and she swallowed back the little whimper that rose in her throat.

"Hold the pole so your two middle fingers are on either side of the reel," he said, his breath warm against her neck.

She tightened her grasp on the fishing pole and heard him chuckle. "Not in a death grip. Firm but not too tight."

She choked back a laugh because it sounded a lot like he was instructing her on something other than fishing. "Okay," she whispered.

"Hold the line against the rod with your index finger and flip the bail with your other hand." He guided her hand to the narrow piece of metal. "Give the line some slack and we're going to bring the rod back and cast."

Her mind was reeling, but she tried to follow his directions. With a shaking finger, she flipped the bail, drew the pole over her head and cast. The line spun, then the bobber dropped with a *plop* into the water only a foot in front of the dock.

"I can't do this," she whispered, trying to hand the pole back to David and move away.

"You can," he said, and tightened his hold on her. He took the rod from her, his arms reaching around her, and reeled in the line. "The motion comes from your wrist and hand, not your shoulder. Now take a breath."

She did and was immediately overwhelmed by the scent of soap and mint gum with the irresistible essence of David thrown in for good measure. It was different from kissing him, of course, but no less intimate. Erin struggled to keep her reaction to him hidden. "I've lived my whole life without learning to fish," she told him. "I can probably manage without the skill."

"Not on my watch," he said, and wrapped her hand around the pole once again. "You're going to catch a fish today."

Erin forced another breath and concentrated on not freaking out any more than she already was. Her goal for the year had been stepping out of her comfort zone, and today definitely counted. She glanced over her shoulder to see Rhett still focused on his rock and stone collection on the bank. "I don't know about a fish," she murmured. "I'll be satisfied if I throw this thing in the water without embarrassing myself."

"It's called casting a line," David said against her ear. His lips brushed the sensitive skin just below her earlobe.

A shiver ran through her in response, and she gripped the fishing pole more tightly. "I can't focus when you do that."

"Then you should stop being so sexy."

She grunted out a laugh at that. Erin was a lot of things, but sexy had never been one of them. The reminder was enough to help her rein in her foolish desire for this man. She couldn't help but think this was another part of his thank-you to her for helping with Rhett. Have a little flirtatious pity on the boring schoolteacher.

She squeezed her eyes shut for a moment and tried to compose herself. He was a man. She was a woman. They were fishing while his nephew—her student—played nearby. A casual afternoon. No need to read more into it than that.

"Tell me what to do again," she told him when she'd pulled herself together.

He repeated the instructions and she followed them, letting out a small cry of delight when the fishing line sailed through the air to land a respectable fifty feet out in the lake.

"I did it," she whispered.

"Now reel it in again," David said.

She did and the zip of the spinning reel was the best thing she'd heard in a long time. She cast twice more, the feel of the rod in her hand more natural with every moment.

"I think you've got it."

She realized David was still standing directly behind her only when he moved away. Her body wanted to protest, but she was too excited about her newfound skill at casting.

"I like it," she told him.

"We'll move to fly-fishing next," he answered with a slow smile. "I'd like to see you in a pair of waders."

Before she could react, the orange bobber floating on top of the water disappeared and she felt a hard tug on the line.

"A fish!" Rhett yelled at the top of his lungs as he ran toward them.

"Reel it in," David shouted as the line made a fast whirring sound.

With a squeak, Erin grabbed the spinning handle of the reel and began to turn it counterclockwise toward her body.

David was behind her again a moment later, his hand steadying her arm.

"Pull the rod against your body," he commanded. "You'll get more leverage."

"Take it," she said in a rush of breath. "I can't—"

"Yes, you can."

"You're doing it, Ms. MacDonald," Rhett said excitedly when he got to her side. He tugged on the hem of her shirt. "Don't let it get away."

"Keep going," David told her, his voice gentler. "You've got this."

Erin felt a grin split her face as she continued to bring the fish closer to the dock. David disappeared for a moment, then reappeared a minute later with a net in one hand.

"Bring him in, sweetheart," he said as he knelt at the edge of the dock.

The fish surfaced and struggled in the water, fighting hard against the hook that tethered him to her line. The sound of splashing broke the quiet of the lake as the water rippled and churned around the fish.

"He's so cute." Rhett crouched down next to David. "He's a boy, right?"

"Hard to tell right now." David grabbed the line, then scooped the net into the water. When it emerged again, the fish was in it, its gills opening and closing in the unfamiliar air.

"I don't want to kill him," Erin said, suddenly having a rush of sympathy for the little creature.

"It'll be fine," David assured her. "Hold the net, Rhett."

"Got it." The boy grabbed the handle with two hands while David removed the fish from the net. He pulled a tool out of his pocket and stuck it into the fish's mouth, extracting the hook.

Then he turned and presented the creature to Erin. "Here you go."

She placed the rod onto the dock and stepped forward. "It's so pretty." She traced one finger over the fish's pink-tinged side.

"It's a rainbow trout," David told her. "Hand Rhett your phone and take the fish. We'll get a photo before we throw him back."

"Or her," Erin said. "He could be a she."

"Yeah, but I don't think you want to cut her open and look for an egg sack."

"No." Erin made a face at the same time Rhett shouted, "Yes!"

She took her phone from her pocket, flipped it to camera mode and handed it to Rhett.

"Hold on tight," David advised as he passed the fish to her.

She didn't have time to think about whether she actually wanted her hands on the slimy, slippery creature before it was in them.

Despite the fact that she was slightly grossed out by holding a fish, she smiled when David took the phone from the boy and snapped her photo.

"Now throw it back," he told her and she flipped the fish into the reservoir. There was a splash, and the fish shimmered on the surface for a few seconds before swimming off.

"Bye, fish," Rhett called, then glanced up at David. "Can we skip stones now?"

"Sure, buddy. We'll collect the fishing gear and head over to you."

"I'll get more ready." Rhett smiled, then walked back toward his rock pile.

"I held a fish," Erin murmured, still holding her arms out in front of her.

"Like a pro," David confirmed. He pulled a bandanna

out of the pocket of his cargo pants and took her hand in his, gently wiping each of her fingers.

"I'm going to need to shower for days to get the fish smell off me."

"One hot shower should do the trick," he said with a smile. "If you're looking for a volunteer to scrub your back…"

She yanked her hands away from his. "You shouldn't tease me."

He leaned in and brushed a quick kiss across her lips. "Who says I'm teasing?"

Heat spiked through her, and her whole body flooded with need. As if unaware of her reaction, David simply grabbed the fishing pole and net and walked off the dock toward Rhett on the shore.

She followed, trying to keep her focus on the boy. That's why she was here—to help with Rhett. Anything more would surely end in emotional disaster.

David climbed the front steps of Crimson Elementary the following Wednesday afternoon, cursing himself for believing he finally had his life under control.

After Sunday's fishing excursion, something had changed with Rhett. His nephew had always been a bit distant, as if Jenna had warned him about coming to rely on Uncle David. Although he understood the sentiment, the tacit rejection still stung. But between the fishing lessons and skipping stones across the placid surface of the reservoir, the boy had started to relax and engage with David in a way he hadn't before.

David gave a lot of the credit to Erin. Her presence seemed to bridge the gap that he couldn't manage on his own. Rhett clearly loved having the attention of his teacher outside the classroom. Her easy smile and gentle encouragement softened the boy, and he was far more connected when she was around.

The funny thing was, David felt the exact same way. Despite a long string of girlfriends, he'd never been one for domestication. He was used to tumultuous relationships—loud arguments and intense make-up sessions that he'd assumed were normal given how he was raised.

Everything in his life had been emotional crisis and big scenes. But Erin made the ordinary bits feel just as exciting as the adrenaline rush that came from being swept along in a drama-filled haze.

He hadn't seen much of her since Sunday, despite dropping off and picking Rhett up from school every day and the fact that the boy had spent two afternoons in her after-school program.

It was a relief to have a safe place for Rhett to be in the hours before David could break away from work. He'd hired another bartender so he didn't have to deal with late nights, but with the plans for Oktoberfest and the festival's highly anticipated beer competition well under way, this wasn't a time he could take an extended vacation from the bar.

Between school, Erin and a couple trusted babysitters, David thought he was successfully managing his newfound role of single parent. Then he'd gotten the call from the school's principal, alerting him that Rhett had been in a fight with another boy during recess, the result of which would be a one-day suspension.

Hell, even David had made it to third grade before he'd been suspended for the first time. So much for having things under control.

He was buzzed into the building and headed for the reception desk. The woman behind it glanced up as he approached. She took him in head to toe and he saw her eyes widen. That's when he remembered the T-shirt he was wearing, which had the words I'd Tap That emblazoned across the front.

Way to make an impression.

Rhett's principal was going to love him. David did a mental eye roll as he wondered what Erin would think.

Probably that she'd dodged a bullet when he hadn't immediately taken her up on her offer to have an affair.

A moment later, an older woman with a sleek brown bob and wire-framed glasses came out of the office to greet him.

"Mr. McCay, I'm Karen Henderson, Crimson Elementary's principal."

"Call me David," he said as he shook her hand.

"Thank you for coming in today. I'm sorry we're meeting under these circumstances. I understand from Ms. MacDonald that there have been some disruptions in Rhett's home life recently."

David gritted his teeth as he followed the woman into her office. "Is Rhett okay? Where is he?"

"He'll be along shortly," she said, moving behind her desk and taking a seat. "He's with the school counselor at the moment. I wanted a chance to speak to you first."

The office was just as he remembered the principal's office at the three different elementary schools he'd attended as a kid. His mom had a habit of moving frequently, taking short-term leases on whatever cheap apartment she could get near her latest boyfriend.

"There's no need to sugarcoat it," he told her. "My sister is getting help for her problems. Rhett and I are coping as best we can. You can be sure nothing like today will repeat itself."

She nodded and opened a file on her desk. "I appreciate that, Mr. McCay."

"David."

"The other boy—the one he fought with—is also being disciplined. He's a second grader at the school."

David felt his temper flare. How had Rhett managed to get in a fight with a second grader?

"Why did it happen?" he demanded. "Rhett's only been at the school a month."

She shook her head, her already-thin lips pressing into a tight line. "From what the teachers and I were able to get out of them, the other boy made a disparaging remark about Rhett's mother."

Everything in David went still—only for a second. Then memories from his childhood, of his mother and the fights he got in defending her honor, crashed through him.

"I want to see Rhett," he said through clenched teeth. "And Erin. Where's Erin?"

The principal's shoulders stiffened. "Ms. MacDonald," she said, placing an emphasis on the name as if to remind him of his place, "is out of the building today."

"Out where?"

"At a district-wide training. Rhett's class had a substitute teacher. Mrs. Mills has been a sub at the school for quite a few years, longer than Ms. MacDonald has been here. She's quite capable."

"She's not Erin," he said. At the woman's frown, he added, "Ms. MacDonald. Rhett has a special bond with Ms. MacDonald."

The woman's frown deepened. "Be that as it may, she's his *teacher*, Mr. McCay. Nothing more. Whether it's with Ms. MacDonald or another member of our staff, your nephew is in good hands at our school."

There was a knock at the door, and it opened to reveal another woman who looked to be about ten years younger than the principal. She was petite, with bright red hair and a kind face. "Rhett would like to see his uncle."

Karen Henderson nodded and the door opened wider to reveal Rhett standing next to the redhead.

David stood, not sure where to start with the conflicting emotions simmering inside him.

To his surprise, Rhett launched himself forward and covered the space between them in a few hurried steps. The boy reached out, and David automatically lifted him into his arms. Rhett held tight, his small body shaking as he clung to David.

"It's okay," David whispered, even though it was a lie for both of them. "You're okay."

"We need to talk about the situation," the principal said softly, and Rhett's hold on David tightened even more. "He has to understand—"

"I'll make sure he understands," David said. "Right now, I'm taking him home."

"Mr. McCay—"

"A one-day suspension." David glanced over his shoulder as he moved toward the door. "He'll be back in class on Friday."

He didn't bother to wait for a response. Settling Rhett's weight on his hip, he walked out of the school and toward his truck, which was parked at the curb. "Let's get you buckled in," he said gently, and after a moment Rhett's arms went slack.

"Are you hurt?"

The boy gave a slight shake of his head.

David settled him in the booster seat Jenna had helped him install and strapped him in, the buckle clicking shut.

Rhett kept his head lowered, and David didn't say anything else. He needed to get away from the school and also wanted some time to rein in his emotions. Anger was part of it—some of it aimed at Rhett for getting into the fight in the first place. But most of it was leveled at Jenna, for putting all of them in this situation.

He flipped on the radio as he pulled onto the road, and a raucous country song about whiskey and women who broke a cowboy's heart filled the cab.

It fit his mood perfectly.

Not that his heart was broken. He wasn't fool enough to open himself up to that kind of trouble. But betrayal swept through him nonetheless. He'd so quickly come to rely on Erin—her sweetness and the kindness she'd shown toward Rhett. He'd wanted to believe…that it was more than a sense of duty. Of course she had other responsibilities, and caring for Rhett was part of her job.

He glanced in the rearview mirror and saw Rhett with his head still down, wringing his small hands together in his lap. His chest rose and fell in shallow breaths, as though he was also struggling to hold it together.

David's anger melted away. He still wanted answers from his nephew, and for the boy to understand that fighting at school wouldn't be tolerated. But the kid was hurting and probably felt totally alone in the world. David knew a lot about being alone.

He didn't want that for Rhett.

Downtown Crimson was bustling as he turned the truck onto Main Street. The weather was perfect for the first week of October, still warm with just a hint of cool to the air. High on the mountain, the aspen leaves were changing from green to gold. Soon the riot of color would extend down into town, and the weekends would be busy with fall tourists and a few hunters on their way to higher elevations.

He pulled the truck to a stop against the curb and punched in a quick text to Tracie. He was supposed to have a meeting this afternoon with the head of a regional bottling company to ensure that everything was on track for the Oktoberfest celebration. He was going to have to delegate, even though it killed him to relinquish that kind of control.

He'd catch up later, he told himself. Right now, the more important work was with his nephew.

"This isn't your parking spot." David undid the buckle of the booster seat, and Rhett climbed out of the truck to the sidewalk.

"I thought we'd stop at Life Is Sweet for a cookie on the way home," David told him, pointing to the sign above the bakery a few doors down.

As they walked, Rhett said quietly, "I got in trouble today."

"I know, buddy. That's why I was at the school."

"Do you still want to get me a cookie?" There was a hitch in his voice that made David's chest ache.

"I sure do." David ruffled his hair. "We're going to need to talk about what happened, but I think a snack will make both of us feel better."

"Yeah," Rhett agreed after a moment, and slipped his hand into David's.

The chimes above the door jingled as they walked in. Despite living in Crimson for almost three years, David had only been in the bakery a handful of times. He wasn't much for sweets and didn't drink coffee. Besides, there was something about the cozy feel of the space that made his skin itch with a need he couldn't quite identify.

The woman who owned Life Is Sweet, Katie Crawford, was always friendly and he'd met her husband, Noah, on several occasions.

But a bakery was different from a brewpub. There was

a sense of community that radiated from it, and David had never had a desire to be part of any community.

Yet somehow he knew it was the right thing for Rhett. Maybe for both of them.

He ordered two chocolate chip cookies and a milk for Rhett, then they took a seat in the small café area at a wrought iron table. There was a young couple at the table next to them, both with steaming coffee mugs in front of them and both tapping away on their phones. David had seen the same thing happen with people in the bar. They came in groups but instead of talking, they spent their time scrolling through social media or dating sites.

It made him feel old at twenty-nine that he wanted no part of online dating. He hadn't even thought about dating since his move to Crimson—at least until he'd met Erin.

With a sigh, he put her out of his mind as best he could and focused on Rhett.

The boy was nibbling the edge of his cookie and had a tiny smear of chocolate at the corner of his mouth.

"A second grader?" David asked casually, figuring the best way to deal with today was to get straight to the point.

Rhett shrugged. "He was only a little bigger than me."

"That's not really the point."

Rhett paused midbite and glanced up. "Mommy said you got in lots of trouble when you were a kid. She told me not to be like you."

David sighed. *Thanks, Jenna.*

"That was probably good advice, but here we are. Want to tell me about the fight?"

Rhett shook his head, his shaggy hair falling across one eye. Add a kid's haircut to the to-do list, David thought.

"We have to talk about it, unless you'd rather go back to the school and talk to Ms. Henderson and your teacher."

"Ms. MacDonald was gone today," Rhett said glumly. "I can't tell her."

Right. Erin hadn't been there to run interference. David knew he had no right to be angry but couldn't seem to stop the feeling of betrayal that washed through him. Erin made him believe he wasn't alone in caring for Rhett. That he had things under control. It was somehow easier to direct his frustration toward her than to any of the other things in his life that seemed beyond his control. "Then tell me."

"He called Mommy a bad word," the boy said, breaking the remainder of his cookie in half. "Real bad."

"What word?"

Rhett scrunched up his nose, as if he'd smelled something rotten. Then he climbed off the chair and moved to David's side. He stood on tiptoe and when David bent toward him, whispered the word *slut* in his ear.

Blood roared in David's head as he stared down at his *five-year-old* nephew. "Do you know what that word means?"

"Isaac said Mommy's boyfriend is his daddy, and she stole him from Isaac's mommy."

David didn't know much about the man his sister had been dating for the past few months. She'd told him he had a good job and they were just having fun together. Either she didn't know or had forgotten to mention that he also had another family. One that was targeting Rhett.

"What's Isaac's last name?"

"I don't know," Rhett answered, climbing back into his seat. "He came up to me when I was on the monkey bars and pushed me and said mean things about Mommy." He gripped the milk bottle tightly. "I got really mad. I didn't mean to get into a fight, Uncle David. Then the teacher came and yelled at me and he cried and she yelled more."

He shook his head. "Ms. MacDonald never yells no matter how mad we make her."

"Ms. MacDonald won't always be there for you, Rhett." David didn't mean for his words to come out harshly, but the boy's bottom lip quivered.

"He shouldn't have said what he did about your mom." David gentled his voice and leaned forward. "Did you explain it to your teacher and the principal?"

Rhett shook his head, and by the set of his jaw David understood why. Rhett was young but still old enough to understand there could be some truth in the other boy's accusations. Not the name-calling. That was inexcusable. But Jenna had a history of making poor choices in men.

Just like David's mother. He'd spent too much of his childhood trying to protect his mom without even realizing he was doing it. Making excuses for why she missed parent-teacher conferences, pretending she was picking him up around the block when in reality he walked home, forging signatures on forms and permission slips every year.

He'd tried to protect Jenna, but in the end he'd failed her.

He wouldn't fail Rhett.

"I'm going to make sure it doesn't happen again," he promised the boy. "But if anyone gives you trouble, talk to a teacher instead of fighting. Talk to me. I'm here to help you, Rhett. It's my job."

"I thought your job was making beer."

David smiled, but the muscles of his face felt stiff. "I do that, too, but nothing is more important to me than you. Nothing."

Chapter Six

Erin walked into Elevation later that night, her eyes scanning the bar for David.

Instead, the gorgeous bartender who'd given her the once-over last Sunday met her gaze.

"He's got the night off," she said as Erin approached.

"I went upstairs and rang the bell," Erin admitted, "but he didn't answer."

"Maybe he doesn't want to talk," the woman said and turned her back on Erin to grab two pint glasses from underneath the shelf behind her. "To you," she added over her shoulder.

Erin felt color rush to her cheeks. She was well aware that David didn't want to talk to her. She'd been trying to get in touch with him since she stopped at the school after her district meeting and Karen Henderson told her what had happened with Rhett on the playground.

The principal had made it quite clear that Erin should

keep her relationship with both Rhett and David professional and not allow herself to become involved in their personal lives.

Smart advice, but Erin's heart was already involved. It killed her to think of the boy in trouble and afraid when she hadn't been there to smooth things over for him.

She stepped up to the bar and waited for the bartender to serve the two beers to the men sitting next to where Erin stood.

"Why don't you pull up a seat and talk to us, darlin'," one of the men, a scruffy-looking guy in a Broncos jersey, said.

Erin swallowed. The only time she'd come to a bar before tonight had been with a group of girlfriends, and no one had paid much attention to her. "Thank you for the offer, but I don't think so." She leaned toward the bar and caught the petite blonde's eye. "I need to see David," she whispered.

"He's no fun anymore," the second man said. "Doesn't live up to his baseball reputation at all."

"Shut up, Donnie," the bartender snapped.

"You know it's true, Tracie," the man shot back. "If half the stories about Dave are true, he got more action than a fox in a chicken coop back in the day."

"Now all he does is work." The first man darted a look at Erin. "No matter how many hot chicks throw themselves at him. We need some excitement around here."

Tracie rolled her eyes, and Erin wasn't sure whether it was in response to the man's complaint about David or the implication that Erin was a "hot chick."

"You'd better not let your wives hear you talking like that," Tracie said.

"Why do you think we want Davey to get some action?"

Donnie took a long pull on his beer. "I don't want trouble at home. But I'm not dead, just married."

The bartender huffed out a laugh and turned away without bothering to acknowledge Erin again.

Erin should give up. David didn't want her, and she could talk to Rhett when he returned to school after the suspension.

Somehow she couldn't force herself to walk away. That was what she'd ordinarily do, but she was done being ordinary.

She stepped behind the bar and followed Tracie down the length of it, tapping the tiny woman on the shoulder when she got close.

"Seriously?" the woman asked as she whirled around. "You can't be back here."

"I need to see him."

"He's used to handling things on his own." Tracie crossed her arms over her chest and glared at Erin. "It's easier that way. No one gets hurt."

Erin was pretty sure the gorgeous bartender wasn't only talking about David. "He doesn't have to do this alone." She made her voice purposefully gentle. "I'm not going to hurt him. I promise."

Tracie studied her for a few seconds, then reached in her pocket and pulled out a set of keys. "The silver one unlocks the office and the staircase inside that leads up to the loft. You'd better make this right. David and Rhett both need that."

Erin had no idea how to make anything right at the moment, but she nodded and took the key ring. "Thank you."

"You're different than you look," Tracie said. "Stronger."

A bit of happiness trickled through Erin at the reluctant compliment. "You're not quite as scary."

Tracie laughed softly. "Don't tell anyone."

Erin closed her hand around the keys and headed through the brewpub. She unlocked the office door and flipped on the light, taking a moment to gather her courage before moving to the wood panel door on the far side. Away from the noise of the bar, every sound seemed amplified and the *click* of the lock as she turned the key reverberated in her ears.

She let herself into the narrow staircase and locked the door behind her, as she had in the office, as well. Before she made it halfway up the stairs, the door at the top opened.

David stared down at her, his expression unreadable with his face concealed by shadows.

"Do you pick locks in your spare time?" he asked.

"Tracie gave me the key," she said, proud that her voice didn't shake. She forced herself to keep moving toward him, even though her knees were practically knocking. As silly as it sounded, it felt like she was going into battle. "You wouldn't return my calls and texts or answer when I knocked."

"Rhett was in the bath."

"I wanted to check on him." She was on the step below him now, gazing up into the hard planes of his face.

"You'll see him when he goes back to school," he said tightly. "Unless there's another sub in his class."

"That's not fair. What happened today isn't my fault."

For a moment she thought he might slam the door in her face, and she wondered what had possessed her to come here in the first place. Maybe her fantasy life had truly taken over and she'd imagined the connection between them. Maybe she was so desperate to be needed by someone that she'd read more into the situation than was really there.

Then he reached out and hauled her against him. His arms wrapped tight around her, and he rested his cheek on the top of her head. She could feel the tension coiled in him, electric and barely contained. And she knew she hadn't imagined any of it. This man needed her, and that understanding made her heart sing.

"You're right. I'm angry at Jenna for putting all of us in this position. I don't mean to take it out on you. I'm sorry."

"Me, too," she answered, speaking into the soft fabric of his shirt. She turned her head so she could feel the warm skin of his throat against the tip of her nose.

He drew back, smoothed his thumbs over her cheeks.

"No. I'm a jerk, Erin. You're right. None of this is your fault. It's easier to be angry at the school and you than to admit how badly Jenna has screwed things up. To admit that I stood by and let her."

"You didn't—"

"I should have known more about her new guy. Should have realized he was bad news and protected her and Rhett. Hell, the whole reason I moved to Colorado was to take care of things, and I let myself believe that just my mere presence here would make everything fine. I was a fool."

"You're here and you're trying. Give yourself a break."

He shook his head. "I can't. The stakes are too high."

She wanted to wipe the pain from his eyes, to take some of that burden and carry it for him. He'd uprooted his life to take care of his sister and nephew. He moved halfway across the country and had become a successful business owner and part of this town. There had never even been a question that he would step in for Rhett and get Jenna the help she needed. David was a good man, but he refused to see that in himself. Erin wished she could find a way to show him.

"I'd like to talk to Rhett." She forced herself to step out of David's embrace. It was too easy to forget that their relationship wasn't actually a relationship. He needed her help with his nephew, and she'd made the commitment to give it.

His attention wasn't about her—not really. She'd had a crush on him for far too long and he hadn't even known she existed. If it wasn't for the fact that she'd inserted herself into his life, he'd still be nothing more than her fantasy man and she'd be…nothing to him.

"We were watching a few minutes of television," he said, then glanced at his watch. "It's almost bedtime." He reached around her to shut the door to the staircase, then led her down the hall toward the main section of the apartment. They passed through the kitchen, which looked like a cozier version of the pub decor. The cabinets were dark wood with dark gray concrete countertops. Four chairs were tucked against the long island, exact copies of the bar stools downstairs.

"Dinner?" she asked, pointing to a half loaf of bread and jar of peanut butter sitting on the cluttered countertop.

David shrugged. "I tried to make grilled cheese sandwiches but burned the hell out of them. PB&J was the best I could do."

"Grilled cheese can be complicated," she said gently, earning a small laugh from David.

"It's better when I bring up food from downstairs," he admitted.

The far end of the kitchen opened to a family room, with wide-plank wood floors and oversize furniture. She could see *The Lego Movie* playing on the flat-screen TV that hung on one wall, and Rhett glanced up as they approached, then did a double take when he saw her.

"I got aspended," he announced, his voice solemn. "I can't come to school tomorrow."

"I know," she said, lowering herself to the cushion next to him. "That's why I stopped by tonight. I wanted to tell you that I'm sorry I wasn't at school today to help you on the playground."

"Uncle David said I can't hit people," Rhett told her, "even when they're mean."

"That's good advice." She reached out and gently smoothed away the hair that was falling across Rhett's eyes. "You can always talk to another teacher or Ms. Henderson if I'm not there."

"I hate Isaac." Rhett held his hands tight in his lap. "He called Mommy a bad word. It's not her fault his daddy wants to be her boyfriend. Lots of people want to be her boyfriend."

Erin heard a sound from David that sounded like a growl but focused her attention on the boy. "You love your mommy very much," she told him. "She's lucky to have you and I bet she's working hard to feel better and misses you so much."

"I miss her," Rhett whispered.

"I know you won't be at school tomorrow, but I hope your uncle will bring you to the community center in the afternoon. You can draw a picture for your mommy that shows how much you love her to give to her when she comes home."

Rhett looked from Erin to David. "Can I go, Uncle David?"

"Sure, buddy," came the rumbly response. "As long as you promise no more fights."

The boy nodded, then yawned. "I promise," he said sleepily.

"Time for bed," David announced.

"Can Ms. MacDonald read me a story?" Rhett asked, scooting off the couch.

David cleared his throat and Erin glanced back at him. He lifted one brow, silently leaving the decision up to her. Her life before last week had been so simple and straight-forward. And boring.

"I'd love to," she told Rhett, and her heart melted a lit-tle when he grabbed her hand to lead her out of the fam-ily room.

She loved the hugs and hand-holding from her students, but there were always some who remained physically dis-tant and she tried to respect that, too. Rhett had been one of those this year, which made the fact that he was reach-ing out to her mean so much more.

Glancing over her shoulder, she saw David watching them with an unreadable expression. Maybe she'd over-stayed her welcome, but it felt right to be part of their lives.

"Are you okay if I check in downstairs for a minute?" he asked. "I'll be back up to tuck him in."

"Take your time." She handed him Tracie's keys and turned back to Rhett.

The boy led her down the hall to a small bedroom with a bathroom connected to it. It was clearly a guest room, with just a bed and nondescript chest of drawers against one wall. Rhett's stuffed blue dog sat on top of the plain beige comforter and there was a basket filled with ran-dom toys shoved in the corner.

Rhett grabbed the same pair of football-themed pa-jamas he'd been wearing the night of his mother's party from a pile of clothes stuffed into a laundry basket and spilling over onto the floor. "I need to get my pj's on and brush my teeth before we read."

"Is it okay if I fold some of your laundry while you do that?" she asked.

"I guess. Uncle David washes my clothes but says there's no point in putting anything away when I'm just going to wear them again."

Erin tried to keep her smile from showing. That was exactly something a single man would say. "Is that what you did with your mommy?"

Rhett shook his head. "Mommy and me folded laundry after dinner. I did the socks."

"Then I'll save the socks for you," Erin said.

"I'm good at them," Rhett confirmed, and disappeared into the bathroom.

She heard the sound of water running and then Rhett brushing his teeth. She folded the clothes and put them away in drawers, hoping that small thing would help him feel more settled.

It made her feel like she was contributing something, making up for how she hadn't been there for him earlier. Rationally she knew it wasn't her fault. Her work on the district planning committee had taken her out of the building for a day of training. Teachers got subs all the time for a variety of reasons. But it didn't change the fact that the boy had needed her, and she'd failed him.

She couldn't let it happen again.

After a few minutes, Rhett returned to the bedroom.

"Dirty clothes in the laundry hamper," she said, pointing to a wicker basket next to the dresser.

"You sound like Mommy," he told her as he went back to retrieve his discarded clothes. But he was smiling as he climbed on the bed next to her. The first smile she'd seen from him tonight.

He rolled the socks into balls, then handed her a Magic Tree House book from the nightstand. She made sure he was snuggled in tight, then started to read about ninjas and two time-traveling kids.

She finished a chapter, then glanced down at Rhett to see his eyes had drifted shut, Ruffie tucked under his arm. She stood slowly and smoothed the covers over both the boy and the stuffed dog. Erin had so much in her life—a great job, good friends, a mom who loved her. But there was nothing she could truly call her own, and spending time with Rhett made it clear how much she wanted that.

The relentless pounding in her chest sounded strangely like her ovaries stomping their tiny reproductive feet, as if to say, "it's about time you remembered we were withering away here." Well, not exactly withering. She had plenty of time to settle down. The scary truth was that she was already settled but seemed destined to be stuck alone.

She wanted to change her life, but maybe it had been a mistake to focus on her professional life when her personal world was so sorely lacking any excitement. David McCay would be an adventure—the kind that could ruin her for any other man. It might just be worth the risk. She shook her head and commanded her ovaries to shut down the party. This was the kind of thinking that had led to her outrageous request, and she didn't need to revisit that moment.

After returning the book to the nightstand, she turned to find David watching her from the doorway. Color rushed to her cheeks as if he could read her thoughts.

He stepped back just enough to let her out, then moved forward to place a gentle kiss on Rhett's forehead and tuck the sheets around him.

When Rhett was settled, David pulled the door shut and motioned her down the hall. "Did I hear you tell your ovaries to shut up?" he asked when they reached the kitchen.

She clasped a hand over her mouth to stifle a hysterical giggle. "Of course not," she said in a rush of air. "That would be crazy. Do I seem crazy to you?"

"At this point," he said after studying her for several moments, "you seem like a gift from heaven."

Oh. Well, that was unexpected. And lovely.

"I'm doing my job," she answered automatically.

"How does finagling the key to my apartment from Tracie fall under a teacher's job description?"

"I wanted to check on Rhett."

He moved closer, crowding her a little. But she didn't step back even though that was her inclination. She stood her ground. "That's not all you want," he whispered.

There weren't enough words in the English language to cover all the things she wanted from David. From life. From this moment.

"Ask me again," he told her, threading his fingers through her hair. The desire she saw in his blue eyes mesmerized her. A longing that matched her own, making her need grow that much more intense. "Ask me to have an affair with you."

"Kiss me," she said instead. Those two words were the only ones she could force her mouth to form at the moment.

He lowered his mouth to hers, claiming her lips with a force she felt all the way to her toes. How could the way he touched her feel both infinitely gentle and demanding at the same time? She wound her arms around his neck and gave herself over to the sensation. It was too much and not enough, and she whispered the one word that pounded through her whole body. "More."

Chapter Seven

It was like the Fourth of July inside David's brain. He'd kissed plenty of women—taken some of them to his bed—girlfriends and baseball groupies who made it their mission to snag a professional athlete. None of them had affected him the way Erin did.

He wanted to blame it on his basically celibate lifestyle since settling in Crimson, but he knew it was more than that. It was the woman in his arms.

A shiver passed through her when he sucked her sensitive earlobe into his mouth. He lifted her onto the edge of the counter and positioned himself against the sweet V of her body, even as he did his best to keep his raging lust under control.

She deserved more than he could ever offer her in life, but the least he could do was refrain from mauling her like some sort of randy teenager. He wanted to savor each moment they spent together, to get down on his knees and worship every inch of her—to beg her to stay with him.

His hands trembled as he undid the buttons of her crisp linen blouse, revealing a pale blue bra covering the most beautiful breasts he'd ever seen. His mouth went dry and all he could do was stare at the creamy skin, flushed with pink.

He traced one finger over the edge of the fabric, earning a whispered moan from Erin.

"Amazing," he murmured, and she shook her head.

"You don't have to say that. My body is average at best." He'd heard plenty of women disparage themselves, mostly fishing for more compliments, but Erin made the statement like it was a well-known fact.

"Nothing about you is average."

She flashed a self-deprecating smile. "Everything about me is average."

"No." He placed a finger to her lips when she would have argued. "You have a gorgeous face and the most kissable skin." He trailed his mouth down the long column of her throat, and it almost drove him over the edge when she dropped back onto her elbows, pressing her breasts high into the air.

"The best part is that the way you look is only part of what makes you beautiful. When we're together, I feel things I didn't know were a possibility for a guy like me." He swirled his tongue around the tip of her breast through the fabric of her bra.

She moaned and he gathered her close, kissing her with all of his pent-up desire, letting her feel exactly how much he wanted her. She tugged on his T-shirt and he pulled it over his head and let it drop to the floor. Her hands smoothed up his chest, making his breath catch. His whole body pounded with need.

He wanted to strip off her clothes and feast on her.

He wanted to lose himself in the moment and take her, make her his.

No.

A woman like Erin would never be his. Reality came crashing down around him, and he jerked back.

She stared at him, her gaze hazy with lust. Her breasts rose and fell as she struggled to make her breathing normal again. She sat on the edge of his counter, soft and sexy and ready for him. Hell, she had no idea how sexy she was.

"I'm sorry," he said, and wanted to punch his own face as her gaze clouded with doubt and then embarrassment.

She scrambled off the counter and turned away, quickly buttoning up her blouse. "Do I thank you now?" she asked quietly, the ice in her tone cutting across his skin. "Are we even? I came to see Rhett and you gave me a little taste—" she waved her hand toward the counter "—of that. I should be grateful, right?"

"Don't say that." He spun her around to face him. "Don't make this into something it isn't."

"I have a pretty good idea of exactly what this is and isn't," she said, her tone miserable.

"You have no idea." He ran a hand through his hair, trying to figure out how kissing this woman had become so complicated. Sex had always been simple. Straightforward. Meaningless. The fact that he wanted it to be so much more with Erin scared the hell out of him.

But the last thing he wanted was for her to believe he didn't want her.

"You mean something," he said. "To Rhett." He cleared his throat. "To me."

She bit down on her lip and he had to stifle a groan.

"I'm his teacher," she said without emotion. "I'm helping you manage these weeks without your sister."

"It's more than that," he said. "I like you, Erin."

"Enough to kiss me," she said through clenched teeth, "but not enough for sex."

"That isn't what this is about. You're not the kind of woman I want to sleep with—"

"I get it," she said, blinking rapidly.

Damn. He hoped like hell she wasn't going to cry. He was making a total mess of everything.

"We're obviously done here." She offered him a stiff little wave. "I assume it's okay if I let myself out the front door?"

He wrapped his fingers around her wrist and pulled her close. "I'm trying to give you a compliment. You deserve more than a quick roll in the sheets after an exhausting day. You're the kind of woman who men take on dates and home to meet their parents. I told you, you're apple pie and white picket fences. I'm late nights wrangling drunk tourists at a bar."

She tugged her wrist out of his grasp. "You're a baseball player," she said, spitting out the words like an accusation.

"Not anymore."

That earned him an eye roll. "You were a famous pitcher for a major-league team. Talk about the American ideal. It's our national pastime."

"I'm not good for you."

She threw up her hands. "Why does everyone think they know what I want more clearly than I do? My mom thinks my expectations of life are too high. My ex thinks I can't be adventurous in the bedroom because I don't have the body of a stripper. You want me up on some holier-than-thou pedestal."

"Your body is perfect," he said, wishing he could punch whatever idiot boyfriend had made her believe otherwise.

"Yeah," she said on a derisive laugh. "Really hard for you to resist. But someone in this town is going to want me." Her voice cracked a tiny bit and she sucked in a breath. "Even for one night. Hey, we're standing above a bar. I bet I can find a guy downstairs willing to be with me."

She turned on her heel and stalked toward the door to his loft. "Bring Rhett to the community center tomorrow at four," she called over her shoulder.

As angry as she was with David, she was still looking after Rhett. Taking care of both of them, really. And David was watching her walk away to find another man.

How big of an idiot could he be?

He caught up to her just as she reached for the door handle.

"Go on a date with me," he said, pressing his hand to the door to keep it shut.

She stilled, but it took her a minute to lift her gaze to his. "What?"

"We can go to dinner or on a hike or whatever you want."

Her eyes narrowed. "Why are you asking me out? Is this more payback for helping with Rhett? I care about him. You don't have to—"

He brushed his lips across hers. "Do you always argue when a man asks you on a date?" he asked against her mouth, then leaned in to press his forehead to hers, the tips of their noses touching.

She inhaled, her warm breath tickling his skin. "I'm not your type," she said.

"No," he countered. "I'm not *your* type. You deserve way better than me. But I'm asking anyway. Go out with me."

She didn't answer for so long he thought she might decline the invitation. He didn't blame her. He knew what he had to offer someone like her. A whole lot of drama and baggage. It would have been smarter to have just taken what she offered earlier. Maybe he could have gotten her out of his system.

But he wanted more.

"Okay," she said when he started to pull back.

He grinned, feeling like he'd just purchased a winning lottery ticket. "I'll call you," he said.

"Really?" She laughed softly. "We could just grab dinner after you pick up Rhett tomorrow night."

"Nope. I'm going to call you, and we'll make a plan and it will be like…"

"A date?"

"Like we're courting," he answered, the sound and connotation of the old-fashioned word appealing to him. Thanks to the baseball groupies who had hung around the fields since high school, David had never had to try hard with women. They fell into his lap—sometimes literally.

The idea of actually making an effort was new and strangely exciting. The thought of earning his place at Erin's side made nerves flutter through his chest.

"Courting," she repeated. "Are you sure?"

"Absolutely," he said, and kissed her again.

Then he opened the door. "I'll talk to you soon."

She looked slightly puzzled, which he found adorable. He wanted to keep her guessing.

She'd just started down the stairs when he called her name.

"Um…" He ran a hand through his hair, uncharacteristically anxious. "I hope this means you aren't heading downstairs to look for a guy. I know you don't owe me anything but—"

"I'm going home. Good night, David."

He blew out a breath as he closed the door. What the hell was he so nervous about? And possessive? He'd never cared before about being exclusive with the women he dated.

But it made him ridiculously happy to consider the possibility of Erin becoming his. He rubbed his shoulder as he moved through the apartment, turning off lights. It was still early compared to his normal hours, but David was tired as hell. All he wanted was to drop into his bed and dream of Erin.

Rhett tugged on Erin's arm as she handed Mari Clayton, the program director for the Aspen Foundation, her grant paperwork the following afternoon. It was just after six, and the other kids who'd come for tutoring and after-school activities had been picked up already. David was running a few minutes late so Rhett had been playing with Lego blocks while Erin began the meeting with the woman she hoped would fund Crimson Kidzone so it could be expanded. Erin needed the money to hire a part-time staff person.

There was so much she wanted to do for kids in the Crimson community now that she'd started, but all of it took money. Mari seemed receptive to her ideas, so Erin had high hopes that the grant request she was submitting would be approved.

"Excuse me for a moment," she said to Mari, and turned to Rhett. "What do you need, Rhett?"

"Isaac is here." The boy gave her a pained look. "And Mommy's boyfriend."

She turned to where he was pointing. Another boy with dark hair and eyes stood in the doorway to the community center's makeshift classroom.

She recognized Isaac Martin, the boy Rhett had fought with at school, although his family had moved to Crimson last year so she'd never had him in class.

He wore baggy sweatpants and a Denver Broncos jersey. Next to him stood a tall, lean man close to Erin's age whom she recognized as Joel Martin, Jenna McCay's boyfriend and Isaac's father. His black hair was slicked back from his face and, although his features were classically handsome, his eyes had a hard edge to them.

He met her gaze and gave her a quick once-over. Goose bumps shivered across her skin, and not the kind she got when David looked at her. This man's stare made her feel uncomfortable and strangely nervous. She saw his gaze switch to Mari for a second before dismissing her just as quickly as he had Erin.

"The lady at the desk said this is where I sign my kid up for day care," the man said, arms crossed over his chest.

Isaac glared at Rhett, who moved behind Erin's legs, holding tight to the denim of the dark-washed jeans she wore.

"I'd be happy to get you an enrollment form," she answered. "Although it's not exactly day care." She threw Mari an apologetic glance. "I offer an after-school enrichment program three days a week and—"

"Whatever," the man said. "Can I leave him now? His mom don't get off work until seven and I have things to do. His sisters are with their dad tonight and he don't want to stay by himself."

Erin had spoken to Melody after the fight about Isaac's family situation. According to her friend, the boy had two older stepsisters but his mother was single and struggling to keep her household together.

"Isaac is welcome to be part of the program," she said, keeping her voice steady, "but it only goes until six and he can't start until the paperwork is completed."

"*He's* still here." The man pointed at Rhett. "Isaac and him can play."

Rhett dug his fingers into her legs, and she wanted to wrap him in her arms. Isaac glared at them both. His father shifted to get a better look at Rhett, then did a double take.

"That's Jenna's kid," he muttered, then swatted Isaac on the back of the head. "He's the one that hit you, right?"

"Mr. Martin, what happened between the boys is a matter for the school to deal with. Rhett is going to be picked up in a few minutes, and I can get you an enrollment form but—"

"How's your mama doing, boy? It was a shame the crap got out of hand that night. I'm looking forward to her getting back so—"

Suddenly Joel jerked back as David spun him around and slammed him against the wall, pressing his forearm to the other man's throat. "You won't see my sister again. You won't look at her. You won't acknowledge her existence. Are we clear?"

Mari Clayton gasped and Erin peeled Rhett's hands off her legs and hurried forward. What kind of example were these two grown men showing boys who had just been disciplined for fighting? Not to mention the fact that the last thing Erin needed was a scene in the middle of her meeting with a potential donor.

Joel coughed and fought, but David had at least thirty pounds on him and showed no sign of backing down.

"Get the hell off me," Joel bit out, his voice hoarse. "Jenna can make her own damn decisions."

"Tell me you're going to leave my sister alone."

Erin didn't recognize this version of David. Gone was the laid-back bar owner or the caring—if sometimes clueless—uncle. Anger and violence radiated from him, making him seem like the man he'd warned her about.

Isaac had moved back into the hall, his small body shrinking against the door frame.

"David." She placed a hand on his arm. "Stop. This isn't the place. You're scaring the boys."

"Listen to the lady," Joel said, but as soon as David loosened his grip, the other man struck out, his fist connecting with David's jaw.

Erin heard a scream and realized it came from her throat. David shoved Joel again, and the tall man stumbled into the wall.

"Enough," she shouted.

Both men stilled at her tone. She might be shaking with nerves, but she had enough experience as a teacher to take command of the situation.

"The community center," she said slowly, as if settling a dispute over a favorite crayon, "is not the place for you two to have this…" She searched for the right word and settled on "conversation. You both have boys watching your every move."

David pressed a hand to his jaw and glanced over his shoulder to where Rhett was staring, wide-eyed, at the scene playing out in front of him.

"Dude grabbed me," Joel muttered. "I got to defend myself."

"Mr. Martin," she said firmly, "you can request a Kidzone enrollment form at the community center's front desk." She turned to Isaac and gentled her voice. "We'd love to have you in the program, but there is no fighting or name-calling here. It's a safe place for everyone. Do you understand?"

The boy's brows lowered but he nodded. His father muttered under his breath a string of expletives so explicit it made her breath catch in her throat. David moved forward again with a growl, and she stepped between the two men.

"It would be a good idea for you to leave now," she told Joel. "Isaac, I hope to see you next week."

Joel's upper lip curled into an ugly sneer as he narrowed his gaze on David. "A real man don't let no woman push him around. Your sister knows what it's like to be with a baller." His mean brown eyes shifted to Erin. "Maybe Ms. Teacher wants something more in her life, too. What you say, baby?"

David snarled and tried pushing around Erin. "I'm going to—"

"No." She took a step to the side so she was still blocking him. "Mr. Martin, you need to go."

With a sickeningly sweet smile and a salute, the man turned away. "Come on, Isaac. Let's blow this place."

Erin stood watching them walk down the hall for several moments, willing her breathing back to a normal pace.

"Erin." David's voice was gentle, but when he went to place a hand on her shoulder, she swatted away his touch.

"I'll deal with you in a minute," she said through teeth clenched tightly so no one would notice how much they were chattering. "Take care of Rhett. I have a meeting to finish."

Nervous laughter sounded from behind her. "I think we're finished here for tonight."

Mari Clayton had gathered her bag and purse and was staring at Erin and David, her cheeks flushed and a hand pressed flat to her chest.

"Uncle David," Rhett called. "You got in a fight just like me."

She heard David sigh as he moved toward his nephew. "I'm sorry about that," he said to Mari. "There was some history there but this wasn't the time or place for us to play it out."

The woman swallowed and nodded. "I understand."

He turned back to Erin, but she gave him a quelling glare, then focused her attention on Mari. "You can't possibly understand."

"You're right. This felt more like *Fight Club* than an after-school program for kids. I applaud what you're trying to do, Erin, and it's clear the community needs a safe place for kids to go. Still, I'm not sure your program and the Aspen Foundation are a good fit."

Tears stung the back of Erin's eyes. It was adrenaline, she knew, but this was not how the meeting with Mari was supposed to end. "I apologize for the scene. But I hope you'll change your mind. I think this demonstrates just how important a community outreach program that brings kids together is for Crimson."

"But can you keep the children safe?"

There was a slight hint of accusation in Mari's tone; Erin's doubts crashed around her like a thousand ocean waves. Her mother's refrain of "be happy with good enough" rang through her mind. Kidzone had been in place one week and already there was a question about whether she could manage it.

"I firmly believe I can," she lied to her potential donor. She wanted to make a safe place for kids to come after school, but Erin knew better than most that wanting something and getting it weren't always the same thing.

"Let's touch base in a few weeks," Mari said noncommittally. "The decisions about our fall funding cycle will be made by the end of October. It may be better to wait until your program is more established."

Biting down on the inside of her cheek to keep from crying, Erin nodded. A moment after Mari walked away, Olivia appeared in the doorway. "Is everything all right? Rita said a guy just stormed by the front desk, dragging a boy along with him."

"A potential client," Erin said, shaking her head.

"Isaac's daddy is mean," Rhett whispered.

"No way are you going to let that kid in here."

She turned from Olivia to see David staring at her, hands on hips, his features hard as granite.

Olivia stepped forward. "Rhett, I was about to box up the cupcakes someone brought in today. Would you help me, and you can take a couple home for you and your uncle?"

"It's fine, buddy," David said when the boy looked up at him. "Ms. MacDonald and I will work things out in here."

Rhett moved toward Olivia.

"I'm going to ask Mommy," he told Erin as he passed, "not to be his girlfriend anymore when she gets back."

"I'm sorry he scared you," she said, reaching out to ruffle his hair. "You know you're always safe with me."

He nodded. "Can I bring a cupcake for Ms. MacDonald, too?" he asked Olivia.

"You bet," she answered and took his hand to lead him away.

As soon as the boy was gone, all of the adrenaline that had kept Erin together through that ugly scene drained from her body. She dropped her head into her hands and drew in a deep breath.

"Erin."

She glanced up to see David taking a step closer. "Don't," she whispered, and automatically moved back. "You don't get to tell me how to run this program. You certainly don't get to make a scene in front of the foundation representative I was hoping would give me the money to hire additional staff and really make this thing work."

"I didn't realize who she was," he said, rubbing a hand over the shadow of stubble across his jaw.

She hated that even now, as angry as she was with

him, the scratchy sound still made her tingle all the way to her toes.

"It doesn't matter," she said, crossing her arms over her chest. "You were out of line."

His head snapped back as if she'd struck him. "You heard what he was saying about Jenna. The things he insinuated toward you. I'm not going to stand by and let a creep like that get away with—"

"You're Rhett's guardian now, David. His role model. How can you expect him to work out his problems without violence when you set that kind of example?" She knew she was being harsh, but her emotions wouldn't let her back down. "Joel Martin is awful but there are better ways to deal with him."

"What ways?" he countered. "Watching the guy get away with whatever he wants? Letting his kid bully my nephew and disrespect you and my sister?"

"I don't need you to protect me."

He barked out a laugh. "It sounds like you don't need me at all."

She bit down on her lip, unsure of how to respond. She didn't want to need him but couldn't resist the current of awareness pulsing between them, despite their differences and her anger.

"Thank you for keeping Rhett today," he said quietly, smoothing a finger over the furrow she knew formed between her brows when she was upset. "I'm sorry I screwed things up with your meeting. I wasn't joking when I told you I was bad news, Erin. This afternoon proves my point."

"David."

He dropped his finger to her lip. "You've gone out of your way to help me, and I'm grateful. What happened here was a crappy way to show it."

Before she could respond, he dropped his hand and walked out of the room, presumably to collect Rhett from Olivia.

Erin wanted to rush after him, to launch herself at his big frame and hold on tight. David didn't belong to her, but her chest ached at the thought of losing him. She'd managed to carve out a decent life for herself, and she should be satisfied with that. It was easier and a lot less pain in the long run.

Chapter Eight

When the doorbell rang that night, David's heart leaped. He rubbed at his chest as he went to answer it, hope rising like a bird on a current of air that Erin was paying him a visit.

He hated himself for hurting her, then walking away. He'd sat on the couch since putting Rhett to bed with his phone in his hand, typing out a half dozen texts but deleting each one.

She'd seen his true colors, although it might be better that it happened now instead of down the road. If he'd actually had the opportunity to truly claim her as his own, he wasn't sure he'd ever be able to let her go.

But hope was a painfully resilient emotion, unwilling to let go of even the briefest glimpse of happiness. If Erin had come to him, maybe he still had a chance. With a deep breath, he opened the door.

"Hello, David. It's been a while."

Without his hand gripping the door handle, David would have stumbled back a step. His mouth went dry and it felt like someone had dropped a lead balloon on his chest. "Mom."

"Are you going to invite me in?" Angela McCay peered around him into the apartment. "Kind of a fancy place you've set yourself up in, even if you're living over a bar."

"Mom, why are you here?"

She smoothed a hand over her hair and flashed him a sad smile. "Isn't it obvious? I'm making things right."

He hadn't seen his mother in over five years, but she looked the same as ever. It was as if Angela drank from the fountain of youth and never aged. Her blond hair was shorter than he remembered, a simple cut that fell to just above her shoulders. Maybe there were a few thin lines etched into the skin around her vivid blue eyes.

But she remained as beautiful as she'd been when he was a boy. At Rhett's age, David would sit on one of the chairs in the kitchen and watch her move about the room—on the rare occasions when she cooked a real dinner—and think how lucky he was to have Angela as his mother. It took him a while to learn that a person's outward beauty wasn't always an accurate measure of who they were on the inside.

Too much had happened in their small family, terrible things and small mistreatments that his mother had either been responsible for or turned a blind eye to as they unfolded. He wished he could recapture some of his unconditional love from childhood, but he was an adult and had spent too long nursing old wounds to let them go so easily.

Yet she was still his mother, so he stepped back to let her into his apartment and, he supposed, his life.

"Did Jenna call you?"

"Yes, and it's about time," his mom answered as she

moved past him. "My bags are in the hall. Be a good boy and bring them in for me."

"Bags?" he asked even as he pulled in the two suitcases and closed the door. "How long do you plan to be here?"

She turned to him. "As long as it takes. Your sister wants me here. She thinks you need help."

"I'm not the one in rehab," he muttered.

"That might have been a bit of overkill," she said, arching one brow. "Jenna could have recovered on her own."

"We've tried that before. It didn't take, and Rhett is old enough now to be affected. She needs to get healthy, and it has to stick this time."

She studied him for a moment, then sighed. "You always were her knight in shining armor." She stepped closer and raised a hand to his cheek. "You took care of both of us."

The scent of her shampoo, honey and almond, drifted up to him, taking him back to sharing a bathroom in their tiny apartment growing up. He'd taken countless luke-warm showers as a kid after his mom and sister used up their limited supply of hot water, but he'd always loved the way the bathroom smelled after his mother got ready.

"I did a sucky job at it," he said, letting his eyes drift closed and losing himself in the familiar touch and scent.

She patted his cheek. "You tried, and that's what counts."

If someone had asked, David would have claimed he didn't need anything from his mother. Not her help, not her approval and certainly not her blessing. Yet those words of absolution seemed to loosen the chains that were locked tight around his heart. They didn't eliminate his guilt and regret, but somehow they made him feel better.

"You tried, too," he told her, his way of offering an olive branch after so many years of animosity between them.

"We both know I didn't," she said quietly. "I was a hot mess, and you and your sister got pulled into it. I thought baseball was your ticket out until the accident…"

"It wasn't an accident." He took a step away and crossed his arms over his chest. "It was a stupid bar fight, and I never should have been there in the first place."

She gave him a speculative look. "And now you own a bar."

"It's a brewpub, Mom. I'm good at making beer." He laughed softly. "Maybe better than I was at pitching."

"How's your shoulder?"

"Fine."

"Do you ever think about going back?"

A familiar tension pulsed through his body, making his blood feel like it was tinged with acid. He'd spent months rehabbing his shoulder with grueling exercise and physical therapy. He refused to believe that stupidity had ended his baseball career in a matter of minutes. Guys came back from injuries and surgeries—sometimes better than they'd been in the first place.

Not David.

He paced to the edge of the living room, glancing out at the view of Main Street from his front window. If it weren't for Jenna's move to Colorado and his frustration over a shoulder that wouldn't return to its normal strength, this town would mean nothing to him. But Crimson had been the best thing to happen to him. It made the ache of losing baseball—his escape and sanctuary—tolerable. Even from his place on the periphery, this community had helped him to stop looking back to what could have been and focus on the life he had.

"Not anymore," he told his mother. "My life is good now. Healthy. I want that for Rhett and Jenna." He moved toward her. "I need help, and if you're willing to give it you can stay. But we're doing things my way. There are rules and structure."

Angela made a face. "I've never been much for structure, honey. You know that. I'm here to bring some fun and sunshine into that boy's life."

Which sounded like his mother blowing sunshine. But if Jenna had called her, he would make it work. "Fun is fine," he said, resisting the urge to roll his eyes. "But he needs a routine. We're giving him that, and we're going to do the same for Jenna when she gets back. She's got to clean up her life, whether she likes it or not."

His mother rose to her tiptoes and kissed his cheek. "Your sister is lucky to have you. It's not too late for our family, David."

He hoped she was right. "You can stay in my bedroom. I'll take the couch."

"I don't want to be an imposition," his mother said, even as she shrugged out of her brightly colored cardigan and draped it over the back of the couch. "Will you be a dear and bring my bags? Do I have my own bathroom?"

Before David could answer, a small voice called his name. "Uncle David?"

He turned see Rhett standing at the edge of the hallway, wiping the back of his hand across his eyes.

"Is Mommy here? I woke up and heard her voice."

David heard a tiny gasp behind him. He was used to how much Jenna and their mother looked alike but hadn't realized they sounded similar, as well.

"Your mom isn't here," he said gently. "But your grandma has come to visit." He moved to reveal Angela standing behind him.

"Hi, sweetie boy," she cooed. "Do you remember your grandma?"

Rhett shook his head.

Angela made a sound of distress, then pasted a bright smile on her face. "You were a baby the last time I saw you. It was before you and your mommy moved to Colorado." She stepped forward. "I'm going to help Uncle David look after you until she comes home, okay? We're going to have lots of fun together."

Rhett slanted his head, studying Angela. "You don't look like a grandma," he said.

David gave a small snort of laughter, earning a narrow-eyed glare from his mother. She reached for the sweater and quickly put it on over the silky tank top she wore underneath. Angela had never dressed like a typical mother, either.

"Doesn't change the fact that I'm yours," she said. "You good with that?"

Rhett's sleepy blue gaze met David's. "Your mom called your grandmother," David told the boy. "So she could stay with us."

After a moment Rhett nodded. "Okay."

"Time to go back to bed," David told the boy.

"I can tuck you in," Angela offered.

"I want Uncle David," Rhett whispered.

David felt his heart clutch, but heard his mother sigh. "You bet, buddy." He put a hand on his mother's shoulder. Although he'd never had much sympathy for her, he understood what it was like to be unsure how to do what was right.

"Give it time," he whispered, and took Rhett's hand.

He led the boy back to his bedroom, retrieved Ruffie from the far side of the bed and settled Rhett under the covers again.

By the time he came out, his mother had moved her bags into his bedroom. She'd taken his clothes out of the dresser and filled a laundry basket.

"I hope you don't mind if I unpack," she said, folding a stack of more tank tops. "I hate living out of a suitcase."

He thought about asking her about her current life and if she had a home base now. Other than a monthly bank transfer into her checking account, David wasn't exactly up to date on his mother's life. But he could save that for another night. Apparently, they'd have plenty if she was here until Jenna returned.

"Rhett doesn't normally wake during the night," he told her. "Since you're here, I'm going to go downstairs and check on the bar."

She raised one finely penciled eyebrow. "Are *you* drinking, David?"

"Mom, I brew beer for a living. I drink, but it's not a problem."

She tsked softly.

He sighed. "I haven't been drunk since the night of the bar fight."

"At least I would have understood if you'd been drinking when you gave that woman and her boyfriend most of your money. I'm not so sure about your decision-making when you're sober."

"I put that man in the hospital for almost a month. Everything changed in one moment. I owed them."

"He fell and knocked his head on the corner of the table."

"Because I punched him."

"After he knifed you."

"I'm not having this discussion again," he said through gritted teeth. "Jenna wants you here, and I'll honor that. But I'm not rehashing old history. I don't get drunk anymore, and I watch my temper. Things are good in Crimson, and I intend to keep it that way."

She studied him a long moment, then nodded. "Fine.

Go do what you need to do. I'll be here if my grandson needs me."

David nodded and headed for Elevation. Halfway down his private staircase, he stopped. His chest rose and fell and it felt like someone had lobbed a grenade at him. How the hell had his life spun so out of control? He was the temporary guardian for his five-year-old nephew and his mother—who had the maternal instincts of a feral cat—was now his child-rearing partner?

He turned and took the steps back to his apartment two at a time. Grabbing his jacket and the set of keys off the hook on the wall, he let himself out the front door and walked toward his truck parked in the alley behind the building.

He had plenty to take care of at both the bar and the brewery, but there was other business that called to him in his current mood.

Erin looked out the peephole of her apartment's front door and sucked in a breath.

"I know you're in there," David said softly, sounding like a man who had the patience to wait all night for her if that's how she played it. "Talk to me, Erin. Please."

Damn her weakness for good manners. A well-timed "please" got her every time.

She opened the door a few inches and tried not to notice how gorgeous he looked standing on the other side. He wore dark jeans, engineer boots and a heavy canvas jacket to ward against the crisp evening temperatures that signaled fall in the mountains. His hair was disheveled, like the wind was blowing or he'd been running his hands through it.

The way she wanted to run her hands through it.

"Can I come in?" he asked in that same quiet tone that made his already low voice sound like a growl.

"Where's Rhett?"

"Asleep," he answered automatically. "My mom is at the apartment in case he wakes up."

"You have a mom?" Erin was so shocked she stepped back and the door opened a little wider.

One side of David's mouth quirked up. "Would you like to see my belly button to prove I'm not an alien?"

Her mouth went dry as she glanced at the edge of his jacket. *Heck, yes*, her body screamed. *Take off your clothes, hottie brewmaster.*

"No," she said, her voice coming out a chirp. "I know you're human, but I didn't realize your mom was coming to visit."

She wanted to smack herself on the head. Of course she didn't know anything about his mother. The intimacy between her and David had developed too quickly and under such strange circumstances.

"If you invite me in, I'll tell you about it." He leaned closer. "Your neighbor's front curtains are fluttering like mad. I swear she's going to call the cops, and the last thing I need is Cole coming after me."

"That's Ms. Kronkowski," Erin said without even having to look at which apartment he was talking about. "Because I'm single she thinks I must be a wild party girl."

David chuckled.

"Hey," she said, pushing at his chest. "That's not funny."

"Yes, it is." His eyes grazed up and down her body and she realized she'd let the door open enough that her Hello Kitty pajamas were on full display. "It's not even ten and you're ready for bed."

"I was reading," she countered.

"Let me guess," he said. "A romance novel."

She narrowed her eyes, not sure how she felt about him pegging her reading tastes so easily. "What do you have against heroes?"

"I don't trust 'em," he said with a shrug. "If a guy seems too good to be true, he probably is."

"Not on my e-reader," she answered, but gestured him into the apartment, both because she didn't want Ms. Kronkowski to go apoplectic and because Erin's ex-boyfriend had seemed too good to be true. And he'd turned out to be a first-class jerk.

"Tell me about the guy who hurt you," David said, pulling the door shut and coming to stand in front of her.

Could he read her mind? She gave a strangled laugh and asked, "Is that why you're here?"

He shook his head. "I'm here to apologize, but I want to know about you."

"There's nothing to know. If you don't believe me, talk to my mother. She'll be happy to tell you how ordinary I am."

When his gaze turned sympathetic, Erin closed her eyes and sighed. "I didn't mean that. I don't want to talk about my ex-boyfriend or my mother with you."

He laced his fingers with hers when she opened her eyes, then led her to the couch, taking a seat and tugging her down next to him.

"I'll start," he told her, using his thumb to trace circles around the center of her palm. The featherlight touch made her skin tingle. "I'm sorry I lost it today at the community center. I was out of line, and the last thing I want to do is jeopardize your program. You've been a lifesaver for me, and you deserve better in return."

"Every kid gets a chance," she told him, "even the ones

with awful parents. I can't turn away a child because you have a personal issue with his father."

"I get that," he said, "even if I don't like it. Hell, maybe if Jenna and I had a teacher like you back in the day, things could have been different for us." He dropped his head to the back of the couch, staring up at the white ceiling in her apartment. "Which brings me to my mother. She showed up tonight because my sister called her to help. She seems sincere, but things have never been great with us. Motherhood wasn't really her thing, so Jenna and I did a lot of raising ourselves."

"You took care of your sister," Erin said quietly.

"Not very well," he told her, pulling his hand away. "I was obsessed with playing baseball. The funny thing was that one of Mom's boyfriends actually bought me my first ball and bat. He was a third baseman in the minor leagues, a decent guy." He gave a half-hearted chuckle. "Of course, that meant he and my mom didn't last long. She was a magnet for losers, just like Jenna. But I kept playing ball."

"And you were good," she said. "I Googled you."

"You Googled me," he repeated softly. "I can't even imagine the crap you found about me online."

She shrugged. "You've had an exciting life."

"Hardly." He shook his head. "I screwed the whole thing up."

"Because of your injury," she prompted.

"I don't talk about it."

"You can with me."

He studied her a moment, then nodded. "It was a stupid bar fight. I'd met a woman after one of our home games and we started hooking up. It wasn't love or dating. I didn't know anything about her other than she was hot. I was twenty-five and stupid as the day is long. I had an

ego to match my pitching talent. The woman had a jealous husband."

"She was married?"

He gave a sharp nod. "I swear I didn't know that, but it
doesn't matter. We were out and her husband came bust-
ing into the bar, hell-bent on beating me to a pulp. He
was a big guy."

"You're a big guy."

"I was also drunk and sloppy. But I'm a decent fighter.
Just not against a knife."

"David," she whispered, noticing that he'd moved his
hand to massage his shoulder.

"In retrospect," he said quietly, "that guy did me a
favor."

"He ended your career."

"My reckless behavior ended it, and who knows where
I'd be if it hadn't happened. I wouldn't have moved to
Crimson to help Jenna." He gave her a lopsided smile. "I
wouldn't have met you."

"Oh," she breathed, because somewhere in his words
was the nicest compliment she'd ever received.

"From my perspective, ordinary is the most exciting
thing going." He draped an arm across the couch cushions, his fingers just grazing her back. The gentle touch
made her body come alive.

"There's nothing exciting about my life," she said,
shaking her head.

"Come on," he prompted. "Give me more than that.
Help me understand you, Erin. I know you're a great
teacher, but I also know the program at the community
center means more to you than just another way to help
kids."

She bit down on her bottom lip, then sucked in a breath
when he ran the pad of his thumb over the same spot.

"I want something that belongs to me," she said after a moment. "I want to do something that my mom can be proud of—"

"She should be proud that her daughter is one of the best teachers around."

If only it were that simple. "We moved to Crimson after my dad died when I was just a little older than Rhett. They were older when I was born." She cleared her throat and added, "I was definitely a surprise. Dad was a college professor and my mom is a psychiatrist. It was clear from the time I was little that I wasn't like them. They loved me, but I didn't quite fit. They were both so smart."

"You're smart."

"My mom is a legitimate genius and I'm—" she shrugged "—average."

"Don't say that."

"It's true. I wasn't the kid she expected to get. After Dad died, I'm not sure she knew what to do with me. I wanted to do things like Girl Scouts and slumber parties, and she thought I should be spending more time with my head in the books. When it became clear I wasn't going to live up to her high standards, she kind of lost interest."

"How could anyone lose interest in you?" He shifted closer, cupped her cheeks in his warm palms. "You're smart and beautiful, and you have the biggest heart of anyone I know."

"Apparently," she muttered, "big hearts aren't as valuable as big breasts."

He blinked and dropped his hands. "Come again."

"Have you heard of Brazen Peaks?"

"The restaurant outside of Carbondale?"

"I think the correct term is 'breastaurant,'" she told him.

"Right. So what?"

"Have you been there?"

He shook his head. "Not my scene."

"My ex met his new girlfriend there. According to him, she's sexy, adventurous and exciting." She made a face. "I'm pretty sure that means I'm none of those things."

"Or it means your ex is an idiot." He leaned and brushed his lips across hers. "Trust me. Your ex is an idiot."

She couldn't stop the smile that tugged at the corners of her mouth. It felt like the door to the cage she'd been living in her whole life had just been thrown open. When her friends told her that Greg was a fool for dumping her, she'd assumed they were just being kind. Her mother certainly hadn't bothered with that sentiment. She'd simply shaken her head and said that until Erin lowered her standards, she was bound to be disappointed by men.

But David made the comment with so much conviction, she believed every word of it. If a man like him found her attractive, what did the opinion of her two-timing ex-boyfriend matter anyway?

"Show me your scar," she said suddenly, then felt her eyes grow wide.

David looked as surprised at her request as she was at making it.

"I'm not sure that's such a grand plan, darlin'," he told her, his voice husky.

"Please," she whispered, hoping the magic word would have the same effect on him as it did on her. "I want to understand what happened to you."

"Isn't it enough to know I'm damaged goods?"

"You're not, and neither am I."

He lifted a brow. "Does that mean I get to see your breasts?"

Her mouth dropped open.

"I'm joking," he said, shrugging out of his jacket. "Although it's not such a bad idea now that I think about it. Best way to prove without a doubt that your ex-boyfriend was a total loser, don't you think?"

Erin swallowed. "I actually can't think right now."

David chuckled. "Then let's do this thing while your brain is jumbled." He grabbed the hem of his dark gray henley and pulled it over his head.

If Erin hadn't been able to think a moment ago, looking at David's gorgeous body made her feel like her mind had just been put in a blender. Every single one of her brain cells chose that moment to go on sabbatical, a fact that made the rest of her body sing with glee.

Because her body wanted things from this man that her brain couldn't handle. She knew David was big and broad, but she hadn't expected the golden skin or the darker hair that covered his chest. His body was all muscle, lean and toned and more delicious than anything she'd ever seen.

He moved, turning so she could see his beautiful back. The hard planes were just as pronounced, but at the top of his left shoulder was a pink scar about three inches long. It had clearly healed, but the color hadn't faded as much as she would have expected. The skin was raised where it had been sewn together.

"It's not pretty," he said over his shoulder. "They call it a keloid scar."

"That's why it's raised?"

"Yeah. They can do therapy to flatten it, but I never bothered. It's a reminder of how stupid and reckless I was."

Holding her breath, she reached out to run her finger-tips along the ridge. His skin was warm, and she felt him stiffen under her touch.

"It's a good reminder that you're human," she told him. "Because otherwise you're a little too perfect."

"I'm far from perfect."

The feel of him mesmerized her. The fact that she was actually touching the man she'd had a crush on for months had sparks flying all through her body. "Hate to break it to you, but your body didn't get that message."

"You like my body?"

She snorted. "A ninety-year-old grandma would like your body."

"I've changed my mind." He moved so quickly all she had time to do was yelp, then she was in his arms with his heat enveloping her. "If I take off my clothes, you have to take off yours."

It was even more difficult to form a coherent thought with his chest hair tickling her cheek. She glanced to one side and—oh my—nipple at eye level.

She didn't even realize she'd licked her lips until David let out a soft groan. "Killing me here, darlin'. I can't even imagine what you're thinking, but I'm guessing it's dirty and I know I'd like it."

"Nothing I want to do to you is dirty," she said, trying to control her breathing. "People do it all the time. It's completely natural."

He lowered his head until his mouth skimmed hers. "What I want to do to you, Erin, is hot and dirty and no one can do it like me."

A volcano erupted inside her body. With just his words, David had her more aroused than she'd ever felt in her life. She brought a hand to her face and patted her cheek.

David smiled against her lips. "What are you doing?"

"Just making sure I didn't spontaneously combust."

He pulled back to gaze at her, his blue eyes warm and full of equal amounts of desire and amusement. "You're something special."

She opened her mouth to automatically correct him. No, she wasn't special. She was average. Ordinary. Boring.

But the way he looked at her made her *feel* special, so who was she to argue? "Fake it 'til you make it" had been her mantra during her first year of teaching, when she wasn't confident in her ability to handle a roomful of kindergartners.

The same principle applied now.

She reached up and fused her mouth to his, sliding her tongue along the seam of his lips. He rewarded her with a groan, and she felt it all the way to her toes. He lifted her until she was straddling him, her knees digging into the soft cushions of the couch.

She draped her arms around his neck and ran her fingers through his hair, every inch of her front plastered to the front of him. He deepened the kiss, making her senses reel. She wanted David with a thundering need that surpassed anything she'd felt before.

Her desire was so all-encompassing that she didn't even hesitate when he tugged at the hem of her cotton pajama top. She raised her arms and allowed him to pull it over her head, then gasped as his jaw grazed her breast.

"I'm not wearing a bra," she murmured, more to herself than him, suddenly remembering that she'd been tucked in bed reading when he'd knocked on her door.

"It's my lucky night," he said against her skin. His mouth closed around one nipple and Erin's body sang with joy. She gave herself over to the sensation of it, the gentle pressure and the sweet words he whispered as he held her.

He claimed her mouth again as his hand trailed under the waistband of her pants and into her panties. She whimpered when he dipped his fingers into her, the fire banking deep within her suddenly bursting into a million flames. He continued to kiss her, his tongue mimicking the motion of his fingers, and she exploded around him on a sharp cry.

It was like nothing she'd ever experienced and more than she would have guessed was possible, and she wanted the moment to last forever.

Chapter Nine

The sensation of Erin coming apart in his arms was pure bliss to David. From the tiny gasps of pleasure to her flushed skin to the way she cried out his name at the end, she was absolute perfection. It beat out the moment he was drafted by the Pirates, the first time he pitched a major-league game and so many wild nights with women he'd lost count. Which only made it that much more difficult to pull away.

Erin had gone pliant in his arms, soft and a little sleepy. He wanted nothing more than to finish what they'd started, to carry her to the bedroom and worship her body from head to toe. But she deserved better than an unplanned roll in the sheets.

She was worth more than she believed, and he was certain that taking her now was something they'd both come to regret.

He picked up her shirt and dropped it over her head.

She automatically pushed her arms through the sleeves, then frowned.

"What's going on?"

Her dark eyes were big and lovely and full of so much trust that he was sure to screw up in the end.

"I'm tucking you in," he said, grabbing his shirt from the floor, then moving one arm around her back and the other under her knees. He lifted her off the couch and started for the narrow hallway he assumed led to her bedroom.

She splayed her hand across his chest, her thumb just brushing one nipple, and he almost stumbled a step. "I'm not sleepy," she told him.

"It's late, Erin, and I didn't mean for things to go so far."

"So this was an accident?" Her eyes narrowed. "Or a mistake?"

He moved into the bedroom, where a lamp on the nightstand illuminated the space in a golden glow. She had a wrought iron bed frame with a patchwork quilt on top—both feminine and classic. Perfect for Erin.

As he lowered her onto the bed, which was unmade only on the side where she slept, he couldn't help but smile at the array of things spread across the quilt on the other side. There was an e-reader with a polka-dot cover, several paperback books, a box of tissues and...

"You have a cat?"

She darted a glance to the ball of fur that didn't so much as offer a tail flick to acknowledge that people had entered its space. "That's Sugar. She's kind of standoffish until she gets to know you."

"See," he said, dropping a kiss on the top of her head, "there's no room for me in the bed anyway." He gestured to the stack of books as he pulled on his henley. "You have too many heroes already."

"You're placating me," she told him, "and I don't like it. That was—" she pointed toward the family room "—pretty darn awesome for me. Beyond awesome. I'm grateful, but I also understand if I don't do it for you. Just man up and tell me."

He grabbed her wrists, pinned them above her head and leaned in to take her mouth, allowing all the frustration and need pounding through his body to transfer to the kiss.

Maybe he was trying to freak her out, to prove that what he wanted was surely more than she was willing to give. Instead, she met his desire with her own, and it tore through him like a brush fire, igniting every part of him until he had to force himself to release her again.

"I want you, Erin. I want us. I want to start with all night, and keep going for as long as you'll let me."

She drew in a breath, pressed her fingertips to lips swollen from his kiss. "Then why…"

"I'm not exactly a stand-up guy, but I know when a woman deserves more than I can give. When I told you I wanted to court you, it wasn't a joke. I want you to feel special—"

"Mission accomplished on the couch."

"I want you to understand how special you are. I wish you saw yourself the way I see you." He straightened, shook his head. "I have to admit I didn't think you'd accept my apology tonight, and I wouldn't have blamed you in the least."

"I'll find another way to get funding," she said, but he could hear the hesitation in her voice. He wanted to kick himself for how he'd acted earlier. He'd spent his whole life dealing with losers like Joel Martin, and had been in more than his share of fights to defend his sister. But he was older now, and he should be smarter. He had Rhett to think about.

And now Erin.

More than anything, David wanted to be the type of man who would deserve her.

"I'll help you," he told her.

"You don't have to—"

"Let me help you."

She gave him a shy smile. "Okay."

"And let me take you out on a real date." When she didn't respond immediately, he added a soft, "Please."

"You're pretty good with manners," she told him, rolling her eyes.

"I'm good with a lot of things." He leaned in and gave her one last lingering kiss. "I plan to demonstrate every one of my skills for you."

To his surprise, she laughed. The sound loosened the invisible band that stretched tight around his heart. "Are you sure you don't read romance novels? Because that sounds like the perfect hero line to me."

"No hero here," he told her. "But I hope you have some sweet dreams tonight."

"Good night, David," she whispered.

"Good night, Erin."

By the beginning of the following week, Erin wondered if she'd dreamed her whole encounter with David.

A sweet dream, indeed, but disappointing to think she'd made the whole thing up in her head.

What other explanation could there be for the fact that she hadn't seen or heard from him in five days? She might not be an expert on courting, but there was no doubt that's not how it typically went.

Each day, regret plagued her. The more plausible explanations for David's silence were a lot harder to take. Maybe she shouldn't have let things go so far on her couch. It felt like he put her up on some pedestal she wasn't interested in standing on, so could it be possible that he'd lost respect for her? The more logical reason was simply that he wasn't interested yet didn't want to hurt her feelings.

Which hurt her more than if he'd been honest in the first place.

She'd thought he might ask her out for the previous weekend, and she'd been fool enough to check her cell phone compulsively most of Saturday, waiting for a call that never came. In the end, she'd ordered pizza and binge-watched *Pride and Prejudice*—both the BBC and Hollywood versions. Then she'd thrown in *Bridget Jones's Diary* for an extra Colin Firth fix.

She told herself she should get in the habit of keeping her books on her nightstand instead of the other side of the bed. But really, why bother when Sugar was the one sharing it?

Rhett had been making progress with his social skills, playing with Elaina during recess and interacting with the other kids in the after-school program.

Joel Martin hadn't been back to see her, but Isaac's mother, Danielle, had signed him up for the program on the two days when she worked until five at the Hair Nation salon outside of town. Other than a subtle side-eye toward Rhett, the woman had been polite and grateful to have a place for her son to go after school.

Isaac and Rhett had seemed to silently agree to a truce. The funny thing was the boys had a lot in common. Both were slow to make friends but craved social interactions. They liked building things and games of any sort. She'd managed to engage them both in a puzzle Monday afternoon and wished their parents could handle things so maturely.

It was nearly five on Tuesday when an older woman with thick blond hair piled high on her head and makeup applied to make her look ten years younger sauntered into the room.

"Rhett, baby," she called, "get your things. Nana's taking you out for a special treat."

Rhett looked up from where he was making a race car out of modeling clay. "I'm 'posed to stay here until Uncle David comes to get me. He's picking me up."

"Change of plans," the woman said. She moved forward and adjusted her oversize purse on her shoulder. "I'm Angela McCay, Rhett's grandma."

Erin felt color rush to her face at the way Angela's gaze seemed to take her in and automatically dismiss her. "David mentioned you arrived in town."

Angela's blue eyes turned assessing. "Oh, did he now?" She shrugged. "I don't think he talked about you. Are you and my son close?"

"Um…we know each other because of Rhett." If David hadn't mentioned her, she wasn't going to give this woman any details of her relationship—if she could even call it that.

Rhett came to stand next to Erin. "I told you Ms. Mac-Donald is my favorite teacher."

"You're in kindergarten," Angela said, reaching out a hand to tousle Rhett's blond hair. "There isn't a lot to compare her to."

"She's still my favorite," Rhett said, his small chin jutting out.

Erin felt a flood of gratitude for the boy and his innocent loyalty.

"Do I need to sign something to check him out?" Angela asked, ignoring Rhett's comment.

"Each parent or guardian submits a form naming the people approved to pick up their child from the program." Erin tried not to fidget under Angela's stare. She could see where David and his sister got their looks.

Angela might be a little rough around the edges, but it was clear she must have been a traffic-stopping beauty in her day. Lines snaked out from the edges of her eyes and around her mouth, but she still had high cheekbones, bee-stung lips and the kind of figure that seemed out of place on a woman with a five-year-old grandson.

She wore a long-sleeved white T-shirt, low-slung jeans and boots. Around her neck were several strands of turquoise layered on top of a couple of heavy silver chains.

"I'm his nana," the woman said, her tone icy. "Of course I have permission to pick him up."

Erin pressed her fingers to the place on her chest where a knot of nerves was forming. "If you'd wait a minute, I'll call David to confirm."

Just then one of the third-grade boys lobbed a purple crayon across the table at one of his friends. Instead of its intended target, the crayon hit the water cup a threesome of girls was sharing as they painted. The dirty water spilled across the table, sending the girls into a screaming panic.

"It's okay, girls," Erin said, holding up a finger to ask Rhett's grandmother to wait a moment. "We can clean things up."

"Are you in charge of all these kids?" Angela asked over the din.

"I have help," Erin answered, trying not to sound defensive, "but she went down to the office to make copies."

"Looks like you've bitten off a little more than you can chew."

Embarrassment rushed through Erin. The old adage was one of her mother's favorite reminders from when Erin was a girl. Every time Erin wanted to sign up for a new activity or try out for a team, her mother had said, "Don't bite off more than you can chew."

She hurried over to the side table and grabbed a roll of paper towels. "I've got it under control."

"While you deal with—" Angela waved her hands at the mess "—I'm going to take Rhett."

"I really need to talk to—"

"My new shirt," one of the girls screeched. "Paint water's ruining my new shirt."

"Honey, let me make this easy on you." Angela reached out and took Rhett's hand. "I'll text my son and let him know the boy's with me. You take care of your mess."

"It's not a mess," Erin muttered at the same moment one of the girls, Ava Elliott, punched the boy who'd thrown the crayon in the stomach.

Erin hurried to them as the boy doubled over in pain.

By the time she looked up again, Angela and Rhett were gone.

Claire Travers, the teenager who was assisting her with the program, came back in the room, her eyes growing wide at the chaos and commotion. "I was gone for like five minutes," she said.

"It's fine," Erin called. "Get Ava and Paige cleaned up, okay?"

She helped the boy who'd been punched, Fletcher, to a seat on the beanbag.

"Can't breathe," he whispered on a gasp.

"She knocked the wind out of you." Erin smoothed his hair away from his face. "Look at me and concentrate on moving air in—" she took a breath "—and out," she said on an exhale.

Fletcher swiped a hand over his eyes and did what she said. After a few minutes he was breathing normally.

Claire managed to calm the girls and soon everything was back under control. Erin grabbed her phone to text David about his mother just at the same time parents started arriving to pick up kids. She meant to get back to the text, but as the last child walked out with her mother, Sara Travers poked her head into the room.

"So this is where the child-wrangling magic happens?" she asked.

"I helped manage a full-blown meltdown today with a couple of the girls," Claire proudly told her stepmother.

"She was brilliant," Erin confirmed, feeling slightly awkward under Sara's gorgeous blue gaze. Sara had been a famous child actor before her career got derailed in her teens. She'd come to Crimson a few years ago, fallen in love with Josh Travers and helped him open the Crimson Ranch guest ranch. Since then, her career had made a resurgence and now she balanced her Hollywood life with her life in the mountains.

Although Erin didn't know her personally, she'd seen Sara around town quite a bit. With Crimson's proximity to Aspen, she should be used to movie star sightings, but it felt different with Sara. She was an integral part of the community after having lived in Crimson only a few years. Erin was still skirting the sidelines even though she'd spent most of her life in town.

Olivia, who was Claire's aunt by marriage, had arranged for the girl to assist Erin in the afternoons. Erin still hoped to receive funding to expand the program and her staff. Until then, Claire was a huge help. The girl was only fifteen but already had an instinctive talent for connecting with young kids.

"Way to go, Claire-bear," Sara said, giving the girl a quick hug. Although she wore a casual pair of distressed jeans with an oversize sweater, she still managed to project a look of subtle glamour. "You're amazing."

The girl rolled her eyes like a typical teenager, but Erin could tell the simple praise meant a lot to her. It seemed to come so easily, and not for the first time Erin wondered what it would have been like to grow up in a household where she'd been valued instead of constantly found lacking.

"Your dad is waiting downstairs," Sara told Claire. "The truck is parked at the curb. We thought we'd grab dinner in town. Why don't you head on down?"

Claire smiled at Erin. "I'll see you tomorrow?"

"I count on it," Erin answered. "I really appreciate your help, Claire."

The girl disappeared through the open doorway.

"She's special," Erin said to Sara.

"I wanted to tell you how much Josh and I appreciate you giving her this opportunity. She loves kids, and has plenty of experience babysitting, but this is different."

Erin gave a small laugh. "Not too different some days."

Sara inclined her head. "When did you know you wanted to be a teacher?"

Erin thought about how to answer the question. She'd played school with her stuffed animals as a young girl, then been the one to ask teachers if she could help with the younger kids at recess as she'd gotten older. But she'd also known being a teacher wouldn't be enough to satisfy her mom, so she'd feigned interest in a variety of more high-profile careers until she'd gone to college and immediately switched her major from premed to elementary education.

"My mother," she said, keeping her tone neutral, "was very much of the belief that 'those who can, do, and those who can't, teach.'"

Sara groaned softly.

"I think I knew—or at least recognized that I liked working with kids—for most of my life. All of my pretend play centered around setting up classrooms for my dolls and stuffed animals."

"I didn't have much of a childhood," Sara said, surprising Erin with her candor. "I was the breadwinner in the family, and whether or not I wanted to act, that was what I had to do."

"Would you have chosen something else if you'd had the chance?" Erin couldn't help but ask.

"Maybe," Sara said with a shrug. "Something normal where I could just be a regular person."

Erin blinked. She'd spent her whole life wanting to be something other than regular. Now a famous actress stood in front of her wishing for normal.

"I've got the best of both worlds now. But I don't want Claire to go through what I did..." Sara paused, then added, "Or what you did as she tries to figure out her path in life."

"She's young and obviously quite intelligent." Erin straightened a stack of papers on the desk, then pulled her purse out of a drawer. "She's lucky to have people in her life who want to support her. She'd be an excellent teacher, and I'm sure she'll succeed in whatever she chooses to do with her life."

Sara drew in an audible breath. "Will you record that so I can play it back to her when the teenage drama and doubts get to be too much?"

"Keep her engaged and stay involved in her life. I know you're busy and have plenty of important things to take care of, but if you ever want to come with Claire, I can always use more hands on deck."

Sara's already huge eyes widened further. She looked around the room, then back to Erin. "Would that be weird? I'm not great with kids. I mean, I was one and I have Claire and Emery, but she's a baby. She can't talk."

"My kids like to talk," Erin said with a smile. "Especially when they have people to listen to them. You're an actress. I'm sure you can fake it."

"I faked it for a lot of years," Sara said, then laughed. "I'm an expert."

"Tell me about it," Erin muttered. It was strange to feel this camaraderie with a woman whose life was so different, but comforting at the same time.

"I'll let you get on with your evening," Sara said, stepping forward to envelop Erin in a quick hug. Sara's fragrance was subtle and earthy but clearly expensive, and Erin couldn't wait to tell her friends she'd been hugged by the A-list actress. "We should get together some time. A bunch of us have regular get-togethers—mostly for Mexican and margaritas but sometimes coffee or yoga. I'll call you before the next one and you can join us."

"Thank you," Erin whispered, feeling better than she had in a long time.

As Sara turned to leave, David rushed into the room. "Sorry I'm late. We were having trouble with fermenting the most recent batch of the wheat beer."

"Hey, David." Sara smiled. "I'm looking forward to watching you win the big prize in a couple of weeks."

"If we sort through the problems with this latest batch, maybe I'll actually have a beer to enter."

"Good luck," Sara said with a grin, and walked out of the room.

"Thanks." He ran a hand through his hair, then turned to Erin. "Where's Rhett?"

"With your mother," she said, her stomach dropping at the way his brows drew down. "She was supposed to call you."

Pulling his phone out of his pocket, he shook his head. "No texts or calls."

"She told me—"

"I thought you weren't supposed to send him home with random people. Isn't that why I filled out the paperwork?"

"His grandmother isn't random," Erin insisted, even though she'd given the same argument to Angela. "She wanted to take him out for a fun afternoon."

David muttered a curse under his breath then said, "You don't want to know my mother's definition of fun."

"I thought she was here helping," Erin said, throwing up her hands. "She's staying with you. You don't trust her with Rhett?"

"I trust her." David paced to the edge of the room. "Sort of. But she's been talking about taking him up the mountain to see the leaves changing. I told her she had to stay in town with him, and we got in an argument about it. My mom is flighty and reckless. For all I know, she'll start a hike with him and lose him in the woods."

"No," Erin whispered. "That's not possible."

"She took Jenna and me to downtown Pittsburgh one year for a Christmas parade. She got sidetracked by some sale at a department store and left us on the street with instructions not to move. Apparently, she forgot that she was doing more than a shopping trip and went home. The police finally picked us up after a street sweeper called them. According to my mom, she thought we were playing in the backyard."

"David."

"It was below freezing," he said, almost as an afterthought. "Just like it gets cold up on the mountain at night this time of year."

Erin shook her head. "That can't be what's happened. I bet she went for an ice cream. If you said not to leave—"

"My mom doesn't give a—" He clamped his mouth shut. "She means well and she's been fine this time around, but she's not always reliable. Not when it counts."

"David, I'm—"

He held up a hand. "It's not your fault. I believed she'd changed. I needed to believe because it's what Jenna wanted and I have no clue what I'm doing with a five-year-old boy."

"You're handling things like a pro," she said, reaching out a hand to squeeze his arm and trying not to take it personally when he shrugged off her touch.

"Clearly, this night is a great example of that." He hit a button on his phone. "Maybe I'll get lucky and she'll pick up."

Erin waited, hoping with every fiber of her being Angela answered. A moment later, David took the phone away from his ear and shook his head. "Straight to voice mail. She's either ignoring me or out of cell range."

"A text might go through," Erin suggested quietly.

He punched in a message, hit Send, and they waited again. David's full mouth pressed into a thin line. "I've got to call Cole and see if he has any deputies up on the mountain. It's going to get dark soon, and I need to know Rhett is okay."

"I'm sorry," she whispered, feeling miserable.

"It's not your problem," he answered even as he continued to stare at the phone. "You're just the teacher."

Erin swallowed. She knew he hadn't meant the words as an insult. He was stressed and worried. But just as he'd wanted to believe in his mother, Erin had wanted to believe in him. In the two of them. He'd said he'd wanted her. Wanted "us."

But once again, she wasn't enough.

He turned away when Cole picked up, and she could hear him explaining the situation to the sheriff. After a minute, he faced her again. "He's going to check out some of the more popular driving routes for viewing the changing leaves. I'm going to look around town to see if they're down here, then head up myself."

"Will you text me when you find them?"

He studied her as if weighing his answer, then finally nodded.

"How can I help?"

"You can't," he whispered, then walked away.

Chapter Ten

The sun had set over the craggy peak of Crimson Mountain, and the sky was aflame in shades of pink and orange as Erin took a curve on the two-lane highway that led up the mountain. Within a half hour, the whole mountainside would be cast in shadow, so there wasn't much time for an effective search.

Her heart felt like it was breaking when David said he didn't need her, but she refused to let that stop her from trying to find Rhett and Angela.

It had been almost an hour since he'd walked away from her, so maybe David had tracked them down by now and hadn't bothered to text her. Erin couldn't take the chance. She was done sitting on the sidelines letting life pass her by, especially when she'd been the cause of the mess they were in.

There were so many service roads and gravel offshoots of the main highway it was difficult to know where to start. Obviously, Cole Bennett and his team of deputies were experts, and she hadn't even thought to ask David what kind of car his mother drove. But Erin had some experience on these roads. She'd always loved the changing colors that swathed the mountains. For a few weeks, the brilliant patches of bright yellow aspens and a few orange and red clumps of scrub oak made the whole valley look like it was on fire.

She turned her car onto a dirt road that led to one of the most picturesque vistas overlooking the valley. It wasn't quite as popular as some of the well-known leaf-viewing drives in the area but remained a favorite with locals.

Angela wasn't a local, but if she'd stopped at the hardware store or the gas station on the west side of town, this was where they would have sent her.

Erin ignored the gorgeous scenery surrounding her and concentrated on scanning the edges of the road and the myriad pull-offs that led to private cabins or trailhead access for hiking.

It was a little bit like searching for a needle in a haystack. When she darted a quick glance at her phone she realized she was out of service range. So even if David had tracked down Rhett and texted her, she wouldn't get the message.

The car climbed almost to tree-line level, Erin growing more frustrated by the second. Why had she allowed Angela to take Rhett? The answer was clear—Erin didn't have enough faith in herself or her authority to stop the other woman. Which was stupid, because of all the things Erin had been too scared of failing at to try, working with kids had never been one of them.

She was a great teacher, and her after-school program was already making a difference. Two of the teachers at school had reported that their students—the ones who'd been identified as troublemakers—were less disruptive and more responsible in class. The kids had cited some of the self-directed exercises for regulating behavior Erin had taught them for the changes.

No matter what her mother thought…or Angela…or David…or her ex…she had value. Maybe if she started believing that about herself, other people would, too.

She was about to turn the car around and head down the hillside when she caught sight of an older-model sedan parked on the side of the road about two hundred yards in front of her.

Adrenaline spiked through her when she noticed the Pennsylvania license plate. As she approached, the driver's-side door opened and Angela stepped out, her pale blond hair shining in the waning light.

Erin breathed a huge sigh of relief as she pulled her Subaru to a stop behind Angela's car. She checked her phone—still no service, but as soon as they got back into cell range she could let David know Rhett was safe.

"Stupid car battery gave out," Angela said sullenly. "And I've got no service up here. We've got satellite radio that can play music anywhere in the dang world. Don't you think they could get some decent coverage for phones?"

Rhett jumped out of the car through the open door. "Ms. MacDonald, you found us."

"Your uncle is worried," Erin said, crouching down to wrap her arms around the boy's shoulders as he ran to her.

"Since when did my son become a worrywart?" Angela retrieved her purse from the front seat of the car and slammed the door shut. "I texted him a message that Rhett and I were getting ice cream and going to look at leaves."

"He never got a message from you," Erin said, feeling defensive on David's behalf. "You promised you'd get in touch with him if I let you take Rhett today."

"Let me?" Angela scoffed. "I'm his grandma and I'll take him—"

"No." Holding tight to Rhett's hand, Erin stepped forward. "When Rhett is at school or with me in the afternoon, he's my responsibility. Unless you have permission from David, I won't allow you to pick him up again."

Angela studied her through narrowed eyes. "Is that so? You do realize my daughter is the one who called and asked me to drive halfway across the country to look out for her boy?"

Erin felt Rhett stiffen beside her. "Rhett," she said, gently taking him by the shoulders, "you should get in my car. It's cold out here. We'll take the booster seat from your grandma's—"

"Nana doesn't have a booster," he interrupted quietly.

"We'll make sure she gets one," she told him. "Your nana and I have a few things to work out and then we'll go find Uncle David."

Biting his lip, the boy looked between Angela and Erin, then headed for the car.

"I'm his grandmother," the older woman repeated as Rhett shut the door.

"I appreciate that." Erin forced her shoulders back and her hands at her side. "I know Jenna is working through her issues, and I understand you're here to help. David does, as well. But he's in charge, Angela. He's balancing so much and trying to do his best by Rhett."

"Sounds like you know my son pretty well." Angela gave her another once-over but before she could continue, Erin held up a hand.

"I hope David and I are friends, but even if we're not, I care about Rhett. He's a great kid and I want to see him through this. We all do." She stepped forward. "I'm not the enemy, Angela. Neither is David."

She saw the woman's shoulders deflate slightly. "Do you know what happened to Jenna when they were in high school?"

Erin shook her head. "I don't, and it's none of my business if David doesn't want to tell me." As much as she wanted to know.

"You should ask him before you get too close."

At Angela's words, a sinking feeling rippled through Erin. Whatever had happened to his sister in high school clearly formed the man David was today. Erin might not know any details, but she understood it must have been traumatic.

"My son is not the type of man who's good for a woman like you." Angela reached out and, to Erin's surprise, patted her softly on the arm. "Rhett is lucky to have you in his life." She took a deep breath, then added, "He's lucky to have David, too. I'm freezing my fanny off up here now that the sun is gone. Let's get back to town so I can make this right with my son."

Erin nodded and they headed to the car. The drive was quiet until they got into cell phone range. Angela's phone was still dead, but Erin's gave several insistent chirps. She took the phone from the console and handed it to David's mother. "You call since I'm driving."

Out of the corner of her eye, Erin saw Angela smile as she looked at the phone.

"What's so funny?"

"You have my son in your contacts."

"Yes."

"His occupation is listed as 'hottie brewmaster.' Is that an official title?"

Erin suppressed a groan. Melody had entered that into her phone, and Erin had forgotten to change it.

"You're stalling," she said as an answer. "Call him."

With a small laugh, Angela hit the button to dial David. After a minute she said, "This is your mother. We're on our way back to town. I left you…" She was quiet for a moment. Erin could hear the muffled rumble of David's voice through the phone but couldn't make out what he was saying. Based on the furrow between Angela's brows, it wasn't good.

"She drove up the mountain and found us," Angela said. Another pause. "It's not my fault the wreck of a car I drive died. Rhett is fine."

"I'm hungry," Rhett called from the back seat.

"He's hungry," Angela repeated, then went silent again as David said something else. "What's that?" She made the sound of static. "Sorry, you're breaking up. We'll see you at home in a bit."

Erin arched a brow as Angela disconnected the call. "Faking a bad connection?"

The older woman shrugged. "He has all night to rip me a new one. I'd like a few minutes of quiet to gather my wits." She pressed her hands to her cheeks. "For the record, my plan was to get a treat and see the leaves, not to get stuck up on the mountain in the cold at dusk."

A rush of emotion flooded Erin when Angela's voice cracked. Despite the attitude, Erin realized David's mother had been more scared than she'd let on to be stranded with Rhett. Erin reached across the console and patted the woman's leg. "It all turned out okay in the end."

"Thank you," Angela whispered and squeezed Erin's fingers.

"Wonder what Uncle David will make for dinner," Rhett said from the back seat. "I'm so hungry even his cooking will taste good tonight."

Erin laughed and was once again reminded how resilient kids could be. "We'll soon find out," she told Rhett, and concentrated on getting them home safely.

David's heart clamored in his chest as he waited on the sidewalk in front of Elevation, and the unfamiliar feeling sent shock waves through him. When was the last time he'd been so worried? The past hour had been the longest of his life. After talking to his mother, he'd gotten in touch with Cole, who had been on the mountain searching for Rhett.

As much as it killed him, David had kept close to town, wanting to remain reachable by his mother if she called. He'd never expected Erin to be conducting her own search, let alone to find his mother and Rhett—especially not after how he'd treated her.

He massaged the back of his neck with one hand. He had the uncanny ability to continuously push away the one person who was quickly coming to mean the most to him.

A small Subaru hatchback pulled to the curb in front of the bar. His mother opened the passenger door at the same time Rhett bounded out from the back seat. David opened his arms, catching the boy and spinning him around.

"Nana's car broke," Rhett said into his neck. "And I'm hungry. Did you make dinner?"

"Even better." David kissed the top of the boy's head and dropped him back down to the ground. "The cook at Elevation made you mac and cheese."

"Mac and cheese," Rhett shouted happily. "Nana, did you hear? Uncle David didn't cook!"

His mother smiled at Rhett. "It's your lucky night." She held out her hand. "Come on. Let's go upstairs."

"I got to get my backpack," Rhett said and turned for the car again.

It was then David realized Erin had also gotten out of

the car and now stood at the edge of the sidewalk. His knees almost gave way from the feeling of longing that charged through him. He wanted to rush forward and enfold her in his arms, somehow knowing that if he held her, his world would fall into place.

Her dark hair was uncharacteristically down, curling over her shoulders and the light jacket she wore. The coat wasn't enough to stave off the cold, and he saw her shiver as a gust of wind whipped down the street. She held out the small Ninja Turtles backpack to Rhett. "Here you go, sweetie."

"Thanks for rescuing us, Ms. MacDonald," Rhett said as he grabbed the pack.

"I'm glad you're safe. See you tomorrow at school."

"Thank you," his mother added, and Erin gave her a little wave. Then Angela and Rhett disappeared through the door that led up to the apartment.

"Erin." David stepped forward, but she held up a hand. "Go take care of Rhett."

"You found them."

"I know you didn't want me involved, but I couldn't just walk away. Don't be too hard on your mother. She's more shaken up by this than she lets on."

He blinked. "Are you defending my mother?"

"I guess I am. She's trying, David. We're all trying. Tonight was my fault for letting her take him without your permission." She laughed softly, then added, "But you know that already."

"No." He reached for her wrist and spun her to him when she turned away. "I'm sorry about the things I said." He brushed his fingers across her cheek. Darkness had officially fallen and her skin glowed under the light of the streetlamps. "I'm sorry my go-to emotion is anger.

It's been that way for a long time, Erin. I don't know how to change it."

She looked up at him through her lashes. "Do you want it to change?"

"For Rhett, yes." He pressed his forehead to hers and whispered. "For you, yes." There was no way to put into words all the things he'd change for this woman if he could. "Why couldn't we have met when my life was simple?"

He felt rather than saw her smile. "Exactly when was your life simple?"

"Third grade," he answered without hesitation. "I had a crush on Brandi Doerger. I chased her around the playground until she agreed to be my girlfriend. Then I kissed her under the flagpole."

She pulled back enough to look at him. "Where is Brandi now?"

"Ours was a short-lived romance."

"And why is that?"

He shrugged. "She wanted me to meet at the candy store across from school and buy her favorite candy bar to prove I was her boyfriend."

"You didn't have the money for a gift?"

"I had a baseball game to get to with my friends."

"So you stood the poor girl up?"

"I was the pitcher," he said, hoping that explained everything. When he was nine, it seemed like a good enough excuse, but as something like disappointment flashed in Erin's gaze, he realized that nothing in his life had ever been simple.

"You don't have anything to prove to me." She untangled herself from his embrace and walked to her car.

He glanced up to his apartment windows and knew he

had to see to Rhett and talk to his mother. But he couldn't let Erin leave like this. Not again.

"Give me another chance," he called.

She stilled in the midst of opening her door and turned to face him. "Why do you even want one?"

A group of twentysomethings was walking toward Elevation and a couple of them hooted with laughter at her question. "She's gonna roast you, dude," one of the taller guys said, slapping David on the arm as he walked by and into the restaurant.

Had he ever been that young and carefree? No, he'd been young and disastrously stupid.

"Because," he said, ignoring everything except Erin's brown eyes, "nothing in my life makes sense right now except you."

He stepped closer but still respected the space she'd put between them. As much as he wanted to push her to let him in despite what a jerk he'd been. It had to be her choice. Never in his life had he wanted a woman to choose him as much as he did now. "Even though I keep finding ways to screw it up, I want you."

Her fingers tightened on her purse strap, as if there was a debate raging inside her brain. It would be the smart thing to walk away from him right now. He sure as hell hoped she wasn't going to do the smart thing.

"Can you define another chance?"

He wanted to pump his fist in the air. She was watching out for herself, but she hadn't said a straight-up *no*. He had a chance, but he had to work for it. David might have made a lot of mistakes in his life, but he could work for something he wanted.

"A real date."

"I've heard that offer before," she countered. "Yet here we are."

Right.

Although he knew how to work, he'd never needed to try to get a woman. "Saturday," he continued. "All day. I'll pick you up at noon."

"What about Rhett?"

David must be more out of practice with women than he even realized. The fact that her first question was about his nephew made his heart clench in ways he didn't want to examine.

"I'll work it out."

She bit down on her lip as her gaze skittered away. "I don't want to force you to take me out. I wasn't lying when I said you have nothing to prove to me. You don't owe me a—"

"I do have something to prove. I need to prove that I'm not the guy I keep showing myself to be. Go out with me, Erin. Please."

She took a deep breath, then met his gaze again. "Do you know I'm a sucker for the word *please*?" she asked, her tone almost annoyed.

He laughed softly. "I didn't before now, but you can bet I'm going to use it to my advantage."

"I'll see you at noon on Saturday," she whispered.

"You'll see me this week," he corrected, "with Rhett. But Saturday is going to be special."

"Can I ask what we're doing?"

"You can ask, but I won't tell. I'm going to wow you. Just wait."

She rolled her eyes and muttered something that sounded like, "If you only knew."

With a small wave, she got in her car and pulled out of her parking spot and down the street.

David glanced up at the apartment windows again but before he went upstairs, took a quick detour into Elevation.

Tracie was tending bar, and he grabbed her shoulders and spun her to face him. "I need to impress a woman," he said. "With a date."

"Take off your shirt," one of the women sitting at the bar told him. He turned to see three women who looked vaguely familiar staring at him. He thought he recognized them from dropping off Rhett at school. Great. Now he was going to be known as the incompetent guardian who couldn't handle women.

Had he really just asked Tracie for dating advice in the middle of his bar?

Two of the women giggled, then the blonde with a short bob leaned forward. "My divorce was final last week." She winked. "I think you're damn impressive just standing there so—"

"Enough," Tracie interrupted the woman, and waved over the new bartender she'd hired to work evenings while David was with Rhett. "Hey, Mark, will you pour these three lovelies a round on the house? No need for the ego-stroking, ladies. I'll take it from here."

She pushed David toward the end of the bar. "What in the hell are you talking about? From the stories I've heard, you went out with half the single women in Pennsylvania in your day. Why do you suddenly need dating advice?"

David gripped the edge of the bar, almost wishing he was still the hot-tempered young baseball phenom who could get away with throwing a fist through the wall. "I asked Erin out."

Tracie stared at him for several moments, then prompted, "And…"

"I told her it was going to be special."

"So make reservations at some swanky place in Aspen," Tracie told him. "I know beer is your thing, but you do remember how to pay for expensive food and wine, right?"

"I need to wow her."

She held up her hands. "Dude, if you're looking for bedroom advice—"

"No," he said quickly. "But Erin is a...a..."

"A woman?"

He blew out a breath. "A lady. I'm not trying to wine and dine her to get into her pants."

One side of Tracie's mouth curved. "You don't want in her pants?"

"Of course I want—" He stopped, growled under his breath. "She's special. I don't want to screw it up. Any guy with a phone and credit card can make a reservation. I need it to be something more."

"I've never seen you like this, boss." She shook her head. "Thank God."

"Forget it."

She laughed, then chucked him on the arm. "I've got an idea. But your prim and proper teacher lady is into you. You know that. I know that. It's a small town, and the school district set likes Elevation. I've seen the way she looks at you when she's here with her friends, and that was before Rhett."

"I never noticed her."

"Because men are idiots." Tracie tsked. "My point is that she's kind of...a sure thing. She crushed on you hard."

"I still need to earn it." He leaned in closer. "Help me. Please."

Tracie rolled her blue eyes to the ceiling. "I bet that sad puppy-dog face and the *please* work on her every time."

"Kind of," he admitted.

"That girl and I need to spend some time together." The new bartender called to Tracie as a line formed in front of the bar. "I've got to get back to work," Tracie said, giving him one of her patented smirks. "Don't want the boss to catch me slacking. I'll come in tomorrow after my run and we can plan world domination—or at least kindergarten teacher domination."

"That sounds kinky."

"You never know," she called over her shoulder as she headed back to the bar. "That might be how she likes it."

David's mind started to wander to an image of Erin dressed in nothing but—

He slapped his palm against his forehead several times. That kind of daydreaming wasn't going to get the five-year-old boy waiting upstairs bathed and ready for bed or his mother dealt with in any sort of productive way.

After scanning the interior of the bar one more time to make sure things were under control, he headed for his apartment. He had to keep things on track this week. He had one more chance with Erin, and he wasn't going to blow it.

Chapter Eleven

"I've never heard of a therapy rabbit." Erin watched in wonder as her Kidzone students took turns petting the bunny that happily hopped up to each of them on the activity rug.

"Fritzi is special." She glanced at Caden Sharpe, the local rancher who also ran an animal rescue center out of his property, his hard features suddenly surprisingly gentle.

Emily Whitaker Crenshaw, the mom of one of Erin's former students, had suggested she call Caden. His manner was gruff, and Erin had been certain he'd refuse her request to bring the kids to his ranch. Instead, he not only set up a time for them to visit but also offered to stop by the community center with a couple of the animals he'd trained as therapy pets.

Caden had been a few years ahead of her in school and had been so surly and mean as a boy she'd barely had the nerve to make eye contact with him. She'd heard rumors that his early life had been tough and wealthy rancher Garrett Sharpe had adopted him when he was ten years old. But even the stable home and the brothers he'd gained in his new family hadn't seemed to settle his restless spirit.

He reminded her of some of the kids she worked with and hoped that meeting Caden, who was also an army vet, would help them realize they had other paths available to them.

Although right now Fritzi the bunny and Otis, the yellow Lab enjoying belly rubs from a group of girls, were the real stars of the show.

"You're doing good work here," Caden told her. Erin realized those were the most words she'd heard the man string together in a sentence.

"I sometimes think I'm in over my head," she admitted. "But as amazing as this community is, there was a need for these kids that wasn't being filled. There are too many who have the potential to get into trouble if no one is watching out for them."

He shifted slightly and she colored under his intense gaze. "I wasn't talking about you."

A noise came from him that might have been a laugh, but it was rough like it had been closed in a drawer and forgotten for too long. "I remember you now," he said. "You were always smiling."

Erin felt her blush deepen. "Did you know that smiling can reduce your blood pressure? Plus it's an easy gift to offer another person."

"People used to be afraid to smile at me."

She raised a brow. "I think that's how you liked it."

He laughed again. "Maybe. The animals help with that."

She gave him her brightest smile. "Thank you for

bringing them here and the invitation to visit the ranch. It will mean a lot to the kids."

He studied her for another long moment. "Would you want—"

A flash of movement over his shoulder caught her eye and she realized David was standing in the door watching the exchange.

"Come on in," she called, glancing at her watch. "I didn't realize it had gotten so late."

"I'm a few minutes early," David said. As he walked toward her, his hand came around from behind his back and she realized he held a bouquet of roses. "These are for you."

"Oh." She pressed a hand to her chest. "No one has ever brought me flowers who wasn't one of my students." She wrapped her hand around the stems, her fingers brushing his. The current of awareness between them zinged to life and she had to fight to remember they were standing in front of ten kids, as well as Caden Sharpe.

"You should have them all the time," David told her.

She heard a sound that might have been a growl come from Caden, but when she turned he was simply watching the kids and the animals.

"Do you two know each other?" she asked, lowering her nose close to the flower petals and inhaling the fresh scent.

"We've met," David answered. "I get all my beef from Sharpe Pointe Ranch."

"Yep," was Caden's only response.

"Great." She glanced between the two men and wondered why it felt like there was some invisible swordplay going on. "Caden brought his animals to visit with the kids."

"I brought flowers," David said immediately.

She nodded slowly. "Um, yes, you did. And I love them."

David leaned a little closer to Caden. "She loves them."

A muscle ticked in Caden's jaw. "I'm going to round up Fritzi and Otis," he told her. "I'll see you when you bring the kids to the ranch. You're welcome any time."

"I definitely will. Thank you."

She watched him turn to David. "She's going to call me," he said under his breath.

David's shoulders stiffened but before he could respond, Erin placed the flowers on her desk and clapped her hands to get the kids' attention. The noise level was surprisingly low given how excited the kids had been to see the bunny and dog. But she had to admit there was something inherently relaxing about the energy of the two animals. She sensed that with Caden as well, despite his gruff demeanor, and was happy he'd found a purpose in life.

"It's time for the animals to go," she announced to a round of groans. "But Mr. Sharpe has invited us out to his ranch for a longer visit." That got some cheers from the kids. "Can you give him a big thank-you for coming to see us today?"

Caden seemed embarrassed by the attention, and left quickly after packing up the bunny and putting Otis on a leash. Parents started to arrive soon after for pickup, and she waved as David led Rhett from the room.

Soon only Isaac remained, and he sat at one of the small craft tables, his head bent forward.

"Your mom will be here soon, sweetie," Erin told him, bending to clean up a few crayons that had been knocked to the floor.

As she straightened, a tear dropped to the desk in front

of the boy. He quickly wiped at his cheeks and turned away from her.

Isaac had been a tough nut to crack. He rarely interacted with the other kids and usually stayed in the corner pretending to read a book that was far above his basic reading level or doing a puzzle. She'd talked to his classroom teacher and the school counselor, but both women had seemed at a loss for how to reach him. Phone calls to Joel and his mother, Danielle, had gone unanswered and voice mails not returned. Both mom and dad shut Erin down when she tried to speak to them at pickup.

It sometimes felt like the only emotion the boy could access was anger, so to see him embarrassed by his tears broke her heart.

"Do you want to talk about it?" she asked softly, resting her hip on the desk across from where he sat.

He shook his head and refused to meet her gaze.

"Fritzi and Otis were really cool. I noticed Otis seemed to like you a lot." What Erin had witnessed was Isaac planting himself at the dog's side and refusing to give up his spot. He'd spent the entire visit gently stroking Otis's furry head and bending down to whisper in his ear. Thanks to his training as a therapy dog, Otis had been patient with the attention. The other kids had seemed to take it as Isaac's due that he got the prime real estate to love on the animal.

"My dad gave away Jack," he whispered, his voice cracking on the last word.

"Was Jack your dog?"

Isaac looked up, tears shining in his eyes. "The best dog ever. But sometimes he got scared when dad yelled and it made him pee on the floor."

"Some dogs get nervous with loud noises," Erin agreed. Like Caden, Isaac rarely spoke more than monosyllabic responses to the direct questions she asked. It both thrilled her and hurt her heart that he was sharing this small piece of his life with her now.

"He barked, too, but never at me. He loved me best of all."

She fisted her hands at her side, every part of her wanting to reach out and hug the boy but afraid of scaring him away if she did. "I can understand why. You were great with Otis."

"We'll get another dog," a soft voice said from behind Erin.

She whirled around to see Isaac's mother standing in the doorway, not bothering to wipe away the tears that stained her cheeks. Danielle Rodriguez was petite, with beautiful dark hair that fell to the middle of her back and wide-set eyes. Erin guessed they were about the same age, although Danielle's features had a weariness and worldliness stamped across them that came from too many years of hard work, hard living and struggling to raise three kids on her own.

"Your father is not living in my house anymore," she said, switching her gaze to Erin, then back to her son. "And that two-timing jerk isn't invited back. We'll start looking for a dog when I get off work tomorrow. I promise."

Isaac was out of his chair in an instant, hurtling toward his mother and wrapping his arms tight around her waist.

She bent to hug him close, and a lump formed in Erin's throat at the tenderness of the moment. Maybe her program was having the impact she'd hoped for after all.

After a few minutes, Danielle straightened. "Get your backpack and lunch box, Isaac," she told her son, dropping a kiss on the top of his head. "Your sister has dinner going at home." Isaac moved toward the row of backpacks, and

Danielle turned to Erin. "I know Joel sees this program as a way to get out of spending time with him on the days when I work late."

Erin acknowledged that truth with a small nod. "Whatever the reason, I'm glad he's here."

"Me, too," Danielle said, squaring her shoulders. "We've got a long way to go, but kicking Joel to the curb was a good start."

"Will he still be a part of Isaac's life?"

Danielle shrugged. "If he gets his act together. My boy wants his father in his life. But I'm done with Joel, and he's mad as hell. Thinks being my baby daddy gives him a right to whatever he wants from me. He's a cheater and a liar. I deserve better than that."

"You do," Erin agreed instantly.

Isaac came over with his backpack. Although the scowl was back on his face, his little shoulders seemed to carry less of a weight than they did minutes earlier.

"We're going to get another dog," he said quietly, leaning in close to his mother and glancing up at Erin.

"I promise," Danielle whispered, ruffling his hair.

"I'll text you Caden Sharpe's number," Erin told her. "He's the man who brought the therapy pets to visit us today. He runs a small rescue organization out of one of the barns on his ranch. Maybe he can help you find a new dog."

"Thank you," Danielle said. "For everything."

Erin nodded and spent another twenty minutes cleaning up and preparing for Friday's class. She trimmed the stems of the flowers David had given her and put them in a vase before leaving the community center. Most nights classes ran past the time she finished, so there was always someone at the reception desk.

She waved goodbye and walked out into the darkening

night. The crisp breeze made her pull in a sharp breath. The change of seasons was a fickle time in Crimson. Summer could linger for weeks, then disappear within a day. Sometimes fall would last just as long, but more often winter inserted an icy blast of cold to remind everyone what to expect over the next several months.

Colder weather made Erin wish for things she didn't have, like someone to cuddle up to on a frosty winter night. Sugar was a great cat, but not much of a snuggler. It was time to put the heavier comforter on her bed and get out her cold-weather clothes. Maybe she needed to give Caden a call and adopt another furry friend.

She knocked her closed fist against her forehead several times to stop pathetic internal ramblings. In her mind, she'd already skimmed past the date with David to when he inevitably lost interest in her. She'd become one of those single women whose only emotionally intimate relationships were with her pets.

"I don't know what you're thinking," a voice said from the shadows, "but I like that head of yours way too much to watch you abuse it."

She looked up to see David standing a few feet away, hands shoved deep in the front pockets of his jeans. He'd put a heavy canvas jacket on over the flannel shirt he'd worn earlier to pick up Rhett. The bulk of it made him look even broader than normal.

His hair was, as usual, casually tousled, and a hint of stubble shadowed his jaw. He was every one of Erin's fantasies come to life, and it positively terrified her.

"Silly thoughts," she mumbled. "What are you doing here? Is everything okay with Rhett?"

"He's fine. The bar is slow tonight so I had Tracie come up to stay with him and my mom for a few minutes." He took a step closer. "I wanted to see you."

"Hi," she whispered as he drew her forward, wrapping his arms around her. She shivered as he nuzzled his nose against her throat. "You're cold."

"I was waiting for you to keep me warm," he said into her skin, and it was like he'd read her mind.

"Thank you again for the flowers," she said, then lifted onto her toes and kissed him. It was the first time she'd initiated a kiss, and he seemed happy to let her take the lead.

Despite the chilly air, Erin's whole body ignited in flames. She was so lost to this man. While it might be her downfall, she couldn't bring herself to care.

"Tell me about Caden Sharpe," he said when she finally pulled back.

It was difficult to remember her own name, let alone anything else, so it took Erin a few moments to answer. "He's a way nicer guy than people give him credit for. I think he's just misunderstood because of his past and the trouble he got into as a kid."

He studied her face as if trying to decipher some sort of complicated puzzle, which was crazy because Erin had always been an open book.

"Do you always see the best in people?" he asked finally.

"I try to. Is that a bad thing?"

"No. It's one of the things I—" He coughed and cleared his throat. "One of the things that makes you special. You realize Sharpe likes you."

"Because he was kind enough to bring a couple of therapy pets to visit the kids?" She rolled her eyes. "He was doing a favor for a friend and I benefited from it."

"I saw how he looked at you and—"

"Are you jealous?" Erin felt her mouth drop open. "Oh my gosh, I got flowers and a man is jealous over me. Those are two firsts in one day." She pulled away and did a little two-step dance routine in front of him.

"I'm not jealous," David muttered through his teeth. "But don't go out with him, okay?"

She stopped dancing and moved closer. "Of course I'm not going to go out with him. I'm going on a date with you."

He blinked several times. "Some women date more than one man at a time."

"I'm not one of those," she assured him, then wound her arms around his neck and kissed him again. She knew her reaction made her seem like the biggest dork in the world, but she didn't care. This man, who made her heart sing, had brought her flowers *and* wanted her for himself. "I only want you. But I'm flattered that you're jealous."

"Flattered?" He gave a small laugh. "You should tell me to mind my own damn business."

"I like being your business, as long as you know I'm going to continue to see Caden. He and the animals help with the kids."

He inclined his head. "I'd never tell you who you can or can't see. I just want to be sure *you* know you're mine."

Erin's mouth went dry. She'd never had anyone claim her before, and the thought of it was both exhilarating and terrifying.

Then a movement behind David distracted her. A man with a dark hoodie seemed to be watching them from the shadows of the nearby alley. "Um, okay… I think."

David looked over his shoulder, following her gaze, and the man quickly walked down the street away from them.

"Did you know him?" David asked gently.

"I don't think so."

"Where's your car?"

"It's fine," she assured him. "This is Crimson."

"Humor me," he insisted. He kissed the tip of her nose, then walked her to her car.

After a few more kisses, she drove home, tingling from the ends of her hair to her toes. She'd been *claimed* and could barely wait to see what that meant for Saturday.

Chapter Twelve

An unfamiliar lightness bubbled up in David at the sight of Erin waiting for him outside her apartment building Saturday morning. It was as if he'd taken a big swig of champagne and the bubbles were rioting around his stomach. His feelings for her were different from anything he'd experienced before. Today was his chance to make her understand how much she meant to him.

But he had no plan to blurt out that he loved her, as he'd almost done when she was in his arms. Hell, he'd known her for only a few weeks and he wasn't built for love in the first place.

Longing was a different story. The yearning he felt for her pulsed through him like blood in his veins. She gave him hope and made him happy in a way he hadn't even thought possible.

It had seemed like a joke when she'd asked him for an affair. Physical desire was one thing, but his need for

Erin transcended what his body wanted. In such a short time she'd become like the air he breathed, necessary for his very survival.

So he had to make this day count.

As soon as he pulled to a stop, she opened the truck's passenger-side door and climbed in.

"I'm ready for our adventure," she said, tossing her tote bag into the back seat.

He grinned and flipped his sunglasses onto his forehead. "I can see that. You know, I would have come to pick you up at your door." He reached into the back seat and handed her another bouquet of flowers. "I brought these for you."

Color rushed into her cheeks as she gazed at them. "I must seem like a total fool," she said, biting down on her lip. "I know the woman is supposed to wait for the man, but I was so excited and it's a gorgeous day and—"

He leaned in and kissed her, breathing in to capture her scent and the sweetness that always seemed to surround her. "I've been watching the clock all morning," he admitted. "I couldn't wait for this date to begin."

"Let me run and put these in water." She opened the door, then looked back at him over her shoulder. "You don't have to bring me flowers."

"I'm courting you," he reminded her.

She flashed a shy smile. "I don't think I've ever been courted before."

"It's a first for me, too."

"You're doing pretty darn well," she said, and hopped out of the truck.

His cell phone rang as he watched her enter the building. Pulling it out of his pocket, he said a silent prayer everything was okay with Rhett. His nephew had been invited to a birthday party for one of his friends from school, and David's mother had promised she'd get him there safely and follow all the house rules David had set.

He'd asked Tracie, who was working all day, to keep an eye on them this morning. Later this afternoon, David's friend Jase Crenshaw, who had a stepson only a year older than Rhett, was going to take the boys to the park and out for ice cream. He'd also asked Olivia Travers to stop by, trying to cover all his bases to make sure Rhett was safe.

Angela seemed to take it all in stride. Since the fiasco on the mountain, she'd been on her best behavior and David had to admit he was grateful to his mother for her help.

It wasn't a local number flashing on his screen, and he recognized the Phoenix area code from where Jenna was doing her stint in rehab. His stomach in knots, he accepted the call, only to have his sister immediately lay into him.

"I can't believe you're messing around with Rhett's teacher," she said, her voice a low hiss.

"Jenna," he said, breathing out a sigh. "Is everything okay?"

"Do I sound okay? I had to trade three packs of Skittles to be able to make this phone call. You know how I love Skittles."

One side of his mouth curved. "I know. Exactly why are you calling?"

"To tell you to leave Ms. MacDonald alone."

"How do you even—"

"Mom told me. She said you've got the hots for Rhett's teacher and you're even taking her out on a date. As far as I know, you haven't dated anyone since you moved to Crimson and you can't start with the teacher. She's off-limits."

"Why?" he asked, trying to keep his temper under wraps. His sister was doing great in her program, but he knew she was still fragile. The last thing he needed was to set her off.

She blew an agitated breath into the phone. "Rhett loves that woman and whatever program of hers he's going to in the afternoons. It's all he talks about when he calls."

"She's great with him."

"Yeah, so if you piss her off by treating her like crap, she could take it out on him."

"She'd never do that," he answered automatically, then added, "Besides, I'm not going to hurt her."

"You hurt everybody."

The words were like a knife to his gut, because coming from his sister they meant so much more. Unwanted memories flooded through him. He swallowed against the bile rising in his throat, trying to forget. Willing himself to forget.

"I know I've messed things up royally," Jenna said in a quieter tone, "and I appreciate you stepping in to help with Rhett. I need his world to be stable, David. I need to believe he's going to get through this. She's a big part of that."

So am I, he wanted to argue, but only repeated, "I'm not going to hurt her."

At that moment Erin emerged from the apartment building, smiling as she walked toward him. If his sister was right, he should throw the truck into Reverse and drive away before this went any further. Because there was no doubt in his mind how far he'd take it if Erin got in next to him.

All the way.

"Promise me you'll leave her alone," his sister whispered.

"I've got to go," he said as an answer. "You take care of you, Jenna. I've got things under control."

He ended the call before she could argue, and he had no doubt she would if given the chance. His sister had seen him at his worst, just like he had with her. How could either of them believe the other had things under control?

Erin climbed into the truck. "I'm ready." She turned to him and her smile disappeared. "What's wrong? I saw you on the phone. Is it Rhett?"

"My sister called." He tapped his fingers on the steering wheel, wishing he hadn't talked to Jenna. All of his happiness from earlier had been colored by her doubts, which mingled with his into some sort of poison that seeped into every cell.

Erin placed a hand on his arm, and the gentle touch felt like a brand through the fabric of his shirt. "Is she okay?"

"She told me not to go out with you," he said quietly. As much as he didn't want to share Jenna's warning with Erin, it was the only way through this.

"She doesn't even know me." Erin drew back her hand. "Is it the mercy date thing?"

He shifted to face her. "What 'mercy date thing'?"

"You taking me out as a thank-you for helping with Rhett." She made a face. "Because of that stupid comment I made about the affair."

David raked a hand through his hair. He hated the doubt that now shadowed Erin's dark eyes. He'd done his best to plan a perfect day, and now it was tainted before they even started.

"She doesn't want me to go out with you because you're too good for me. She thinks I'm going to hurt you."

When Erin didn't immediately refute his sister's claim, David slammed a hand against the steering wheel. "Damn it," he muttered. "You agree. We haven't even started and you think I'm going to hurt you."

He stared out the front of the truck, unable to look at

her and see the truth on her face. This was his chance. *She* was his chance to finally get something wholly right in his life. And not one person believed he could do it.

"David."

"We should end this now," he told her. "I don't want to hurt you."

"There are no guarantees in life." He felt her press closer. "Please look at me."

He gave a small laugh, then turned. "I can't resist a 'please,' either." Her face was only inches away from his and, once again, her beauty slayed him. He focused on the tiny flecks of gold at the edges of her dark eyes and tried not to think about losing her before she was even his.

"My life has been safe for as long as I can remember. I didn't risk anything and had little to lose. My job is stable, my boyfriend bored me to tears. Typically, the most excitement I have is when a new book from one of my favorite authors comes out."

He smiled. "I'm going to read one of those romance novels so I know what all the hype is about."

She rolled her eyes. "My point is that with you, I feel like I'm living the adventure I've always wanted."

"You're doing that on your own," he countered. "You're helping with Rhett. You've made a difference in the lives of the kids in your program. It's you, Erin."

"Then I'm happy to share it with you." She sat back and arched a brow at him. "You know, I could be the one to hurt you. I could break your heart."

David opened his mouth to tell her his heart was too closed off to be in any danger of breaking. But at that moment a flash of pain pierced his chest so sharply it made his breath catch. "Anything is possible," he answered instead, struggling to keep his voice neutral.

"That's right," she agreed, thankfully oblivious to the

strange things going on inside him. "Anything is possible. Life is a gamble. I want to take a risk with you, David. No matter what the outcome."

Despite his reckless youth, all his life, David had made decisions based on keeping himself or the people in his life safe. Baseball gave him a way out of his tumultuous childhood. Moving to Crimson had made it easier to watch out for Jenna and Rhett. The brewery gave him a stable income doing something he was good at. He'd always chosen women who wanted nothing more from him than a good time. Being with Erin wasn't safe—for either of them.

But she was worth the risk.

He leaned in and kissed her deeply, realizing he'd quickly become addicted to the taste of her. The more time he spent with her, the more he wanted.

How could he consider pushing her away? She was too important, and he wasn't going to hurt her. He wouldn't let himself.

"Are you ready for the best day of your life?" he asked, finally pulling back and shifting the truck into gear.

She laughed. "Pretty confident in yourself."

"I'm confident in us," he corrected and turned the truck toward the highway.

Butterflies danced through Erin's stomach as David drove out of town. It had been easy enough to toss off the comment about either of them getting hurt, but she had no doubt her heart was on the line.

As much as she'd tried to stop her feelings from spiraling out of control, Erin was falling for this man. Hard. If this day was half as good as he promised, she'd be a goner for sure.

But she hadn't been lying when she told him he was worth the risk. Her life had been spent taking the safe path, but the only things that had gotten her were frustration and discontent.

Even if she lost her heart, at least she could say she tried.

They headed up the mountain, and he turned off at the sign for Cloud Cabin.

"This is private land," she said, even as she leaned forward to gaze up at the tall pines arching over the road.

"I know," he answered.

"Crimson Ranch owns Cloud Cabin. Josh and Sara opened it last year for their guests. I guess a lot of family reunions and corporate events are held there in the summer."

One side of his mouth crooked. "Yep."

She figured David must know what he was doing, but curiosity niggled at her. "Are we trespassing?"

"Nope."

"Are you going to tell me anything?"

"You look beautiful."

Erin sat back in her seat and didn't bother to hide her smile. Even if David had doubts and his sister had doubts and everyone around them had doubts, this day felt perfect to Erin. "It's an adventure," she whispered.

A couple of miles in, a driveway split off to the right. David took the turn and within a few minutes they arrived at Cloud Cabin. The house was magnificent, large without being ostentatious and made completely out of hewn logs. A patio wrapped around two sides of the cabin on the second floor, and she could see a fire pit and several pieces of outdoor furniture arranged at the far end.

"It's amazing," she whispered.

David parked the car in front of one of the three garage bays on the lower level. "Some famous architect Sara knows designed it. They brought in the timber from Montana, but sourced the rock locally from the quarry near Meeker."

"What's that?" She pointed to the small cabin that sat at the other side of the clearing.

"Caretaker's cabin," David told her. "When they have big groups at Cloud Cabin, the staff stays there."

"Is anyone up here now?"

"You and me." He bussed her cheek.

She found herself unable to move even as he got out of the truck and came around to open her door.

"You okay, honey?"

She bit down on her lip. "I've lived in this town most of my life, so I'm used to seeing rich people. I've had wealthy students and walked the streets of Aspen, but I've never… I've never actually been in a place like this."

He leaned in and whispered in her ear, "You have to get out of the truck if you're going to make it to the cabin today."

She laughed and pushed him away. "You make fun, but that's because you were a rich and famous baseball player. You probably hung out on yachts and stuff."

"A few speedboats in Miami, but no yachts." He took her hand and tugged until she stepped out onto the gravel driveway. "Money makes things easier, but it's not important beyond that."

"What people do with it is important," she corrected. "Like fund an after-school program."

"And that," he agreed. "This place is ours for the day. Let's go explore it."

He laced his fingers with hers as they walked up the flagstone path that led to the front door. David produced a key from his pocket and unlocked the door, holding it open for Erin to walk in.

She wasn't sure what she expected, but it wasn't a space

that immediately seemed to wrap around her and make her feel at home. The foyer was cozy and bright, with framed paintings of mountain vistas on each wall. The family room was situated to one side. Rich, colorful rugs covered the hardwood floor, and overstuffed furniture had been arranged to make a cozy sitting area in front of the massive stone fireplace.

"What do you want to do first?" he asked. "There are ATVs in the garage, a hot tub out back." He led her into the kitchen, where wood cabinets and gorgeous marble countertops balanced the industrial feel of gleaming stainless steel appliances.

"I could make us something to eat."

She glanced up at him. "You're going to cook?"

"Let me rephrase that," he said. "I could heat up the food that the head chef at the brewery prepared for us."

She grinned. "You've thought of everything."

He turned to her fully, wrapped his arms around her waist. "I wanted this day to be about you and me. No distractions. No real life butting its ugly head in. You and me."

"You and me," she repeated, and held on tight as he claimed her mouth. It was like they were the only two people in the world, and she let all her worries and doubts drift away. He lifted her into his arms, then sat her on the edge of the counter, pressing himself into the V of her legs.

Her body tingled with need and awareness, and she could feel that he wanted her, too. It made her want to forget everything else and beg him to take her to the bedroom. What would it be like to spend an entire day in bed with this man?

The air seemed to get caught in her throat at the thought, because what if she ruined everything by not knowing what she was doing. Kissing was one thing, but the rest…

"ATVs," she blurted, wrenching herself away from him.

He stared at her as if she were speaking a foreign language, then laughed softly. "ATVs it is."

Chapter Thirteen

David breathed in the pine-scented air and tried to keep his focus on the path in front of him, and not on Erin's body pressed tight against his on the back of the ATV.

Once again, his desire for her had almost gotten the best of him. If she hadn't stopped it, he would have taken her right on the counter…or the floor…or wherever she would have him. He'd arranged with Josh to borrow the cabin so he could give Erin a day away from the responsibilities of life but still remain close to town if Rhett needed him.

It was becoming more and more difficult to keep his mind on anything except what she would feel like under him and how much he wanted to explore every inch of her beautiful body.

She shifted behind him, and he slowed the powerful machine, not wanting to scare her. Instead, she leaned in closer and shouted, "Faster." That was all the encouragement David needed to hit the throttle.

He tightened his grip on the ATV's handles and maneuvered through the pine forest and out into a clearing that overlooked the valley below them. As soon as he pulled to a stop and cut the motor, Erin jumped off the back.

"That was so cool," she cried, bouncing up and down on her toes. "We were flying."

He grinned at her happiness. Everything with Erin felt new and made him want to shake off his typical attitude and see the world through her eyes.

"Can I drive on the way back?"

"Of course." He gestured to the meadow behind them. "The trail loops around this field. You can use it like a practice course."

"On my own?" she asked, her eyes bright with excitement.

He laughed. "Ditching me already? Yes, I brought picnic supplies. I'll lay everything out while you take this baby for a ride."

He unloaded the soft-sided cooler and blanket he'd packed in the ATV's cargo area. Despite the fact that it was early October, they'd been blessed with a summer-like day. The sun shone brightly in the clear blue sky, and even the breeze that whispered through the trees felt warm.

"Climb on," he told her, then stifled a groan at the way her eyes widened. "The ATV," he clarified, wishing he'd locked her in the cabin and had his wicked way with her when he had the chance.

Instead he watched her position herself on the ATV. He gave instructions on how to put it into gear, braking and steering around turns. Erin's fingers trembled slightly as she gripped the handlebars. He wrapped his hand around hers. "Don't be nervous."

"I've never even driven a stick shift," she admitted.

"We'll put that on the list," he assured her, "and this is way easier. Just don't make sharp turns going fast."

"Because I'll flip it?" she asked, biting down on her lip.

He couldn't resist the urge to brush a quick kiss across her mouth. "You're not going to flip it. Go get 'em, Erin Earnhardt."

She turned the key, then shifted the machine into gear. He gave her a thumbs-up when she glanced over at him, and with a nod she hit the gas and took off down the path.

The ATV lurched forward several times as she got used to driving it. But after a few minutes, she was moving at a steady pace around the perimeter of the meadow. Slow but steady.

She pulled to a stop in front of him when she'd circled the entire path and clapped her hands together. "How'd I do?"

"Great. But you can go a little faster if you want."

She scrunched up her nose. "That was boring, right?"

"Watching you is never boring, but trust yourself. You can handle the machine." He reached out and tugged on the end of her ponytail. "You can handle anything."

Determination seeped into her gaze, lighting her eyes with a fire that made him want to shout for joy. This was the woman he knew and...

Once again, not going there.

She steered the ATV down the path once more. Within minutes, David regretted his words as the ATV went faster and faster around the dirt trail. He motioned for her to slow down as she sped past him, but she either didn't see or chose to ignore the warning. Her hair came undone and flew out behind her, like she was some ancient Amazon warrior racing into battle.

He held his breath as the ATV suddenly veered sharply to the right, and two of the wheels lifted from the ground.

"No," he shouted, already running toward her.

At the last second, Erin shifted her weight and the machine straightened on the path once more.

David bent forward, placing his palms on his knees as he struggled to pull air in and out of his lungs. The ATV was at his side a moment later, and he quickly turned the key, then hauled her into his arms.

"What the hell happened?" He hugged her close, then gripped the sides of her head with his hands, moving her away enough that he could examine her face. "Are you okay?"

She grinned up at him. "Did you see me go up on two wheels?"

"See you," he shouted. "I almost had a heart attack watching you. I thought I said no sharp turns."

"A chipmunk ran across the trail."

He couldn't understand how she remained so calm when his heart was rioting in his chest. "I didn't want to hurt him."

"So flipping the machine seemed like a better alternative?"

She laughed and smoothed the hair from his forehead. "I didn't flip. I had the whole thing under control. Remember, I can handle anything."

He stared at her for a moment, taking in the pure joy on her face. "You're really okay?"

"Maybe your mom was onto something when she said you were a worrywart."

"My mom has no idea what she's talking about."

Erin reached up and covered his hands with hers, a frown pulling on the corners of her mouth. "You're shaking," she whispered.

"You scared the hell out of me." He closed his eyes

and leaned in to place a kiss on her forehead. "Adventure is fun, but it would kill me if I couldn't keep you safe."

He touched his lips to each of her eyelids, then trailed kisses down her cheek and along her jawline. It was as if he needed to touch every part of her to reassure himself she was okay.

"I'm fine," she assured him. "I'm sorry I scared you." She tilted her head so that her mouth met his, and the kiss quickly turned molten. He couldn't wait anymore. His body still shook from fear of her being hurt, and he channeled his thundering emotions into the kiss. Scooping her into his arms, he strode across the field to the place he'd spread out the blanket and lowered her to it.

The sun remained warm on his back and he buried his nose in the crook of Erin's neck, breathing in her scent mixed with the smell of pine trees and fresh mountain air. It was intoxicating in a way not even the finest liquor or the most powerful drug could be, and he was an instant addict.

His body trembled as he tried to control his need, to take things slow, to allow this to be her choice. More than anything, he wanted her to choose him.

"I want you," she whispered into his ear, and it was like every prayer he'd never had the guts to say had been answered.

For a moment Erin wondered if she'd said the wrong thing. David stilled above her, the muscles of his back going rigid under her hands.

He lifted his head, the intensity in his blue eyes stoking the fire inside her almost as much as his kisses had.

"I had a plan for this," he told her, his voice rough. "Champagne and rose petals and—"

"Actual rose petals?" she asked on a hoarse laugh.

To her surprise, pink tinged his cheeks. Who knew she could make David McCay blush?

"It seemed like something one of your romance heroes would do," he told her.

"You're the only man I want." She ran her hands down his back and up under the hem of his sweater. He gritted his teeth as she drew her nails along the bare skin of his back. "And I've waited long enough, David. Please don't make me wait anymore."

"I guess I can't refuse since you said please," he whispered against her lips.

Then he kissed her again and all her senses began to sing, a choir of desire and lust building in her body. After a few minutes he sat back, straddling her legs as he knelt. He slowly unbuttoned her denim shirt, his gaze fierce as inch by inch, her skin was revealed to him.

She shrugged the shirt off her shoulders, any wariness she had about being with a man so much more experienced than she was forgotten because of the longing reflected in his eyes. Longing for her.

The sun was like a warm bath on her skin, and she reached forward and tugged his sweater up and over his head.

She'd seen his chest before, but the sunlight casting his body in silhouette was perfection. He rolled to one side and quickly toed off his boots and undid his jeans, pushing them down over his lean hips.

Reaching behind her back, she unhooked the clasp of her bra and let the soft satin material fall away from her body, then shimmied out of her jeans and panties. David let out a small groan as he knelt at her side again, a condom packet held between two fingers.

"You make me want to lose myself," he said, covering

her body with his. "You make me forget everything except this moment."

"I think that's the point," she said, then gasped as he filled her. She wound her arms around his neck and kissed him, arching up so that every part of her touched every part of him.

He groaned in response and she felt an unfamiliar surge of power lick through her. She could feel that he was holding himself back, trying to take it slow because that's what a woman like Erin would want. But she wanted *more*. She wanted everything, and David was the man she wanted to give it to her.

Or even better, she'd take it from him. She moved her hips at the same time she raked her nails over his muscled shoulders. "Let go," she whispered, and without even having to add "please," he gave her exactly what she wanted.

They found a rhythm all their own, deep and intense and exactly what Erin craved. Her pleasure built in thick waves and she lost herself in the sensation of it and the fact that David seemed as overwhelmed by desire as she felt. He whispered her name like a prayer and buried his face in her neck. Then he nipped at the sensitive flesh of her ear and Erin spun out of control, gripping him tighter as she hurtled over the edge of passion.

He followed a moment later and Erin wasn't sure if it was her own heartbeat or his she heard pounding through her head. He continued to kiss her throat as she came back down, humming soothing little sounds against her skin.

"That was incredible," David whispered into her hair. "You were incredible."

Erin still felt like she was floating through the air, and the only thing that tethered her to earth was his deep voice. It was as if she'd shrugged off the old, boring version of herself and had begun to step into becoming the person she was meant to be.

"*We* were incredible," she corrected him, because she knew that nothing in her life would ever compare to this moment. Whether they lasted another week or for an eternity—and how she longed for an eternity—he would always hold her heart.

Even though he hadn't said the words *I love you*, she had to believe he felt something for her. It was in the way he looked at her, the intensity of his touch, the way her body came alive as he moved inside her.

"Are you hungry?" He trailed his fingers over her stomach in small figure-eight patterns. "You distracted me with your race car ATV driving and I never got the food unpacked."

She kissed his shoulder. "I think you distracted me by getting naked," she said, earning a rumbling laugh from him. "But now I'm starving."

After several long, lingering kisses, he rolled away from her and she grabbed her clothes. As she dressed, Erin looked around in wonder. She'd just had the most amazing sex she could ever imagine in the woods. Outside. She almost giggled at the thought of it. Talk about an adventure.

They ate the lunch he'd packed, sandwiches, fresh fruit and the best chocolate chip cookies she'd ever tasted. After repacking everything into the ATV, they took a short hike up to another overlook. Erin told him more about her relationship with her mother and her friends at school. While David peppered her with questions, he offered little about his life in return.

"What happened to Jenna?" she asked finally, as they stood together gazing out over the valley.

"You were there that night," he said casually. "You saw her apartment and—"

"I'm not talking about recently." She made her voice level, even though nerves tumbled through her. "I mean years ago. Something happened, and I don't know what it was, but it's clear you feel responsible for it."

He dropped her hand and stalked toward the path that led to the ATV. For a moment she thought he was going to leave her standing by herself in the woods. How was it possible he'd willingly shared his body with her but not whatever it was that so obviously burdened him about his sister?

Just before disappearing around the bend, he turned and walked back to her, his gaze fierce.

"I've never talked to anyone about Jenna," he said.

"Let me be the first."

He was silent for so long she thought he might refuse. Then he gave a jerky nod. "I started playing for a club baseball team in high school. Kids from the area, but no one from my neighborhood. These were boys whose parents could afford to sponsor the team, buy us the best equipment and make sure college scouts took notice. I knew my only chance of getting out of our crappy neighborhood was a scholarship." He shook his head. "Jenna didn't like the team because it took me away from home. We were on the road a lot during the summer."

"It was your dream," Erin said softly.

"Yeah," he agreed, his voice filled with bitterness. "My dream. Mom had started dating a new guy around that time and it got serious real quick. I didn't mind the guy— he wasn't as bad as some of her boyfriends—but Jenna didn't like him. He got too into the 'father' role, trying to impose house rules and curfews."

"This man lived with your family?"

David shrugged. "Not officially, but he stayed over a lot. Mom definitely knew how to pick the losers. Jenna asked me to kick him out or talk to Mom about kicking him out, but I was too busy with baseball to even care. The dude left me alone. It was Jenna he wanted to fall into line. Her wild streak had always been blatant and she was mouthy with anyone who gave her grief about it."

"She sounds like a lot to handle."

"We mostly raised ourselves, so she wasn't much into being 'handled.'" He gave a small laugh. "She still isn't. But it doesn't excuse what happened to her."

His shoulders rose and fell, as if he was struggling to catch his breath. Suddenly all of it came together. His protective instinct around his sister while holding tight to the belief that he'd failed her. The ambivalence toward his mother. Her mouth went dry but she forced out the words, "Did your mother's boyfriend—"

"He tried but Jenna fought him off." His hands fisted at his sides. "He knocked her around pretty good, but my mom came home from work. He went after her, too, but a neighbor called the cops and he was arrested." He turned to her, his eyes bleak. "I should have been home that day after school. We didn't even have baseball practice, but some of the guys were hanging out so I went with them instead."

She grabbed his hand and forced open his fist, lacing her fingers with his. "It wasn't your fault, David. You were a teenage boy. How were you supposed to know something like that would happen?"

"Jenna asked me to walk home with her," he whispered. "She didn't like being alone in the apartment with Mom's boyfriends. I told her she'd watched too many after-school movies and she was just trying to get attention." He blew out a breath. "She never forgave me."

Erin moved so she stood directly in front of him and waited until he finally looked down at her.

"She hasn't forgiven you? Or you haven't forgiven yourself?"

Chapter Fourteen

David stared down into Erin's luminous brown eyes, unable to speak. To his knowledge, Jenna and their mother were the only people in the world who knew about what had happened that afternoon. They were the only ones who truly understood how badly he'd failed them.

Until now.

He'd been reluctant to share the memory with Erin, terrified it would change things between them. How could she not despise him after how much his selfish choice had cost his family?

But instead of judgment, her gaze was filled with sympathy and…could that possibly be understanding he saw when she looked at him?

"What's the difference?" he asked when he finally found his voice. "I failed her. I failed my mother."

"Your mother's boyfriend was at fault. You were a kid."

"I was the man of the house," he insisted, because that

was the truth he knew. A tear spilled from the corner of her eye, and he caught it with his thumb. "Why are you crying? The last thing I want to do is make you cry."

She gently pushed at his chest, but when he started to take a step back, she leaned in and wrapped her arms around his waist. "You big oaf," she said into his jacket. "I'm crying *for* you. For all the years you've carried that guilt around inside you and punished yourself for something that was *not* your fault."

Her words stunned him. He'd never cared about anyone's opinion of him. David made his own luck in life—good or bad—and he told himself that's how he liked it. But something unfurled in his chest as he held Erin, looking out to the town that had become his true home. She still wanted him despite his failures, and the realization made him almost dizzy with relief.

"Don't cry, sweetheart," he whispered, resting his chin on the top of her head and rubbing her back. "I'm not worth a single one of your tears."

"You are," she insisted, sniffing loudly. "You're worth a lot more than you believe. I hate that you can't see the man that I do when I look at you."

He closed his eyes and breathed in the scent of her, let it wash away all the bad things he believed about himself—if only for a short time. Hell, it was good to feel truly happy. "I think that makes us even," he told her, "because I hate that you think you're ordinary."

She gave a soft laugh and wiped her face on his jacket. "That's different."

He tipped up her face and kissed her. "You are beautiful, extraordinary and special to me."

Her lips curved into a smile against his. "This is the best date ever."

"And we haven't even hit the hot tub," he said, earning another laugh.

Feeling lighter than he had in years, David led her back down the trail to the ATV. He insisted she drive back to the cabin, a fact he was pretty certain thrilled her given how many times she let out whoops of delight as she maneuvered through the trees.

They changed into bathing suits kept at the cabin for guests, and he opened a bottle of wine before climbing into the bubbling hot tub with a breathtaking view of the surrounding peaks.

The wine lasted longer than the bathing suits, and it wasn't long before he carried Erin into the cabin's master bedroom and made love to her again.

He'd assumed being with her would make the pounding need inside him lessen, but every touch and whisper that crossed her lips only made him want her more. There had never been anyone like her in his life. For the first time ever, he wanted to claim a woman as his and never let go.

The sun dipped over the mountain far too soon and they made their way back down to town.

He'd called both his mother and Tracie from the cabin's landline to check on Rhett and how the day was going. The boy had been thrilled with all the attention he was getting during the day, but when he heard his uncle was with Erin, he begged David to bring her home to have dinner with them.

"Is your mother going to be okay with that?" Erin took his hand as they drove down the mountain road.

"My guess is she'd rather have you there than me," he told her.

"That's not true. She loves you." Erin squeezed his fingers. "She's your mother, David."

"Right. And when do I get to meet your mom?"

Immediately she tried to pull her hand away from his, but he quickly interlaced their fingers.

"My mom and dad wouldn't believe we're together," she told him.

He felt embarrassment wash through him and struggled to keep his voice even. "Because I didn't graduate from college?"

"No," she insisted. "Not at all. You're a former baseball star and you own the hottest bar in Crimson. She's even been to Elevation. My mom likes the honey wheat beer and the artichoke dip."

"It's a real crowd pleaser, but I think you've got it all wrong. I could throw a ball and now I make beer. It's not the same as what you do, Erin. You change kids' lives."

"Kindergarten is just colors and shapes and noise control according to her."

"It's a big deal," David told her, willing her to believe him. To recognize how amazing she was and all she'd accomplished. "How long have you been a teacher?"

"Seven years."

"So your first class of students is in sixth grade?"

She nodded. "Their last year at the elementary school before junior high."

"I bet more than a few of them still visit you."

"Of course. They come in at recess or help me during my planning session."

"Do they do that for all the teachers?"

He studied her face as he waited for an answer. He could see her mulling over the question and how to respond. "It's just that I'm the most accessible," she said finally.

"Crimson Elementary is one building. All the teachers are accessible. You make an impression, Erin. How many famous people have you heard refer to teachers who made a difference in their lives?"

She rolled her eyes. "They're talking about college professors like my father was or acting teachers or vocal coaches. Not kindergarten."

"You're making a difference to Rhett."

"Because he's a great kid."

"Jase Crenshaw told me his stepson with Asperger's still asks for you to be his teacher."

"Davey is really special, too."

"Which kids aren't special to you?"

He turned down the alley behind Elevation and parked in his spot in back of the kitchen.

"They're all special," she answered immediately.

"You have to admit some of them are little pains in the neck. I know I was." He turned off the ignition and braced himself for her response.

"Don't say that. I'm sure you were adorable at five."

"I was a hellion."

"The kids I have are amazing."

"What about Isaac Martin?"

She hesitated, then said, "Well, I never had him as a student because they moved to Crimson last year. But I've been getting to know him in the after-school program and he's actually quite sensitive. I think the trouble between his parents caused him to act out, but his mom changing things around will help."

"You proved my point." He hopped out of the truck and walked around to her door. When she climbed out, he took her hand. "You're the kind of teacher who believes in the potential of each of her kids."

"Kindergarten is all about potential."

"Tapping into that potential is all about you."

She opened her mouth, as if to argue with him, then

snapped it shut. Her eyes widened and a smile lit up her entire face. "I'm good at what I do," she said softly, as if it were a new revelation to her. "I'm really good."

"The best," he agreed. "Don't let anyone make you feel like you don't matter. You do."

They walked through the narrow space between the buildings, and David unlocked the door leading up to the apartment.

"This day was perfect." Erin leaned in to kiss him.

"You're perfect," he said. And for the first time in forever, David felt totally at peace with his world.

The following week, preparations were well under way for the town's Oktoberfest celebration, although that meant Erin hadn't seen as much of David as she would have liked.

She'd had dinner with him, as well as Angela and Rhett, most evenings and last night he'd knocked on her apartment door at nearly midnight. He'd clearly been exhausted but showed up holding a small bouquet of flowers, which had become his calling card.

"Courting," he whispered into her hair as he wrapped her in a tight hug. "I hope I didn't wake you. I know I should have called or texted first, but I had to see you." He kissed her, then stifled a yawn.

"If this is the kind of energy you put into a booty call," she said with a laugh, leading him into the apartment, "you need to work on your skills."

He nuzzled his face into the crook of her neck. "I have mad skills."

"Trust me, I know." She set the flowers on the counter and turned in his arms. "But you also have dark circles under your eyes."

"Are you offering me makeup?"

"I'm offering," she said, tugging him toward the bedroom, "a few hours of decent sleep. In a real bed, not the couch."

He let out a soft moan. "I hate to admit how good that sounds. I came here with every intention of having my wicked way with you."

"Save your energy for Oktoberfest."

"Only if you promise to wear a dirndl to the competition."

"To match your lederhosen?" she asked, pushing him down onto the bed.

"You know you love my lederhosen," he said sleepily, bending forward to take off his boots.

Erin's heart swelled as she watched him undress. There were so many things about this man that she loved. The way he tried so hard at everything he did—from the brewery to taking care of Rhett to repairing his relationship with his mother. The way he made Erin feel both cherished and challenged—as if he had no doubt she could handle everything life threw at her.

She would have never guessed that the crush she'd had on him for months could so quickly turn into a much deeper connection. But somehow they fit together perfectly. She softened some of his rough edges and he'd helped her unlock her confidence. His belief in her helped her realize she needed to believe in herself.

She'd even gone to see Mari Clayton from the Aspen Foundation, asking the woman to reconsider funding Erin's after-school program. Before David, Erin would have simply accepted the foundation's declining her request. But the program with the kids was too important to give up and she had no doubt any longer that she was the one meant to lead it.

Sugar rose from her place on the pillow next to Erin's

and slowly walked over to rub against David's back. He'd even won over Erin's cantankerous cat.

The past month hadn't been easy, and they were both being pulled in a hundred different directions. But the time they spent together was precious, and Erin wanted to believe they had the basis for something strong and lasting.

She was already in her pajamas, so had no issue crawling into bed next to him when he held up the sheet and comforter. He pulled her in close so her back was against his chest, then draped an arm around her.

"I really did mean to ravish you," he said, dropping a featherlight kiss at the base of her neck.

"Sleep," she whispered, and within seconds felt him relax and heard his breathing slow.

She snuggled in tighter and closed her eyes, happy to fall asleep in David's arms and even happier when she awoke an hour later to find him unbuttoning her pajama top.

"I got my second wind," he told her, and proceeded to make good on all his promises about ravishing and wicked ways.

They made love deep into the night, but he left at dawn, wanting to be back at his place before Rhett woke up.

"Jenna will be out of rehab soon," he told her as he put on his jeans and boots. "She's doing well and can't wait to get back to her son."

"Do you think she's going to be able to stay healthy this time?"

A shadow passed over his face. "She loves Rhett more than anything." He sighed. "I definitely hope she loves him enough to make the alcohol and drugs a thing of the past. My mom is going to stay in town for a while, and I plan to be more involved in Jenna's life, whether she wants it or not."

"You're bringing your family back together." She sat up in the bed, tucking the sheet under her arms. "I'm proud of you."

He stilled as color crept into his cheeks. "Thanks."

"I like making you blush."

"I don't blush," he said, sounding offended, which made her smile.

"You're definitely blushing," she told him with a wink.

Pulling his sweater over his head, he moved toward her, then tugged on the sheet.

Erin yelped and held it tight to her body, but let it slip when he kissed her deeply. "First you hint that I need a nap and now you accuse me of blushing. What's next?"

"Next is you go home before *I* have *my* wicked way with you," she said, squealing when he tickled her.

"So tempting," he whispered. "When my life gets back to normal, I'm taking you away for the weekend. You and me and a hotel room all weekend long."

"I think I'd like that."

"I think you'd love that."

She had to bite her tongue to keep from whispering, *I think I love you.*

But he must have read something in her eyes, because he pulled back suddenly, like she'd scalded him. Definitely too soon for *I love you*, but he was planning weekend trips, which meant something.

He brushed her hair away from her face. "Thank you for tonight."

"Literally my pleasure."

He flashed a lopsided grin, then walked out of her bedroom. She waited until she heard the apartment door close then threw on her robe and went to lock the door. She parted the front curtains and watched him drive away, wondering if she'd ever get used to the thought of David McCay belonging to her.

Chapter Fifteen

"Stop messing with your hair," Melody told Erin Friday night as the two women walked toward the park at the center of downtown Crimson. "You look beautiful."

Erin immediately pressed her hand to her side. "I wasn't messing with my hair. I'm just not used to wearing it down and styled."

"It looks pretty," Melody's daughter, Elaina, told her. "Like you're a princess."

Erin felt a bit like a princess tonight, the first evening of Crimson's Oktoberfest celebration. Melody had convinced her to have her hair done at a local salon and buy a new outfit for the event. Although it was out of her comfort zone, Erin had chosen a chic but casual fitted sweaterdress from the small boutique they'd gone to in Aspen. It had been over her budget but too perfect to pass up. Paired with her vintage cowboy boots and some chunky jewelry she'd borrowed from Melody, she felt amazing and couldn't wait to see David's reaction.

"Thank you, sweetie," Erin said, and smoothed a hand down the girl's blond braid. She nudged Melody, who was pushing her son, Lane, in the stroller. "Do I look like the kind of woman who could attract the town's hottie brewmaster?" she whispered.

"I don't think you need to worry about that," Melody answered with a laugh. "You've already caught him—hook, line and sinker."

"That's right." Erin took a deep breath and whispered, "David McCay is mine." A tiny bubble of happiness floated up inside her. She'd done it. In the space of a month, she'd turned her ordinary life into something extraordinary. It wasn't just David. Karen Henderson, the elementary school's principal, had called Erin into her office the previous afternoon. Apparently she'd fielded calls from several families requesting to be put on a Kidzone waiting list.

While Karen admitted she'd been skeptical at the beginning, Erin's program was turning out to be a valuable asset to the community and great PR for the school district. Mari at the Aspen Foundation had agreed to do another site visit and allowed Erin to resubmit her grant proposal along with letters of recommendation from eight of the ten families who had kids enrolled in the program.

"Where's Daddy?" Elaina asked, gripping Melody's leg. "There are lots of people here."

"He's keeping everyone safe," Melody said gently. "We'll see him when he gets off duty in a little while."

Erin looked around the streets of Crimson, with the shops still brightly lit to take advantage of the Oktoberfest crowds. She hadn't seen so many people converge on downtown since last year's Christmas festival. "It's huge," she said, clapping her hands. "I knew it would be, but I'm so happy for David. He worked hard to make this event a success."

"Apparently lots of people like beer and German food." Melody smiled. "When are the beer contest winners announced?"

Erin glanced at her watch. "In about ten minutes. Let's head to the grandstand. I want to be there when his name is called."

"The supportive girlfriend," Melody said, gently elbowing Erin in the ribs. "It's a good look on you."

Suddenly there was a commotion on the sidewalk in front of them. Melody gripped the stroller as Erin grabbed Elaina's hand, pulling the girl toward the side of the brick building.

A moment later, Joel Martin stood directly in front of her, and she gasped as she saw the flash of a blade in his hand.

"You did this to me," he said, his voice an angry snarl.

Erin's throat went dry even as her heart pounded in her chest. "I don't know what you're talking about," she whispered as she pushed Elaina behind her. "Please put away the knife."

"The hell you don't," he said, his eyes narrowing. "My old lady kicked me out because of you. My kid don't want to talk to me. Your boyfriend made sure I lost my job at the tire store, and now I got nothin'."

She could see a crowd beginning to form in a wide circle around them, and met Melody's gaze behind Joel's shoulder. "Elaina," she whispered. "Go to your Mommy, okay?" She started to give the girl a gentle push but Joel stepped forward.

"Don't move," he shouted. "You don't get to tell no one what to do tonight. Not until I'm done with you."

The little girl buried her face against Erin's leg with a whimper, and Erin saw Melody's face turn white as ash.

"I can't talk to you when you're waving a knife at me," she said, willing her voice to be calm. "Please let the girl go to her mom. She has nothing to do with this."

"You and your damn kids," he muttered. "You think you're so great, like you rule the school."

She shook her head. "I don't think—"

"All this started with that stupid McCay boy. His mama was a hot little piece, but I didn't want nothin' to do with the kid. Now I've got the sheriff breathing down my neck every time I turn around, and my life is in the toilet."

"I'm sorry," she said automatically. Was there anything she could say to this man that would stop his tirade?

"I'm going to make your boyfriend sorry for messing with my life. You'll all be sorry if you don't help me fix it."

Erin swallowed. She hadn't realized David had been in contact with Joel since that day at the community center. What had he done to make this man so angry?

"What can I do?"

She could see more people beginning to gather around them. One man called for Joel to set down the knife, but Joel only brandished it more erratically. Where was Cole Bennett or Melody's husband, Grant, when she needed him?

"You gotta talk to Danielle. Get her to take me back. Tell her I'm a good daddy and I got a right to see my son."

"I don't think—"

"Tell her," he shouted, taking a menacing step forward. At the same time, the crowd parted and Grant Cross muscled his way into their small circle.

"Drop the knife," he commanded, his gaze white-hot.

"Back off," Joel answered, slashing at the air with the weapon.

Elaina let out another little cry and whispered, "Daddy."

Before Erin could stop her, the girl tore away from Erin's embrace and ran toward her father. Grant's attention switched from Joel to his daughter as he moved forward.

Joel thrust out the knife again, just as Elaina ran past. The girl screamed as the blade sliced into her side. Then she crumpled to the ground.

Erin heard another scream that she recognized as Melody's.

Joel was momentarily still, clearly shocked by what he'd done. In those few seconds, Grant made his move, grabbing Joel's wrist and twisting it away from his body. Although Joel struggled, the knife clattered to the ground, and Erin kicked it out of reach. Cole came through the crowd and slapped cuffs on Joel, reading him his rights as Grant bent to his daughter, calling for an ambulance.

Erin rushed toward Melody, who had pulled Lane out of the stroller and was elbowing her way through the crowd to get to Grant and Elaina.

The next few minutes were a blur. Erin took the boy from Melody, who maintained more composure than Erin could have ever imagined. Joel was taken away by another deputy, and Cole turned his attention to crowd control, instructing onlookers to give the Cross family space. Two EMTs were on the scene soon after, and Elaina was placed on a stretcher, then into an ambulance.

Erin handed Lane to a tearful Melody and promised to call Melody's parents and come to the hospital.

As the ambulance disappeared around the corner, Erin felt her knees start to buckle. A strong hand wrapped around her shoulders, and Cole led her to a bench outside one of the nearby shops.

"Is Elaina going to be okay?" she asked, fighting back tears. The EMTs had loaded the girl into the ambulance, but she'd looked so pale against the bright streak of blood staining the front of her unicorn T-shirt.

"The blade penetrated high," Cole said, rubbing a hand over his face. "We've got to hope it didn't hit a lung or major artery."

Nausea washed through Erin, forcing her to bend forward and swallow hard to keep from throwing up all over Cole's shiny black work boots.

"I should have never let her dash away from me," she whispered.

"Don't blame yourself." Cole reached out a hand and squeezed her shoulder. "Joel Martin might be pissed about his life, but he had no business with that knife."

"He reeked of liquor."

"Probably high on something, too." Cole sighed. "I know you want to get to the hospital, but I need to ask you a few questions first."

"Of course. Let me call Melody's parents, then I'll talk to you."

Cole nodded. "I've got to do some crowd control and make an announcement to keep everyone down here calm." He looked out toward the center of the park. "I can already see the news moving through the crowd. Are you going to be okay?"

Erin wanted to scream that she wouldn't be okay until she knew Elaina would recover, but nodded instead.

Cole studied her a moment longer. "My squad car is parked at the curb. If you want to avoid talking to people, I can put you in there for some privacy."

"I'm fine. Go on, Cole." As he walked away, she managed to get her phone out of her purse. Unfortunately, her hands were shaking so badly she couldn't hold them steady enough to access Melody's parents' number in her contacts. Tears spilled onto the phone's screen, and she tried to blink them back. Now was not the time to lose it.

She finally made the call, her heart breaking as Melody's mother began to sob loudly on the other end of the line. She spoke to Melody's father, who remained calmer and promised to get his wife to the hospital.

She'd just returned her phone to her purse when David raced up to her and hauled her into his arms. "Did that scumbag hurt you?" he asked, breathless as he held her tight against him. "I'll kill him if he hurt you."

She wanted so much to sink into him and take the comfort that he offered. Instead, she pulled back. "Did you get Joel fired from his job?"

"What?" David seemed confused by the question.

"Joel said we'd ruined his life and that you made him lose his job."

His gaze turned steely. "Yeah, I talked to the guy who owns the tire store—told him he needs to pay attention to the sort of people he hired."

She moved away, out of the warmth and safety of his embrace. "Why would you do that?"

"You're kidding, right? I did it because the guy screwed with my sister, then his son bullied my nephew." He held out his hands. "Clearly tonight is evidence that Joel is a loose cannon. I figured he'd move on if he didn't have a job. You'd already told me his girlfriend had kicked him to the curb. I didn't like the idea of him being anywhere near Rhett or you during the after-school program or still in town when Jenna returns."

It felt like her heart had taken a direct hit. "I shared the information about Danielle Rodriguez in confidence. If you had concerns about Rhett's safety while under my care, you should have come to me about it."

"What would you have done?"

"Assured you that I had things under control," she answered, trying to ignore the fact that he hadn't denied having doubts about her ability to keep his nephew safe.

"Like things were under control tonight and a little girl ended up in the hospital?"

"That wasn't my fault," she insisted, even though she'd said almost the same thing to Cole minutes earlier.

His blue eyes turned hard. "Are you saying it's mine?"

"I'm saying that by trying to control everything without talking to me, you put me at risk."

"I was trying to protect you," he said, his voice tight.

There had been a time when Erin believed she needed a man to take care of things for her, and she still wanted someone to rely on in her life. But not like this. She'd just come to realize her self-worth and wasn't about to let anyone, even David, diminish it now.

"I don't need you to protect me," she whispered. "I need—"

"Join the club," he muttered, walking away several steps before stalking back to her. "My sister didn't want my help. My mother thinks she can handle everything just fine without me. I thought you were different."

"I thought *you* believed in me," she countered.

"I do."

She shook her head. "Not if you're going behind my back to handle things that involve me. That isn't trust."

"It's how I take care of the people I love."

Silence stretched between them, fraught with tension.

Was she included in the people he loved? Was he actually trying to say the words she longed to hear? She shook off her curiosity because the whole thing was twisted now.

"You didn't think I could handle it." Her voice shook as she said the words, but she tipped up her chin, refusing to ignore the crux of the problem.

"You're a kindergarten teacher," he said, as if that explained everything.

She felt her eyes widen and he quickly added, "You have no experience dealing with people like Joel Martin."

"Really?" She stepped forward and jabbed her finger into his chest. "You think I don't see bullies working at an elementary school?"

"He's more than a bully, and we both know it."

"And apparently because I'm *just* a kindergarten teacher, you don't have to share things with me."

"I never said *just*."

"I know what you meant." She shook her head. "I've got to give a statement to Cole so I can get to the hospital."

"I'll drive you."

"No. Tonight is important to you."

"Not as important as you."

She studied him for a moment, willing those words to be true. But everything he'd said to her earlier seemed to refute that. Even the way he'd used the word *love* seemed wrong.

"I thought you were different," she whispered. "I thought you believed I could handle anything. That I was strong and capable." She gave a quiet laugh. "You made *me* believe in myself. And now…"

"Now what?" He moved closer, but she didn't back away.

"Now I can't go back to who I was before. I want more, David. I deserve more."

"I thought I could give you that."

She lifted her hand and trailed her fingers over the rough stubble that shadowed his jaw. "I did, too. We were both wrong."

Then she turned and hurried to where Cole Bennett waited next to his patrol car.

"Everything okay?" the sheriff asked, one brow raised as he watched the place she knew David stood behind her.

"No," she answered honestly. "But it will be. I'm ready to answer your questions."

"You won!" Tracie raced from behind the bar and threw her arms around David when he finally made it back to Elevation after Oktoberfest ended for the evening.

There was a loud round of applause from the bar's patrons, many of whom had come to Elevation to celebrate after the event.

He gave them a half-hearted wave and tried to muster a smile, but his insides were churning with a mix of guilt and regret. He'd beat out two dozen other breweries to win top honors at the festival and a nationally known distribution company had approached him about bottling not only his Altitude IPA, the award-winning beer, but two of his other more popular selections.

He couldn't care less.

"What's wrong?" Tracie asked when she took in his expression. "Did you hear an update on the Cross girl?"

"As far as I know, she's still in surgery." Bile rose in David's throat as he spoke the words. The knife blade had nicked Elaina's right lung, and she'd been rushed into the OR as soon as she arrived at the hospital. Cole Bennett had driven Erin to the hospital, then come back downtown to oversee the end of Oktoberfest, but David knew the sheriff would be back with the family and the Crosses' friends now, waiting for word on the little girl.

"She's going to be okay," Tracie whispered, with more confidence than David felt.

"It was my fault." He rubbed a hand over his face. "If I hadn't antagonized him…"

"You didn't put the knife in his hand or tell him to come after Erin."

"I knew he was unstable and a drug user. I wanted to mess with his life, to make him angry for his role in Jenna's relapse and how he'd treated Erin. I should have let it go."

"You couldn't have known how he'd go off."

"No," David agreed, "but it doesn't change that he did."

He'd told Erin he wanted to protect her, and that was true, but it had been anger fueling him when he'd interfered with Joel Martin's life. Now an innocent girl was paying the price for David's mistake.

Elaina was the same age as Rhett. His nephew had talked about the girl several times, and David couldn't imagine what that family was going through right now because of him.

"David."

"I'm fine, Tracie," he said when the bartender continued to study him. "Don't worry about me. Get back to work. I need to go upstairs and check on Rhett."

She watched him a few more moments. "I'm still happy for your success tonight," she said, squeezing his arm as she moved past him. "You've worked hard for it."

One of his regular customers walked by and patted him on the back. "Nice work tonight, McCay. Why don't you come to the back room and have a celebratory drink with us? One of the ladies is asking about you."

"Thanks, Brad." David forced a smile. "I'll be over in a minute."

This had been his life before Rhett and Erin, and up until a few weeks ago, he'd been happy with it. Or at least he hadn't realized what he was missing. He'd been given a taste of how much better his life could be, but somehow he'd managed to muck up the whole thing before he'd even had a chance to truly claim it.

Maybe this was all he was meant to be. The local brewery owner who'd share a couple drinks with patrons or a few hours with a willing woman before retreating to his solitary existence.

No harm, no foul. Nobody got hurt.

Which didn't explain the searing pain that burned across his chest, refusing to ease.

Brad turned and gestured to him, hitching his thumb at the cute blonde standing at his right side. The woman offered David a slow, sexy smile full of promise. The exact kind of promise he needed to numb his brain and his body and forget about the things he couldn't control and what he'd lost because of it.

David slipped into his apartment later that night—or in the early morning hours of the following day, to be exact. He'd stayed at Elevation until closing but had refused the lovely blonde's offer of a nightcap in her hotel room.

His life might be in the toilet, but he was no longer the man he used to be—the one who would flush it away with no thought of the consequences.

Cole had texted to say Elaina was still in surgery, so David grabbed a pillow and blanket from the side table and started to make up his temporary bed on the couch.

Once Jenna returned, he'd have his apartment to himself again. He had visions of Erin spending the night here in his big bed and the thought of waking up after a full night's sleep wrapped around her body still made his heart clench. After tonight, he wasn't sure his fantasies would ever become a reality.

"Uncle David?"

Rhett stood in the doorway to the hall, sleepily rubbing his eyes.

"Hey, buddy, why aren't you asleep?"

"Is Elaina going to be okay?"

"The doctors are doing everything they can for her," he answered, moving toward the boy. He crouched down until they were at eye level. "I know she's a friend of yours."

Rhett nodded. "She was my girlfriend but then she started dating Micah from the other class. We're still friends, though. Her favorite color is purple."

"Then let's go out tomorrow and buy her a get-well gift that's purple." He lifted the boy into his arms and walked toward the bedroom. "Do you have a different girlfriend?"

"No, I still like Elaina. She got mad when Isaac and I got in a fight."

"You're definitely my nephew," David muttered. "Sorry to tell you this, but you're in for a lifetime of girl troubles if you take after me. So don't, okay?"

"Is Ms. MacDonald your girlfriend?" Rhett asked as David lowered him to the bed.

"I don't know," David answered honestly. "I think I messed it up."

"By fighting?"

"Sort of," David admitted.

He pulled the sheet around the boy and leaned in to drop a kiss on Rhett's forehead.

"Will you stay with me until I fall asleep?"

The nightlight plugged into an outlet on the far wall cast a soft glow across the room. Rhett looked so small and innocent tucked into bed, and it killed David how much the boy had seen and experienced during his young life. Childhood was supposed to be about building forts and sneaking an extra cookie after dinner, not having a mother taken to rehab and a friend stabbed on a busy street.

When bad things had happened to David as a kid, he'd had Jenna to lean on. He couldn't even count the number of nights he'd dragged his pillow and blanket into her tiny room and slept on the floor next to her bed so neither of them had to be alone.

But even though he might not be the world's best role model, David was the person Rhett had as his own.

He toed off his boots, then drew back the covers. "Scoot over," he told the boy, and got into the bed. His feet hung over the edge and Rhett had left him only a small corner of the pillow, but when the boy reached out in the dark and wrapped his small hand around David's larger one, there was no place in the world David would have rather been.

He closed his eyes and tried to control the emotions pummeling him from every angle. In the dark, listening to Rhett's steady breathing, it was difficult to tamp down the regret and pain coursing through him at the knowledge that he'd very likely lost Erin.

Maybe he could find some stupid late-night movie on TV and try to forget—or at least ignore—the mess he'd made. His plan was to leave as soon as Rhett fell back to sleep, but the next time he opened his eyes, light streamed through the curtains.

"You snore," Rhett told him matter-of-factly.

David blinked at the boy, whose face was directly in front of his on the pillow. "I don't snore," he said, his voice rough. How had he managed to sleep the whole night in this tiny bed? "And you kicked me."

Rhett grinned. "I know. Mommy says I sleep like a starfish."

"You remember she's coming back in a week, right?"

"She said we can move into our new house."

"Yep." David pulled in a deep breath. He'd finally convinced Jenna to let him help her with rent on a cozy du-

plex on the south end of town. The three-bedroom house
had a small fenced yard in the back and was in a neighborhood of young families, stable professionals and a few
older couples who had been there for decades.

Angela was going to stay with them until Jenna was
ready to handle life on her own again. They had a lot of
work to do to keep his sister on the right path, and David
hoped a decent rental house was a good first step. At least
it was something he could control, unlike everything else
in his life.

"There's a yard and a park at the end of the block," he
told Rhett. "The last time I drove by I saw kids playing
soccer on one of the fields."

Rhett scrunched up his nose. "I'm not good at soccer."

"Says who?"

The boy shrugged. "I never played."

"Well, you can learn." David sat up and stretched his
legs. His back ached and there was a kink in his neck,
but it was worth it because Rhett seemed happy. "We'll
buy a ball today."

"You play baseball."

"I can play soccer, too." He moved to the edge of the
bed. "At least I played when I was your age. I must remember something."

Rhett looked unconvinced. "That was a long time ago."

"Thanks for the reminder." David grabbed his phone
from where he'd left it on the dresser. Several texts had
come through overnight, but the one that made his heart
lighten was from Cole. He turned back to Rhett. "Elaina
made it through surgery and is resting now."

"She's okay?"

"She's going to be fine."

"We can get her a purple soccer ball," Rhett announced

as he placed Ruffie on top of the pillow. "Me and her can both learn to play."

"She and I," David said automatically, then swallowed. He was correcting the boy's grammar like a parent would do.

"I thought I heard voices," his mother said from the doorway.

Rhett pointed at David. "We had a sleepover."

A smile tugged at the corner of Angela's mouth. "Your Uncle David snores."

Rhett laughed. "I told you so," he said to David.

David bent and gathered the boy in his arms, lifting him high in the air then pretending to let go before catching him again. "I'll teach you to make fun of me."

Rhett squirmed and giggled and finally shouted, "I got to pee."

David immediately set him on the ground. "Well played, buddy."

"Go to the bathroom and get dressed," Angela told the boy. "I'm going to take you and your uncle out to breakfast."

"Pancakes," Rhett yelled, then grabbed a wad of clothes from the floor and ran toward the bathroom.

"Clean clothes," Angela called after him.

David smiled. "I don't think I cared about clean clothes until—"

"You cared about girls," his mother supplied.

"True enough." He massaged a hand along the back of his neck and turned to make Rhett's bed. "I can't believe I slept the night in here."

"You'll be glad to get us out of your hair when Jenna comes back."

"It hasn't been so bad," he said, surprised to find he

meant the words. "But living above the bar isn't the best for a five-year-old boy."

"You've taken good care of him," his mother said gently.

David's chest pinched as he thought of the price an innocent girl had paid for him trying to protect his nephew.

He turned to find that his mother had stepped farther into the room. "Last night wasn't your fault."

"She's going to be okay," David said, not addressing her comment directly. "She made it out of surgery."

Angela nodded. "Still doesn't make it your fault."

"I wanted to hurt Joel Martin." He swallowed to stave off the anger that rose in his throat at the thought of the man. "I purposely messed with his life to get back at him for giving Jenna the drugs."

"She took them," Angela said. "Your sister has to work out her demons on her own, David."

"Demons that are there because I didn't protect her," he countered, then added softly, "Because I didn't protect either of you."

Tears shone in his mother's pale blue eyes, still so striking after all these years. "How do you think I feel? I was the one who trusted that creep around my daughter. I let him into my home and—"

"You didn't know."

"I should have." She gave a humorless laugh. "Jenna knew. She hated him from the start."

"You did the best you could at the time."

"How is it you can forgive me but not yourself?"

Her voice was like a caress, the gentle motherly tone he'd always wanted to hear when he'd been a kid. The way he heard Jenna talk to Rhett. For all of his sister's problems, she loved her son. David hoped for all their sakes it would be enough to help her vanquish her issues once and for all.

But he couldn't release the belief that he'd failed his sister and his mother. Just like he'd failed Erin last night. No matter what his intention had been, the outcome was what mattered.

"I'm going to take a quick shower," he told his mother without answering her question.

He started to walk past her, but she threw her arms around his waist and hugged him tight. "You're a good man, David. I love you."

Emotion rushed through him like a tidal wave, turning him into the vulnerable boy he'd been so many years ago. He couldn't remember ever hearing his mother say she loved him, and so he'd convinced himself he didn't need the words.

One more delusion shattered.

He hugged her back and whispered, "I love you, too," then broke free of the embrace and left the room. If he allowed himself to feel anything, there was a good chance he'd have to feel everything.

And an even better chance he'd never recover.

Chapter Sixteen

A week after the accident, Erin parked her car outside the Crosses' two-story house in a newer subdivision west of Crimson. She opened the back of her car and pulled out gifts from the staff and students at Crimson Elementary that she'd offered to bring to the family.

Elaina had been released from the hospital the previous afternoon but still had a few more days of rest at home before she could return to school.

Erin had canceled Kidzone for the week, and quite possibly for good. She couldn't bear the idea that Elaina had been injured because Erin had angered a parent and he'd come looking for revenge.

What if she couldn't keep them safe? There were district-sponsored security measures in place at school, but the responsibility for her students during the after-school program was completely hers.

She wanted to believe she could handle anything, but

Friday night's tragedy had rocked her confidence to its core. Her mother had always told her to be satisfied with good enough, but Erin hadn't listened. She'd wanted more from life—to be more.

But not at the cost of a child's life.

She had two big boxes filled with stuffed animals and games plus several trays of meals to deliver. Instead of making two trips, she piled everything into her arms, trying to distribute the weight as best she could. A few steps up the front walk she realized her mistake. One of the boxes began to teeter, and she tried to adjust her hold so everything would fall back into balance.

Instead, the lasagna she'd placed on top of her load started to slide and would have splattered to the ground if a set of strong hands hadn't stopped it.

"Whoa, there," David said against her ear, his arms coming around her to steady the pile. "You may have bitten off more than you can chew with this one, darlin'."

Erin gritted her teeth. Didn't that just about sum up her life at the moment?

"I've got it under control," she said, even though it was obvious she didn't have anything under control.

"I know you do," he agreed, "but can I help anyway?"

She wanted to turn down his offer, to prove that she could handle this one tiny task. But a homemade lasagna would inevitably end up all over the concrete.

"Thanks," she muttered as he took three boxes off her pile.

"We got Elaina a purple soccer ball," Rhett said as he skipped up the walkway next to her. "'Cause Uncle David is going to teach her like he teached me."

"He taught you," Erin corrected with a smile. "I saw you playing at recess today."

"I made a goal." He held up an oversize gift bag. "I

bringed her a pink baseball bat, too, so we can learn to play baseball."

"Brought," both Erin and David said at the same time. One small word, yet Erin felt the connection between them zing to life and did her best to ignore it.

David had made his choice by not believing in her, and she'd made hers as a result. There was no going back now.

She knocked to announce their arrival, then they walked into the house together. Lane toddled down the hall toward them, followed by Grant.

"Whett, Whett, Whett," the boy called.

"I don't know who's more excited for your visit," Grant told Rhett. "Elaina or her brother." He glanced at Erin. "Thanks for bringing all of Elaina's stuff. Did you guys come together?"

"No." Erin and David answered simultaneously once more, and Erin felt a blush creep up her cheeks.

Grant looked between them with raised eyebrows. "Okay, then. Elaina's on the couch in the family room," he said to Rhett. "Lane can lead you back there."

"Come on," Lane shouted at the top of his lungs, because he seemed to have no volume control. Rhett followed the boy, leaving Erin standing with David and Grant in the small foyer.

"I'm going to put everything in the kitchen," she said, feeling suddenly self-conscious. She'd spent a lot of time at the hospital with Melody but hadn't talked to Grant since the night Elaina was hurt. Not since he'd watched Erin let his daughter run past the man holding a knife.

One glance at David showed he looked as uncomfortable as she felt. Instead of taking solace in that, Erin wanted to reach out and comfort him.

"I have something to say to both of you." Grant moved to block her way down the narrow hall.

"You don't need to do this." David shifted slightly to stand between her and Grant, as if shielding her from whatever the stoic deputy might tell them.

"I don't blame either of you for Elaina's injury," he said, ignoring David. "And it's obvious you each blame yourself or each other. I can't tell which it is, but I want you to stop."

"I should never have let go of her," Erin blurted, fresh tears clogging her throat. She'd already cried so much since Friday night but her heart was a bottomless reservoir of guilt.

"No one would have been in that situation if I hadn't antagonized Martin," David said, more to her than Grant. "If anyone is at fault—"

"Someone is at fault." Grant's voice was firm. "Joel Martin. We're going to make sure he pays for what he did to my little girl. But the blame is solely his, and I want you both to understand that. I've had the worst couple of days of my life and I'm not going to stand here and argue. Do I make myself clear?"

Grant might not be in uniform at the moment, but he still commanded respect. Erin knew it was pointless to argue with him.

"Thank you," she whispered. Trying to discreetly wipe her eyes on her sleeve, she moved past him to the kitchen.

As she placed the packages on the counter, she felt David at her side.

"Listen to Grant," he said, setting the boxes he carried next to hers.

"I could tell you the same thing."

"But you won't," he countered, "because we both know I set off that guy. I only wanted to—"

"Don't say 'protect me.'" Fists clenched at her sides, Erin turned to him. "I can't do this with you again, David."

His lips pressed together in a firm line, but he nodded. "When are you going to reopen the program?"

The question caught her off guard.

"Rhett keeps asking," he added. "I guess he's been working on something for Jenna when she comes back."

Erin smiled even as a band of emotion tightened around her chest. "It's an adventure book—pictures of all the things he wants them to do together. He's been putting a lot of time into it."

"He's worried about finishing before she returns."

There were so many things unfinished right now. Erin hated letting go of Kidzone, but panic pounded through her every time she thought of Joel Martin and what could have happened if he'd chosen to confront her during her program hours at the community center. "I'll bring it to school, and he can work on it there."

"You didn't answer the question," he said softly.

"I'm a kindergarten teacher." She cleared her throat when her voice cracked. "You said it yourself. I'm not a social worker or someone trained to work with families in crisis. I had an idea for a way to help but…"

"It was a great idea." He leaned in so they were at eye level. "It still is."

"Maybe Olivia can find a person better qualified—"

"Kidzone belongs to you."

Her heart squeezed at the tenderness in his tone. She'd wanted the program to be hers, just like she'd wanted to believe David belonged to her. But in the last few days she'd never felt more alone.

"I've got to go," she whispered, turning from him. It was too hard to pretend she was fine when her heart wouldn't stop breaking. "Tell Melody I'll talk to her later."

"Erin," he called as she hurried away, but she didn't

stop. Couldn't stop. Not when she might crumble into a million sad pieces if she did.

"You turn your foot just a little," Rhett shouted, "then look up and kick!"

Elaina Cross clapped as Rhett shot the soccer ball toward the goal David had set up on the far end of the backyard. She sat bundled up on a patio chair watching Rhett teach Lane how to kick the ball. Both boys ran across the yard, Rhett slowing his pace to match the toddler's. David's stomach tightened when Lane stumbled, but Rhett took the boy's hand and they continued together.

"He's sweet with Lane," Melody said gently.

"Yeah," David agreed, pride creeping into his tone. "He's a good kid. Thanks for letting him visit Elaina."

"She's thrilled. Now that she feels better it's difficult to rest all day."

"She looks good." David glanced at Melody. "She'll make a hundred percent recovery, right?"

"According to the doctor," Melody answered.

David nodded. "I have to tell you how sorry—"

"Grant spoke to you," Melody interrupted.

"He did."

"Then no apologies. There's only one person responsible for Elaina's injury, and it isn't you."

"Or Erin," David added automatically.

"Of course not," Melody agreed with a sigh. "Although I can't get her to believe that."

"You have to convince her to reopen the Kidzone program."

"What are you talking about?" Melody turned fully to face him, shock and concern warring in her tone.

"She isn't running the program. You didn't know?"

Melody shook her head. "I've been kind of preoccupied."

"I thought it was temporary, but the way she sounded today…"

"We can't let her do that."

Lane shouted for his mommy to watch him kick, and Melody called out a few words of encouragement. When the boys were occupied again, her gaze swung back to David. "Crimson needs that program. *Erin* needs that program."

David rubbed a hand against the back of his neck. "I said some things Friday night," he admitted.

"I'm guessing they were stupid things?" Melody crossed her arms over her chest.

"Really stupid," he agreed.

"Fix it," she told him.

"I can't. Erin ended—"

"Do you love her?"

"I don't… I mean…she deserves more than—"

"Simple question. Do you love her?"

David felt himself shift uncomfortably under Melody's steely gaze. The woman barely reached his chest, but she was a force to be reckoned with nonetheless.

"I love her," he whispered.

"Then fix it," she repeated.

He opened his mouth to argue, then shut it again. He was used to working hard but had never had to put himself on the line emotionally. Hard work and commitment, he was quickly discovering, were two different things.

Yes, he loved Erin. She was the best thing that had ever happened to him, like winning the relationship lottery— unexpected and wholly life-changing. But what if he tried to make things right and she still said no?

What if he wasn't enough?

He started to shake his head, but Rhett looked over at that moment, flashing a wide grin as he dribbled the ball toward Elaina. Joy radiated from the boy with such intensity it stole David's breath. A month ago he would have never guessed Rhett could look that happy. David might not have known what he was doing when he stepped in to care for his nephew, but that hadn't stopped him from trying.

And he sure as hell had no idea how to be a man worthy of Erin's love, but he knew for certain he couldn't win her back if he didn't try.

He glanced down at Melody, already feeling a strange sense of accomplishment, and grinned when she gave him an approving nod.

"I have an idea," he told her. "But I'm going to need a lot of help to pull it off."

"You've got it," she answered immediately. "Anything for Erin."

David took a deep breath, resolve filling him. *Anything* to win back Erin.

"Any place but Elevation." Erin refused to budge from where she stood on the sidewalk as Melody and Suzie tried to tug her forward.

"I'm craving artichoke dip," Melody insisted. "You can't deny me after what I've been through."

"Seriously?" Erin glared at her best friend. "You're using Elaina's injury as a ploy to force me to see David? That's shameless."

It was Friday night, exactly two weeks after the confrontation with Joel Martin, and her girlfriends had wrangled Erin into agreeing to a happy hour downtown. The truth was she needed a night out and away from her lonely apartment.

Even the promise of a BBC movie marathon had done little to lift her spirits. All she could think of was the nights she'd spent with David and how much comfier her bed was with his arms wrapped around her.

She hadn't seen him since the afternoon at Melody's house, although Rhett and a few of the other kids continued to ask when Kidzone was going to open again. Even Erin's principal had gently suggested she continue the program, but Erin couldn't bring herself to take that chance again.

How could she expect parents to trust their kids with her when she didn't trust herself?

"I'm not forcing you to talk to him," Melody argued.

"Even though," Suzie added, "you're clearly miserable without him."

"I'm not miserable." Erin bit down on the inside of her cheek to keep from saying more. She was *beyond* miserable, brokenhearted in a way she hadn't known existed. How had she ever believed falling in love was worth this kind of pain?

"Artichoke dip will make you feel better," Melody said, wrapping an arm around Erin's waist.

Erin gave a small laugh. There was no sense arguing, and she couldn't avoid David forever. Crimson was too small a town for that kind of blessing. "Fine. He might not even be here. His sister is home now. They're probably out as a family."

"Probably," Melody said, her voice uncharacteristically high-pitched.

"What's the matter?" Erin asked. "You sound strange."

"I'm hungry," Melody said. "For—"

"Artichoke dip," Erin said, then stopped outside the brewery's front door. "Are you pregnant again? I've never seen you with such a strong craving."

"Just go in already," Suzie muttered.

"Fine," Erin agreed, throwing open the heavy walnut door and striding through. "Are you both happy now?"

"Yes," Melody whispered over her shoulder. "And I hope you will be, too."

Erin didn't have a chance to ask what her friend meant because a loud chorus of cheers rang out from the crowd filling the bar.

She glanced around and saw people she knew from every facet of her life. Teachers, parents and kids from the elementary school; Karen Henderson, the school's principal; as well as Sara and Josh Travers and their group of friends. There were people she'd gone to high school with and even her mother waved to her from a seat at one of the high-top tables in front of the bar.

"What is this?" She automatically took a step back, but Melody pushed her forward.

"You finally taking center stage," her friend whispered as David came out from behind the bar.

"It's a fund-raiser," he said, moving closer. "For you and Crimson Kidzone."

"But the program isn't—"

"Going to start up again until next week," he said loudly. "That's what I told Ms. Clayton from the foundation."

He gestured over his shoulder to where Mari Clayton from the Aspen Foundation stood at the edge of the crowd. The woman gave Erin the thumbs-up and Erin waved in return before her gaze slammed into David's once more.

"This town needs Kidzone," David continued, taking another step toward her, "and the program needs you, darlin'. Everyone in Crimson agrees." He lifted his hands. "Don't we, everyone?"

There was another round of applause and shouts of support. Erin's heart thudded and she pressed her fingers to her wet cheeks as a hush fell over the room. "I don't know what to say," she whispered.

"Say you won't give up." David reached out and covered her hands with his, wiping away her tears with the pads of his thumbs. "On yourself or on me."

A woman's voice cut through the quiet. "Even though he sometimes acts like an idiot."

"Thanks, Mom," David muttered, lacing his fingers with Erin's.

Erin tried not to laugh as she met Angela's brilliant blue gaze across the bar. The older woman stood next to her daughter, who was holding tight to Rhett's hand and looking somewhat uncomfortable as people turned to stare at their small group.

"Mommy's back," Rhett shouted to Erin.

Erin saw color flood Jenna's cheeks, but the woman stepped forward. "I'm very grateful to you and your program," she said, clearing her throat when her voice cracked. "I'm grateful for the support you gave Rhett while I was getting help. This community needs more people like you."

There was another round of applause, and Erin felt her face grow hot. "Everyone is staring at me," she said quietly.

"Because you're amazing," David said. "This town needs you." He pressed a gentle kiss to her knuckles. "But not as much as I need you."

She sucked in a breath at his words. "David."

"Don't say no yet." He squeezed her fingers. "I know I've said stupid things and done stupid things, but please give me another chance. I love you, Erin. I love who you are—your heart and your beauty. I love that you make me want to try harder than I ever have. You make me believe that I can be the type of man you deserve. Let me prove it to you."

She swallowed against the sob that rose in her throat. "You don't have to prove anything to me, David. I love you just the way you are."

"I'm not perfect," he told her.

"You're perfect for me," she countered.

"I know you want a hero."

She lifted up on tiptoe and kissed the corner of his lips. "I want *you*," she whispered, then laughed as he enveloped her in a hug so tight she knew he'd never let her go.

There were more cheers but Erin barely heard them over the wild beating of her own heart. David kissed her deeply.

"Forever," he said when he finally pulled back to look at her. His blue eyes shone with so much love. The intensity of it made her breath catch.

"Forever," she agreed, knowing this moment was just the start to the grandest adventure she could ever imagine.

* * * * *

Love this book? Look for Caden's story,
available December 2017 from Mills & Boon
Cherish!And catch up with all the residents of
Crimson in previous books in the
CRIMSON, COLORADO *series:*

CHRISTMAS ON CRIMSON MOUNTAIN
ALWAYS THE BEST MAN
A BABY AND A BETROTHAL
A VERY CRIMSON CHRISTMAS

MILLS & BOON®

Cherish™

EXPERIENCE THE ULTIMATE RUSH OF FALLING IN LOVE

A sneak peek at next month's titles...

In stores from 7th September 2017:

- **Whisked Away by Her Sicilian Boss** – Rebecca Winters *and* **The Maverick's Return** – Marie Ferrarell
- **The Sheikh's Pregnant Bride** – Jessica Gilmore *an* **A Conard County Courtship** – Rachel Lee

In stores from 5th October 2017:

- **A Proposal from the Italian Count** – Lucy Gordon *and* **Garrett Bravo's Runaway Bride** – Christine Rimmer
- **Claiming His Secret Royal Heir** – Nina Milne *and* **Do You Take This Baby?** – Wendy Warren

Just can't wait?
Buy our books online before they hit the shops!
www.millsandboon.co.uk

Also available as eBooks.

MILLS & BOON®

EXCLUSIVE EXTRACT

Crown Prince Frederick of Lycander needs a wife and an heir, and discovering he has a secret son with beautiful supermodel Sunita makes him determined to claim both!

Read on for a sneak preview of
CLAIMING HIS SECRET HEIR

'You have a baby?'

Frederick's hazel eyes widened in puzzlement, a small frown creasing his brow as he took another step into her sanctum. His gaze rested on each and every item of Amil's.

'Yes.' The word was a whisper, all Sunita could manage as her tummy hollowed and she grasped the door jamb with lifeless fingers.

'How old?' Each syllable was ice cold, edged with glass and she nearly flinched. No, she would not be intimidated. Not here. Not now. What was done was done, and, rightly or wrongly, she knew if she could turn back time she would make the same decision.

'Girl or boy?'

'Boy.' Each question, each answer brought them closer and closer to the inevitable and her brain wouldn't function. Instead, all she could focus on was his face, the dawn of emotion – wonder, anger, fear and surely hope too? That last was so unexpected that it jolted her into further words. 'His name is Amil.'

'Amil,' he repeated. He took another step forward and instinctively she moved as well, as if to protect the life she had built, putting herself between him and her home. 'Is he mine?'

For an instant it was if the world went out of focus. She could almost see a line being drawn in the sands of time – this was the instant that separated before and after. For one brief instant she nearly took the coward's route, wondered if he would swallow the lie that Amil was Sam's. Then realised she could not, would not do that. 'Yes. He is yours. Amil is your son.'

Now she understood the origins of a deafening silence. This one trolled the room, echoed in her ears until she wanted to shout. Instead she waited, saw his body freeze, saw the gamut of emotion cross his face, watched as it settled into an anger so ice cold a shiver rippled her skin. Panic twisted her insides – the die had been cast and she knew now that whatever happened, life would never be the same.

Don't miss
CLAIMING HIS SECRET HEIR
by Nina Milne

Available October 2017
www.millsandboon.co.uk

MILLS & BOON®

Why shop at millsandboon.co.uk?

Each year, thousands of romance readers find their perfect read at millsandboon.co.uk. That's because we're passionate about bringing you the very best romantic fiction. Here are some of the advantages of shopping at www.millsandboon.co.uk:

* **Get new books first**—you'll be able to buy your favourite books one month before they hit the shops

* **Get exclusive discounts**—you'll also be able to buy our specially created monthly collections, with up to 50% off the RRP

* **Find your favourite authors**—latest news, interviews and new releases for all your favourite authors and series on our website, plus ideas for what to try next

* **Join in**—once you've bought your favourite books, don't forget to register with us to rate, review and join in the discussions

Visit **www.millsandboon.co.uk**
for all this and more today!

Join Britain's BIGGEST Romance Book Club

50% OFF your first parcel

- **EXCLUSIVE** offers every month
- **FREE** delivery direc to your door
- **NEVER MISS** a title
- **EARN** Bonus Book points

Call Customer Services
0844 844 1358*

or visit
millsandboon.co.uk/subscriptio